# STORMS AND EMBERS

## C.D. BRITT

Copyright © 2022 by C.D. Britt

www.authorcdbritt.com

Cover Artwork by Hannah Sternjakob

Map by GermanCreative

Editing by Rain Brennan & Niki Fixtion

Proofreading by Kate Popa

Published by C.D. Britt

ISBN (eBook): 978-1-7372652-4-5

ISBN (Print): 979-8-9918574-3-7

To my husband, my muse in creating Viktor.
Thank you for always pulling me back into the light after I fall into darkness.
I love you more than you could ever know.

**Playlist:**
The Beginning of the End by Klergy & Valerie Broussard
Queen by Loren Gray
Castle by Halsey
Up in Flames by Ruelle
Desire by Meg Myers
In Flames by Digital Daggers
Paranoia by Neoni
Start a War by Klergy & Valerie Broussard
I Scare Myself by Beth Crowley
Rival by Ruelle
Play With Fire by Sam Tinnesz & Yacht Money
Pyrokinesis by 7Chariot
New Rush by Gin Wigmore
People I Don't Like by Upsahl
Gasoline by Halsey
You Belong to Me by Cat Pierce
Legendary by Welshly Arms
Bad Side by CRMNL
The Fire by Bishop Briggs
I am not a woman, I'm a god by Halsey
Legends are Made by Sam Tinnesz
Empire by Beth Crowley
Trouble by Valerie Broussard
Headcase by Kailee Morgue & Kayley Kiyoko
Numb by Carlie Hanson
Goddess by Jaira Burns
Gallows by Katie Garfield
All Eyes on Me by CRMNL

STORMS AND EMBERS

Warfare by Katie Garfield
Journey (Ready to Fly) by Natasha Blume
Without You by Ursine Vulpine & Annaca
Even If It Hurts by Sam Tinnesz
Burn by Astyria
Caught in the Fire by Klergy

# CONTENTS

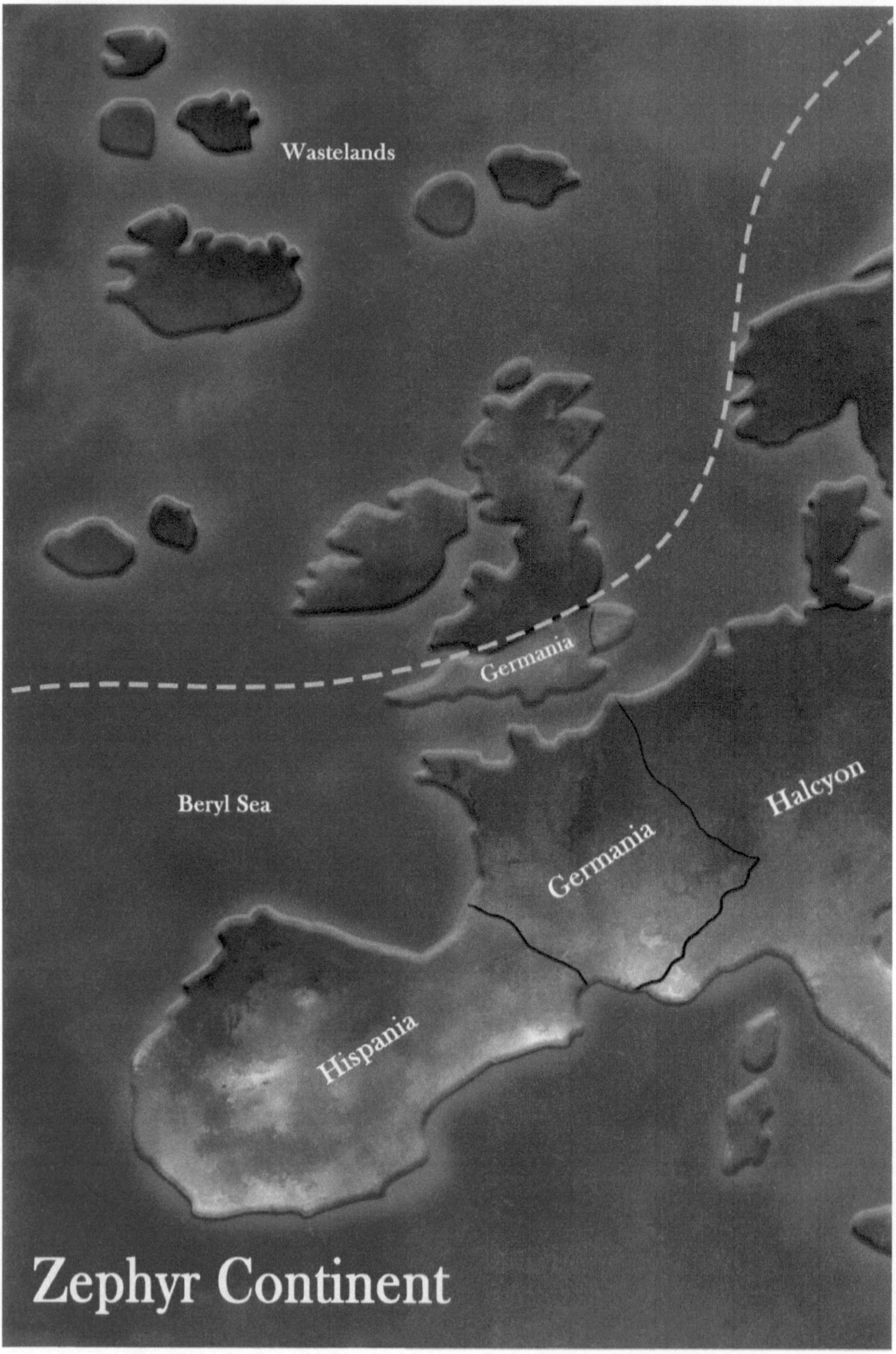

Wastelands
Germania
Beryl Sea
Germania
Halcyon
Hispania
Zephyr Continent

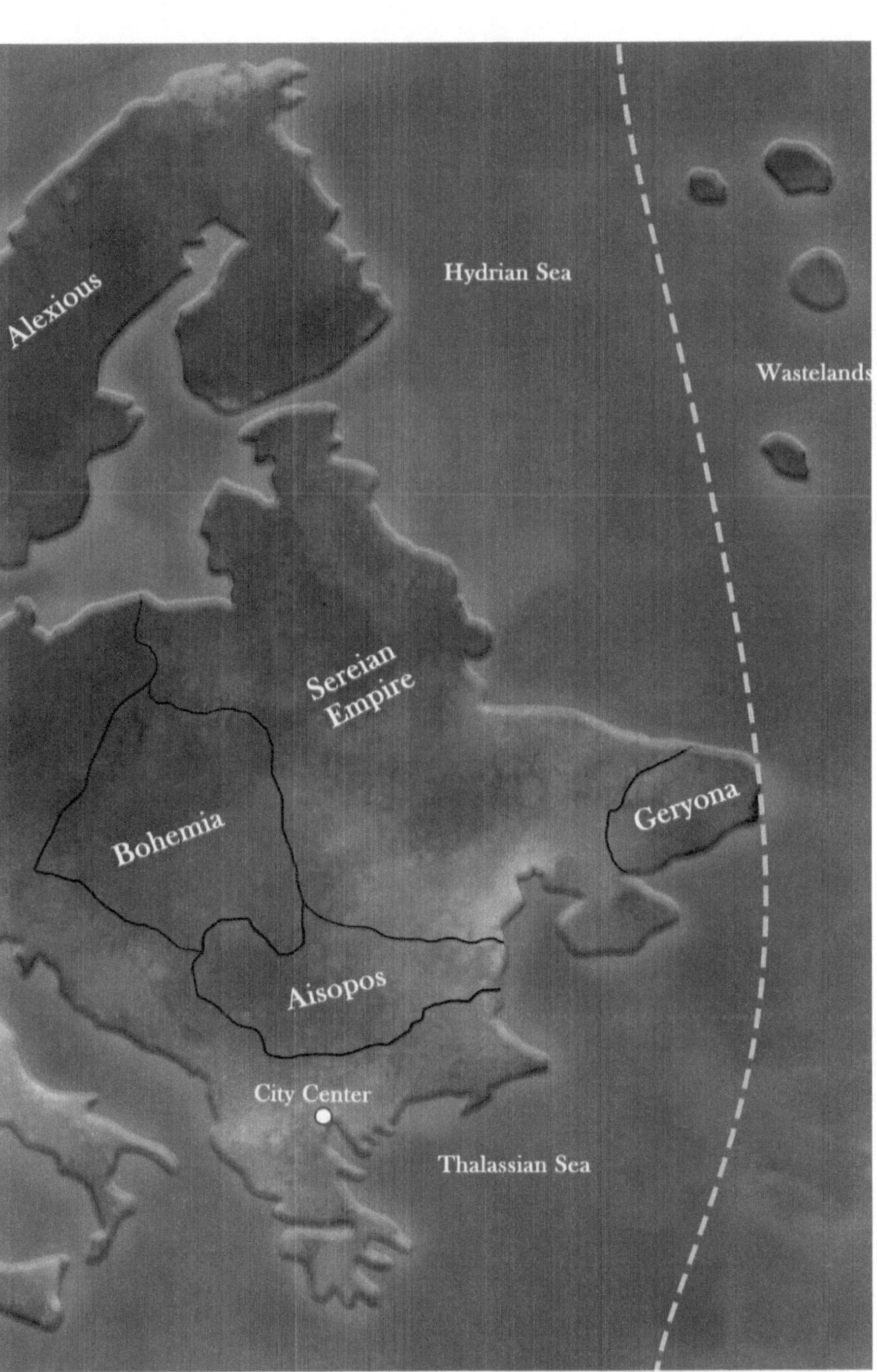

Alexious
Hydrian Sea
Wastelands
Sereian Empire
Bohemia
Geryona
Aisopos
City Center
Thalassian Sea

# PROLOGUE

## GREECE, SOMEWHERE AROUND 3000 BCE

THE SUN HAD LONG since set, then risen again, painting the sky with soft hues as Hera rested her head on a cool, flat stone. She watched the wind blow through the field of wheat and waited for the birthing cry. The cry that would signal she and Mother could finally go home.

Her mother had warned her that Chaos was fickle about when a babe would be born, and the health of the mother and child would be determined by the Moirai. She'd said the primordial gods would come with their blessings or curses upon the birthing hour.

Hera, unlike her sisters, thought that was a load of bull. To prove it to herself, and her sisters, she'd decided she would join their mother on the next birth she attended to see if anything actually happened. So far, she had yet to see anything but the father pacing, drinking, and praying.

Pushing up from the hard-packed earth that had been her bed that night, Hera wished she had stayed home. At home, she had her sisters to keep her from the devastation that was boredom. A chance to terrorize them in only the way the youngest child of the family could.

Closing her eyes, she imagined her sisters in that moment. Hestia was probably cooking something over the fire to break their fast, tending to the food diligently as Demeter wove baskets at her side. Amphitrite and Persephone were undeniably outside and far from the village as they separately followed their own pursuits: Amphitrite most likely sat by the lake's edge, plotting another one of her forbidden midnight dips she thought nobody knew about; and Persephone was probably holed away under a tree somewhere, listening to the screeching owl's call before her early morning hunt.

As the youngest, Hera spent much of her time chasing after her sisters, eager to learn from them. To do something with them. To belong. She danced around the hearth and raced Amphitrite up and down the shore. When Hera got lost in the woods after following Persephone into the leafy shadows, Demeter always found her to bring her home. But the woes of pestering her sisters were worth the excitement. And more often than not, her antics pulled their attention away from chores and tasks, much to her mother's chagrin.

A loud, piercing wail permeated the silence, and both Hera and the husband let out a sigh of relief.

Him, knowing his babe was healthy and hale. Her, knowing she could finally go home and never have to attend another birth. She did not know how babies came about, but after watching the stress age the father's face overnight, and those awful screams, she was certain it was nothing she wanted to deal with.

Another hour passed before Rhea stepped outside through the modest home's curtained doorway. Hera always thought her mother looked like one of the goddesses of old, the ones the village elders always sang about, with her long, auburn hair and sparkling brown eyes. She had a light about her that called to something deep inside Hera. Something deep that her young mind didn't quite understand as much as her sisters might, since they were nearing womanhood, and Hera had not yet passed her twelfth summer.

"Come. It is done, and the gods have blessed both the mother and child this morn. Let us not stay about and bring bad omens."

"I saw no gods this morn," Hera said as she skipped around her mother, another wave of energy electrifying her small body.

Though her mother was tired, she still laughed. "Dearest, you will not see the gods. They have no desire to be called away from their duties by a youth with too much zeal and far more curiosity."

Hera smiled, not minding the gods' neglect overly much. She found she liked her mother's appraisal of her inquisitive mind. When she spotted the entrance to their property, she ran ahead of Mother until she saw her home buried in the forest. The trees were too thick and densely packed to see their house from the road; the familiar stone and mud bricks covered by the thatched roof. A large oak tree stood tall next to the house, with its twisted and gnarled bark, waving in the breeze as if welcoming Hera home.

She paused and looked over her shoulder for her mother, who had been waylaid far behind her by a woman in the wheat fields that bordered their land. Hera cringed at the sight; she didn't want to be delayed by a local matron and whatever boring business she and her mother were chatting about. Impatient to return to her older sisters, she sprinted the rest of the way home.

A horrible scream rent the air, stilling Hera in the middle of the dirt pathway. Before she could move forward, another piercing scream followed on the heels of the first. This time, she knew the voice as it begged their father to stop.

Ignoring her instinct to run in the opposite direction, to find her mother, Hera ran to the great tree that grew next to her home. She clambered up the branches, the rough bark scraping against her skin, each movement a familiar ache in her muscles.

Reaching the branch to the window overlooking the hearth, she peered into the house, her eyes squinting in the dim morning light. As she leaned forward, she lost her grip on the branch and barely caught herself. Steadying her hold, Hera held her breath and watched for movement.

She could see a blood-covered hand grapple with the edge of the window. Black hair and a tear-streaked face came into view as her sister pulled herself up, anchoring her elbow over the edge, and reaching for Hera.

Persephone.

Catching a glimpse of her in the tree, Persephone found her gaze and mouthed, "Run."

Hera's heart raced. Run? Run where? To whom? How could she run when something was so, so wrong?

Her sister, her serious and beautiful sister, slumped forward, unconscious. The slight movement of her hair against her mouth from her shallow breaths was the only indication that she was still alive at all.

The fear that crowded her mind was intense, and Hera trembled, nearly losing her grip again. All she could see was Persephone not moving and covered in blood.

Suddenly, a thump and several screams rang in her ears. Screams she knew would haunt all her days. High screams. Young screams. And deep, wordless shouts of a man's rage.

It was the silence that followed that punched her into action.

Turning, she scrambled down the tree and ran to the wheat fields where she had left her mother chatting. Her feet pounded the earth as she ran faster than she ever had, tripping over vines in her haste. She ignored the pain of the rocks digging into her flesh, desperate to get to her mother.

Before she could reach her mother at the end of the path, a large figure emerged from the line of trees ahead of her. A chill ran up Hera's spine, and she dug her heels into the dirt, pivoting to hide behind a fallen log as she watched her father step out onto the road. Her thoughts raced—how had he gotten to the road before her?

Father raised his hand, revealing in his grip a knife dripping with blood. She knew at that moment her sisters were dead, grief rising and overtaking her small body.

Her father turned slowly, his eyes scanning the tree line.

"Hera, Hera, Hera," he called out in a singsong voice. "I saw you running, dearest. I know you are here. Come on out and talk to me. I promise you are safe, darling."

Her stomach dropped through to the earth below at his bold lie.

Crouching, she quietly moved to the end of the log, keeping herself as covered as possible by the bracken around her, and the road insight. Father was on one end and her mother, farther down in the opposite direction. Could Mother see him yet? Would she look over and see Father in this mad state?

Hera knew she was taking a risk getting her mother's attention, but she had to do something before Father found her.

She backed deeper into the woods, careful not to step on fallen leaves and twigs. Father paced the road, knife still in hand. If she could get closer to her mother—

*Snap.*

Dread struck her chest as her father whirled toward the sound with stunning speed, and Hera's heart raced. She'd been able to get closer to her mother by creeping through the undergrowth, but had she gotten close enough?

It would have to do. As her father started in her direction, Hera burst out onto the road.

"Mother!" she cried out, straightening and preparing to run to her. Her mother turned abruptly, her smile faltering as she caught sight of the murderous presence behind Hera.

In a split second, her mother disappeared, only to reappear beside her. Stunned, Hera faltered and blinked at the empty space where her mother had been. Before she could rationalize what happened, she was shoved back, her mother widening her stance over where Hera had fallen to her hands and knees.

Her mind spun. Her mother's speed. Her father's rampage. The sight of her sister's bloody hand and the sound of their screams. Hera was confused by all of it.

"You swore they were human," he growled.

*Human?* Of course, they were human. What else could they be? Was there something about her parents that she and her sisters had not known?

Her sisters. A sob escaped her lips, but her parents did not seem to notice her any longer. She knew she should run, but her mother... *no.* She would not leave Mother to the same fate as her sisters.

"They are!" her mother yelled. Cronus grabbed her arm in a bruising grip, and his purple eyes lit up in a way Hera had never seen. He was no longer her father, but some terrifying entity. Some monster from the scary tales her sisters had told around the fire.

"Then explain, wife, how my brothers came and felt a power inside them. One that was not of this world."

"They lie! You know how they lie. They want the power of the Primordials, and any children you have would be a threat to that." Her mother reached out to grab the knife, but her father held it out of reach. "You did exactly what they wanted!"

Father shoved her mother away, but she latched onto his arm, pulling him to the ground. Her mother gave Hera a wild look as she stumbled to stand, Cronus behind her.

"Run, Hera. Run to the mountain. Find Themis!"

"Themis?" Hera rasped, barely able to force the question from her dry mouth. She didn't know anyone named Themis, having never even heard the name before.

Her mother stumbled toward her and shoved Hera away as Cronus attempted to snatch her with his free arm.

"Go!" she yelled again, and this time, Hera ran. There were mountains in the distance, far enough away, she imagined she'd never make it in time.

When her mother screamed, she ran harder, pumping her legs without stopping as she tripped and scraped across the landscape. Tears burned her eyes, blinding her, but she refused to stop. Hera didn't realize she was screaming for help until she collided with someone that manifested from thin air, knocking the breath from her lungs and silencing her. She fell back, gulping air, and gaped at the stranger. A woman in robes of an unfamiliar deep indigo, her braids adorned with silver beads, stood before her.

"Hello, Hera." The women kneeled in front of her before reaching out to brush the tears from Hera's face. Hera, frozen from shock and exhaustion, let her when normally she would have fought anyone trying to touch her outside of her family.

"Who are you?" Hera sobbed. "My mother said I must find—"

"Themis. My name is Themis, and I am a friend of your mother's ... and a Titaness far more powerful than your father. You are safe now with me. Rest, child."

"But ... a Titan?" Hera whispered shakily, pulling away from the woman. The Titaness.

Instead of anger, the woman only looked at her with calm resolve, and Hera grew foggy. It had to be something this woman, this Titaness, was doing to her. Hera knew they were powerful enough to bend the mortal mind to their will.

"I am the Titaness who balances the universe. I right the wrongs, I find justice above the law of man and god, and I was the one who worked with your mother to bind your powers."

Hera's entire world was slipping through her fingers. Everything she had known until now, about her sisters and herself, was a farce.

"My powers?" she echoed. "I ... am not human?"

Themis shook her head gently, her hands cupping Hera's elbows as she wavered. "No, my darling. You were born from the Titan blood of both your parent's lines."

Hera let out a sob, then a gasp. Her parents? Her mother? Her father? She squeezed her eyes shut, able to see only flashes of blood glinting off the edge of a blade.

"My father," she stammered, unsure of how to put it into words. "He—"

Themis hushed her soothingly. "I know. I feel it, little one. Now, I need to take you to the mountain to make sure Cronus cannot find you."

The Titaness steadied Hera as she stood, her touch surprisingly light as she released Hera, before offering a hand. The silence was punctuated only by the distant birdsong as Themis waited.

Lost and confused, Hera looked up at the woman who had thrown her whole identity into a state of upheaval—but no, her father had done that, had he not?

"My sisters..." She stared in the Titaness's eyes, needing this one answer before making a decision. Yes, this woman felt safe, but hadn't her father before today? Who *could* she trust anymore?

"You will see them again soon. That I can promise."

Without another word, Hera sucked in a deep breath to gather her strength. Stepping forward, Hera slowly placed her hand in the Titaness's offered palm as the world spun then went dark.

# Chapter 1

## 2138 A.D., CITY OF HALCYON

### <u>Viktor</u>

Taking another drag of the cigarillo, Viktor stared at the senate building. He was disappointed in himself for giving in to a vice he had long since banished from his repertoire of coping skills. But for the first time in decades, his nerves were well and truly rattled.

Having made the choice to out himself as the person holding Hestia's power, he now needed to stand before the goddesses and explain his lengthy silence over the eras. Something he had been both anticipating and dreading for hundreds of years.

Thankfully, he would only be meeting the goddesses and not the entire senate, but it would still be an interrogation. An interrogation he knew would happen from the moment he let Amphitrite, the goddess of the sea, in on who he was.

Putting the cigarillo between his lips, he let the tobacco fill his lungs once more as he prepared himself to walk into the lion's den.

He hated any type of attention, and standing before the queen goddess, her entire focus solely on him, would be challenging for a man with his proclivity to remain in the background.

As a human child, he was happy to sit back and observe as opposed to being in the center of a situation. Time had not changed his personality much in that respect.

Just as he had been doing for two years now, watching from the shadows, and waiting for his moment to bring awareness of his power, *of his true identity*, to the goddesses.

Having made the choice to leave breadcrumbs for Amphitrite was a gamble. One he wasn't sure he had won or lost yet. Viktor thought he had more time before he needed to step into his role alongside the deities of their very small world, but when he felt the loss of Oceanus's power, he knew he couldn't wait a moment longer.

Damn the curse that tore at his soul. Literally.

The moment he had uttered 'Little Fish' to Amphitrite only a few days ago, he'd had to escape, unable to stick around to explain himself. As if he even could.

Dropping his cigarillo, he looked at his watch as he stomped out the embers with his boot. It was time to go in. He'd waited long enough.

*Centuries too long.*

Viktor strode toward the entrance, since opening a portal into the center of a room full of jumpy goddesses would most likely not end well for him.

He knew the situation with them was tense, and not just because they'd been trying to find their sister Hestia's power for so long. They were still trying to regain their balance after the recent battles at sea and in the Underworld.

Viktor walked toward the statue of Themis that stood large and prominent before the senate steps, slowing to touch the stone scales, silently asking for her blessing. He needed her intervention, her ability to see to justice on a level higher than the humans, or even deities themselves, could. A divine justice that could only come from Chaos.

While his past with the Titaness was fraught with complicated emotions, he could admit it was her justice that would help them in the coming days.

Or so the fire had told him.

Yet, no one had heard from the Titaness in so long, most had assumed she was dormant or dead. Who really knew with the Titans, though? The ones who stuck around had shown themselves to be either neutral or horribly violent; bent on the destruction of the goddesses and retaking control of the world.

When he neared the vast doors at the top of the marble steps, Viktor was met with highly reinforced security. Armored and alert guards were stationed on either side of the entrance with guns strapped to their sides. Steel, vault-like bolts on the doors made it clear that Halcyon valued their senate, and he couldn't help but agree. Until the war was over, the senate would need to be protected from the Titans.

One guard widened his stance in front of the entrance, most likely the senior officer, judging by the bars on his uniform.

Before he could inform them that the woman they knew as the archon would very much like for them to let him through, a familiar voice spoke up from behind him.

"He is cleared to go in." West stepped up next to him and, with a slight nod, the guards moved their hands from their weapons to the steel door handles. The doors opened to a white marble foyer, where a woman sat behind a desk made of the same stone.

She stood when they entered and scurried from around her desk with a smile. The kind that Viktor had long ago deemed a 'court smile'. It was overly friendly and completely fake. A poor attempt to create a false sense of security for those awaiting trial.

"Dr. Alden! Come right this way. Our Archon is awaiting you in the senate chambers."

"I've got it. I can show him," West replied, sending the woman a charismatic smile. The secretary wobbled with a wide infatuated smile before she returned to her seat, wearing a dreamy expression as they walked down the statue-lined hall.

Ah, so they would not speak in the Archon's office, but in the grander chambers. An obvious show of power on Hera's behalf.

The message was clear; Hera was in charge, and he would heed her authority.

"Real therapist or fake?" West asked, his tone jaunty for such a serious question, breaking Viktor from his thoughts. It was a question that Viktor had known was coming.

"Real," Viktor answered, unsure of how much he could say. The curse had never been tested as much as it had been in the last few months.

"So, you were aware of who I was before I became your patient? *What* I was?" West asked, and Viktor felt like he was walking through a field of landmines. How did he answer without painful repercussions?

"Your father found me. It worked for both of us if I involved myself in helping you find your place among the—" Viktor choked around his words and swallowed down the bile that rose in his throat. He was treading far too close to the curse's limits.

"So, Amphitrite was right. My dad was looking for Hestia's power. And he found it," West whispered, turning to look at him. "He found you. He set everything up..."

Viktor wished he could explain how he had maneuvered the best he could into their lives; painfully and impulsively. How he had to make everything, every decision and step, as spontaneous as possible since planning would only make the curse's retribution that much worse.

Viktor had taken the job with Theta, West's mother, at Halcyon General doing psych intakes when he was called to the goddesses' human home, compelled to be closer to them and his end goal.

While he couldn't walk up and directly ask about how to work his way into their lives, he gleaned information here and there, until one day Oceanus stood at his office door, offering him the chance he needed to start on the path he had foreseen in the fires. A chance to make peace with the broken part inside of himself. To find his equilibrium again after so many lifetimes. The chance he had been waiting for since he set out on his own so very long ago.

Thinking back to that first time meeting the Titan, he knew somehow Oceanus had sensed Viktor's magical signature, even with the curse's repressing power. Somehow, he had known Viktor could say nothing about himself or his past. And *somehow* Oceanus had foreseen his death. He refused to let his son fight a war without all the help he could get.

Which was where Viktor came in.

Viktor had agreed to take West on as a patient and keep their secrets. He was used to secrets, and he was even more familiar with the tingling sense of precognition. Oceanus had not found him alone. He'd had help. The neutral Titan was powerful, but he hadn't been all-knowing, and there were less than a handful of entities on the planet who could give him that information.

"He knew what was coming—the Titans, the war—and he wasn't sure if he would be there to stand beside you, as much as he wanted to. He needed to make sure you were ready," Viktor said. "Even if it meant forcing you to our appointments, so that you were mentally capable of taking everything on."

West closed his eyes, his features twisting with grief. The loss of his father was still so fresh for him and would be for quite a long time. Oceanus had loved his son so deeply that he worked to ensure West was cared for even after he was gone. Viktor felt a tinge of jealousy. While his father cared, it was nothing like what West had with Oceanus.

West sighed, and Viktor could see the sadness pass through him, his signature smile forced as he changed the subject.

"I am not calling you Dr. Alden anymore," he said, warmer than Viktor expected he would be after learning of such deceit.

"Viktor is just fine," he replied. It wouldn't do him any good to imagine more of a friendship with the young Titan than he had, especially as they turned the corner and faced the senate chamber's doors. At the sight of them, guards on each side pulled the doors wide open, waiting for them to walk through and find out Viktor's fate.

Stepping into the domed part of the building, he took in the rows of curved benches lined up before a raised platform, where a long table overlooked the would-be crowd. For a moment, he was distracted from his ordeal by the gravitas of the chambers. He'd seen much of human civilization, and now he stood in a place that held such importance to the much smaller version of the world.

But for all the power he felt in the air, every bit of it radiated from one person.

Hera, the archon and queen of the goddesses, stood in the middle of the long table. It'd been so long since he'd seen her in the flesh and not on a screen or a paper. Her blonde hair fell in curls around her oval face and grazed her shoulders. Her stormy gray eyes pierced him with the intensity of a predator spotting its next meal. She was gorgeous; he would never deny that, but she was intimidating as well.

When they approached the center of the chambers, West gave him a short nod, and left his side to join Amphitrite, who stood at the first row of benches with her arms folded

On the opposite side of the aisle was her other sister, Persephone, ruler of the Underworld. A male with dark blond hair stood next to her. His green eyes were not hostile, but watchful, much like the guards out front. Viktor felt the man's power thrumming around him, searching and seeking. If he remembered correctly, this was Devon, West's closest friend and Demeter's scion.

As he took in the people around him, they all stared back at him pensively, as if struggling to reconcile him with Hestia's power—or perhaps the memory of Hestia herself, for the goddesses. Questions were obvious in their eyes, but the answers were unattainable, and he was unsure how they would react when he couldn't give them what they wanted.

The room remained quiet for so long that when Hera finally spoke, he caught West jumping a bit in his periphery.

"Dr. Viktor Alden, according to Amphitrite, you hold the power of our sister, Hestia. Is this correct?"

Words could trigger the curse, and he was going to play it as safe as he could. So, he silently extended his hand and ignited a flame in his open palm.

A small smile crept along the archon's face.

It was both alluring and dangerous.

## <u>Hera</u>

It was him. It had to be. They had found Hestia's scion, and now they had the power to do something about the Titans blighting humanity and her rule.

They were no longer guaranteed to lose this battle, not with Hestia's power in tow. Now, they had a fighting chance. A chance to protect the people of the world from the Titans.

Finally, there was some good news.

Hera could almost taste victory. She would send each and every Titan trying to break her father out to their own eternal damnation in Tartarus.

*Sweet, sweet damnation.*

As the flame danced in his palm, she looked up to see the fire reflected in his eyes. No ... not just a reflection. Instead of the glow the rest of them had, the doctor's eyes were lit with real flame. Viktor must have noticed her rapt attention and calculation because he quickly closed his fist, extinguishing the fire in his hand and his eyes. Lowering his arm, his eyes returned to a human blend of colors. Green, brown, and blue all mixed.

It wasn't until then that she realized how long he had held her gaze without blinking, without cringing away in intimidation. Hera frowned, a twitch of her eyebrows, before she schooled her features back into a blank expression.

She lowered herself into the chair behind her, the seat she used when the senate was in session. Her *true* seat of power, her throne, waited for her on Olympus.

"Tell us about yourself, Dr. Alden," she said in a steady and emotionless voice.

"I am a therapist who has lived in many places. All over the world before the Great War, and all of Zephyr in the years after."

His voice was deeper than both West and Devon's, and his words were measured, thought-out. Precise. Amphitrite had warned her he was a man of few words, but this was ridiculous. That was a vague answer if Hera ever heard one.

Still, she got one piece of information she needed. *Before the Great War*, he'd said. The near loss of humanity had been generations ago.

"When were you born?" she asked, and he adjusted his stance, as if preparing for some physical response. Hera narrowed her eyes, but he simply maintained eye contact, though his jaw was clenched.

"I was born in Zephyr before it was even Europe," he gritted out between his teeth.

"Born human?" Amphitrite cut in, earning a nod from Viktor.

"When did you ascend?" Hera asked, her tone stiffening with irritation. Just how long had Hestia's scion been a god among them without them knowing?

"Long ago," he replied, and Persephone's eyebrows furrowed at his lack of explanation.

"So, you ascended and came into your powers well before now?" Persephone asked.

With a sigh, Viktor showed the first sign of defeat by rubbing his nose with his thumb and forefinger under his glasses, but it was not enough to quell Hera's building frustration.

"Not long after birth," he replied, his voice barely above a whisper. His skin appeared to grow paler with each word he spoke.

Everyone in the room gaped at him, and Hera could feel his discomfort, but it was apparently not enough to break him and obtain the information they wanted. *Needed.*

Hera ground her teeth. Something was not right, and the more he dodged answering, the more Hera lost that tiny thread of hope.

Which only ignited her anger.

"So, you have lived centuries as a god. Many mortal lifetimes. How have you hidden your powers from us?" Hera asked, watching Viktor closely.

"With great control," was all he said, and something like a rock hit the bottom of her stomach. She had been so hopeful only moments earlier.

Joke was on her. The joke was *always* on her.

"If you ascended, as you said, we should have felt it. Any new god leaves a ripple of power through the universe, and I *always* catch it. Explain how you ascended without me knowing," Hera growled as sparks of lightning flickered out from her clenched fists.

Viktor stumbled over his answer. "I was hidden by someone more powerful than you."

"Who?" she demanded; her hackles raised at the audacity of him implying there was someone stronger than herself.

Instead, he gave only a slight shake of his head, and her anger and mistrust took hold, anchoring themselves in her chest. Her sisters' power nudged against hers, trying to calm her before she sent a million volts of electricity into Viktor.

"If he had ascended already, that would explain why we were unable to find him. We were looking for a mortal," Amphitrite stated with no small amount of irritation as she placed herself between Viktor and Hera. As if Hera couldn't find a way through her sister to the man Amphitrite was needlessly protecting.

"All this time," Persephone whispered as Devon placed a hand on her forearm.

*Wasted*, Hera finished for Persephone in her head. Because he'd been hidden. For centuries. Perhaps even millennia.

Hera wondered why the man had even walked in here, why he'd revealed himself to Amphitrite at all. Why not stay hidden?

As she stared at him, her anger lashed within her, begging to break free. Ever since the latest battle with the Titans, exhaustion had tattered her already threadbare patience. She couldn't afford any missteps or any weaknesses.

And she was looking right at one.

This Viktor Alden had shown up at the wrong time—or the right one, depending on whose side he was on. Had the Titans hidden him this entire time? Were they sending him to get close enough to spy on their plans?

It would not be the first time a man stabbed her in the back. It started with her father and then many more men following in his footsteps in the millennia since. All of them hoping to use her power and status for their own gain. Hera had learned long ago that no one did anything without a motive, most especially not when they had the chance to take everything for themselves.

"Is there anyone that could corroborate your story that you did, in fact, gain the powers of my sister from an ascension centuries ago? I know several demigods who descended from Titans that can manipulate fire," she challenged.

"I created the fire. I did not call it from a spark already lit," Viktor replied as he pressed his hand to his chest and rubbed at his sternum, before folding his arms across his chest. She caught the fingers of his right hand tapping against his left elbow, a tune of anxiety.

Hera scowled. "Answer me straight, scion of my sister. Who witnessed your ascension?"

Viktor stiffened but remained silent.

Hera leaned forward in her seat. "Who has guarded you from our notice?"

The muscle in his jaw twitched.

"Why were they hiding you from us?" she pressed, her voice rising as she gripped the arms of her seat. "Why were *you* hiding your power from us?" Hera tried to restrain herself, but something about his stubbornness got under her skin. Maybe it was disappointment. Maybe it was annoyance that he still had yet to cower from her gaze.

"Hera, my hair is standing on end, and it took an hour to tame this morning. Please cool your static down," West snapped as he ran his fingers through his hair. Hera straightened in her seat and touched the lightning necklace at the base of her throat, calling back the electrical charge she had let loose in her agitation. The tension that had thickened the air lessened.

She narrowed her eyes at Viktor.

"Are these questions too difficult for you?" she asked, giving him a tight smile. "Perhaps you need a break to come up with some better answers? Or perhaps you need to step outside to discuss your next steps with your Titan handler. You know, to clarify exactly how he wants you to glean information from us?"

Alright, so maybe she hadn't restrained herself enough.

"Hera," Amphitrite snapped, but Hera ignored her as she stood and walked around the table toward Viktor. His knuckles were white from holding his hands in tight fists at his sides, and his chest heaved with laborious breaths. As she neared, he appeared to brace himself, widening his stance, which caused his well-fitting jeans to strain across strong, surprisingly muscular thighs.

Her steps faltered for a mere second—she was *not* checking him out. Treasonous immortal. Stubborn therapist.

When she stopped in front of him, his eyes lit up with small orbs of dancing fire.

Did he perceive her as a threat? *Good.*

The only way to get an answer was to delve into his mind, which was something Hera usually did not enjoy. Some people were absolutely disgusting when they thought no one could see into their inner selves. But she enjoyed letting a spy roam free around her city even less.

"You can't hide everything from me," she warned, and then she pushed into his mind.

Instead of seeing the realm of his innermost thoughts and motivations, her vision instantly exploded with red, followed quickly by white.

Clutching her head, she jerked her mind away from his so hard she physically took a step back. Her sisters shouted in surprise and concern, but Hera could only see Viktor. The guilt in his expression surprised her, but it was gone quickly, replaced by indifference.

Moving back another step, she gathered herself, but she was unable to stop the rapid heartbeat pounding in her head. She couldn't look away from him. He was incredibly dangerous, but she would not be held hostage to fear.

If he was a threat, then he needed to be eliminated.

"Who are you?" she whispered darkly, throwing her hands out to her sides as lightning danced along her fingertips.

"I am who I said I am," he growled back, eyes narrowed, flames brightening within his irises.

Viktor's power simmered around him. But even as the air heated between them, his energy roiled close to his skin, not lashing out.

His body was coiled tight, twitching with tension, and although she had thought it was from irritation at her interrogation, she realized that he was in pain.

With her next breath, clarity washed over her, and she lowered her hands. She wasn't sure if it condemned him further or not, but the man was not being evasive of his own volition.

The pain, the resistance, the minimal answers, the smothered power signature, the instantaneous pain when she probed for answers... Hera had seen such measures taken before, but rarely—and never on someone with a god's power.

"You're under a binding oath. Is that why you cannot speak of your past?" she asked, stepping back from him, but not going far. If he were to lash out at her observation, she wanted to be the one who took the brunt of it.

His breathing was heavy, his chest rising and falling quicker by the minute, but he gave her nothing.

"Who? Why?" she asked, though she knew he would not answer. His lips pressed together in a thin line, confirming her thoughts. At some point, Viktor had sworn not to reveal any information about his past or his powers—perhaps it went so far as to force him not to reveal himself at all.

The electricity left Hera entirely, and Viktor's shoulders dropped.

"Well, that is absolutely fantastic," she chuckled mirthlessly.

She had been wrong. They were not saved.

They were doomed.

# Chapter 2

## <u>Hera</u>

H ERA STOOD FACING A group of humans armed to the teeth, those horrid machines humans called tanks behind them. They were here to destroy Greece, but the hell if Hera would let them.

The buildings around her had been blown to rubble, and the citizens of the city were hidden in the mountain, huddled and afraid.

The world to the east and west was gone. Europe was all that had survived, and what was left was dismal: no clean water, fresh food, or order; a pandemic wiped out those who hadn't died from combat; extreme weather and explosives ruined the infrastructure.

When she'd walked along the streets after the first bombs fell, the sight of the dead and dying had snapped something in Hera's psyche.

And these assholes thought she'd let them waltz in and take over?

No.

*For months, Hera had been on a rampage, fueled by rage for the loss of life, a deep feeling of failure and helplessness. How had humanity reached this point?*

*The first ones she killed were the officials who'd ordered the bombs, who ordered the demise of innocents for their own power and greed. Then she worked her way through the chain of command before eradicating all the military.*

*And each of them had died looking into the eyes of a goddess. She didn't bother hiding herself any longer.*

*"We are here to—"*

*"I don't give a shit why you are here. This is my territory now, and you made the decision to show up on my doorstep. That was a terrible idea." She knew she looked terrifying, but as she stepped forward slowly, letting the goddess come to the surface, she could only smile as their fear permeated the air.*

*Movement flickered to her right, but she didn't dare take her eyes from the men in front of her. The creature in the rubble held no ill intentions, though she felt a small pulse of power from them. They were not strong enough to be a threat to her. A man. She could sense that now, but not a hostile. He felt ... familiar somehow, but perhaps he was a citizen she'd met moving away from the battle she was about to unleash.*

*And Hera was going to make these people pay. Oh, how they would pay.*

*Flames suddenly engulfed the tank at the exact moment the front of the army started toward her. The men inside the tank tried to get out, but to no avail.*

*Having no idea where the fire came from, and not caring enough to find out, she unleashed her power, calling upon her lightning to strike the soldiers. The screams pierced her ears while her power was fed by her rage.*

*Hera hoped Chaos was listening as she obliterated the war-hungry army. As she fed the Underworld thousands of souls, sparing only those who dropped their weapons and fled.*

Hera woke with a start, realizing she'd fallen asleep in her office. The nightmares plagued her at night, but now she was reliving them during the day, too?

She put her face in her hands, attempting to pull herself from the dark memory, but was distracted by the sheet of paper stuck to her cheek.

Sighing, she pulled the paper from her face, loath to admit a goddess might drool when sleeping.

She'd come to her office after the debacle in the chambers and passed out after toiling over the situation with her sisters for hours. While Devon and West watched over Viktor to make sure he didn't commune with their enemies, Hera went over how screwed Halcyon was with them at the helm of this sinking ship.

When Hera took over their little world after the Great War, she'd thought she had it all figured out.

Humans would make their typical horrid decisions, and she and her sisters handle it before going home for a glass of wine. Done. Being that humans killed themselves almost to extinction, it should be easy enough to run the whole of the continent of Zephyr with such a small population, right?

No. No, it was not.

It kept Hera up many a long night—even before the Titans started slinging crap her way.

And that crap included an attempted jailbreak in the Underworld and a coup at sea. The most recent battle, where they had lost

Oceanus just when it looked like he would break his neutrality to join their side fully, had been devastating. Although they had lost such a strong potential ally, they had gained an alliance with Atlantis, the small island kingdom West had reawakened with his birthright. While it was an alliance, she didn't have to question—West was wholly, disgustingly devoted to Amphitrite—she wasn't sure how much the Atlanteans could offer in a conflict when they were still rebuilding.

And they were down one guardian because of some misguided power grab by Amphitrite's best friend and lieutenant spymaster, Medusa. A loss her sister felt keenly. Hera thought she was granting the women a boon by not sending Medusa to Tartarus for her crimes, but as usual, Hera wondered if she had it all wrong. It seemed to hurt her sister still far too much to know Medusa was right there, but out of reach.

Through their losses and gains, Hera felt like she was struggling to figure out a complicated equation. All she knew was that Perses, a Titan who'd disguised himself as General Olethros of Goryeo, was still out there in the world, recovering from their battle and plotting to unleash the remaining Titans from Tartarus.

Was he the one who held the key to Viktor's magical gag order? The one who hid Hestia's power from her and her sisters for centuries?

If he was, why hadn't he called upon Viktor sooner? Before his mother Eurybia, another disguised Titan, was destroyed by West's leviathan? Perhaps, they'd been overconfident.

*Overconfident.* Like Hera was when she'd learned Hestia's scion had finally been located. Before everything was thrown into doubt.

Rubbing her temples, Hera tried to focus, but her brain was still crispy from the fire that had ignited inside her skull when she tried to look inside Viktor's mind.

Normally, she would clear her thoughts by talking through strategy with Finley, one of her senators, but Finley had yet to return from her latest mission to find Hestia's scion. Which, clearly, she had not found since Viktor was here with them. It had been far too long for one so adept at finding people to be gone. Even a mortal would have been back by now.

Yet another concern that ate away at her in the dark hours of the night.

Where the Fates was her senator? If the person holding Hestia's power had been in Halcyon this whole time, where had Finley gone? Finley was the best at pulling people from their hidey holes into the light of day. The best at doing so, at least as far as Hera had ever seen. As a demigod, she was able to do far more than human investigators, but it was a blip on the radar compared to what a goddess could do.

The five senators representing their respective countries in her cabinet were all demigods with some power—not much, but enough to put them slightly above the human population in talent, skill, and lifespan. As much grief as she gave her senators, and they her, she was fond of them. But that fondness had the same limitations as all her relationships did—Hera never showed vulnerability in front of others.

Sure, she loved her sisters, but she wouldn't even let them in on her true feelings and fears. No one was privy to the inner workings of her mind. Her soft underbelly would stay well and truly hidden from the world should someone mistake her for prey.

If there was a predator, Hera would make damn sure it was her.

Just then, a vision, not her own, came over her. A mere flash, but enough of a warning that she knew Edie was on her way.

Hera stood and threw open the window to her office just in time to see the golden eagle, her companion for many lifetimes, flying from the forest near Mount Olympus.

The moment Edie touched her claws to the windowsill, she linked with Hera's mind, sending all the information she had gleaned on the uprisings in Goryeo from the past few weeks. Nothing had died down there, and, in fact, the dissent was growing. Rapidly, too. Chaos and conflict spread far and wide, and based on Edie's perspective from the sky, it seemed to reach all levels of society.

Unease trickled down Hera's spine. Her suspicion that the Titans were involved somehow, either causing the turmoil or prodding it to a frenzy, strengthened.

Edie's intel made her question Finley's disappearance even more since the demigod represented Goryeo in the senate. Had the Titans taken out Goryeo's only connection to the senate in order to cut the country off from the rest of the continent? If that had happened, was Finley gone in a more permanent sense?

An image of humans attempting to strike Edie down with arrows and bullets made Hera's fists clench, but the scene changed quickly. More visions of the border between Aisopos and the Sereian Empire came through her link with Edie, and Hera felt like she'd been struck by her own lightning.

The conflict was no longer just in Goryeo. She watched the small army grow in size as it moved across the continent, absorbing bodies and chaos like a living creature. Her own soldiers, dispatched to guard the borders in an event such as this, were either struck down or joined the opposing army without a fight.

Why would the people just blindly follow an army on foot? If the Titans were somehow behind this unrest, how were they directing the mass of violence? Their bids for power so far hadn't been successful, so where were they getting the capacity necessary for this kind of influence? Hera knew she was missing something important, but she didn't know what.

And finally, she watched the last vision with a painful pull in her chest. The forces were crossing the border into the country of Halcyon.

"They are almost here," she whispered, and Edie let out a cry of agreement.

Back in the present and in the world around her, she lowered her head. Edie shuffled her claws along the windowsill until she was in front of Hera, placing her feathered head against hers.

"Thank you, my friend. You put yourself in great danger to bring me this information. I owe you much," she said, earning a small nip from the raptor. Edie despised when Hera stated her debts. She wasn't sure why the large bird refused it, but she had a hard time accepting that a creature such as Edie would have any loyalty to someone like her, goddess or not.

The eagle had been with her for as long as she could remember her life as a goddess. Although she couldn't fully recall her ascension, she knew she'd had the magical bird since she first sat upon Olympus. Edie only communicated through images, but she understood Hera's words, which was enough for their relationship to last millennia.

"You're almost as stubborn as me. Go rest. You've traveled far," Hera said softly. Edie tilted her head regally before she took off, sending her relief and love through their bond. Hera tried to hold on to it, only allowing such affection from Edie and none other.

How damaged was she that only Edie, a bird, could be privy to her vulnerabilities and affection?

As Edie flew off to her perch on Olympus where she bedded down most days, Hera sent out a call with her power for her sisters. Before the echo of the call had finished, her sisters and their partners were standing before her.

She raised her eyebrows. "Impatient, I see," she stated as she sat back down behind her desk. The others sat across from her, lowering into the velvet seats. Hera's entire office was decorated in deep purples, emerald, dark blue, and gold. Much like her penthouse high above them, where Hera guarded her city from above.

Placing her hands beneath the desk where no one could see, Hera gripped the armrests of her chair until her knuckles went white and bobbed her knee anxiously. Meanwhile, to the rest of them, she was calm and unaffected.

"We were curious if you were planning to have the new guy flogged," West said, earning an elbow from Amphitrite.

"If I were to do that, I would have to make sure you and Devon were not left out of the fun," Hera replied with her typical snark, hoping the small tremble of her lips looked like a smile trying to break free instead of fear.

"Don't threaten me with a good time." West wagged his eyebrows at Devon, and Amphitrite rolled her eyes at her husband.

Devon only shook his head in response, his arms folded across his chest as he leaned against the wall next to Persephone.

"Edie has returned," Hera stated, lacking the mental energy to continue the banter. She enjoyed verbally sparring, and loath as she was to admit it, her sister's soulbonds gave as good as they got—they were certainly more game than her sisters, but she would never say it aloud.

"Have the uprisings ceased?" Persephone asked, leaning forward pensively.

"No, in fact, they've moved closer. They've just crossed the border onto Halcyon land. I cannot imagine it will take them much longer to reach the city center."

Hera waited a beat as what she'd said dawned on everyone: they were going to be under attack.

"From the border, on foot..." Devon both stated and asked, earning a nod from Hera that they were, in fact, traveling that way. "Coming in from somewhere along the border of Aisopos, if I am assuming this group is from the original uprisings in Goryeo?" Another nod. "Two weeks if they barely break for camp."

"Well, shit," West muttered as he leaned back in his chair and ran his hands through his dark brown hair.

"Yes, my sentiments exactly," Hera deadpanned. "So, from what has been transpiring with the Titans and Hestia's—"

"We need to take Viktor to Olympus and put him in a seat of power," Amphitrite interrupted.

The nervous energy in the room ratcheted up in response to her suggestion. West leaned away from Amphitrite, and she cut him a look. He simply gave her a shrug as if to say, 'If she lights you up, I am not going down, too.'

*Smart decision.*

Hera only stared, an eyebrow slowly arching up her forehead.

It was official. Her sister had lost her Fates damned mind. The soulbond with West was clearly leeching the incredibly sharp brain cells from the once-clever spymaster.

"Obviously, spending so much time with West, frolicking and humping away under the sea, has deteriorated your ability to reason. That is quite possibly one of your worst ideas, and if the list I've compiled since the dawn of our powers is correct, there have been some serious errors of judgement on your part," Hera replied caustically, staying perfectly still. Perhaps if she struck her sister with lightning, it might restart her brain.

"I agree with Amphitrite," Persephone chimed in, and Hera turned her sharp gaze to her. *Both of them were going down with this sinking ship?* "And I have not been frolicking and humping away." Devon let out a cough that sounded suspiciously like a laugh. "My list is probably much shorter than Amphitrite's, as well."

"Yes, I do not need to be reminded of how boring you are. Still—"

"Olympus will judge if he is a threat, will it not?" Devon inquired, throwing his hat into the three-ring circus that was this discussion. Hera stared at him with eyes that could have killed lesser men.

Interrupted three times in a row!

Annoyed, she sent a zap of electricity from a nearby outlet to hit Devon before she heaved a sigh and looked up at the ceiling.

Trying to think while they made a fuss over Devon getting a slight jolt was proving difficult.

"I miss when it was just us girls," Hera muttered, scraping a hand down her face.

"Hera, just think about it. Devon is right. Olympus won't give him a throne if he's not meant—" Amphitrite started, but Hera held her hand up to stop her.

"Amphitrite, I adore you, truly, but two strays on Olympus are enough." She eyed West and Devon, who was patting down his hair unruly from static.

"I'd argue with that if I wasn't so pathetic in the beginning of all this," West laughed, but he went serious at the look from his wife. Clearing his throat, he sat up straighter in his chair.

"Why not? What is the real harm in trying?" Devon asked her, his hair still not lying down.

"The harm, dear brother, is *if* he is a traitor. That he has Hestia's power, and a Titan got to him before we did. We give him anything, and he runs back to his master to spill it all. *Someone* hid him from us. Someone holds the reins of that oath," she growled.

"Are we sure it is an oath?" Persephone chimed in, breaking the stare off between Hera and Devon.

"What else could it be but that? You saw him, he was almost on his knees from me asking him his favorite color and which hand he uses to debase himself."

Amphitrite turned slightly red at Hera's commentary, but Persephone was unaffected as she moved on.

"An oath would be done on the river Styx by someone with our power level—"

"Like a Titan?" Hera asked sarcastically with a tilt of her head.

Persephone just waved her away.

"The river has a history, one that tells of the souls lost to it and the oaths made. I checked in the Underworld after we parted. There have been none performed by anyone other than myself since we took over."

The entire room went silent at that.

Leaning forward, Hera narrowed her eyes.

"And that is supposed to push me *in the direction* of putting him on Olympus?"

"It means it is possible he was cursed," Persephone responded.

Amphitrite swung her head to gape at Persephone as Hera sat back in her chair.

"And why, my lovely and very cold sister, would he be cursed?" Hera asked with a raised eyebrow, but it wasn't Persephone who answered.

"To keep him off the Titans radar," Devon looked to Hera as he said this, his hair finally calming down enough for her to focus on his words. "If someone knew the Titans were watching for Olympian power, perhaps the curse was meant to keep him from falling into their hands. To hide him." Devon shrugged. "It worked on us, didn't it?"

"Then how did my father know about him?" West asked, a shadow flitting across his face. "Curse or oath."

Amphitrite leaned forward. "He was able to give me enough of a hint to figure it out," she said.

Hera frowned. "It's suspicious he waited this long to reach out. So, whether he's cursed or voluntarily entered into an oath with his master, it doesn't matter since we still can't trust him."

Persephone shook her head. "It does matter, Hera," she countered. "It means the man with our sister's power is trying to help us, in truth, and is defying a restrictive power to do so."

"I am not comfortable with any risk relating to the Titans and their grandiose agenda. We do not know the perimeters of the curse. Part of the curse could be to kill anyone who finds out." Hera sat back, but felt her hackles go up when she watched Amphitrite's body language. Her sister was digging her heels in.

"Devon was right earlier, and you know it, that is why you electrocuted him," Amphitrite snapped.

"A little melodramatic, dear sister," Hera rolled her eyes, but Amphitrite stood up and the temperature in the room elevated.

"Olympus will not, and has never, let someone unworthy step on it, and you Fates damned know that!"

Hera stood quickly, slamming her palms down on her desk.

"Tread carefully, Sea Goddess," she growled as the goddess inside her came to the surface, and Hera felt no need to stop her. As Amphitrite's eyes flashed aqua, hers flashed gold.

The temperature in the room dropped as Persephone stepped between her sisters.

"You know what the right thing to do is, Hera," Persephone whispered, her eyes calm in the middle of the hurricane between her and Amphitrite.

"It's a horrible idea," Hera growled through clenched teeth.

Persephone only gave her a small smile.

"When has that ever stopped you, dear sister?"

Hera narrowed her eyes, but Persephone was right. When had Hera ever walked away from a bad idea? Her track record of horrid decisions was legendary compared to her sisters', though she would hardly admit that aloud.

"Fine, but I will drag him there myself," she conceded, her tone brokering no argument.

All four of them looked at each other with unease in their eyes.

"I am not going to eat him," she muttered, pushing away from her desk.

"That is actually the least concerning scenario that crossed my mind," West mumbled as he leaned back again in his seat across from her.

They were right, and Hera mentally chafed at losing the argument. Viktor could not cheat Olympus; he could not lie and manipulate the mountain blessed by Chaos.

If he tried, then they would know if Viktor was a threat, and she'd fry him where he stood right before Olympus flung him off the mountain.

And it would be her absolute pleasure to do so.

## <u>Viktor</u>

*"Your metal contraptions are death traps."*

Viktor waited until Nyx, a small black cat and his familiar, trotted over from the detached garage where she was currently complaining about his 'art' for the third time this week. Why she went in there when all she did was complain was beyond him, but who knew the true intentions of the feline?

"You have no reason to bother going into the garage aside from needing something to complain about," he replied, taking a drag of the cigarette. He knew he should stomp it out and be done with it, but his nerves were still getting the best of him. He had waited his entire immortal life to work alongside the goddesses, and the time was here. It was absolutely taking its toll on his psyche.

So many years of doing well, and here he was, smoking again.

*"You've taken up the disgusting habit again. Weak,"* the feline commented into his head.

"Not now, Nyx," he sighed, shooting her a look. She had been immensely loyal to Viktor's mother, so devoted that she'd taken on the role of Viktor's familiar when his mother died. But he could not remember his mother ever saying the tiny beast gave her this much sass.

*"I am the one to burn down barns, as I hope to take out that infernal one you make those horrendous metal monstrosities in, but perhaps you will do so for me with your need to inhale chemical fire into your lungs. Perhaps you will forget, leaving it lit, and I have no cause to complain further. Take out that dratted barn, Viktor."*

Shaking his head, he looked out into the forest surrounding his small cabin home at the base of Mount Olympus, close to his office.

"For one, *again*, the garage is not a barn. Two, just stop—"

"You talk to cats now? That explains a lot about your social skills."

Viktor froze, reeling that he hadn't felt her power sneak up on him. That was not a good thing. His survival to this point had been about keeping himself completely aware of other potential threats, others with powers that rivalled his, before they had a chance to eradicate him.

"I didn't feel your power," he said, cramming the butt of his cigarette into a dish next to him on his porch. He turned to look at her fully.

Hera, arms folded, raised an eyebrow.

"You're not the only one who can dampen your powers."

"Are you making a point?" he asked, leaning against the porch's wooden column.

*"She is fire even if that is not her power. She will give you much more 'sass' than I do."*

Viktor snorted, earning a glare from Hera.

"Something you'd like to share with the class?" She narrowed her eyes.

"Nyx, this is Hera, and if she wasn't dampening her own power, she would hardly have to be introduced. Hera, meet Nyx, my familiar."

*"Ah. Yes, Hestia's kin. She seems meaner."*

"You have no idea," he murmured to the cat, remembering their meeting earlier in the Senate chambers.

"Are you done having a conversation with your kitten?" Hera demanded, but Viktor remained silent as he crossed his arms, mirroring her body language.

"She is not quite a cat. She is an Ovinnik," Viktor stated before Nyx could start pelting his mind with obscenities at being called a kitten. "An Ovinnik is a spirit," he clarified. "They attach themselves to families, protecting them from evil if they are treated well."

Hera raised her eyebrows. "And if they're not?"

"They burn everything down," he said. "She finds being referred to as a kitten deeply displeasing," he added for good measure.

Hera's eyes moved to the familiar, and Viktor wondered if there was a kinship there. Hera seemed the type to do that same, burn down someone's house that had crossed her.

"What are you doing here, Goddess?"

"I am here because my sisters thought it would be a brilliant idea to bring you to Olympus and see if you deserve a throne."

"Your sisters? Not you?" Viktor inquired.

"I have reservations. Huge, *gigantic* reservations, but it calms my nerves to know that should you be devious, Olympus will throw you off the mountain like a sack of shit, and I will never have to deal with any of this again."

*"I am starting to actually like her."*

Viktor shook his head. "I do not need to sit on Olympus. I can access my powers just fine," he responded, even though that wasn't necessarily the entire truth. He could access his powers, but he couldn't reach his potential. Not while the terms of the curse hung over him.

Needing some tea, since coffee would only agitate the emotional input he was taking in from the goddess, he turned to head back inside to decompress. This woman was messing with his mind and the walls he had built long ago to keep people from reaching the empath inside of him did not seem to work as well with her.

"Wait," Hera stopped him with that single word as she stepped closer. "Why would you not want to sit on Olympus? Is this some form of reverse psychology? Are you pretending not to want this, so I'll beg? Or do you know that Olympus will not accept you, and you'll have to crawl back to Olethros with your tail between your legs?"

*"What is she on about?"*

Turning to her, he caught a calculating gleam in her eyes. Hera was baiting him. If he didn't want to go to Olympus, he was admitting guilt to whatever little conspiracy she had going on in her mind.

Whatever it was she was telling herself so she didn't have to trust him.

He wanted to scoff but held himself back from doing so.

"I have no idea who or what you're talking about," he said levelly.

Some hesitance flickered across her expression. "You don't want a position of power? Power that you're due as Hestia's scion?"

Disappointment suffused through him. The Queen probably was not willing to split her power with others, to lessen her hold on deities and humans.

"No. I just have no interest in *that* kind of power," he told her honestly. "I know that may be strange to you, *Queen* and *Archon*." He was frustrated at the thought of her being so power hungry. "I have only ever wanted to help."

"And you assume I don't? That I will stay on Olympus and watch my people battle in my place?" she asked, and he watched her metaphorical hackles go up. "I see..."

She stepped closer to Viktor, and he was taken aback by the sincerity in her eyes. "At the end of the day, I don't care what you think of me, Viktor. I don't care if you think I sit around being fanned and eating bon-bons." She shrugged. "Olympus needs our power as much as we need it. We feed each other and adding your power to it would only make all of us stronger."

Tilting his head, Viktor opened his mouth to speak before Hera's eyes went hazy, the stormy bluish-gray igniting into orbs of pure gold.

"Hera?" he asked, reaching out to touch her before he caught himself. He knew when the goddesses were calling their power, their eyes lit with what they called godfire.

She shook her head, and her expression smoothed, her face losing all the taut lines and irritation before going to something akin to fear.

Not an emotion he would ever imagine her outwardly allowing. Especially not in the presence of a god she was unsure of, but she shuddered her expression so quick that he questioned if he actually saw anything there at all.

"I have to go," she stated, and her gold and white power flashed, leaving a tiny ball of electricity arcing out and dissipating where she had just been.

Closing his eyes, he felt for her power.

Then, he followed.

## Hera

Hera light jumped to the border of Germania, the country to the west of Halcyon.

Standing atop a hill, overlooking what looked similar to a military camp, she clenched her fists. She knew of the people coming in from the east, but to have them on her western border, too, ignited her anger ... and fear.

Below her, there were thousands in Germania and Hispania military uniforms.

She extended her vision, taking in the entire mass, and nearly fell back. *Halcyon colors.* Her own damn military was down there, moving in on the country it was sworn to protect.

The rest of the people in the camp looked as if they had dropped their farming equipment and paperwork, stood from their desks, and left their jobs and families to march the borders. As if they just stopped their entire lives, not packing or making plans, and walked out the front door to join the army marching through. No questions asked. Mindless.

Her military was defecting, and she'd had no idea. But these people were like puppets—had they actually defected or were they under the same influence as the civilians beside them? Was that just what she wanted to believe, though, instead of admitting her own people would turn on their country?

Hera didn't allow herself to feel helplessness, not since she was just a human girl, so she decided unmitigated rage was the go-to response for this evening's events.

A pulse of heated power thrummed behind her, and she swung around to find Viktor.

Good. She needed a target for her growing anger, and he would do just fine.

"What in the fresh fucking Fates do you think you are doing here?" she seethed, grabbing her lightning bolt necklace. She was ready to strike the world around her with her power, leaving nothing but ash and fried traitors in her wake.

Completely unperturbed by her anger, he walked to the edge of the cliff and looked out over the encampment. His response, or lack thereof, made her falter.

She knew she was radiating like a beacon for anyone with power to see. Who knew if there were Demigods down there, or hell, any number of other deities? She needed to tone it down before she found herself in a battle she was not prepared for. Damn it, had Viktor not shown up, staying completely calm, she could have stayed in her rage filled bubble.

Now she just felt like she was overreacting, and that made her even madder.

Watching Viktor closely, she stepped up next to him. He was preternaturally still as he looked over the camp beneath them with a critical eye. They both watched the people cleaning weapons, making food over campfires, brushing down horses. A large canvas tent stood out among the lean-tos, and Hera knew, just knew, there were officers in there planning an ambush. She doubted Perses was among them. No, that would be too easy; plus, she did not feel the power of a Titan nearby.

"I should zap them all into oblivion," she growled.

Viktor turned to face her instead of the encampment.

"Take me to Olympus," Viktor demanded. "Please," he tacked on, the word seeming foreign on his tongue. "You are right. It is not the power or prestige of the throne, but the fact I can feed my power to Olympus." He looked back at the camp. "Maybe I can help stop this, stop the attack on Halcyon before it happens, and we can take the Titans down once and for all. Together."

Hera considered him silently, watching him work his jaw. She didn't trust him, and though it made no sense, she felt that any betrayal from him would wreck her. She was brought back to their meeting in the Senate chambers when her hope had first turned sour. If he was so serious about helping now, why had he waited so long to join them?

Perhaps sensing her train of thought, Viktor broke the silence.

"This is more than me," he said. "More than my power. More than my past." He gestured broadly around them, seeming to take in the entire world. "This is for the future."

She wished she could believe in him. And she hated that she wanted to.

Without thinking, she grabbed his shoulder, sinking her nails in and light jumped them to Olympus.

Her fury riding close behind.

# Chapter 3

## <u>Viktor</u>

VIKTOR WAS NOT A fan of opening portals, and even less so when he was forced through one made of electricity.

He was sure his hair was sticking up everywhere.

Hera ignored him as she walked toward a stone door with pictorial engravings that were quite obviously ancient. The door was nestled between two large marble pillars. He forgot his hair, forgot the portal—hell, he even forgot about the infuriatingly beautiful goddess.

He had finally made it.

Olympus was more than he ever dreamed of on the lonely nights when he made camp alongside Nyx and stared up at the mountain. More than he knew was possible when he was a child, roaming with his tribe to find a place they could stay without Romans invading and stealing their women, killing everyone else.

The mountain represented a stability his mother only ever saw in the fires of her visions, desperately trying and failing to find an end to Viktor's story that she could live with.

In the end, she would give her life to bring him to ascension.

And to curse him.

Between the pillars of the hallway leading to the door, he could see out over Halcyon and beyond. Water fell from the mountaintop where he was sure there should be snow. Peacocks ambled about along the vine-wrapped pillars framing the giant open hallway.

Viktor followed Hera, who shoved the marble doors open as if they were made of simple wood. The marble creaked open, and the light of the room beyond was blinding. Holding his hand up to cover his eyes, he could still see the shadow of Hera shift as she turned to look back at him.

"Well, come on," she called, not sounding enthused. "If I have to do this, let's at least make it painless." She strode into the room, not waiting for him any longer.

Letting his eyes adjust, he walked forward, careful to review his surroundings lest Hera decide to unleash something less than desirable on him.

He may be immortal, but he could be hurt ... severely. Enough that it would take a long time to recover.

Once he passed the marble doors, the room opened. The space was encircled by stone pillars, and though the room was already bright with light, sconces were lit along them. Five thrones filled the platform at the center.

When Viktor stepped fully into the throne room, a not-so-unfavorable tingling sensation filled his extremities. He flexed his fingers, releasing a long exhale.

Hera stepped up to the tallest throne, one decorated with carved lightning bolts, and lowered herself on a golden cushion. A sudden and bright flash of light seared his already abused retinas before it faded away, leaving Hera in all her Queen Goddess splendor. A white gown flecked with gold flowed down her curves, leaving one shoulder bare, held only by a golden laurel belt at her waist. Her blonde hair fell in ringlets past her shoulders, her eyes alight with the godfire. A crown of white and gold fire flared over her head before cooling into a laurel crown with diamonds.

Viktor found himself breathless and in awe of the sight before him.

When she placed her hands upon the throne's armrests, flashes of colors lit the room: dark blue and aquamarine on one side of Hera; green and the darkest of blue, almost black on the other.

Had Viktor been mortal, he was sure that the enormous rush of power overtaking Olympus would have turned him to dust.

As the light once again faded, Devon, Persephone, Amphitrite, and West materialized on their thrones.

Viktor was standing before the goddesses and gods of the world. He had known this day would come, had seen it in the fires of his youth, and yet, seeing it was nothing close to living it. His mind and body froze in disbelief as he stood in the middle of the vision made real.

"Dr. Viktor Alden, step forward and let Olympus deem you worthy ... or not, of your throne," Hera called, her voice booming through the mountainside as her power pushed her intention beyond words or volume.

He took a steadying breath and stepped forward onto the platform.

Nothing happened.

Olympus had chosen not to give him a throne, and everyone but Viktor and Hera looked around in surprise. Hera only sat with a smug look on her face, her nails tapping on the armrests of her throne.

Viktor's heart sunk with disappointment. It still allowed him to stand upon it without issue. But what else should he have expected? The familiar sensation of his curse's burning power settled into his chest as if in warning. How could Olympus allow him to sit upon it without his given name? His true name. At Hera's smug look and the others' confusion, he chafed against his chains.

*Damn this curse.*

Staring right at Hera, he caught her smugness give way to resignation. There and gone in a second of time as if she knew this would happen but had actually held out hope that it would not. When her eyes caught his, she gave him a smirk that he now knew with absolute certainty was for show. A mask. Who knew what truly went on in that head of hers? He doubted anyone took the time to find out.

Sighing, he knew he belonged here, but only as himself.

The confused gods and goddesses murmured to each other, all except Hera, who continued to stare at him in return.

Finally, when the voices rose in volume enough that he knew they would not hear him, he whispered his true name to the mountain. A whisper only Olympus could hear.

And then the earth shook.

## <u>Hera</u>

Viktor's lips moved. Not that Hera was looking at his mouth.

Viktor had whispered something, and Olympus had responded, but what was it? Knowing him, and his many curse-bound secrets, she would never know the truth. Frustration flared in her chest, but it paled in comparison to her shock and anger when the throne beside

her—Amphitrite's throne—shifted several feet away, moving with the sound of grinding rock.

A massive flame ignited in the space between the two sisters, the fire nearly passing the pillars before dissipating and forming the shape of a...

*No. Absolutely not.*

A new throne sat where the fire cooled.

Viktor should be at the end near one of the other men, not near her. Not at the center where Olympus seated those with the most power to draw from and give to.

Amphitrite gave Hera a quizzical look, but Hera had nothing to give her, no explanation on how someone who walked around with a demigod's level of power would in any way be more powerful than one of her sisters.

However, Olympus did not bow to her as much as she wished it did. Most especially not today.

The throne cooled completely, revealing a symbol at the top.

"It's a bird on fire," Hera observed.

"*Pták Ohnivák*" Viktor said at the same time. "Fire bird," he translated, voice tinged with awe.

Unless he turned into a bird of fire, it made no sense. Or did he have another familiar?

"Like a phoenix?" Devon asked, leaning forward to see the throne better. She had never heard of an actual phoenix existing, and Hera doubted his cat would do well with a bird like that hanging around.

"Not quite—"

Hera cleared her throat and motioned for Viktor to step forward, yet he continued to stand there. His eyebrows furrowed and his fists clenched at his sides, as he stared at his new seat of power.

As if Viktor had some plan, yet it did not work out in the way he thought. For all she knew, he was behind everything and laughing to himself every night with his cat about how absolutely naïve and dumb the goddesses were.

Olympus had proven him an ally. But Hera was stubborn, and it would take more than that to prove his usefulness, even if he wasn't working with the Titans. Letting the anger burn enough to make her hostile, she snapped at Viktor.

"Feel free to have a seat whenever you like, Fire God. We are simply here for your leisure and amusement."

She hated the words as they left her mouth, but she hated vulnerability even more, and she found nothing moved a man faster than taunting. Their precious little egos could hardly handle it.

He finally shook his head as if physically shaking his thoughts away.

Slowly, he stepped to the throne, his eyes roving over everything in a way that made Hera think that perhaps at some point in his long life he had been a soldier. It was an assessing look she had seen on Devon more than a few times.

Or, perhaps Viktor was as weary of her as she was him. That gave her back a bit of her good humor.

When he finally lowered himself onto the throne, flames erupted all around him, but he didn't flinch as one would with fire on all sides, much less touching them.

The fire did not bother him. Hera could somewhat understand that, as her electricity was a comfort to her when it was also a threat to others. In that, they were the same, much as she loath to admit any similarities between them.

His clothing changed to dark red formal garments not unlike Devon and West's. A crown of flames erupted upon his head, and as it cooled, it looked like living flames made of gold.

That, she could admit, looked pretty amazing. A part of her was drawn to the way the dark golds and red complimented his complexion, and how the crown seemed to emphasize his sharp bone structure. Her emotions were in complete turmoil as she looked upon the new god. Something in her chest begged her to trust him. To see him as not only an ally, but something more.

Hera shoved the attraction deep down, throwing it in a box marked 'Bad Ideas'.

"Looks like Olympus will accept you, even if I do not," Hera said tightly.

"Was it ever your choice?" he asked, settling into his throne.

She heard a sharp inhale from Devon, and a "Good luck, man," whispered by West.

*Yes, good luck indeed.*

"Maybe it was not my choice whether you managed to gain a throne on this mountain, but it is my choice to trust you. And, surprise, surprise, *I do not*." Hera straightened her shoulders. "But we have bigger problems than just you to deal with," she said, remembering his words on the hilltop.

Viktor shifted in his seat, perhaps not completely comfortable with it yet, and nodded once. The message had been received.

Shoving herself off her throne, she called on the globe they used to keep an eye on the world. As it rose from the center of the throne room floor, she purposely kept her eyes off Viktor. She did not need him trying his therapist mind magic and taking a look into her very confused and unsteady psyche when she had to focus.

Just as she predicted, the man was becoming quite the unwelcome distraction. She hated being right all the time.

Scratch that, she loved it. It was other people that hated it.

"We've had movement on the west and eastern portions of Halcyon. Devon, I sent Cassandra to you to discuss the protection and defense of Halcyon."

Devon nodded. "We've met and are going to meet again after this meeting concludes. She has some good ideas."

Hera agreed. That was why Cassandra was the senator of Bohemia and Aisopos, the two countries bordering the Sereian Empire. The latter being the one place she did not have absolute control of.

Not for lack of trying, of course, but the people there had been under the old emperor's thumb for so long at that point. They resisted a new regime after some humans took the opportunity during the Great War to assassinate him. Having been cut off from the rest of civilization for so long, they were scared and unsure of their place in the new post-war world they'd found themselves in.

So, for once in Hera's long life, she'd compromised. The son of the current emperor would take over in his father's stead if he declared a truce and allowed her to place a senator as liaison. And that was why her senator, Kiran, was only a liaison for the empire due to the decades old truce she knew would be broken at any moment should the emperor decide it was worth the hassle of war.

The son did fine. It was his offspring that gave her troubles and had her reminding them every quarter century of how quickly she could sweep in and upend their little world.

"Yes, well, Cassandra was the top professor of War Studies and Tactics at Zephyr University. She should have some decent ideas, I'd hope."

Devon stood from his throne and moved toward the lit globe. Her heart beat a little faster at the sight of the clear ocean water, her eyes cutting to Amphitrite to see a relieved smile cross her sister's face. West reached over, taking Amphitrite's hand, and pressing the back of it briefly to his lips.

There were also some patches of green in the wastelands of what used to be North and South America. Devon had been busy trying to bring Earth back to life in the areas that had taken the brunt of the fallout after humans used their weapons of mass destruction.

Devon used his hands to zoom in on Halcyon, halting the globe's slow turning and moving in to bring a clear picture. Hera watched the red dots, life signatures of the forces that had been in Goryeo not long ago, move closer and closer to the city center. Moving in from the western and eastern borders, just as she had seen with her own eyes, and Edie's, earlier.

"Fates…" Amphitrite muttered.

Fates was right. They were surrounded by the enemy.

"Who are these people?" Persephone asked, her voice low and dangerous.

"That is a good question," Devon replied, zooming in further. "I've light jumped and looked at these locations, and as they move through towns, it seems to increase, but it's all random on who joins. Many from each town just drop whatever they are doing and join in, seemingly unaware of the cause they march toward. It's like a snowball going downhill, growing larger the more distance it covers. As for leadership…" Devon sighed and ran his hand through his hair. "Honestly, there never seems to be anyone higher in rank than a captain there—"

"How are they moving so quickly?" Amphitrite interrupted, looking around at each of the goddesses and gods on Olympus. "You cannot tell me that moving from Goryeo to the borders of Halcyon in a matter of weeks is normal for humans?"

"If I can light jump all of you places, could a Titan ... say ... that idiot Perses masquerading as General Olethros, not do it with an army? Perhaps if he had other Titans..." Hera let the thought drop off as she paced the throne room. "But even more so, how the fresh Fates is he using humans? They cannot all be so willing to take down the first governmental structure to know true peace since the war! Is their memory that short? Or is something more at work here than we thought?"

With her temper rising, Hera turned to the others, aware that her eyes glowed gold. She didn't care. They had worked so hard to create this new world, and the humans were willing to tear it apart because some idiot was whispering in their ear. What was Perses even offering them for their allegiance? Or was he even giving them a choice? Never had Hera heard of such a large group of people being controlled, so how would it be possible now?

A sudden vision entered her mind, the familiar angle from above telling her it was her link with Edie. The mountains of Germania stood in the distance ... No. Those were not the mountains of Germania. Her mind only associated them with those mountains because the last time she had seen the army was at the border of Germania.

No, that was Olympus. Hera knew all too well that beyond that mountain range was Halcyon city center and the Thalassian sea. Her arms and legs felt shaky as she watched Edie swoop around and move back toward the encroaching army. They were not marching but sitting around and not really conversing either. Unfortunately, Edie wasn't close enough to see their facial expressions.

An arrow whizzed by her, and she cut the connection so Edie could focus on getting away.

Realizing she had gone quiet with thought, she took a deep breath and looked up, her eyes catching Viktor's. Something deep inside of her settled, like a wild animal finding its calm. She must need to work out some of her sexual energy if her body kept reacting this way to Viktor.

"Then they could light jump here at any point in time?" Persephone spoke up, the room coming alive again with her words. Hera hadn't realized how tense it had become in her contemplative silence.

"Yes, and with that, we need to not only increase our defenses for those staying here but find somewhere for our citizens to go who are not staying to fight, as I assume some will. Stubborn lot, these Halcyonians."

"The ones left behind. How do we make sure the titans, if they are the ones running this show, do not compromise them, too?" West asked the room. He wasn't looking at Hera, but she knew he felt her glare. Why would he question if it was the titans? Of course, it was. How else would they move so quickly?

"We need to find out how they are being compromised first," Hera interrupted as she ran her index finger lightly over the red dots closest to Halcyon. Still a distance away, but there were too many to fight should they descend on the city proper all at once. And what damage were they doing along the way to the people who chose not to follow? "But first and foremost, we need to evacuate the city and set up a curfew for those who remain. Shut everything down that is not critical."

"And send them where?" Amphitrite commented. "Where in the entirety of Zephyr is a safe place at this point?"

Alexious was the only part of the map that seemed to not be overrun. Though there were some red dots here and there, they were few as compared to the many overtaking the continent. The northernmost country of Halcyon looked to be the safest. Hera could only hope her senator there, Ryder, kept it that way.

Hera turned to Devon and saw the same answer in his eyes before he gave a nod of agreement.

Turning to West and Amphitrite, she spoke.

"I need all your ships to cease movement of goods. We will transport people via boat to Alexious. That way, we bypass coming across any of the armies moving in on us on foot. Persephone," she added, looking at her sister, "please inform Ryder that we will be relying on his hospitality in the interim." Looking back at Devon, she gave her orders. "Meet with Cassandra and pull in the people she knows are loyal to our military. Plan a defensive stance and report back to me."

One by one, everyone in the room disappeared until it was just Hera and Viktor. Hera continued to stare at the globe as it turned again, trying to realign her thoughts with her next move.

"And how shall I help?" Viktor asked.

Slowly, Hera turned to face him, her hands clasped behind her back.

"You and I are going to visit the second most annoying deities on Earth."

Viktor raised his eyebrows but said nothing.

Damn. Hera had set that trap up so perfectly for him to fall into.

"Just come on," she growled, reaching out to him to lead the light jump since she knew their destination.

He was making it difficult to mess with him. No fun at all when one had to explain the joke.

*Damn therapist.*

# Chapter 4

### Viktor

VIKTOR WAS BETTER PREPARED this time for Hera's abrupt portal than the last time she had pulled him through.

"Far less nauseating to go through a portal when prepared for it," he commented as his feet once again stepped into a foreign room. Foreign in the sense that he had never been to this specific place personally before today, yet, once the women chittered, he knew exactly where they were.

"We call it a light jump," Hera murmured as she straightened her suit jacket, as if preparing for some boardroom battle.

"I have fire—"

"It's a light jump," she grumbled. "You do not need to contradict me on everything just for the sake of fighting."

Viktor didn't laugh, but he privately enjoyed this new bit he learned about the goddess—she didn't know she was a terrible contrarian herself.

Hera turned to the three women sitting in white chairs facing them. The windows behind them let the light shine through, catching on an unbelievable number of gossamer strings that had been strung along the wall. The strings were in various states—some gleaming and new and unblemished; some frayed and darkened.

"You've come! Oh, how we've missed you!" one called out as she clapped her hands with childlike enthusiasm. Though she may look like and act like a child, Viktor knew she was ancient.

"Shut it, Clotho," Hera snapped, catching Viktor off guard with her hostility.

"These are the Fates, and you speak to them as if they were errant children?" he asked before he could catch himself. It stunned him that Hera, who was in fact old, but not as old as them, was not in complete reverence of the deities before them.

"They are three idiot beings sharing one brain cell." She looked over her shoulder. "Now shut up so I can drag information from them." Turning back, she stared down the immortals.

Raising his eyebrows, Viktor looked at the beings, who seemed completely unperturbed by Hera's outburst. Shaking his head, he crossed his arms and stood back to let Hera frontline this theatrical performance she was intent on making.

"We have forces coming in from all sides and I need some information, should you be capable of giving anything that makes a lick of sense, so I can protect this city. And you. If I have to." It did not sound like she wanted to in the slightest, but she went on. "We have Hestia's power now, so we have all the people you hem and haw about being players on some board."

"No, all the players are not on the board," The middle-aged woman stated, and he watched Hera's shoulders draw up. Electricity flickered over her form.

"Do I have even more sisters I was unaware of?" Hera asked in a low, deadly tone.

"No, but you have ties that are unraveled and need to be braided back together again," the oldest one said, her voice ancient. "And the other player hasn't set up their side of the board yet, either."

A growl left Hera, and the temperature in the room increased. Pushing out his senses, he felt the ward. Ah, so at least they protected themselves. Hera could not do much more than give a spectacular light show. They must have gone toe to toe before.

"I would like to not have them set up their side if at all possible. That is why I am wasting my precious time, instead of planning, standing before the three of you useless hags—"

"Hera..." Viktor warned. His mother spoke of the Fates, or the Moirai, with extreme respect, and that had stayed with him.

"—hoping to ring that one precious brain cell for all its worth," she finished, staring daggers at Viktor before she looked back at the Moirai.

"Hera, darling, the embers are still hot, but the fire is weak. You must fan the flame."

"Clotho," she sighed. Hera didn't even continue, choosing instead to pinch the bridge of her nose. Viktor appreciated her control.

The three women looked at him simultaneously as if he had spoken aloud.

"You have such a large job in front of you, and not one you are new to. The pain will be immense, the sacrifice more than you think you can withstand. You will have to let yourself burn to know that another will not. Let the error of your past, and the ghost you love and mourn lost to that error, go. Trust yourself."

Viktor's heart stopped and then accelerated, his skin going cold, his thoughts frozen. The ghost he loved... he had to let her go. Coming back to himself, he looked to where Hera was staring at him. He wasn't sure if the look on her face was confusion, concern, or irritation at the prophecy having nothing to do with what she came for. He bet it was a little of each.

The Moirai's eyes moved back to Hera all at the same time, not a second's delay between the deities.

"Trust what you see in the flames, child. Weather the storm, but do not let yourself be swept away by the call of the past. Stay true and hold on to the future. Hold true in the fire and be reborn!"

Hera threw her head back with a growl and scream mixed, staring at the ceiling with the last of that diatribe.

"Blood." The oldest one stood up abruptly, and Hera's head snapped back down to look at the deity. "Blood is cast. Ruins. Freedom."

The way she said freedom was not inspiring any sort of awe, but fear. Freedom that sounded ominous.

"The opposing players have made the final move to set up the board," they spoke at once, all standing now, their eyes milky white.

Chills ran up and down Viktor's arms as he watched them walk in a circle in front of him and Hera.

"They've never been this weird and creepy before," she stated as she stepped back to stand beside him, giving the deities more room.

They muttered, "Time will tell," in perfect unison.

"Bat shit crazy, but not *this*," Hera added in a whisper.

The Moirai suddenly began moving jerkily, and they started chanting in a language Viktor had never heard spoken before. A language Hera seemed to recognize.

"They're done. Time to go," she announced, grabbing his arm to portal them out of there.

All at once, the three heads snapped up and completely focused on Viktor with milky white eyes.

"The curse dies in the fire," they whispered. "But not the bond."

The three women moved together to form one being, a being who moved across time, from youth to old crone in a matter of seconds before going back through time again.

Viktor stared at them as light flashed in his eyes, and they were gone from the strange women known as the Fates. The Moirai.

He knew how the curse could be undone now.

And it would not be easy.

# Chapter 5

### <u>Hera</u>

DAYS LATER, THE EVACUATION of the city center had begun. Hera was watching from her office window when she felt Viktor light jump into the suddenly way-too-small space.

"I've closed my practice down temporarily. What should I do to help with moving everyone out of Halcyon?" he asked, his voice ringing with concern.

As she turned to order him about, or tell him to screw off, she wasn't sure yet, a sharp pain crossed through her connection with her sister, causing her to gasp.

*Persephone.*

More pain burst through her body, a horrible alarm. Persephone had to have just been injured and Hera's mind spun.

Suddenly, her office was a blur. She saw her desk. She blinked. She saw a bloody hand. She blinked again. Viktor's face. Another blink. Her father's face.

Hera tried to breathe but struggled through the flashes of memory that assailed her anytime her sisters were in danger. Except this time, she wasn't alone when it happened.

Her heartbeat raced, panicked, and suddenly she felt pressure around her chest. Warm, strong bands wrapped around her. A familiar scent of pine and spice. Viktor. She hadn't noticed him move. His lips forming words that her panic didn't allow her to hear.

Moving his hand, he pushed her hair back and took her chin, his eyes full of concern. She jumped away from him and whatever look was on her face had him holding his hands up, palms out.

"It's alright, Hera," he soothed as he took a step back. "I just want to know what's wrong."

*Who the Fates is this man? Why does he care?*

Shaking herself, she let the pull of her sister's power take her to Persephone. The moment her light jump was completed she came face to face with a very irate Devon. His eyes flashed bright green, and his godform raged against his skin to be let out, the green dragon tattoo moving over his skin in agitation as if Devon were not allowing him to form.

"Persephone was attacked," he growled before Hera could say a word, his voice not his own, but the god beneath. Ancient and wise, but incredibly angry.

"What happened?" she asked, realizing her voice had also changed. Her goddess was set to go off like a grenade at any point in time. It was always defensive, the cranky she-demon, but so much worse when something was wrong with her sisters.

Looking around, she noted they were in Alexious, but she didn't see Persephone right away until she moved around Devon, who had blocked anyone from getting to her. Ryder came up from a side street with some bandages, looking like he took some hits himself if the blood on his shirt and face were any indication.

"A group of people, humans, surrounded her. She didn't engage, and they slashed her arm with a knife." Devon growled, his voice animalistic now as he stepped into Hera's personal space, getting into her face.

"This was planned, Hera," he seethed through clenched teeth. "I refuse to lose her again."

She stepped closer, their noses almost touching as she let the goddess take a tad more control, lighting her eyes with gold. The static in the air increased.

"As do I, but watch where you step, little god, because she may not be the one in danger should you keep taunting me with your little power plays."

"He is worried. Perhaps it would be best if we took Persephone home where Devon felt there was less of a threat?" Ryder asked as he handed Devon a cloth to clean up the blood, not going near Persephone while Devon was in such a protective state.

"Devon, I told you I would be fine. Hera, it is alright," Persephone finally spoke up from where she sat, running a cloth across her arm to remove the blood that had already stopped seeping from the wound.

The shirt she wore was torn, stained with blood, and her normally perfectly coifed hair was askew. Tendrils of black fell from her chignon; the only sign of her power was her eyes that were fully black. Devon handed her another and took the soiled one from her, his power decomposing the cloth as if thousands of years had passed.

"I am going back to the Underworld while you two toss your power around like children," Persephone grumbled as she called the shadows to take her away.

Viktor showed up a moment later in a light jump, and Devon's shoulders tensed again before he realized that Viktor was not a threat. Hera wished she could feel the same way about the man.

Hera looked from Devon to Viktor. The concern on Viktor's face told her he knew exactly what Devon was going through, and the Moirai's words moved through her mind once again. *The ghost you love and mourn.* Were they referring to his mother? A lover, perhaps? It was most definitely someone he loved deeply. Ignoring the little stab in her chest, unsure of why she should feel anything, she grabbed both men by the sleeves and pulled them into a light jump. One that was slower than usual, as she was tiring- out from moving all these people around town like a damn ferry.

In the Underworld, a place Hera dreaded going, she took them to Persephone and Devon's bedroom, where Hecate was already waiting to look over the very unmarred arm, Persephone's power having healed the wound almost immediately. Turning her gaze to Devon, Hera raised an eyebrow, waiting for more information.

Only narrowing his eyes at her in return, he said nothing as he walked to where Persephone sat on the bed. Sitting next to her, he put his arm around her and pulled her against him. Hera was sure it was Devon who needed the comfort and not Persephone, but she decided to say nothing and let that little vulnerability lie unspoken.

"She looks fine now." Hera stepped forward, a low growl coming from Devon, and a flash of her teeth in response culled anything further from him as she sat on her sister's other side. "What happened?"

Hecate stepped away and moved to the wall Viktor currently occupied. He leaned against it languidly, but his crossed arms and assessing eyes showed how alert he actually was. A flash of black and shadows filled the room before Thanatos appeared near the doorway.

"Alexious is an absolute wreck," Thanatos announced, his deep booming voice filling the entire room. His eyes landed on Hera after the words left his mouth, and his steps faltered for a heartbeat. "Oh, hey Hera. Probably not great that you're here."

Hera shook her head, rolling her eyes privately at the frustratingly loveable idiot. The reaper was the only immortal she wasn't related to who could speak so flippantly with her—who wasn't deeply afraid of her.

"What do you mean?" Persephone spoke up, scooting forward with the barnacle that was her husband attached to her.

"Overrun, just like Goryeo was oh-so very recently," Thanatos responded, simultaneously jocular and deadly serious. "I am not sure anywhere is completely safe to evacuate to now. Everywhere is far too dangerous and the proof of it is filling up the River Styx. I'm gathering souls as quick as I can... but I'm struggling. They are coming in almost non-stop, Persephone."

Silence engulfed the room at the revelation.

"Are the people..." Hecate started but seemed unable to finish her sentence.

Thanatos only nodded gravely. "They do not seem to be aware of who they cut down... or truly do not care."

Fates, the people were murdering their own. Neighbors turning on each other. Husbands turning on their families... Hera felt a knot form in her chest before she threw out a pulse of power, causing everyone aside from her to jolt at the abrupt, and excessive, call.

Amphitrite and West were there mere seconds later, their eyes moving to Persephone and Devon, before taking in the room around them.

"I felt Persephone's pain and went to the site where the echo of it came from. You were quick to move here," Amphitrite muttered as she moved closer to Persephone, placing her hand on Persephone's shoulder.

"Amphitrite, I need your help to figure out who attacked Persephone and why," Hera ordered and was given a strong nod by Amphitrite in return.

"How were you attacked, exactly? And are we no longer moving citizens out of the city?" Amphitrite's eyes moved over Persephone, searching again for any proof of her injury.

"Someone stabbed her in Alexious. We were working with Ryder on setting up the safest place to evacuate and were overrun with humans," Devon responded. Hera could tell Devon had held off on killing them all—had they not been innocent humans being used as puppets for the Titans, he would have obliterated them. And Hera would have been glad for it, though she'd never speak those words aloud to Devon.

"I was not stabbed, I was cut, and not that badly." Persephone darted a look at Devon, but he ignored it, continuing to seethe. Green light flickered around him, projecting from his eyes, as the tattoo of his dragon writhed along the surface of his skin.

Amphitrite gave Hera and Persephone a meaningful look of concern, and her sister's worry slammed into her. Hera nearly went cold. She truly did not want to contemplate the possibility. Not with everything else going horribly wrong.

"I do not believe it was to create a blood bond," Persephone stated, catching on to the non-verbal communication going on between the sisters.

"What's a blood bond?" West asked, cutting a look to Devon, who only shook his head. Both men had most likely never heard of it, having only been gods for the blink of an eye. She wondered if Viktor knew about blood bonds since he had been around far longer.

Hecate, who'd been observing the room quietly from her stance by the wall, stepped forward. It was the closest to her expertise, after all.

"It's an ancient spell," Hecate said. "Perhaps the first. If one cuts oneself before using the knife to cut another, in conjunction with a spoken incantation, you can create a connection between two souls. Where one goes, the other goes, too." Devon whipped his head from Hecate to Persephone, his face paling.

"It was something I used long ago in my witchcraft to ensure people were together in the afterlife," Hecate continued. "I stopped when the Underworld judges became agitated about it," Hecate responded with a shrug.

Devon's expression was dark. "You think someone is after her blood?" His hand seemed to go to his soulbond mark subconsciously, and Hera knew that her brother-in-law raged at the idea of another bonded to Persephone.

Persephone placed a calming hand on his shoulder.

"No," she assured. She looked at Hera and Amphitrite. "There was no incantation."

"Did you feel the power of a Titan nearby when the attack happened?" Hera asked, unfolding her arms and trying to relax her pose. She had noticed as a younger goddess that her sisters reacted to her mannerisms, even if they were unaware of it. She needed to keep her cool so that her sisters kept theirs.

"No, they were... human. At least as far as I could tell," Persephone answered. "Which is why I am sure I was caught off guard. Had an immortal or Titan been anywhere nearby, I would have been more watchful."

"You should always be watchful, damn it," Devon growled.

"Calm yourself, Devon," Viktor interrupted. Hera was surprised he would insert himself into such a sticky situation, especially as she watched Devon's eyes light up. *Uh oh.* Someone is challenging the alpha on his territory.

Absolutely ignorant of this fact, or just not caring, Viktor went on. "This is a situation that is now within our borders. I do not know what happened in the past, but you must stay rational in order to stay vigilant. If you want her to remain watchful, you must remain calm."

"You should listen to him, otherwise he will drone on and probably make you do a round of meditation," West piped in with his two cents.

Viktor simply tilted his head, giving West a look of reproof, but said nothing more.

Hera could feel the power building around Devon, and without thought, she stepped between the two men to stand in front of Viktor. Shock stole through her at what she had just mindlessly done.

*Now how will you play this off, huh, Hera? Idiot.*

She did not look at her sisters, as she knew they felt the same shock at her instinctive reaction. Hera had no idea why she stepped between them instead of letting them duke it out. That would have been far more fun to watch.

Hera was beginning to think she was losing her mind.

Thankfully, Devon got himself back under control, which took the heat off Hera. Shaking his head, Devon took a deep breath and relaxed his body, his arm unwinding from around Persephone.

"I'm sorry. I've never felt for another as I do her and it just..." Devon trailed off, running his hands through his hair as Persephone ran her hand over his back.

"Understandable," Viktor chimed in as he stepped out from behind Hera, which she was glad for. "You are bonded to her and put her safety above all else."

She tried to ignore that Viktor was standing flush with her now, his elbow grazing hers and she stepped away, all the while she felt his eyes on her.

"I could attempt some form of a veil around Halcyon, but it would weaken the one in the Underworld," Hecate stated from behind her and Viktor.

"I prefer not to have to hunt all the dead that escaped because you split yourself too thin, Hell Cat," Thanatos replied. Hera could hear the smirk in his voice and the subsequent thump and wheeze. Hecate gave as good as Thanatos had.

"I am going to hunt down Perses, A.K.A. General Olethros. I know he has everything to do with this... at least in some form," Amphitrite ground out, disappearing into aquamarine light before anyone could say anything. Hera understood why. She didn't want anyone to talk her out of it, to tell her it was pointless. Amphitrite needed to do something instead of sitting around and staring at their sister. Though Persephone was fine, Hera knew it brought back the horrid memories of their past. She could empathize with that.

"Shall I begin operations again?" West asked, not following Amphitrite. Smart man. He knew Amphitrite needed this time to gather herself. She was more likely to drown him right then than hug him.

"No, I need to pull the Senate together and form a plan on how to address the citizens," Hera said, ending on a sigh. "Until then, hold off on restarting. It is not like we can do much anyway, since every single fucking city is a war zone now."

Her hands clenched into fists at her words, a light misty breeze hitting her as West light jumped too. The man was getting smarter about when to joke and when to skedaddle.

"Devon, once you are done playing nursemaid, and once I finish the Senate meeting that I am sure will go off without a hitch," she said sarcastically, "I would like you and Cassandra to come before the Senate with your plan on the defense of Halcyon. Kiran is trained in triage and one of our most renowned surgeons, he will be able to help with medical."

Finley... was still missing and oh, was she needed. Again, damn it, where was the girl? At this point, with the latest attack on Persephone, she feared the worst.

Hera turned to her remaining sister and raised a brow. "Not too scared to return to the field, are you?"

Persephone gave her a baleful look in answer.

"Triple check the gates to Tartarus," she told her, stiffening her tone so the fear didn't shine through. If things went... wrong, she wanted to make sure the final reinforcement stood.

Persephone nodded and caught the gazes of Thanatos and Hecate. The immortals who were the closest things to deputies there were in the Underworld.

Hera tried to reassure herself that they would find answers, but she was failing. She knew they all thought it was Perses, cursed son of Crius, perpetrating this, working as the puppet master, but her gut told her it was much bigger than that. *So much bigger.*

The Titans had been building their alliances in the background for a while now. It could be any number of the older immortals doing this. It could be a team of them—Fates, it could be *all* of them outside of Tartarus. Hundreds, perhaps even thousands, of ancient deities could have placed their loyalties with Cronus right under her nose.

They were going up against an enemy far larger than themselves in numbers. And perhaps with power. Even taking into account Viktor's power now, too. Hera couldn't pinpoint when she started assuming him as a number on their side, or even thinking of it as his power instead of Hestia's, but she knew that they needed him.

"We will find a way through this intact. Us and Halcyon," Viktor whispered near her as Persephone and Devon became engrossed in discussing something she was sure was tooth achingly sweet. Some profession of love and all that crap.

Turning to Viktor, she let out a small laugh.

"You cannot know that." She shook her head, her body finally feeling the drain of fatigue and depression.

"I have my ways," he returned, a small smile on his face.

Oh, this man and all his Fates damned secrets. She hoped he was right.

### <u>Viktor</u>

Sitting before the fire, Viktor chanted the words of his people, of his mother's power. The visions were not consistent, but sometimes Chaos blessed him with enough information to give him something to work with. His power for foresight was as strong as his father's but just as inconsistent.

He may call the fire to tell him of the future, but it was the whim of the universe on if it answered, or even gave him anything tangible to interpret.

Under the blanket of darkness, Viktor watched the fires, hoping for a vision that never came. Sitting back, he put his face into his hands, frustrated at his lack of ability to gather something, anything, to help them figure out the next step in the battle currently making its way to their doorstep.

Out of all his powers, precognition would be the most beneficial right now.

The Fates-damned curse was keeping him from telling the goddesses anything relevant in regard to himself, so even if he did see something in the fire, would he be able to actually tell anyone without horrible repercussions?

Hera didn't trust him, not in any real way, and why should she? How much had he given her to trust him with?

Growling, he pulled his knee up and laid his arm on it, looking at the fire, but not seeing it.

Complex though the woman was, he had to admit he was intrigued by her. Called to her. He wished he could earn her trust enough for her to confide in him, and hopefully, should they survive this war, something could come of it. If nothing else, at least a friendship where she wasn't tempted to electrocute him every fifteen seconds.

It had been years since he even allowed himself to think about something like that. He had been a nomad up until he crossed the border of Halcyon and set up shop. Using his powers of empathy, he could gauge people's moods enough to manipulate them into hiring him without looking too much into his background.

It would have been extremely suspicious if they had, since he hadn't stayed anywhere more than three years since he ascended.

Thinking himself simply the son of a fire priestess, he had spent his youth at his mother's ankles, pestering his mother's familiar, and being the center of attention when it came to the elders. Children did not always survive, or at least not for long, when they were nomads and unwelcome everywhere. The environment was not conducive to child rearing, but his mother always managed to keep Viktor safe until she settled them, so he was seen as something of the heir of his people and treated as such.

He'd lived his life normally, blissfully unaware of the powers that simmered dormant in his blood. Until the day he died and came back to life, only to never die again.

His mother must have known well before they were invaded, but she said nothing, teaching him the craft of manipulating fire as she did.

It was the day his mother died—the day his father came—that it all changed for him. When he was told the whole truth of who he was.

By the time he was well into his forties, he looked as he did in his late twenties, and stayed that way, confirming the words of his father that he was immortal. Powerful. *More.*

How had Hera felt when she realized she was more, too? He thought of a much younger Hera, and he wondered if she'd entered her immortality as she was now—shut off, guarded, confusing, sarcastic, infuriating, gorgeous—or if she'd changed over time.

As much as he knew about her, he couldn't know what happened internally. He had watched her, needing to know when to make his leap into her orbit, and had slowly seen her for more than she was. Unbeknownst to him, his regard for the goddess had grown over time. And for most of it, the icy goddess had been unaware he even existed.

*What a stalker*, he laughed to himself.

But the truth was, he kept all the goddesses in his line of sight, knowing he needed to be up to date on everything for when the time came because of what the fires had said so long ago.

Hera was just the one that caught his attention.

And held it.

# Chapter 6

## Hera

ADAM GROANED IN HERA'S ear, moving his big frame against her, and she wished that her body would stir for him like it used to, but nothing happened. With a sigh, she shoved him away and stood up from the bed to pace his bedroom, unable to look at him. Adam was one of her... friends that she came to on a somewhat consistent basis, but tonight, it all felt so off.

So *wrong*.

Coming up to stand behind her, he kissed along her neck, took her hand, and spun her back around to look at him.

"Let me take your mind off things. That is why you are here, no?" Adam asked, his voice smooth as silk.

When she closed her eyes, he moved his kisses from her neck to nibble at her ear, focusing his attention there before attempting to move to her lips. He was one of the ones who tried to push kissing, but she wouldn't budge on that. It was just a line she refused to cross.

It was too intimate, and her dealings with the opposite sex were more akin to business transactions, as crass as that was to admit.

Long ago, when Hera first took power, she'd trusted and done more with her partners. She'd allowed men to sleep in her bed, to stay until morning, but that ended when she took the mantle of Archon. Then, those same men would needle their way into her political affairs, releasing secrets that hurt her image as the pious and benevolent leader. They painted her as a harlot who couldn't be trusted instead of a woman doing the same as all her male counterparts: enjoying herself and her sexuality.

Her response was to stop hiding her affairs. Let the world see she was equal to the male leaders of the past with nothing to hide.

The men who had tried to twist her reputation, the ones who coveted her title, took it to another level. Had she been mortal, she would have been assassinated more than a few times. She'd woken up to a knife against her throat by a male paramour she had trusted. Her date for a political evening had stabbed her in the back, literally, as they made their way home.

Creating Zeus all those centuries ago had backfired in some ways as well. The large deity had become a scapegoat for men to do evil things and blame an entity that could not be held accountable. Women used Zeus as a way to work around the laws pertaining to adultery.

For a short period of time, she'd allowed people to think she was favored by Zeus, hoping that would cull some of the more brazen assassination attempts. Alas, they only increased. She'd started to resent Zeus, the imaginary male deity, who'd seemed more powerful in humans' minds than she actually was in life. He'd been accused of horrendous crimes yet was still worshiped and honored. While the real goddess, working at keeping the humans from destroying themselves, was branded as weak, useless, and nothing more than a wanton political operator.

So, she stopped having relationships in the public eye, and then relationships period. Now, she was left with a few lovers, who she only met when she needed to let off steam. But she didn't love them. And she never, ever trusted them.

Trust. Something she lost the ability to do. When her father killed her sisters. When all the men in her life used her, discarded her, then tried to kill her.

So yeah, she wasn't interested in making deep connections.

"Sorry, I am just not as much into this as I thought I was." She placed her hand against his chest, leaning in carefully to touch her lips to his cheek in a soft kiss. She knew she would need to evacuate him soon, so it would be a long time before they saw each other again. If ever. "I need to go."

"Why do I feel like this is goodbye?" he asked with a smirk. Hera knew he understood their arrangement as a mutually beneficial good time, and they would both miss it.

"Because, darling, it is," she whispered, stepping back.

The words rang with truth, and Adam accepted it with a nod. He grabbed his shirt, buttoning it back up, as she did her own and retrieved her purse from the side table. Before she left, she turned and took in the tall, dark, and handsome friend who gave her body comfort when it was maxed out and never asked for anything in return.

"Stay safe, Adam," she said finally. With that, she walked out of his home and started walking down the empty night-time street. She couldn't light jump yet since he was probably watching. Turning to look, it was confirmed when he waved from his window, and she gave a small wave in return.

An odd sense of loss overcame her. She wasn't just walking away from a lover; some part of her life was over. It didn't make sense, but nothing much did these days with her emotional state.

Hera wanted to say her lack of libido was all due to the stress of what was coming, and yes, that was a major part of it, but the truth was that she couldn't focus on Adam when she kept seeing Viktor for some Fates-damned reason. Her attraction to the infuriating man was causing issues with the other men in her life.

That pissed her off more than anything. Never, ever, had she had a problem losing herself to pleasure before. Not until that tight-lipped man walked into her senate hall. She couldn't lose herself in bliss to ignore everything weighing so heavily down on her.

The streetlight above her flickered before exploding and raining glass down onto the street.

She scowled at the broken glass. That was Viktor's fault, too, and it was going into her mental book full of all the things she would lay at his feet when given the opportunity.

Regardless of her feelings, Olympus had accepted him, and they needed him in the fight to come.

Releasing a sigh, she tried to center herself.

Tomorrow morning, she would get to the bottom of his oath—or curse—and find a way to work with him once she knew everything. Once she finally had her answers.

And if there wasn't a way around the damn thing, she would have to figure out how to trust him without all the details she really needed.

As much as she did not want to admit it, she needed Dr. Viktor Alden.

Somewhere nearby, another streetlight exploded.

## **<u>Viktor</u>**

Half asleep, Viktor rolled away from where Nyx swatted his cheek with her paw, trying to ignore her. She took her attempt to wake him up a tad further by jumping onto his back, her claws digging into his skin. When he jolted at the stabbing sensation, Nyx flew off his back in an arc, spitting and hissing, her fur standing on end.

"If you choose to wake me up that way, be prepared for the consequences," he grumbled, shoving himself up to a sitting position and rubbing his eyes. Light filtered in through the window, letting him know it was early morning. He could have slept for at least another hour if Nyx had not decided to wake him up.

*"The angry female is here,"* Nyx announced, her telepathic tone seething. He knew he would have to beg Nyx for forgiveness, or he would be looking over his shoulder all day long. She would finally go through with her plan to reduce his garage to cinders.

"Hera?" he asked, lowering his hands and looking at the feline now at the foot of his bed, who was licking her paws as if nothing had transpired. That was dangerous. The more affronted she was, the easier to apologize. When she acted like nothing was wrong ... he was doomed.

*"Yes. She seemed upset, so I thought I should wake you. The power running through her could easily demolish this house."* Dropping her paw, she met his gaze with her fiercely intelligent feline eyes. *"As you know, if anyone is to burn this place down, it will be me."*

With that, Nyx jumped from the bed, trotting off like only a feline of incredible self-importance could.

"Warning noted," he whispered with a shake of his head before standing to throw on some sweatpants and a shirt.

As he walked out of his bedroom, his bare feet hit the hardwood floors, announcing his approach as Hera swung around to face him.

And said nothing. Something in her eyes held him still.

"Huh," she said aloud, obviously not as much to him as to herself. "You look different without your glasses..."

Narrowing his eyes, he observed Hera as she stalked toward him, suddenly feeling very much like prey caught in a predator's sight.

"You are quite attractive, Viktor," she whispered as her eyes roved over him, wishing he could reciprocate the attention without feeling like he was taking advantage. He knew more about her than she knew, so it felt incredibly wrong to act on it.

But what if she took the first step in that direction? Was he morally obligated to step back until she did?

Fates, he didn't want to. He wanted desperately to give into the pull Hera had on him. To know her in every aspect a man could know a woman.

Shaking his head, he stepped back, though it took a herculean effort to do so.

"Uh, thank you? Is this why you barged into my home so early?" He wasn't sure of himself as she looked him over. Perhaps he should make some quip? What did people normally do when caught in her trap?

Chew their own leg off?

"No." She turned, breaking the tension, but it did not soothe the beast inside of him that saw her perusal as both a challenge and an invitation. She was gorgeous, no doubt about it, but dangerous. As so many of the most deadly creatures in the wild were.

"We need to talk," she said. "As much as I loathe Olympus giving a throne to everyone like a participation trophy, there are things you should know." A brow raised. "There are things both of us should know, really, but we can start with the basics."

Viktor withheld a sigh and looked out his window at the forest and mountain beyond.

"The Titans attacked the Underworld to get your father out, then there was the attack on the oceans to nullify Amphitrite and West's power. Now, we have human hordes, ostensibly created by the Titans, coming at us from all sides," he stated with little fanfare before returning his gaze to Hera. His stomach churned and sweat beaded on his forehead as the curse caught up to him.

Frozen and staring at him with her mouth slightly ajar, she said nothing. She was a vision even when in a state of shock, her blonde hair pulled back in a ponytail that he wanted to release from its tie and run his fingers through.

"How? Or am I allowed to know that?" She laughed, but it did not sound like it held any true mirth. "Oh, of course not. For all I know, you're a stalker-spy combo who knows enough to get past my boundaries so you can find the most opportune time to turn on me." Her look cut through his own thoughts.

"Why can you not trust anyone? Not even truly your sisters?" he asked, knowing he shouldn't say anything, but he had to get to the heart of this issue with Hera if there was any hope of them defeating a Titan, much less a legion of them. "They died and became goddesses, too, and they are not having as much of an issue with trusting people as you are."

Lightning danced between Hera's fingertips, and he knew immediately his words had threatened the very delicate grasp she was holding onto the edge of an emotional cliff with.

*Great.* He was not the best at the same communication he so often berated his patients about. A very pot meet kettle situation he would need to remedy in the future—if he had one.

"You know nothing about me," she seethed. "And I know nothing about you, *Viktor.*" She took a slow step forward. "You showed up out of nowhere, after centuries hiding from us, right when my rule is destabilized. For all I know, you're behind this with the Titans." She scoffed, "Are you really even a therapist? Is your name even Viktor?"

She put a mocking emphasis on his name. He knew she was dangerous right now, but he walked up to her, anyway. Olympus had shown that card for him by not allowing him to have a throne by his chosen name. It had most likely only reinforced she knew nothing about him, which was not going to work in his favor.

*Thanks for the extra work, Olympus.*

"You are right. My name is not Viktor." He swallowed the bile that tried to rise as he came close to the boundaries of his curse. "My real name doesn't change that I am who I say I am, the bearer of your sister Hestia's power. I am here to help, but it would be a damn sight easier if you'd let me in enough to do so."

"Then there cannot be secrets."

"And how many of your secrets are known to the world, Zenovia?" he asked, using her alias name in a mocking tone as she had done his. "Archon Zenovia Quinton, am I correct in the name? Cute that the name means 'life of Zeus'. A fun little play of words."

Narrowing her eyes, she stepped into his personal space. It was the closest they'd been, and yet she meant to intimidate him. As she opened her mouth to let loose some witty comment, he was sure, the retort died on her lips. A flicker of something crossing her face, as if she were having a conversation with someone else who Viktor wasn't privy to.

Watching as her fists unclenched, the electricity disappearing from her hands and a look of … fear? Hurt? Shock?

A myriad of emotions crossed her face.

"They're here."

### <u>Hera</u>

Edie was in the middle of Halcyon, looking down at a crowd of people moving into the center of the city. The horde's last known location was not anywhere near the city center. They were moving fast, but not that fast—so where did these people come from?

They were making their presence known by lighting fires, fighting people trying to stop them, and in an almost animalistic manner, making their way to the empty senate building.

The building she would have called her senators to later that very same day, and she was so thankful she had decided to stop by Viktor's home first even if they had only managed to irritate each other. She could at least acknowledge she kept her claws sheathed, which was a huge show of willpower for her these days.

Without sparing a glance at Viktor, she light jumped to the senate building, not surprised to feel Viktor's fire following her.

Time for him to prove himself both loyal and useful.

"They were at least a week away. Looks like that confirms your theory of them using portals to get here," Viktor said as he rushed after her to the window, looking out onto the main street, the line of people just visible around the corner.

"Now we need to find out the why. Why are humans jumping into a battle, they should be running in the opposite direction from," Hera muttered as she ran to the double doors, pushed them open, and ran to the middle of the road to take the mob head on. Sending out a call to her sisters, the oppressive humidity stifling her. She tried again; nothing. As if there were a block on their connection and she was unable to call or be called by her sisters.

"Damn it," she muttered as Viktor came up beside her, a questioning look in his hazel eyes. "I cannot call to my sisters."

Viktor stopped and evaluated the chaos around them, his eyes brightening with fire, and he shot off a fireball from his hand that hit an invisible dome above them. The fire blasted apart and rained down sparks, blinking out before hitting the buildings of Halcyon. A dome covered the entire city.

The Fates-damned Titans had trapped them. It was the same as the dome that cut off communication when Crius went to the Underworld and battled Persephone. Unable to call to her sisters, only their familial link told them that she was in trouble. Something similar happened when Amphitrite went against Crius's wife, Eurybia, who turned the waters in to a cesspool of death until she was defeated by West's leviathan. Which Hera had found amazing but refused to tell West, lest he develop more of an ego.

Hera gaped at the dome, confused about which Titan they were dealing with. A witch could also create a shield, but Hera was unsure if it could be of this scale. Crius had executed a shield before—but had he gathered enough power to encapsulate an entire city? Perses was his son—did he inherit that same power?

Oh, how she wished she'd known General Olethros was Perses before the battle for the sea. The Titan had been exposed to the highest levels of power in Goryeo, where the unrest had started. She didn't know how the conflict had grown at this unnatural rate, but she had a strong feeling she knew who had initiated it.

But she hadn't known who he was until he'd exposed himself in battle. The Titan had been able to shield his powers, not as effective-ly as Viktor though. The thought had her stumbling over another suspicion—was the mysterious deity who'd hidden Viktor actually Perses? Viktor had known to look for the dome, hadn't he?

She didn't want to keep suspecting him, but how could she not when they both could shield their power signatures better than any deity she knew aside from her father, and she knew damn well what side *he* was on.

Fates damn it! More questions than answers. Questions that would have to wait until they handled this bit of fighting and could get to her sisters to make a plan, depending on the outcome of this battle. And a battle it would be. Groups of the mob were starting to notice them in between destroying the city center.

"Guess you better get ready to fight," she told him. "Aside from fire, what else you got? I know you're a therapist, so I am hoping your fallback isn't to discuss these people's feelings on killing us. I doubt they give a shit."

Cutting his eyes to hers, he said nothing and moved to hold a combat stance beside her as the army encroached on them.

Hera called her lightning, and the comforting feel of the electricity skittered over her skin. She knew her eyes were blue and full of electric sparks, as opposed to her godform's normal gold light when she called on her full goddess form. These were humans, so they needed to show some caution—she didn't want to raze them, given the chance that they were acting against their will, and she didn't want to reveal the truth of her goddess, either.

She thrust her hands out straight above her, and her lightning came down around them, sending the closest combatants back and away from the center of the city where they could do the most damage.

Noticing that Viktor had not called on his power yet, she turned to snap at him, but her eyes caught his.

"Now!" she yelled, her heart thumping quickly and not all of it having to do with the battle at hand. What if he turned on her? What if she had to fight all these humans *and* the man carrying her sister's power?

If that happened, she had already lost and should probably accept she was going to meet Chaos a lot sooner than she expected. Because if she went to the crossroads, she might just let herself die the final death and be done with it. She was Fates-damned tired.

Shock stole through her at the feel of his magic completely unfurling. Flames licked over his skin, filling his aura with heat. His was a purely raw elemental form of power, whereas her electricity was more dependent on her goddess manifestation, the same as Amphitrite, Persephone, and Devon.

Not West, the son of a Titan.

The damn sense of betrayal bit at her again, but she shook her head, knowing there was nothing she could do to get the answers right then, and faced their invaders.

Both she and Viktor sent warning strikes, but they kept getting closer. The nearer they got, the more Hera could see that something in their expressions wasn't right. Their faces were slack, their eyes blank. Not the look of someone in battle, of someone wrecking the city with a destructive vigor. These people were not out acting foolish because some idiot Titan offered them something their selfish human nature couldn't say no to. They were not there for power like her father would have been.

Stepping up next to Viktor, Hera tried not to feel slighted when he stepped away, since he was most likely keeping her from becoming an immortal bonfire.

"Look at them ... something isn't right," she whispered, hoping he could hear.

Viktor scanned the crowd for several moments, taking in the same mindless stumbling that Hera had. The vacant expressions on their faces and jolting movements. Clothing that looked like it hadn't been changed in weeks, covered in grime, blood, and other very unsavory body fluids.

They were more puppet than human.

As Viktor took in the behavior of the mindless servants the Titans had made them into, the humans took that opportunity to advance forward and beginning their attack.

Without a word, he moved toward them. The people didn't halt as Viktor approached, and she tried not to scream at him to get back before they covered him. All at once, like a coordinated dance, the people brandished their weapons, aiming for Viktor.

A few shot off some bullets, ones that melted before they even came close to the God of Fire.

*Now*, she was going to yell at him.

"What are you doing, you fool?" Hera yelled. Was he trying to get sent to the Underworld? Was that how he would screw them all over? They find him only for him to then kill himself before they had even begun.

Oh, that would be the irony the crazy old bats called the Moirai would thrive in. Chittering away while Hera burned their tower to the ground with them in it.

Ignoring her, he held out his hands, palms facing up, and called upon an unnatural fire, one that moved through all the colors of the rainbow. As the colorful flame flickered, he began chanting in some long-lost language she hadn't bothered to learn.

Honestly, there were so many damn languages out there, it was pointless to even try at a certain point.

One by one, each person dropped their weapons. The clattering of weapons hitting the ground all at once was an explosive sound on the nearly silent street. Viktor's low chanting tapered off as the flames in his palm went out, his voice drifting off until he was done.

When Viktor's hands closed, the mob shifted, transforming. Some shook their heads like they were coming out of a strange dream, some fell to their knees, others rubbed their temples, and many were crying.

Hera jogged over to Viktor, watching the crowd with wide eyes.

"What did you do?" she asked.

"They had a spell of some kind cast over them. I simply ... released them," he whispered in a voice full of pain.

"*How* did you know how to do that?" Her confusion turned into frustration as she stepped closer, readying her lightning.

Sad eyes turned to hers.

"Because I have seen them use it on people before. *My* people." His voice hitched on the end, and he turned away from her as she took in the scene before her.

A spell. So, there was a witch involved.

An anger bubbled up in her. One she knew was not good. Nope. She was dangerous right now, and she did not want the humans to take the brunt of what she owed the Titans.

She tested the bounds of her power—whatever Viktor had done, he'd eliminated the shield, too. Without saying a word, she light jumped to the coast of Germania off the mainland of Zephyr. No one inhabited the healthy parts of it, as it was far too close to the wastelands to maintain any growth.

With a loud scream, she released her goddess's form and let her anger at being helpless explode into the world around her. A tornado formed above her, throwing up rocks and dirt.

She was tasked to protect her people, and she was failing. It was only the beginning of this war, and she could already see the losses on both sides. Fear palpated under her skin. Her bones felt like liquid as she fell to her knees, a sob that could only have come from her leaving her lips.

Digging her hands into the soil, she offloaded enough electricity into the earth that the ground and thin trees around her lit up blue and gold.

Her sisters. She wouldn't see them lost again, but how did she fight when she was still so weak?

A blast of power from behind her caught her off guard, and her tornado moved back into the clouds at her distraction.

Standing on wobbly legs, she turned to see Viktor staring at her from twenty feet away, his expression full of agitation and disappointment. He began walking toward her, but she felt vulnerable and unable to keep her rage as a shield in place, so she stepped back. He light jumped and was on her before she could escape. Grabbing her by the shoulders, she took in huge gulps of air as he let the fire grow in his eyes.

"You are not giving up," he growled, as if he knew her and her thoughts. He kept her pinned as he looked into her eyes, his hands too strong for her to break away from. "You are the strongest of us all, yet you think of yourself as the weakest. Continue to think so and so you shall be."

Hera growled, hating that he could see her so vulnerable. The primal part of her wanted to lash out at him, angry he saw her weakness, but something deeper wanted to bask in his warmth and comfort. To let him help her fix her problems. She wanted so badly to trust him, but she didn't trust these feelings were real and that he wasn't her enemy. That he was just toying with her brain ... and other parts of her anatomy that seemed to stop working unless he was around.

Those parts of her lit on fire then. As if called to do so, lust stirred in her belly, and her eyes dropped to his lips. His proximity called to her, but her damn brain came up with all the reasons she needed to keep her lust in check, clicking her good sense into gear before she did something stupid and reckless.

Reminding herself of what she had learned during their battle helped; him not having a godform and stopping a massive spell in its tracks.

Earlier, when they were arguing, he'd known about the clashes with the Titans. He'd admitted Viktor was an alias.

All signs pointed to him being attached to an unknown Titan. Why would Olympus allow him to have a throne?

A sob left her lips as Hera pulled in more power and broke free of his hold finally. The conflicted part of her roared inside her brain. Pain and fear flowed from her soul and engulfed the world around her.

She sprinted away from him, but she fell to her knees again as she expelled a wave of power so intense that it sounded like a thunderclap. When the thunder lessened, she could hear a groan of pain from Viktor. When she whirled around, falling on her hindquarters, he was doubled over. As if her torment was somehow affecting him. As if she were forcing her pain into him.

And yet he still walked to her. She watched him warily, unsure if he would pin her again. Why did he have to be so unpredictable? Why couldn't he be afraid of her like everyone else?

He took her shoulder with his free hand and squeezed lightly.

"Call the senate and let's discuss our next move," he whispered sadly. A full-blown sadness bordering on depression looked back at her from his eyes.

Without another word, Viktor light jumped away, leaving Hera in a mess of her own making.

# *Chapter 7*

<u>**Viktor**</u>

**V**IKTOR SLAMMED HIS BEDROOM door shut and fell to his knees, the anger and fear under his skin like a living fire.

*Damn, Hera. Damn her!*

He felt Nyx's power sidle up beside him as he half-crawled to the bathroom, slamming that door by falling against it.

"Not now, Nyx," he pleaded, leaning on the stone counter with his elbows and rubbing his eyes.

*"You got too close. You need to release it all into the fire and not involve yourself intimately with the Queen. Physically or mentally. You knew the toll it would take before you started this. You are taking the steps out of order!"*

A rage like Viktor hadn't felt in hundreds of years bubbled beneath his skin. He was out of his mind with Hera's emotions right then, but some of it was his if he looked around the edges of the pain in his mind. The ones she had offloaded onto him in that moment of self-deprecation. The ones he had dumbly allowed into his mind so he could get a grasp on her mental state before he left her to own devices. And so, he could figure out his next move with her.

If he were being honest, he also hoped to take some of the heavy burden from her shoulders. Taking some of it had left him in this state, and he became incredibly aware of how much pain she lived in all the time. Every day.

Suddenly, the bathroom door was thrown open. Nyx sat in the doorway; her small feline head tilted in question before her eyes glowed with fire.

*"Outside. Garage. Now."*

He let out a growl, one that Nyx met. Yet hers was not that of the domesticated house cat she seemed to be.

Fire broke out along his skin, coming from his pores as the tension built.

How did Hera feel this all the time? How did she keep it hidden?

How strong was this woman?

*"Now!"*

Nyx was done talking at that point. She lunged at him, taking him down, and his back hit the garage floor instead of the bathroom tile where he had just been.

Flames erupted around them, and Nyx let out a roar, her true form standing over him.

She looked like a black jaguar, but as tall as a horse with fire for eyes and tail.

*"You took on emotions. You have been so good about leaving the humans on their own. Why did you allow her past your wall?"*

His adrenaline was fading, and Viktor could feel the physical and mental exhaustion overtaking him.

Letting his head thump back on the garage floor, he watched one of his metal sculptures melting. *Damn it.* He had spent a month on that. Thankfully, the garage was flameproof for this very reason. Sadly, his work was not.

A paw hit him across his face, bringing his focus back to the very large, very angry jaguar standing over him.

*"Already, you forget what the fires told you. You know the end to the story if you make even one misstep."*

Closing his eyes, he tried to push out the images that Nyx forced into him. A curse cast on him by his own mother with her dying breath long ago in an attempt to save him. A curse that cost him the love of his life.

It would have changed so much had they allowed him to continue on his path. Yet, he knew she would die either way.

Pinching the bridge of his nose to keep out the visions of the woman he had held night after night, promising her forever before her death took her from him. Losing control, he let out an agonized wail as he slammed his hands on the ground next to him. Staring past Nyx's head to the ceiling of the garage, he watched the burning flecks of fire swirl in the air above him.

"I know, Nyx. Please get off me," he ordered, his voice so low no mortal would have heard a word, but Nyx stood off him, quelling the flames as he sat up. His elbows on his knees, he put his head into his hands.

*"It makes you vulnerable when you take their emotions into yourself. You know better. Do not do that again."*

Giving Nyx a nod, Viktor refused to promise anything.

If the fires were correct, the curse would need to be broken soon. The visit to the Moirai had only confirmed what he already feared was true.

He just had to figure out how exactly to break a centuries-old curse in less than a few days.

## <u>Hera</u>

Sitting in the senate chambers, Hera stared straight ahead at the doors, the room empty of all but her.

Unfortunately, her mind was anything *but* empty.

It hadn't been since the dawn of her powers that she had felt so conflicted and lost. Anger and fear were her constant companions now, and the one person she didn't truly trust had given her what she never expected.

Comfort. Almost a sense of belonging.

Yet, the reason for her turmoil still boiled her blood as she thought back on what she and Viktor had seen.

A horrible spell. A massive trap. These people were not fighting because they wanted to. They were being played as puppets by the Titans. Killed for the simple fact that her father's people wanted chaos, needed a foothold in their world, and held no love for humans. This was exactly what she feared would happen should the Titans win the war. This world would no longer be for the humans who inhabited it, but for the Titans to glut themselves on everything in it.

Perhaps the Titans felt this way because they never knew what it was like to *be* human.

Hera was human for longer than her sisters. Years longer. She was the only sister to make it to adulthood before she ascended, though her memories of that time were foggy. Living in the mountain next to Olympus, Themis kept her hidden from her father as long as she could. Until Persephone and Amphitrite offered her a chance to take Cronus down.

No power pulsed through her then, only her own human blood. Though her human memories of her ascension were lost to time, the days and nights blending together, there was one thing she remembered well.

Grief. That was one memory that still tore at her, that kept her eyes full of tears as she tried to sleep, missing her mother and sisters. Missing her life from before her father had turned on them.

The grief turned sharper, more painful, and angry when she felt like she'd been too small to fight back. That she failed her sisters by not saving them. It was all a huge, knotted ball in her chest, every day and every night still.

Weak. Her proud, sarcastic femme fatale was all a cover, so no one knew how truly pathetic she was.

A fraud.

"Hera," a gentle voice called to her.

Blinking, she realized her sisters, Viktor, Devon, and West, were all in the room with her.

Scanning over them, she flinched at the concern on their faces. She wasn't brave enough to look at Viktor right then. The mix of vulnerability and suspicion was too combustible in her veins.

She cleared her throat, but she was cut off.

"The human hordes are not just being *prodded* by Titans. They are being directed by them. The humans are all under a powerful manipulation spell. I was able to pull them out of it, but I can almost guarantee every one of those uprisings was at the hands of the Titans, with humans as the casualties," Viktor reported to the rest of their group.

Viktor was taking control of the situation and giving her time to gather herself. Hera wanted to be thankful, but her embarrassment was fresh. Then she wanted to lash out, but her sisters turned their focus to Viktor as he apprised them of what she should have herself.

"Can the humans fight it? Do they remember enough that we can find the Titan responsible?" Persephone asked, yet Hera noted Amphitrite's narrowed eyes. She was already planning whose door she would be breaking down for answers. Hera would have to pick her brain later on what all she had planned.

"Nothing," Viktor said. "When they came to after I broke the spell, they only remembered what they were doing before it all happened. Farming, working, caring for the youths, they couldn't say what or who they had seen prior to it all aside from their normal day-to-day socialization."

"Devon," Hera spoke up, her thoughts following along with Viktor's words. "If we take you to the humans we have, can you check for power trails?"

"I can," Devon said with a slight nod.

She noted that Viktor did not seem at all surprised they had someone who could see the power trail of a Titan, or god, long after they had left the area.

How did he know so much when she knew so very little?

"Persephone—"

"Tartarus is secure, and I have extra guards posted. Hecate is currently weaving a spell that can notify us of a breach, should someone show up."

Nodding, Hera sat back.

"They are using our own people against us, using them like puppets and throwing them away," Hera seethed, and the lights of the Senate chambers flickered.

"It won't be humans forever," West piped in from where he sat on the bench with his arm thrown behind him. "If they can warp the minds of humans with this spell, can they do the same to deities? How much longer until they can control us? Are we immune to it? If we think so, do we know for sure?"

The lights flickered again, nearly going out completely as Hera clinched her armrests tightly. "I do not know for sure," she growled. "Whatever spell this is may not even be cast by a Titan. They could have witches on their side now. Whoever it was though had cast a powerful shield over the city during the attack, keeping me from calling you."

"Then we need to be even more vigilant," Amphitrite stated, and Devon gave Persephone a slight shove, earning himself an eye roll from his wife. "We need to make sure we are not alone like we were when the attack on the Underworld and the ocean happened. They can cut us off from each other."

"Agreed," Everyone but her and Viktor stated. Looking over at him, she caught the look of annoyance on his face. It figured that a man who lived in the mountains by himself would, of course, be averse to the prospect of people entering his domain. Or, from the look on his face, people existing in general. Goddesses included.

"You are welcome to hang out in your hovel and grumble at trespassers, Viktor, but should you be turned against us, I will be first in line to kill you," Hera stated, though her heart was not in it like it had been in the past.

*She* didn't even believe herself anymore.

Being callous and cold-hearted was her armor, and she wore it always.

"Thanks for the warning," Victor said flatly.

"Adjourned. Now, go away. I have things to handle before I call the senators." Hera stood, shooing everyone out. They disappeared two at a time, aside from Viktor. He cast her a quick look before the fire engulfed him, and he was gone.

Calling her own power to light jump to her office, Hera opened her window the moment she was corporal again and sent out a call for Edie. The raptor must have been nearby since it took her a mere minute to accept her call.

"Hey, pretty lady," Hera cooed as the bird allowed her to run her fingers over the golden feathers of her head. Edie gave a chirp, rubbing her head against Hera's hand in an affectionate manner. "I've yet another favor to ask, and I apologize for so much work in such a short period of time. We will celebrate our evisceration of the Titans with a girls' night in. Perhaps I will have steak and you some type of large rodent?"

Edie shuffled her head, making an enthusiastic nodding motion.

"Good." Hera laughed at the raptor's enthusiasm. "I need you to keep an eye on Viktor. Make sure no one goes near his cabin, or any spells are woven around it."

Edie's wings ruffled, her sign she was in agreement and ready to go. It was helpful that Hera could share her thoughts with the bird so that Edie knew who she was looking for. She sent her images of what Viktor looked like and his home until she felt a pushback when Edie had all the information she needed.

With a sigh, Hera stepped back, and Edie took off. Watching until the golden eagle had disappeared into the forests beyond. She told herself this was because she needed to know when and if he turned on her, that she was keeping her enemy close. But deep down, something called her a liar.

A part of her that knew a truth that the rest of her did not.

# Chapter 8

### <u>Viktor</u>

VIKTOR WORKED TO CALL upon the flames as Nyx faced off with an eagle. He knew it wasn't an ordinary eagle since no ordinary eagle was gold, or as big, or felt like it carried Hera's power. So, naturally he concluded Hera had sent her to check up on him.

Unsure how he felt about that, Viktor continued to stoke the fire in the hopes something would come of it. It was pointless to speculate about the bird's presence since he was unsure in general when it came to the goddess.

*"Make this infernal beast leave!"* Nyx growled into his mind, disrupting his work.

Pinching the bridge of his nose, realizing he had been forgetting to put his glasses on since he hadn't been working, he shook his head. Wearing them helped him play the part of a human doctor, helped him feel more mortal to have a disadvantage like poor eyesight, something an immortal god would not have to deal with.

Viktor looked over to where Nyx stared at the eagle as it cleaned its feathers high up in the tree. It was next to the garage doors he had opened to let the mountain breeze in.

Shaking his head with a sigh, he knew Nyx was bored and looking for dramatics. The eagle was nowhere near the Ovinnik.

"It is not bothering you at all," he stated, watching the powerful creature continue to act like a disgruntled house cat.

Without another word, the Ovinnik made a running leap for the tree, but the eagle only tilted its head in response, and Nyx came to a sudden stop. Her hackles lowered as she laid down against the ground, making herself smaller, her head tilted to the side. Now *that* had Viktor's attention. Nyx didn't look scared, but curious.

"What?" he asked, standing, the fire all but forgotten.

*"She is as ancient as I..."* Nyx's voice trailed off in his mind as the Ovinnik moved to a sitting position, no longer in an aggressive state. Viktor really looked at the eagle then, taking it all in. A memory flashed in his mind of the eagle, this exact one, sitting upon the branch of a tree near him when he was a youth. Then the many times that he had slept fireside, the bird doing nothing more than it was now, but a deep comfort had come over him.

A guardian. Edie was a guardian.

"You've been taking care of Hera," he whispered, his eyes closing as the curse came dangerously close to being triggered. He knew who the eagle was now but seeing her after so long took him off guard. He'd assumed she had been killed.

A powerful feeling, one like the shock of a mild electrical current ran over his skin, and he turned to where Hera stood a few feet away from him.

"We have called the senate and, though I am loath to admit it, you are needed there."

The eagle took flight and landed near Hera, an obvious familiarity there between the goddess and the raptor.

"What is her name?" he asked, not acknowledging what Hera had just said. He needed her to confirm what he thought it was, and when she did, he needed to look into her eyes. Needed to see if Hera could push through his curse even just a little bit.

Hera's eyes flashed before she looked at the bird. Her fingers gently stroked the soft feathers of the bird's breast.

The name sounded in his mind at the same time it came from Hera's lips.

"Edie."

### Hera

Hera walked into the senate hall with Viktor following behind her. She kept her back straight and her haughty expression in place.

Her armor.

None of what she would be speaking to the senators about was going to go well. They were the descendants of the Primordial Gods, their bloodline watered down with mortal blood until they were barely more powerful than the average human.

Even so, they themselves had the same tempers as the gods of old, which meant Hera always had to keep her head clear and never let them see an ounce of weakness. Not if she wanted to keep her position at the top of the pecking order.

Not for the power, though she did allow them to think that was the reason, but because it was the only true way to protect the sisters she had failed once. She would not fail them a second time.

"Cassandra had updated us on the breach in Halcyon's borders," Kiran started, not giving Hera a chance to even sit before he started. "What are your plans to protect our people, Archon?"

Keeping her eyes on Kiran, she moved to her seat, not allowing him the satisfaction of submission. She was the alpha between the two of them, and every once in a while, she had to remind him of exactly that.

Seating herself, she caught Viktor's eyes from where he stood next to a pillar at the side of the room, not bringing any attention to himself. Viktor no longer wore his glasses, and she assumed it was pointless now to pretend he was human when everyone in the room knew the truth about him holding Hestia's power.

He seemed to naturally fall into the shadows, much like her sisters, who were there, but up front with their soulbonds. Seated on the benches. Like normal people.

"As Archon, I open this meeting," Hera started, shooting Kiran a look of reproach that did nothing to mute the man's derision. Deep down, she felt that his resentment was somewhat fair since she had been the one to send his sister out on the mission she'd disappeared on. She really needed Finley to return. All the spies and Edie as well had failed to find the missing senator, but they had also returned already. "I have called this emergency meeting. As Kiran felt the need to state without letting me open the meeting, our borders have been breached. Our people are being used by the Titans as mindless puppets, attacking one another and our infrastructure. Not only are they killing each other, but they will die when they meet our defenses."

"You'd kill your own citizens?" Kiran asked, his fingers balling into fists on top of the table.

When Hera shot him a look of censure, his eyes finally moved away, and she nodded. Let him think her cold and heartless, but she would not allow the Titans to make it fully through. She would not allow them to control her in any way, would not let them rule once again, which would cause many more deaths in the end.

"If it comes down to it, I will, but I would rather them not be a sacrifice."

Silence stilled the air in the room as everyone took in the information that Hera had given.

Her eyes moved to Viktor's, and she wondered how many others there were that could break the spell. Or was Viktor the only one able to?

"I propose that we call upon all of our army—"

"You would kill them before we even—" Kiran attempted again to interrupt, but Hera did not have a chance this time to admonish him.

"Kiran, I did not think it was yet your turn. It seemed your Archon was speaking," Persephone stated in a low tone that had all the same effect as yelling.

Kiran sat back, his eyes on his fisted hands upon the tabletop.

"I propose," Hera waited a beat before continuing on, "that we call upon, and activate, what is left of our army. Cassandra will, of course, work with Devon on logistics, but if Hecate could find more spellcasters, I'd like one with each regiment. If we can break the spell, we have no reason to lift our weapons until we face the Titans themselves."

From the corner of her eye, she could see Ryder and Calista both nodding. Hera didn't need to see Cassandra since she was already coordinating and strategizing.

Without Finley, she did not know which direction Kiran would go. He was a wildcard these days without his twin next to him. His anger was palpable, and she wondered if he wouldn't argue just for the sake of sticking it to her.

Grinding his teeth, he looked at everyone in the room.

"All those in favor..." Before she finished, every voting member, sans Kiran, raised their hand.

Kiran locked eyes with her, glaring, but he slowly raised his hand in the air too.

"Let's hope you do better for our people than you did my sister," he rasped.

And even though they were said quietly, she was sure the words had echoed off the walls of the senate chambers.

# Chapter 9

### Viktor

VIKTOR WAS CONFUSED WHY Hera did not tell them that he had been the one to pull the humans from their spelled minds. Was she keeping it a secret to be used later at her convenience? He might have thought that a year ago, after watching her in action at gatherings and galas, but he was starting to see the true Hera shining through the armor she wrapped so tightly around her.

If he didn't know better, he'd think she was actively protecting him, which he needed to be honest with himself about. Hera would rather dig his grave than give him an ounce of trust—much less protection, unless she considered him an asset, which was entirely possible.

Still, Viktor let himself smile at the thought that he might be wearing her down, for it meant more than she could know. Catching his smile, she narrowed her eyes his way. He didn't care. She was obviously feeling something for him, and that was a step in the right direction.

It meant he hadn't totally ruined everything earlier in her moment of vulnerability. A moment where he wanted more than anything to hold her and make it all okay again as she fell apart on that shore, her power creating chaotic storms, as he took in all her pain.

The fires had told him a different story, and it was aligning with her actions.

Relief flooded him that he had not stepped off the correct path.

"Then we are in agreement. We will activate our army, and Hecate will call upon the witches of this world. Since we will need to continue meeting, please consider staying in Halcyon and allowing a trusted second to take your place in your territories."

The senator next to her, Kiran, was bristling enough that Viktor was feeling less than confident of the senate's loyalty toward their Archon.

His mood darkened at the thought of one of her own betraying Hera. Viktor would have to figure out the story there before they found a senator on the opposite team. He cut his eyes to West, who was standing next to Amphitrite with his own gaze narrowed on the senator.

What a difference from the West of only months ago. It seemed only yesterday West was stumbling drunk through the city. But when given such a huge responsibility, he took hold and became a leader. Viktor was impressed by the male and only hoped that he was part of what had contributed to such growth.

"This meeting is adjourned, and we will reconvene tomorrow at the same time. Stay safe, everyone," Hera ordered.

The senate doors slammed open, stopping all movement in the chambers. Every person in the room watched in absolute shock as a female walked down the aisle toward the senators. Her body was extremely thin, as if she had been lost for days in the forest without proper sustenance, and her mind was pushing off more emotions than Viktor would have been able to deal with had his shield not been in place. He knew who she was without anyone saying a word, though the fires never gave him exact information. It was enough to glean who they were dealing with here.

That thought was confirmed when Kiran stood up, his eyes wide, his anxiety palpable.

"Finley."

## Hera

Hera watched closely as Kiran stood and walked around the large curving senate table, his footsteps light as if walking toward an injured animal, not wanting to scare it. She could *feel* the power pulsing from Finley, a power the woman had not held before she left to find Hestia's scion.

As Kiran approached his sister, Finley raised her head from where her weakened body had fallen into a kneel. Or so she had thought until Finley looked up at her. Godfire was in the senator's eyes and Hera felt the room around her slow. Finley had ascended and her kneel was to a higher goddess. To Hera, as the queen.

Hera looked at her own sisters and saw it in their eyes as well. They knew what had happened, but not the how.

"Finley, what happened?" Kiran whispered as he moved to touch his sister's shoulder, but her flinch made him stiffen. She watched Kiran swallow whatever words he had been about to speak, his hand hovering there a moment before he pulled it back.

Calista suddenly came up between Kiran and Finley, the brave woman that she was, and walked Finley to the closest bench to be seated. Ryder was there a mere second later with a glass of water he helped her shaking hands take.

Hera could only watch, unsure of how to address this. She felt so much concern and guilt at the vision of the woman in front of her, but she never knew how to be sweet and caring in these situations. It was so much easier to demand answers and face the problem head on. Hera had been caught off guard, and she did not appreciate that. A little heads up from the Moirai would have helped so she could be ready to assist the newest goddess in her transition of power instead of standing there like a Fates-damned idiot.

"I..." Finley's voice was hoarse, as if she hadn't spoken in weeks. Perhaps she hadn't.

"Did they capture you?" Hera asked the words before she could think better of it.

Kiran shot her a look of fury over his shoulder as he knelt before his sister.

The idiot could be mad all he wanted. She needed to know what happened to Finley as much as anyone there did. A demigod with hardly more power than the average human now sat before them a full-fledged goddess. Let him think it was for her sole purpose of knowing the Titans and their whereabouts, but she really needed to know where Finley's head was at so that she could address the situation properly. She did not want to inflict more trauma on the girl.

Hera knew all about forced ascensions and the trauma they could bring if one's mind was not ready.

Humans died and could ascend if there was latent power, but demigods would only become gods in their own right if they were changed by a higher power—one that even Hera and her sisters had not reached.

"Did the Titans change you?" she demanded, an uncomfortable feeling in the pit of her stomach whenever she had to push for information in such a delicate situation. She hoped she wasn't wrong in her assumption, but when the fire and determination lit in Finley's eyes, she knew she had chosen the right path. Finley gave a slight nod of thanks. Hera was unsure if it was for her treating her as she always had, or for the fact that Hera's voice distracted her brother, who was currently hovering over the woman like the old machines called helicopters.

"Could you give her a damn minute!" Kiran yelled, his fists clenching as he swung around to face Hera. She let her electricity build up along her arms in preparation for a fight. She wouldn't kill him, but she would give him enough of a shock to shut him up for a while. He was really starting to give her a headache with his constant whining and attitude.

Kiran fell back as she started toward him, letting out a small amount of the electricity building under her skin as she moved.

"Have you forgotten who rules here, demigod?" the goddess in Hera chastised the senator as he scrambled back, the look of fear in his eyes giving her goddess a rush.

"Stop," Finley ordered, the power of her own goddess resonating in her voice. The shock in Kiran's eyes would have been comical had the situation not been so grim. She had used her new power to hold her brother back from turning on Hera, and he was now catching on to what most likely everyone in this room already knew.

Hera gave him another zap, just so she could feel a tiny bit better about him turning his fool back on her. Shooting her a look over his shoulder, it turned apologetic once his eyes caught her gold ones. He bowed in submission and Hera finally felt the relief of her goddess pulling back. Nodding to him that he may continue, his shoulders sagged in relief.

"Finley..." His voice broke as he turned back to her again and fell to his knees, the sound of them hitting the marble floor, the cracking noise, painful.

Now he saw the godfire. Now he understood.

Hera actually felt her heart squeeze at the look on the man's face. The pain, fear, anger, and confusion she knew all too well from learning the same had happened to her sisters while she'd been unable to stop it. To protect them.

She knew he felt like he had failed to protect her, but in the larger scheme of things, she was probably safer now than he was. She could hold her own in battle and possibly assist in rendering the Titans powerless once again.

"I don't know what happened. It was only one day after I left to find Hestia, and I awoke in a place with darkness. A woman was there ... and she told me I was finally ready."

Finley took a deep breath. This was most likely the most she had spoken in weeks. There was not any physical weakness within Finley, not any that wouldn't heal on its own soon with her immortality, but there was mental trauma, and she was working through it far better than Hera would have.

Being alone, ascending... *Oh, Finley.*

"I do not have complete control over my power, but enough so that she felt I was safe to leave and ask the goddesses for help. I don't remember much more than that. I cannot even remember her name..." Finley's face pinched in confusion when she realized the name was lost to her.

Her story had all the hallmarks of a certain Titan, but Hera said nothing. A clearing of the throat had Hera looking at Viktor, and she saw the same thoughts in his eyes.

"The goddesses," Kiran whispered. His shoulders bunched up and his hands clenched into fists as he turned toward Hera. Sneering, he stomped his way toward her, getting as close as he could with a table between them. Hera threw out a stream of electricity around Kiran should he try anything stupid. Hera did not necessarily want to hurt him. She could empathize with him, but she would also not back down and show weakness.

A threat was a threat. Friend or foe. That never mattered to Hera, as one could easily become the other and vice versa.

That was one life lesson she had learned well.

"You are the reason Finley is..." His anger seemed to spike at his loss of words.

"More powerful? More likely to survive the upcoming battle ahead?" she snapped back, light jumping over the table to face off with him.

"Dead!" he screamed, the echo from the marble increasing her already rampaging headache. He had done it. He had finally given Hera the migraine he had been working toward giving her for years.

"She is very much alive, you pompous ass. Pay a bit more attention. If the situation is beyond your scope, sit down and raise your hand like a good little boy until called upon to ask your questions."

Kiran stepped closer until his face was a mere inch from hers.

"Kiran, stop!" Finley shouted, disrupting a fight before it could start. A fight he could not, would not, win. "Just ... stop." Her voice weakened as she spoke.

It was taking too much energy, energy that should have been replenishing immediately, but wasn't—not even enough for her to make even the smallest attempt to stop her brother. Hera had figured her weakness was from trauma, as a goddess would have been well on her way to fully recovered by now. How much was done to Finley in the time she was gone?

"If she is such a powerful deity, why is she so weak?" Kiran asked, looking back at his sister over his shoulder before turning his angry gaze back to Hera.

*Well, question of the day and all that.*

"She needs to go to Olympus and, for lack of a better word, connect to her power there," Amphitrite stated, looking back at Hera with something akin to fear in her eyes, and Hera realized what she was thinking.

Their sisters, Demeter and Hestia, had been incredibly weak, unable to hold their power even once they were upon Olympus. It was not something she wanted to discuss in front of an irate Kiran, but she would need to get Finley there soon.

They could only hope that Finley's power didn't overtake her, that her soul was strong enough to contain the great volume of power. If not, they would have to take her to the Underworld, to her final death, and place her powers in a worthy human and wait for ascension.

Hera's heart hurt at the prospect of losing Finley. No, Hera would make damn sure tethering her power at Olympus would be enough.

"Then, let's go! Now!" Kiran yelled, moving away from Hera to help his sister up.

Persephone and Amphitrite intervened, pulling him away from the young goddess.

"You cannot go with her. Olympus is only for those with the power of the gods," Persephone stated to Kiran, and his head snapped up.

"If you think for one second I will let you take my sister anywhere without me—"

"Oh, shut up, Kiran," Hera ordered sharply. "We take her, she lives. We listen to your childish threats, she dies."

Kiran glared at Hera, working his jaw.

"Then take her," he snarled. "I'd ask you to keep her as safe as you can, but I have no faith in any of you anymore. No faith, and obviously no choice." His eyes flashed with anger and fear as he squared his shoulders. "I resign as senator. I will no longer work beside you, and as soon as I am able, I will take my sister and leave you all to rot here in this goddess-forsaken city."

Hera listened to the rhythmic tap of Kiran's shoes as he marched to the doors and slammed them open, the echo of it bouncing through the deathly silent chambers.

Silence reigned at his departure. Gathering herself from the shock of the proclamation Kiran had made, she wrapped the thoughts and worries and pushed them aside for her to ruminate on later in the privacy of her own home.

"Well, that was a fun little dramatic play courtesy of our former senator Kiran, but let's get to work, shall we?" Hera asked, her false sardonic smile on her face belying her racing heart.

She hated the role she played, but she played it well.

## Viktor

Viktor was once again pulled to Olympus by Hera. The force of the jump was abrupt, and the anger radiating from the queen was not lost on any of them as they settled once again onto their thrones. Now that he sat next to her, the full force of her emotions hit him.

How Persephone was able to keep her face straight was beyond him. He was flinching every time she moved, her power engulfing him in angry energy. Even with his wall up against her emotions, they held a physical presence around him, making it difficult to concentrate on the proceedings.

They were about to add a new throne and, hopefully in the process, save a fledgling goddess.

Finley stood just before the platform, a small and worn figure. He resisted the urge to help her stand, curled into herself as she was. She had to do this on her own, and they had no time left to wait. The woman could fade, and the Titans were pounding on their door.

"Finley, you may step forward and see if Olympus has a throne for you as a new goddess in your own right," Hera stated, her bland tone in great contrast with her intense emotions.

Finley stepped forward with a look of determination she hadn't had until Hera spoke to her in the senate chambers.

The moment her weight settled on the platform, the throne room shook. There was the deep rumbling sound of stone against stone as the area next to Devon's throne transformed into Finley's new seat of power. The throne rose from the marble, engraved with the symbol of the moon with an arrow piercing it. As Olympus finished creating the throne, all the seated goddesses and gods looked to Finley.

Breathing rapidly, Finley straightened her shoulders and approached her throne with measured, careful steps. When she lowered herself into the seat, a bright light of shimmering gold flashed, illuminating the already bright room to an even higher level of retina-searing light. As the light faded, it left Finley in a shortened silver chiton with her tan legs on display, the extra fabric wrapped around her waist. Where she'd worn dirtied sneakers a moment ago, she now wore sandals. Upon her head, a lunate crown had materialized. The waxing curve of the crown mirrored a crescent moon.

Finley touched the crown on her brow with wondering eyes. She seemed stronger than she had minutes ago. Her skin was cleaned of dirt and filth, and she seemed to have returned to her original weight, the unhealthy pallor and hollows of her cheeks vanishing completely.

A shuddering breath left the new goddess, breaking the silence. "It worked. I'm…"

"A goddess," Hera finished. When Viktor looked at the Queen Goddess, she wore a gentler expression than he'd seen in ages. Interesting—she was fond of the senator.

"How are you feeling, Finley?" she asked.

Finley looked herself over, curling her hands into fists as if checking her strength. "Better," she answered. A small laugh left her. "The best I've ever felt. Strong."

Hera nodded, her shoulders lowering an inch—something that wouldn't be visible to the others. A look passed between the sisters. "Even still, come back here whenever you can find the time," Hera said. "The support the mountain can offer in these early stages cannot be underestimated."

Viktor knew what had happened to Hestia and Demeter, holding Hestia's power as he did, and he knew that Hera would do everything to keep Finley from the same fate.

Finley agreed, her fingers still exploring her goddess garments and her throne.

"Devon and West," Hera called, and the gods turned to her. "Since you've been where she is so very recently yourselves, you will train with her, find out what her powers are. Keep her with you, as well, Devon," she added. "Finley's keen mind is a boon to operations and strategy."

Finley seemed to glow with the praise, looking even more determined. The two men nodded and shared a look, perhaps remembering their own recent training.

"Did I say later?" Hera smiled, showing her teeth like a wolf might when needing to assert its dominance.

Gold, green, and blue light flashed brightly before disappearing. He knew more than felt that it was Hera that had pushed them into light jumps when they had not heeded her command fast enough.

"Amphitrite, please continue searching for any clue as to the Titans' whereabouts," Hera ordered, and as Amphitrite disappeared in a flash of aqua mist, Hera turned to her other sister. "Persephone, set more alarms along the river and have your harpies guard the gate to Tartarus. The Titans would have all the power they need to defeat us should Cronus escape." The shadows took Persephone in an instant.

"And me?" Viktor dared to ask, staring at the goddess's profile. She finally turned to look at him, her eyes pure gold.

"No more surprises in battle. You're going to show me everything you can do, Fire God," she ordered.

When he opened his mouth to remind her of the curse, the light in her eyes grew brighter.

"Even if it kills you."

# Chapter 10

### <u>Viktor</u>

VIKTOR WASN'T SURE WHICH was worse: triggering the curse or disobeying Hera. Both could kill him.

They light jumped to the clearing outside his home, the one with his fire pit. The air felt strangely still, something more than the normal high-altitude chill, as if the mountain sensed the curse's power readying to strike down on him.

Hera stood nearby at the tree line, watching him closely. Viktor could still see the worry weighing down on her; Finley may have successfully accepted her throne, but there was still a chance she would not survive the war as an untrained goddess.

"Let's get to it," she said firmly. "Time is running out. You were able to break the spell in the city center, but I can't afford to not know your full abilities once we're facing off with Titans instead of humans."

Viktor stiffened, already feeling the curse threatening to burn him with the strong desire he felt to tell Hera the truth. His powers. The curse. All of it.

She seemed to judge his silence. "Since you are unable to *tell* me anything with this bloody magic bondage of yours, curse or oath ... *show* me what you can do."

*Oath*, he mentally swore. As if he would do this to himself by swearing an oath.

Taking a deep breath, he centered himself and closed his eyes, trying not to focus on the powerful goddess beside him. He was not used to people watching him call his powers, and it made him a lot more nervous than he had anticipated. As he began unbuttoning his shirt, he heard the intake of Hera's breath. Opening his eyes, he looked at the wide-eyed goddess.

"What are you doing?" she demanded. Ignoring her, he shrugged off his shirt before sitting on the log next to the fire to take off his boots, her eyes staying on his chest as he did so.

"Only my pants are flame retardant. It's cold, and I'd rather not be completely naked."

As he finished taking his boots and socks off, he looked up to see Hera glancing away with a slight blush on her cheeks.

This woman, who had seen plenty of nudity over her very long life, was blushing at him being shirtless? She was an enigma, and the therapist part of him wanted nothing more than to dig into her psyche. Another part of him wanted nothing more than to crush her body to his.

Turning away from her, he called to his fire, and it answered.

### <u>Hera</u>

For the first time in far too long, Hera was shocked. Both from the lust she felt at seeing him half naked and the depth of his power. A rush of desire like she'd never felt before burned through her, but a greater fire transformed Viktor.

The absolute power that this man held inside him, that he never let seep out, was unfathomable. Fire moved over him until his entire body became a flame itself. His veins blazed as if even his blood had become fire, too. A gush of heat radiated from him, stinging her eyes.

Hera stepped forward, closer to the warmth. Closer to him. She could still see the man in the flames, but he was like burning coals in the shape of a human, fire dancing around him. His eyes, though, burned brighter than the rest of him.

She'd never seen a power so transformative.

Realizing she was sweating, she stepped back, and his fiery eyes followed her as she moved out of the danger zone. As soon as she was far enough away, he threw his hands up, and fire launched into the air and danced around him. Large flames moved around like streamers before they flew into the fire pit and erupted into a large blaze.

In that moment, when she thought he could change no more, he changed again. His figure was no longer like coals banked in a fire; now, Viktor was alight.

Viktor's entire body was now pure fire, white like the hottest flames.

"Amazing," she whispered, her heart racing with excitement and awe and, yes, a small amount of fear.

The flames moved with his hands as if he were the conductor of an orchestra, and at first, it seemed they were simply dancing as they had been just moments ago, but then she saw it. She watched the flames take shapes and forms, the fire cooling and heating to create different colors. Hera gasped when the fire shifted into an image, an almost dream-like scene.

A small boy dressed in animal pelts, moving with a group of people through snow. A thriving village. A woman with light auburn hair who took a young Viktor's face into her hands.

"Believe what the fire tells you, my little firebird. You have so much more power than you can even understand," she whispered, and the scene before Hera blew away as if smoke.

Again, the fire grew, and the village from the previous vision was once again before her. This time Viktor looked as he did now, only dressed in a tunic and pants, holding a bow with a quiver of arrows slung across his back, as he was running and yelling for his mother.

Hera watched as he fell to his knees next to his mother, his hands slipping in her blood as he tried to pick her up. The people of his village ambled around mindlessly, just as the people in Halcyon had done. She remembered how he had told her that the Titans had done something similar to his people when he broke the spell cast over the humans in the city center.

"They wanted you," she whispered, her bloody hand touching his jaw. "They know who you are. Know of your power. You must hide from them so they cannot use you."

"Who?" he asked, trying to get a better grip on his mother and settle her on his thighs.

"I am so sorry, my little firebird. Sorry for what I have to do to protect you." She closed her eyes, and Hera thought she had passed until she watched the world around him and his mother light with fire.

Words like song whispered on the wind from her bloodied lips.

Hera did not need to speak the language to know what she was doing. She felt the magic through the vision. This was the root of the curse. His mother had sacrificed herself and cursed Viktor.

*To protect him.*

Fear coursed through her as she watched everything burn around Viktor, his scream breaking her heart, as the fire simmered down, and he was left naked and covered in ash.

His mother gone as well as his village. The people around him had been so far out of their own minds she never even heard them scream.

Flame erupted, changing the scene.

Viktor sat under a tree, his face wet with tears and his eyes swollen from what had to have been hours of crying.

"I am so sorry I couldn't protect you," he whispered, but the flames didn't show who he spoke to.

Suddenly, everything cut off, the flames disappearing as if in a vacuum.

For a moment, Hera just blinked at the empty clearing; the visions in the flames were so entrancing, she'd forgotten where she was. Turning to Viktor, her heart ceased beating all together when she saw him, now in his mortal form again, seizing on the ground.

"Viktor!" she yelled, collapsing to her knees before him and rolling him to his side. From the forest, a small shape bounded into the clearing. His cat—the familiar—ran to him and placed her paw on his shoulder. The contact seemed to ease the seizure enough that he slowly came out of it, but his eyes were still disoriented.

"I am going to move him inside. Try anything, and I will fry you straight to Tartarus," Hera warned the feline before pulling them into a light jump.

# Chapter 11

### <u>Viktor</u>

VIKTOR COULD TASTE METAL in his mouth, and the light from the window was far too bright for his eyes, which told him all he needed to know about what had happened.

He had tested his curse once again and been laid out flat for his trouble. Letting his eyes adjust slowly as he opened them, he took in the room around him. The window to his room was open. Not unusual for him to leave it that way during the day, but not normal for him to do so when the night chill hadn't yet lessened.

Rolling to his side, Viktor noted he was only in his boxers, and his eyes moved to the chair beside the bed where Hera was asleep with her hands clasped against her cheek.

So very innocent looking, yet so very dangerous.

*"She disrobed you, but I was here to keep your virtue intact."*

Viktor let out a small snort at the idea he had any virtue left. Looking to where Nyx had made herself comfortable at the foot of his bed, he raised his eyebrows at the Ovinnik.

"She stayed?" he knew Nyx would understand why that was a question. Why would the queen, the one in the middle of preparing to defend her city against the war working its way to her doorstep, take the time to watch over him? Viktor figured she would have run at the first opportunity.

*"It was worse than it had ever been. It was more than you losing the contents of your stomach and passing out like a youth full of too much ambrosia. You were ... in a state she referred to as a seizure. She also dared to threaten me."*

"Why would she threaten you?" he whispered.

"Because," Hera's sleepy voice came from the leather chair in the corner, "I have a feeling that cat is not all she seems to be."

Nyx hissed at Hera, and Hera's eyes narrowed back at the Ovinnik as she straightened in the seat.

"What was her name again, Viktor?" she asked, her eyes narrowed on him now. She knew Nyx's name, but he was sure she wasn't asking because she had forgotten.

"Nyx," he whispered, looking between the two females.

Hera laughed out loud, making Viktor jolt, which sent a shard of pain through his already aching head.

"You blasted—" Hera didn't finish her sentence, instead jumping up to pace the room. "Have you been earth side this entire time, you little demon?" Turning back to Viktor, she said, "Did you realize your *cat* is a primordial god?"

"What?" He spun back to Nyx. "Why would a primordial wander around like a simple familiar for hundreds of years?" He wasn't sure who he was asking at that moment, but no one answered him.

There was no way it was *the* Nyx that had been at his side for so long.

*"Tell the young queen that if she is to call me cat again, I will remind her why she fears me so."*

Turning her feline head to Viktor, she padded over to him across the bed and rested her paw on his arm.

*"I made my own oaths to my favored mortals when my fellow gods found themselves against the very Titans you do now. In time, you will understand the what and why of my decisions, and those of the other deities who have not sided with the Titans."*

"Can you clue me in on what the all-powerful furball is saying?" Hera demanded, earning a hiss from Nyx that had Hera stepping back and slightly paling. He would have to ask later why someone as powerful as Hera was cowed by a being that spent the better part of the millennia as a feline familiar to a fire witch and her son.

"She is saying she will reveal everything when the time comes. She made her own oaths."

Hera's hands went to her hips, and an anger radiated from her that had Viktor throwing up his shields. He was not able to handle any emotional overload after challenging the curse.

"Well, you two were meant for each other. I am done playing all these damn games. Unlike my jackass of a father, I do not enjoy the constant fuckery of the primordials and Titans." Her eyes met Viktor's. "You've proven you're cursed, but don't think for a second you're off the hook. Now, I've seen your true form, and it's obvious you have Titan blood in you, *Fire God.*"

The bright flash of her light jump pierced his retinas before he could close his eyes and look away.

*"She will find trouble, that one. She always has."*

Viktor knew that all too well.

But for now, he needed to find answers to his own questions. He hadn't foreseen the change in Olympus's power structure with Finley's addition, and that was a problem. Viktor couldn't afford to stray from the path laid out in the fires.

Unfortunately, he had a strong suspicion of who was the cause of it.

### **<u>Viktor</u>**

Viktor found him in an empty art gallery, abandoned in the midst of evacuation.

"Are you kidding me?" Viktor shouted, striding over to the lone figure.

"I rarely kid, as you well know," Prometheus stated as he stood in front of a well-known painting, his hands behind his back, his suit pressed. He looked to all the world like a collector of fine art. A wealthy aristocrat looking for another overpriced painting to adorn his ostentatious manor.

"The senator? Finley? Did you have a part in her ascension as a goddess?" Viktor demanded, reaching to grab the man's shoulder, only to have the Titan light jump several feet away. He observed another painting, as if Viktor hadn't tried to grab him.

"The future is difficult to pin down, but when I see something clear as day, I know I must follow the guidance of Chaos."

Viktor pinched his nose, trying to abstain from obscenities. Prometheus never responded well to such language.

"Oh, so, it was Chaos who determined my mother should die that day?" Viktor knew it was useless to instigate a fight with the

Titan, especially one they'd had a million times before. Prometheus wouldn't give, no matter how much Viktor laid into him.

"She was part of a bigger plan," was all the Titan said as he moved on to look at the bust of some general from centuries ago.

"She didn't need to die," Viktor whispered, and Prometheus finally turned to face him.

"She did, and while you may not agree with my methods, they will keep you from falling in battle. You hold the key to ending the threat of Cronus's reign once and for all."

Prometheus approached him, his shoes clicking on the marble floor, the echo bouncing around the room. Viktor kept his eyes on the Titan, so he could see even when the man wasn't using his power. Prometheus's mind was in the future, not the present.

"There will be so many things in this battle that seem truly unfair. You have no idea the paths that I wrote off and why I chose the ones I did."

"To see the Titans thrown into Tartarus," Viktor stated blandly.

Prometheus gave a small smile and nodded to the wall behind Viktor. Turning, Viktor took in the painting.

"How did Francisco Goya know of such things?" Prometheus asked as he settled closer behind him and placed his hands on Viktor's shoulders. The piece was one of Cronus, or Saturn, in Roman mythology, eating his child. "It was said that Saturn ate each of his children. Though the end result was the same, the humans did not know the true nature of the gods. The *actual* story."

Viktor stayed silent, knowing interrupting the man would just send the Titan on another path, and he would have to corral him back to the point he was trying to make. Thankfully, Prometheus did not bother to stop talking.

"People throughout time have foretold of saviors. Born. Leading. Dying. Fanatics hold to the idea of these beings, creating laws that punish people they deem inferior. Keeping people down so that they may stay on top."

"Your point?" Viktor growled as he stepped out from Prometheus's grasp and turned to look at him.

"Hera hasn't kept her people down. As much bravado as she throws around, her people have thrived in a way that never happened under the Titans. She allowed humans their choices, and like errant toddlers, their war taught them a lesson. A lesson that allowed Hera to bring a sense of peace to this world."

Sighing, Viktor crossed his arms and leaned against the gallery wall. It might take a minute since seeing into the future scattered the mind slightly. Viktor tilted his head from side to side, popping his neck as he waited for the Titan to finish.

Prometheus moved closer again. Not normal behavior for a being who was avoidant of touch, knowing it could send him into a vision. When Viktor looked into his gaze, he saw the clarity there and knew what Prometheus said next would be important.

"You and Hera will save this world. You will lead with integrity. People will not know the true story, as they never do, but do not discount them as being unable to comprehend. Your story will be told for millennia and painted by artists all the same. But the end of it all? It cannot happen if you ignore what the universe tries to tell you. If you let your human side stand in the way of the hard choices."

"Like murder? That kind of hard choice?" Viktor growled. Prometheus simply tilted his head.

"So much like Relbeo. So much, yet ... the emotions did not linger inside her the way they do you. She was content with her choice to burn alongside those who invaded your village. She knew you would live, and that was all that mattered to her," Prometheus said, referencing Viktor's mother.

"You do not get to talk about the woman who sacrificed herself for our people!" Viktor yelled. "Not when you could have stopped it!"

"She had to die by the same fire that gave her power," Prometheus stated in an even voice that only increased Viktor's anger.

Viktor got into the Titan's face now, but Prometheus did not step back. Of course, he probably saw this confrontation coming well before Viktor even stepped foot into the gallery.

Perhaps even before he'd moved to Halcyon.

"Did she have to stand in the pit of it? Did the Romans have to invade our territory and trigger the event that led to her death? You couldn't step up and save her?"

Prometheus looked at him as if he had lost his mind.

"No, I could not. It would change the future far too much. Relbeo saved her son. She saved *you*. A sacrifice that was not made in vain, as you were able to escape without anyone knowing where the line of Hestia went. The Titans lost track of you, and so it worked out as it was meant to."

Prometheus placed his hands on Viktor's shoulders again.

"You know the cost of foresight. We cannot make our destiny what we want. To do so would cost us greatly. You thought you were using your fires to save the woman you loved, when in all actuality, it took her from you."

Viktor closed his eyes at the reminder, his teeth grinding.

Nodding in understanding, he opened his eyes to Prometheus and stepped back from his hold. He knew to continue in anger would do nothing to change what Prometheus foresaw. No, he would only end up hurting himself in the end.

"Use what you are given. No matter the shape of the path, the fires tell me it is needed," the Titan said as he clasped his hands behind his back again.

"Why? What did you see?" Viktor asked, but once the words left his mouth, he remembered it was pointless to ask Prometheus a direct question. He would not receive a clear answer.

"I see both the end and the beginning," was all Prometheus said before flames erupted around him, taking the Titan from the gallery, and leaving Viktor to stand in the floating ashes left behind.

# *Chapter 12*

### <u>Hera</u>

*S*HE WALKED ALONG THE *bloodied path. Her father was long gone, perhaps in search of her. Or perhaps he had given up.*

*It no longer mattered.*

*Walking into the home that had once harbored the laughter of her family, she breathed in the stale air and took in the dried blood that painted the walls and floor.*

*Hera wondered if it had all happened as she remembered, or if it had been her youth that had colored her visions of what had happened.*

*In the end, it did not matter. They were gone.*

*Wiping fresh tears away from her face, she sat in the middle of the common room. The hearth was empty, the frigid breeze of the last of winter hitting her skin, yet she felt nothing but the soul deep pain.*

*Arms wrapped around her, and she turned into them, losing herself to her tears.*

*"Shh," they whispered, the scent of pine and wood smoke calming her nerves.*

*"Yes, one must be quiet when they are being hunted," another voice, her father's, piped in, and Hera tried to inch closer to the person holding her, but she was ripped away from their arms by her hair. She was pulled forcefully around to face her father. Struggling, she tried to escape, but he twisted her hair around his wrist and gripped it tighter.*

*"I've waited so very long for this." He smiled, manic glee in his purple eyes as he shoved a knife into her heart.*

Hera bolted upright in bed, her heartbeat racing through her as she shoved the covers off, her body overheated from the terror of her own mind. She breathed rapidly, trying to catch her breath and fight off the imminent panic attack.

*Water first. Then get on the ground. Rinse and repeat all the damn time.*

"Cronus is not here," she reminded herself as she threw a robe around her and padded to her bathroom. "He is in Tartarus, and I am safe."

The nightmares had been a common nuisance since even her human life. In the past, she would have shrugged it off, but now it was all too close to reality. If Cronus were free, her nightmare would pale in comparison to his rule as king.

But that was only if he broke free ... and if she were gone in a more permanent fashion.

Shuddering, she ran the water in the bathroom, splashing it on her overheated face, though the drying sweat from her night terror had made the rest of her body far too cold. She looked at herself in the mirror, seeing only a ghost of whom she portrayed to the rest of the world. Her hair was a mess, the curls frizzy and untamed. Her eyes were bleak, and her skin was sallow.

Unable to look at herself any longer, she sat down on the floor of her bathroom and reminded herself of the world around her. Felt the cold tile, the warmth of the rug she was sitting on. Keeping herself in the now as she tried to work her way out of her terror.

Her mind snagged on the familiar scent of pine and wood smoke that had penetrated her nightmare. Why the hell had she conjured up Viktor in one of her reoccurring nightly terrors? Was she actually beginning to believe he wouldn't stab her in the back?

Hera let out a disbelieving laugh. She knew better. It was this damn obsession she had with the man and his secrets. They were haunting her even in sleep now. Letting her head fall back against the bathroom wall, she closed her eyes and tried to come back from the trauma of her youth.

Easier said than done.

### <u>Hera</u>

Hera had made sure that every storefront was closed and boarded up, having told the citizens that the Sereian Empire was making moves to invade Halcyon.

Was it the truth? Kind of, in that many of the forces were from the Sereian Empire ... and Goryeo ... and others, but with the Sereian emperor not sending any correspondence to Halcyon on the matter, her assistant having informed her this morning about how eerily quiet the emperor had been, she decided to use the pompous ass emperor as her scapegoat.

Screaming, "Leave, Titans are coming!" seemed counterproductive to keeping the panic level down.

Unable to move people to Alexious, Hera had sent Calista and some of Amphitrite's spies to the countryside to set up temporary refuge camps for the people who lived in the city center, effectively making Halcyon a ghost town. People still lived on the outskirts, but Devon and Cassandra knew as much as Hera did that the Titans were coming for Olympus, and it was best to have the humans gone and safe.

One item checked off her itinerary of oh-so-many.

Pacing around her living room, Hera thought of her next problem. Viktor.

Viktor and his primordial cat were not going to let anything slip, and by the reaction he had by the fire, it was obvious that he would likely die if he ever did manage to say a word against his curse. For all her bluster, she did not want that for him.

Seeing him like that broke something in her. Hera was thankful that he didn't seem to be aware of her tenderly moving a lock of hair off his forehead, or the tears that sprang to her eyes when she watched him in so much pain, unable to do anything to stop it. It was time to admit to herself that her craving to know about his past wasn't purely practical. She wanted to know *him*. She wanted to carry his secrets alongside hers. And she wanted to see how close she could get to his warmth and feel her libido spark again, like it had last night when he removed his shirt.

But she knew she was not going to let that happen, so why bother stewing over it?

Rubbing her face, she groaned, wishing she had let Adam take the edge off, even if it felt wrong somehow. Obviously, sex during preparation for war would be weird, but a girl needed release.

The light salty breeze that came with her sister blew into her living room, and before Amphitrite had formed fully before her, Hera was in her face.

"What do you have?"

"Hello to you too." Amphitrite rolled her eyes before taking a seat on the eggplant-colored couch, moving a peacock feathered pillow out of her way as she sat.

"We do not have time for niceties. We have a war brewing, dear sister."

"I hadn't noticed," Amphitrite mumbled. "But yes, there have been sightings of deities with Titan-level power. None of them are Perses. Devon couldn't spot any power signatures on the humans, either. My guess is he is hiding out and planning some huge reveal on game day." Amphitrite's expression was stormy—she had a personal score to settle with the Titan who'd destroyed Atlantis in a bid for power and let her take the blame for centuries.

Hera let loose a disappointed breath and lowered herself into an emerald armchair. "I was hoping there would be some power signatures on the humans, at least enough to give us an idea of how many deities they had. But they had a witch do the dirty work for them." She crossed her legs. "Any progress on breaking the spell?"

"Hecate is working to gather some of her better-known witches, but so far, the people they have broken the trance on did not recover."

"What do you mean?"

"They are broken," Amphitrite said. "That is the only way to describe it. There is no longer a person inside of them, almost as if their soul was stolen while they were still alive."

"But Viktor was able to bring the humans back when he did the same thing."

Shaking her head, Amphitrite leaned over, her elbows on her knees. "I am not sure if they changed their tactic, or if Viktor has some spell breaking magic that we are lacking."

"I will speak with him," she said. She'd meant to extract all the details of his abilities from him last night, but his seizure had completely changed the ambiance of the evening. Instead of grilling him, she'd watched him sleep.

*Pathetic.*

Her heart beat a little quicker at the thought of seeing him again so soon, and Hera wasn't sure if it was in anger or something else altogether. Something in that fire, in his power, pulled her into a place she couldn't describe. For once, all the voices and pain in her own head were quiet.

As she had settled him into bed, she'd been overwhelmed with a concern she felt only for her sisters, yet it felt ... different in some way. How could a man she had just met, with so many damn secrets, pull her in a way she had never felt?

"Hera!" Amphitrite yelled, snapping her fingers in front of Hera's face and pulling her from her thoughts.

"Yes! What?" Hera snapped back, embarrassed by losing her train of thought at such a moment.

Viktor had taken over her thoughts far too much recently, and it was going to cause her to make horrible choices in the long run.

She needed the man out of her system. When was the last time she had been intimate? Not since this whole Titan debacle had erupted. Her sex drive was making her lose her focus, simple as that. Nothing directly related to Viktor.

*Liar.*

"Focus!" Amphitrite yelled again. "What is wrong with you?"

Shaking her head, Hera took a deep breath and looked at her sister.

"Sexual frustration. I apologize. The Titans have been consuming so much of my time lately that I haven't found myself under a man in a while. Or on top of one."

Amphitrite's look of irritated resignation almost made her smile.

"Well, forget men and sex for a moment and listen," Amphitrite chastised.

"That's a tall order, but you have my full attention," Hera replied, earning a quick eye roll.

"Finley's training is underway. I've had my spies try to follow her steps for any indication of the circumstances around Finley's kidnapping." She shook her head. "No trail left behind."

"Who changed her?" Hera wondered aloud. "No Titan would change someone who is so clearly on our side—" Hera stopped at that thought, her mind circling back to a time before she held her own power.

"With Oceanus gone, no," she agreed sadly. "The Primordials are quiet."

Hera's eyes snapped up to Amphitrite, her thoughts moving in another direction now. "Nyx is Earth side."

"What did you do now?" Amphitrite groaned, leaning back on the couch, pinching the bridge of her nose.

"Nothing!" Hera defended. When Amphitrite shot her a look of distrust, she said, "Really! I was at Viktor's, and when he woke up this morning, I found out his *pet cat* is Nyx. I mean, of all the crazy crap we've been dealing with!"

Amphitrite sat up straighter, her eyes pinned on Hera.

"You slept with Viktor? The man you all but murder with your eyes when he speaks, or ... doesn't?"

That was what her sister chose to focus on? Not that the primordial goddess showing up as a long-lost god's cat? The same Primordial who'd promised long ago to have Hera's head should she choose to step over the line and trespass on to her domain, the night. But as a young goddess, she'd tampered with more than just the clouds in the sky. Messing with night had come at a price that led to Themis having to keep the two away from each other for a few hundred years.

"No," she said adamantly. "He was showing me his power, and I guess something he did pushed far too close to the fine line of his precious little curse." At Amphitrite's raised brows, Hera sighed and added, "Yes, I now agree it's a curse." She shook her head. "He passed out. I guess, technically, it was more of a seizure, but he calmed as Nyx pushed her power onto him. I fell asleep in a chair by his bed, making sure he..."

Hera stopped speaking at the look in her sister's eyes.

"What?" she demanded.

"Nothing." Amphitrite broke her stare, looking away. "Sorry, I just ... well..."

"Didn't think I could be around a man without trying to screw him?" Something in admitting those words hurt, but the lack of denial on Amphitrite's part hurt worse.

"Crass, as always, but yes, that was my first thought. Is he alright now?"

"Yes, he is hale once again." Hera pasted on a fake smile and glanced out the window of her penthouse overlooking Halcyon.

She could still feel her sister's eyes on her, so Hera dared to look back at her and instantly regretted it. Amphitrite didn't look away this time. In fact, she seemed to be studying her.

"Do you care for him, Hera?"

"What?" Hera started laughing. She was unsure if she was sincerely tickled at the thought or trying to avoid the conversation. How did she feel about the irritating bundle of mystery that showed up on

Olympus's doorstep? "We need him alive to fight the Titans, dear sister."

"I just … he… well, we need West, but I hardly see you tucking *him* in at night."

Hera sent her a predatory smile.

"No, Amphitrite, that's *your* job. Keep him happy and on our side. That's all I've ever asked of you regarding that man."

Rolling her eyes, Amphitrite finally gave up her questioning. Hera breathed an internal sigh of relief that her sister was finally letting it go. Her sister was right about one thing. She was confused on how Viktor had made it so far under her skin.

Watching as her sister light jumped away after a moment of silence, Hera turned to look outside again, finding her thoughts once more on the Fire God. He was taking up too much headspace, and that would not work for her.

It was time to work the god out of her system so she could focus on keeping her people alive.

# Chapter 13

### <u>Viktor</u>

THE FLAMES ERUPTED, THE metal melting as Viktor worked on a new piece of art in the garage behind his cabin. Thankfully, the garage was fireproof since his mind was all over the place.

"Shit," he grumbled, realizing he had heated the metal to a temperature that caused more than the weld to melt.

Instead of welding the pieces together, he had made a pool of molten metal on the floor. He most likely should not be playing with fire while unable to focus, but this was usually a hobby that calmed him. Or it had been until today. Sitting back on his heels, he pushed the palms of his hands into his eyes before shoving himself up to standing. Stepping back from the molten puddle, Viktor took in the mess around him that was the physical representation of the state of his mind.

"What is all this?" a feminine voice asked from behind him, shocking him into swinging around, his hands already holding fire.

Hera sat on one of his work benches, her legs crossed at the ankles and swinging as she took in his art, unphased at his defensive response to her sneaking up on him. Having no idea how long she had been there was worrisome. Was he that consumed with his thoughts that he had missed one of the most powerful deities sneaking into his sacred space?

"Hera," he simply said her name, and her eyes locked on him as he stood all the way up. She looked him over, and he knew what she saw. A man in a frazzled state of mind. It didn't take looking into a mirror to know his hair was sticking up everywhere. Ash was coating his skin, and he was only in a pair of work pants and boots.

Yet, something in her eyes went wild after her perusal. Pushing herself off the workbench, she sauntered toward him, and his heart rate increased with each step.

"You are becoming a problem for me, Viktor," she whispered, not taking her eyes off him as she moved into his personal space.

"How so?"

She reached down to pull her sweater up and over her head before tossing it away.

"Oh." That was it. That was the extent of his verbal capacity at that moment.

*Eloquent as always*, Viktor chided himself, but his mind quickly moved from chastisement to *her*. She was all curves, blonde hair, stormy gray eyes, soft skin, and...

Her pants were gone next, and he let out the kind of awkward groan a virgin might make. She stood before him in a pair of dark blue panties and a bra. His tongue felt too big for his mouth. Words were not coming—and did he just grunt? *Fates*, he hoped not.

Trying to gather himself, he looked down and realized she was barefoot. Why? There were metal shards everywhere—

His thoughts were cut off when she grabbed his face and pulled his lips to hers. His mouth immediately opened and allowed her tongue to push in, giving the kiss more intimacy.

As if his brain was slow to catch up, Viktor finally realized her hands had gone to his pants, pushing them and his boxers down. As much as logic was telling him to stop and regain control of the situation, he was done listening to that part of him for a while. He had listened to his logical brain for hundreds of years. No, he was going to do this. With that thought, he was picking her up around the hips and placing her back on the workbench, not breaking the kiss once.

She ripped her underwear off and leaned back, giving him a face full of curves as his hands moved to the back of her bra. He worked to unclasp the bra, and her mouth found his neck. She bit down lightly, making him groan. Viktor pushed away the memories of another time, another place, another bite so similar to this one. He wouldn't, couldn't, think of her. Not when he was with Hera right now.

"Infernal devices created to stop a man from enjoying himself," he growled as he worked at the clasp, his mind overrun with arousal to make sense of anything but his need to be inside her. With a laugh, she released him, unhooking it herself, and tossed it aside before pulling him to her again in a rough kiss.

Viktor realized he was not in charge at all, but he couldn't find it in himself to care. She pushed a hand between their bodies and moved him to where they would be joined. A breath was all it took before he was one with her, his hips moving of their own volition.

"Goddess," he moaned at the feel of her around him, his head falling to her shoulder as he was overcome by his emotions and the sensation of being with her. *In her.*

Hera's heels pushed into the back of his thighs, and he moved faster, trying to stay in the moment with his mind and emotions stuck between two lifetimes.

"Má lásko," he growled as his thrusts became erratic, his mind still lost between two worlds until he opened his eyes to meet Hera's. She quickly covered whatever was there. Perhaps the fire in his eyes, this close up, had scared her. He wouldn't burn her. Would never let his fire touch her. Nothing would harm her. *Ever.*

Hands in his hair now, Hera pulled him in for a kiss that was rough and dangerous, like *he* was on the edge of burning alive. A soft moan left her mouth, her body tightening around him before her back arched. His mouth descended on her neck, kissing and licking as she yelled out his name for all of Halcyon to hear, her nails digging into his back as she reached her peak. Pleasure surged through him as he let go, his head snapping back, neck muscles straining, and everything around him became a kaleidoscope of bliss and light.

Coming back to himself, his breathing ragged, he looked down at Hera, who had pressed her forehead against his shoulder. Placing his fingers underneath her chin, he gently lifted her head to look up at him, but she jerked away and shoved him back. He didn't make another move toward her, his confusion and concern overtaking the blissful state he had just been in.

"I am sorry if I hurt you," he whispered as he pulled his pants back up and redid them, unsure why the seductress of moments ago would not look at him.

"You..." She swallowed. "You didn't. It's..." Her eyes finally connected with his, and he could see her attempt to act like everything was fine written across her tense features. It was not working, and he knew she would make a run for it now. Once she escaped, there was no chance he would garner any answers from her after that.

"I did something, and I need you to tell me, Hera." He stepped forward, but she jumped from the bench and began gathering her clothes. "Hera," he growled, not liking what was happening.

He was a therapist for Fate's sake, and this woman was absolutely baffling him.

Throwing her sweater on without a bra, she turned to him.

"Look." She pulled on her pants, stuffing her panties in the pocket of her jeans. "I needed a release. I've been pent up and unable to focus on ... anything and everything. You gave me that, and I gave you that too. Let's not make this a huge thing, okay?"

Viktor felt like he had taken a hit to the stomach. He started to talk, but Hera's confused expression told him he had slipped into the old language of his people. The only way anyone ever knew he was truly frustrated.

"You came here to ... find release? That is all? That is what just happened here—" He waved to the workbench, "between us?" He hadn't realized he was growling his words.

Her eyes softened before a hardness moved over them.

"Yes. I don't do forever. And I don't do it more than once unless there is an understanding—"

"Lies," he snapped before he could think better of it. His emotions were gathering up for an epic headache later.

Hera stepped forward, anger sparking in her eyes, and he wanted to pull her to him and kiss her out of her tantrum.

"You do not know me, Viktor, so quit pretending that you do," she whispered to him, so close he could smell her. Smell the scent of him on her, mingling with hers.

"Like I said before, I probably know you better than you know yourself." He looked into her eyes, and this time the fear was stamped plain on her face. Almost as if she had seen a ghost, her eyebrows went up, her body rigid.

Shaking her head, she stepped back, and light jumped away.

His stomach churned. He had gotten far too close to giving a voice to the words his curse had bound long ago.

### <u>Hera</u>

Landing in her bathroom, Hera slid down the door, her hand over her mouth as she tried to quell the urge to scream. She needed to clean up and get herself together, but something in his eyes had felt so different, yet the same.

Her plan to screw the frustration out had failed. Epically.

Confusion flooded her, chased by panic. Holy shit, had she kissed him? When was the last time she had been so caught up in passion that she forgot her rule?

Thoughts she didn't understand whirled in her mind, and the only reaction she could give anyone was anger and dissociation. She had been weak and vulnerable in his arms. She'd let him too close.

Hera had gone to find release, to get the man out of her system. It was working out just fine until she felt him. Not just physically, which was obviously her goal there, but felt him in her emotions... in her head. A deep, searing pain had ripped through her, one she couldn't place. It had been his.

Why had she thought it a good idea to do what she did? Why had she decided to let herself feel anything? How and why was he causing such havoc on her emotions when she had been able to keep herself closed off for so very long?

*Damn it. Damn him. Damn the Fates.*

Slamming her fist on the tile from where she lay, she let out a scream of anger, all directed internally. The yell was loud and long, and she was glad no one was anywhere nearby to hear her.

Letting it roll through her, she pushed herself up to her feet. Moving to the shower, she threw open the glass door and twisted the handle to the hottest setting possible. Shedding her clothes, she stood under the spray of water, letting it take her tears down the drain.

Hera was done with letting people in. It was time to focus.

She had a war to fight.

# Chapter 14

### <u>Hera</u>

WALKING TO HER OFFICE with a cup of coffee in hand, Hera turned the corner to see Viktor standing between her and her office door.

"I was hoping we could wait to do this song and dance until the second Tuesday of never." She rolled her eyes as she continued walking to her office. He could either move or end up covered in steaming hot coffee. Perhaps that would burn him, the almighty Fire God.

Viktor followed her into the office, the soft click of the lock echoing after he shut the door behind them.

"Hoping for another go?" She smirked as she placed her cup of coffee on the desk and turned, hands on the edge and leaning back.

His eyes went to her breasts before he looked back at her face. "Hera..." His face broke her phony smile to pieces.

"Don't," she snapped out before she could think. Her defenses were all on alert now. She had spent the better part of the evening building more walls and tightening up her defenses, only for him to come in and tear them down simply by speaking her name. "I need no explanation. We enjoyed each other's bodies. That was all."

"Stop. I need you to listen."

"Oh? Are you actually going to tell me something? Well, this time, you can save it." She crossed her arms. "I already know you didn't enjoy it."

*Fates damn it.* She'd said that aloud, hadn't she? So much for separating oneself from the issue.

Viktor's eyebrows went up.

"How could you possibly think I wasn't enjoying myself?" he asked, but his voice was not angry. In fact, the man sounded almost hopeful.

"I felt your pain," she admitted reluctantly. "No one feels like that while they are in the middle of getting laid."

"You ... felt me? My emotions?"

That was not a denial. Damn it. She needed to finish this conversation quickly and help him find his way out the door before she embarrassed herself.

For whatever Fates damned reason, probably some screwed up joke by Nyx, this man was breaking through her walls, and she did not know why.

It was *really* making her mad.

"It doesn't matter. None of it does. I wanted an itch scratched before battle in case it was the last time I had the chance. Thanks for taking care of that for me." Hera winked at him. "Now, I have a lot of work to do—"

"I did enjoy it," he cut her off. "Last night was one of the best I've had in *centuries*, Hera." His eyes darkened and his voice took on a deep, intimate quality. "It's all I can think about. Any pain I felt … it was pain from the fear that it may not happen again."

Hera sucked in a breath, but before she could speak, he light jumped away.

In his absence, something in her felt heavier than ever before.

### <u>Viktor</u>

*"I believe that is enough wood for many winters, Fire God."*

Ignoring Nyx, Viktor swung the axe again, his body pumping enough adrenaline through him that he was able to cut off the storm of emotions Hera wrought within him.

*"Fire God! Stop!"*

"My name is Viktor!" he yelled, slamming his axe down, finally splintering the log down the middle.

*"It is not."*

"You know," Viktor said, turning to face Nyx. "You have a lot of nerve telling me who I am when you've kept your own identity a secret for *millennia.*"

Giving Nyx his back again, he split the wood the rest of the way before throwing it into the massive pile. He needed physical activity when he was wound up. It was not a common occurrence, as he was usually able to keep impeccable control of himself, but the queen of goddesses was undoing eras of work.

*"The annoying goddess is changing you. Perhaps it was a mistake to come so soon. Perhaps we should have waited until the battle started and slipped in unnoticed, as I had planned all along."*

Viktor stared off past the growing pile of firewood, up and through the trees to where a sliver of Mount Olympus could be seen. He had made the call to come here, knowing his curse would torture him, but knowing they needed him.

*"You are coming dangerously close to stepping over the parameters of the curse. A step that may very well end in your demise."*

Looking past her, Viktor stared up at the mountain again.

"Then, so be it."

# Chapter 15

### <u>Hera</u>

THE SENATE TOOK THEIR places, all except Kiran, whom no one had heard anything from since the day he had resigned. Not even Finley, which surprised Hera, as she was sure the man would latch onto her like a parasite after almost losing her.

But Hera did not have the mental capacity to worry about him. He would need to be dealt with, and hopefully someone from the meeting would be so kind as to throw an idea out so she didn't have to. Or, even offering to track him down for her and have a little chat would be great, as she wasn't doing so well communicating with anyone right now.

Exhibit A of that fact was leaning against the pillar as usual. She tried to ignore Viktor, unsure of how to address him since their last discussion. Hera had winked at him, being flirtatious, and he had simply stared at her in return, giving nothing away of his thoughts. What did the man want from her?

The doors opened, and Finley walked in, looking better, her skin brighter and her hollowness gone. The storm in her eyes was still there, and Hera knew after the war, it would only get worse as Finley lost mortals she cared about.

Devon and West followed her in and took their seats next to her sisters on the benches. Finley stood in the center of the chambers, looking from senator to senator. Hera wondered if Finley had been transformed because she'd been the senator of Goryeo, where all the conflict had started.

"Finley, what progress have you made in learning your powers?" Hera asked, keeping herself as professional as possible, though her heart was thumping with anxious nerves.

Finley looked up, meeting Hera's gaze with her brown eyes. Hera was once again struck by the difference in her appearance from such a short time ago. Her tan skin glowed, looking young and supple. Her straight black hair glimmered down her back. She very much held the look of her ancestors, who'd come from what was once Korea.

"After training, we discovered that I can communicate with animals. And not only can I communicate with them, but I can also take on their form," Finley stated.

Hera straightened in her seat, as did most everyone else, aside from Devon and West.

"Explain," Hera ordered.

A flash of light filled the room and revealed a giant stag made of silver. A startled Ryder jumped in his seat.

Another flash, and Finley stood there again.

"Interesting. Can you form any animal?" Hera asked.

Nodding, Finley became a silver bear before quickly changing back.

"When I communicate with the animals, I call to them as their own pack would. Though my hounds have ... brought me into their fold, made me a leader, much as wolves have an alpha. They call to hunt whenever I am near. When they do ... others join us."

"Others?" Calista asked, leaning forward.

"Incorporeal animals," Devon interjected. "She can call the spirit of animals lost to the Underworld."

"Fates, you have animal wraiths hanging out down there?" Hera stared at Persephone in bewilderment.

"We have all living things. The soul need not be human, sister."

Hera felt a shudder. How her sister sat down there for months, years, at a time before Devon was a mystery.

"Speaking of hunting. Do you have an arrow and bow?" Cassandra asked, her strategic mind going straight to weaponry.

Finley made a gesture of her hands, and a silver bow with one arrow appeared.

"Moonlight. She has a bow and arrow made from moonlight. I have no fucking idea how that works, but it does," West stated, shrugging from where he stood on the left side of Finley.

Another flash of her hands, and the bow and arrow were gone.

Hera looked at Cassandra sitting at the end of the table. Without a word from Hera, Cassandra knew what she was asking and nodded.

Good. She would bring Finley under her command and teach her to wield her new weapons with precision and accuracy.

They would find a way to not only use Finley's new powers to win this war, but to bring everyone back from the battle alive.

"Thank you, Finley," Hera dismissed her. Giving a hesitant nod, Finley sat beside West on the bench.

"You may retain your seat on the council, senator."

Finley looked up at Hera, something in her eyes saying everything she couldn't give a voice to.

She was lost. Scared. Alone. She needed normalcy, and Hera was offering just that.

Hera gave her a slight smile of reassurance, and Finley slowly moved to her senatorial seat, her steps growing in confidence. A small smile of relief passed the woman's lips as she seated herself among the rest of the senators.

Hera could only hope that little bit of familiarity would help Finley find her footing.

Turning back to Devon, Hera listened as he went over his and Cassandra's plans for defense with the senators, plans that she was already privy to.

"My army is on standby should they be needed," West piped in, his shoulders straight, no longer slouching in his seat. Devon looked from West to Hera, his eyebrows raised as he waited for her to make the call.

"We will need everyone. I will come to the island and meet with the highest officer in charge to discuss our plans. Cassandra and Devon will join me."

West gave a small nod, but she saw a new light in his eyes. He was helping, and that was also something the trauma of the past year had taken from him. A sense of control and the ability to find his place among them. She only hoped his story did not end as his father's had.

Sighing, Hera adjourned the meeting. Everyone but Viktor and Amphitrite filed out of the chambers.

Of course, he would stay behind when she was trying to ignore him. He was not playing by the new rules, his face changing from stone once the meeting started, and he gave her intense looks from the corner while she was trying to focus on her meeting. They were not the looks of someone who showed up for some nightly fun and went their own way. They were almost ... possessive.

Standing and walking to Amphitrite, she stepped off the dais and met her sister.

"You have information or just want some sisterly bonding time?" Hera asked, slightly turning her back to Viktor, who sidled up behind her. She had never behaved this way around a man before, preferring to make *them* uncomfortable until *they* relented, but of course Viktor would find a way to have a word with her, and all her work in shoving her feelings into a deep, deep dark pit in her psyche would be undone.

"Dolus has made a request for an audience," Amphitrite said. "He seems to know something, so I was planning to go tomorrow to gather whatever intel he has."

"Why the wait?" Hera asked, folding her arms across her chest as the heat of Viktor's power rolled across the back of her neck. He was standing close enough that she could smell the pine and smoke that was his natural scent. It reminded her of camping in the woods, something she used to do as a youth with her sisters.

"Reaver's Paradise is in full swing at this time of day. I would be safer going during the daylight hours when there is not a giant drug-fueled orgy going on."

"Right," Hera agreed easily, and Amphitrite narrowed her eyes. An eyebrow went up when she caught on to the reason behind Hera's agreement.

"No. Absolutely not," she growled. "Hera..."

"What?" Viktor chimed in, walking around to see Hera's face. Sneaking a slight peek at the man, she winked at him.

"I will see you two later."

With that, she disappeared in a flash of light before anyone could stop her.

### **<u>Viktor</u>**

Whirling on Amphitrite, Viktor demanded, "What is she about to do?"

Amphitrite just stared at where Hera had been with a slightly stunned look on her face.

"Something incredibly stupid. I have to go!" Amphitrite called her power for a light jump.

Viktor's hand shot out to grab her elbow. Using his power, he pushed hers aside so she would be unable to call her own until he let go.

Amphitrite's eyes went wide, the whites of her eyes dominating.

"How are you this powerful?" she gasped, staring at him in complete awe and with a little fear mingled in there.

"Where is she going, and what is she doing?" he demanded again, not answering her.

If Hera was in danger, he needed to know and find a way to stop her. The longer Amphitrite stood there, the longer Hera was doing something incredibly stupid.

Amphitrite looked deep into his eyes.

"Viktor, do you care for my sister?" she asked as she held an almost hopeful look in her eyes.

Waiting a beat, unsure of if the truth would make a difference, he looked away from the goddess and gave a slight nod.

Truth it was, then.

At his acknowledgment of his feelings, her shoulders relaxed slightly. Obviously, Amphitrite had no idea what had transpired between them if she was happy about this, but Viktor was not going to bring up last night. The idea that last night was meaningless, just something to work out the tension, was ludicrous, and he was going to prove it to Hera.

He refused to take any less than all of her. Thorns and all.

That meant making sure she survived this war and her own perilous tactics.

"She is going to go to Reaver's Paradise alone to face a trickster of a Titan. I hardly trust Dolus, but most of the time, he holds important information that we can in some ways use. As of right now, we are in desperate need of something to plan our next move."

"Can Hera not hold her own against one Titan?"

Amphitrite shook her head, the weight returning to the woman's shoulders.

"She does not have permission to carry her goddess form in there. She will be wholly mortal until she crosses the veil back into our world from there."

"Why would you allow such a place to exist?" he asked, honestly flummoxed.

"Look, for a while, there were deities who would drink the blood of humans and other deities in order to gain power. We were not strong enough to stop them, so we pushed them underground, where people interested in the vampiric exchange would be able to find them. Now they are mostly what the mortals call demons."

Viktor stepped away from her.

"Can you use your powers there?" he asked, hopeful that someone could.

She shook her head again. "But I am going to at least help my sister, even if it means..." she trailed off, but she did not need to say the words. They would both die in a pit of powerful beings if they were unable to call on their goddess forms.

"Who can walk in there without being rendered mortal?" he demanded.

"Titans, unless they have been forbidden. Oceanus was never allowed after having crossed Dolus too many times in the past, therefore permission to enter the Den with his power intact was not given to West since he was his son."

"Only Titans?" Viktor asked, feeling like he was being sucked into a vacuum of despair. He could not lose Hera, and the damnable woman decided to walk to her death.

"Only Titans, should the Titans or their offspring have not enraged Dolus." A tear slipped from Amphitrite's eye; her hand was quick to wipe it away.

Viktor felt her fear as sure as his own.

Hera was walking into a trap, and Viktor was unsure if he could do anything to stop it.

# Chapter 16

### <u>Hera</u>

Hera was never the patient sister, and nothing showed this more than her walking into Reaver's Paradise during happy hour. She had electrocuted the giant satyr that was attempting to deny her entrance. She knew she'd have to do it again once he regained consciousness, but hopefully she would be long gone before that happened.

When she entered the dark hall leading to the doorway of sin, she knew she had made a mistake. She pushed through the shimmering veil that separated the den from the narrow tunnel leading to it.

Pressing through, she felt as the wards pulled at her power, rendering her almost as mortal as she'd been as a human girl.

The magic of the veil was sticky, and she felt its tackiness all over her body. There was no going back now.

Her sensory system was immediately overwhelmed by the den's flashing red lights, the smell of drugs and sex, and the random strangers trying to touch her ... everywhere.

She hated people touching her. Absolutely despised it. The fact she was without her power down here, unable to zap any wandering hands, made it so much worse. If she wasn't almost to Dolus's hidey-hole, she'd turn around and go home.

It had been so long since she had stepped foot down here. Amphitrite was the only sister insane enough to attempt speaking with the drug-addled humans and deities who frequented the Reaver's Paradise. The den, which was more like a street market for everything sinful, wasn't just a haven for predatory deities and their prey, and not just for feasting on blood. The deities fed on mortals for the power and sustenance, yes, but many also fed on other deities for the drugging effects.

There was a compound in the blood of deities—from the weakest demigod and demon to the oldest Titan—that put anyone who ingested it, even mortals, in a mindless haze. Some immortals used it to make their humans more impressionable, like brainwashing, but others just wanted it for the euphoria.

People called it the nectar of the gods, or just ambrosia, and it had developed into an unsettling underground market, with the Reaver's Paradise at its center.

And she'd just volunteered to enter it, to make herself mortal for the time it took to speak with Dolus, a trickster and a demon.

As Hera pushed through the crowd, she could feel the eyes of many of the males, and some females, on her body. She wished she had been able to bring Viktor, pretend he was her plaything, and they could have dry humped to Dolus's door without a problem. It would have been infinitely preferable to this, but she couldn't have brought herself to ask him, not after knowing what he felt like so intimately.

An incubus moved towards her, his eyes revealing just what he'd been partaking in. His pupils were blown wide, and they looked glassy, as if he hadn't blinked for a while. But the most sickening sight was the color—his irises were deep red, and crimson veins spiked out into the surrounding whites. Ambrosia.

Hands wrapped around her waist, moving faster than she could fight off with her mortal reflexes, and pulled her into the incubus, who rubbed himself against her backside as he ran his nose over her neck. Doing a quick spin out of his arms landed her in another man's lap. She was thankful that he was at least clothed, unlike the very naked and aroused incubus now in front of her.

Before she could jump out of the man's lap, he grabbed her arm and licked her neck, nuzzling before scraping some seriously sharp teeth across her flesh. She shoved at him, but he was stronger since he had full use of his powers. Her stomach churned. This man was trying to take the scent of Viktor off her, trying to claim her.

A panic flared in her stomach. The thought of getting taken advantage of making her nauseous and she realized she only ever wanted Viktor's hands on her from now on.

She grunted with her pathetic attempts to escape, hating her mortal form. Hating her mortal weakness more. No amount of combat or physical conditioning would be enough to fight even the weakest demon in the hellish situation she had found herself in.

"Sorry boys, I'm not on the menu. I have nothing but good old-fashioned human blood." She gave a false smile of bravado as she tried to pull away from the one behind her, but he only held her wrists tighter as the other one crowded her front and licked his lips.

"We don't need the taste of ambrosia," one of them said. "We've had enough. Some blood and sex will do us just fine."

"Gentlemen, let's not accost my guest before I can speak with her," a deep baritone voice moved through the crowd, and everyone stopped their playtime to see why Dolus had come out from under his rock.

Amphitrite had told her that Dolus was usually in a state of undress, but the man before her wore a suit like he was running late for a business meeting. His dark hair was smoothed back, and his blood-red eyes stared daggers at the man holding her, not giving her even an inch to escape him.

"Enough, Sadric. I called for her. If anyone gets a taste, it is me," Dolus stated blandly, and the man behind her—Sadric—immediately released her wrists, letting her escape his lap.

"Oh good, I won't have to sex my way to you after all." She smiled, not showing the pain in her wrists or any strain in her bravado. Giving the incubus in front of her a pat on the pectoral, she sneered. "Try that again when we are topside, asshole."

Hera used the sleeve of her jacket to wipe the man's saliva from her neck. *Gross*. She needed a shower.

Looking back at the man that had held her, she realized he had opened his pants, his exposed erection touching her jeans. Great, she would have to burn them, and they were the only pair that did her butt justice.

Hera pushed away from the men and stepped up to Dolus, who, of course, had to put his hand to her back and guide her toward his office. She wouldn't complain though, since the crush of demons eyeing her up like a treat parted for them to pass, and she realized she would need to fight her way out if it went south with Dolus.

"Come to my office." He offered her his arm, and though she hesitated to take it, she knew she was out of her league here. To be on his arm offered her a tad bit of protection.

Not much, but enough.

His office was not what she expected from the man dressed to the nines. He had a desk, but he also had a large bed, which currently had quite a few naked women sleeping in it, and an area for drinks and drugs to be dispensed. Next to it was a large lounge area that also held several naked sleeping women.

"Not enough money to properly clothe your people, huh?" she asked nonchalantly as she looked around the room.

"Hera, Hera, Hera..." Dolus sat back against his desk and crossed his arms. "How I have wanted a visit from you for so very long. Your reputation precedes you."

Turning her head to look at him, she gave him a smile full of teeth.

"You had plenty of opportunities to come topside, I'm sure, but I am guessing you'd rather play with them instead." She gestured at the various women.

"It takes a lot to satisfy me." He smiled with blindingly white teeth.

"I gathered. My sister stated you had information, and I came here to collect," Hera told him as she moved around to sit in the chair in front of him. She had hoped he would take the hint and sit behind his desk, but she was low on luck these days.

A feral smile crossed his face as he pushed off the desk and lowered onto his knees in front of her, her pulse racing at his proximity. And not at all because she wanted him there. Unsure of his motives, she let a small, sardonic smile tilt her lips from the side, keeping an air of bemusement around her.

His hand went up and pushed a lock of her hair behind her ear. She prided herself on not flinching.

"You are such a beauty, Hera. Such a shame your father chose to kill you and your sisters. I could have had fun with all of them, but most especially you."

"Get to the information you told my sister you have, Dolus," she ordered, shoving his hand away.

Dolus only moved closer, an inch from her lips, and his hands lowered from her temple to her thighs. The urge to fry him was strong, but there was a void where her powers should have been.

Fates, she had not thought this through at all. So hasty to get away from Viktor. To do something—anything—to prepare for this war, that she hadn't thought through the consequences of her actions.

"Your sisters are attached, their souls bound, yet you continue to stay unattached. The queen. How will you have heirs?" He licked his lips, his mouth so close that his tongue almost touched her skin.

Instinct was screaming at Hera to get out. Now. Grabbing the arms of the chair, she struggled to keep calm as his hands moved under her jacket, his fingers running over her skin.

It was nothing like with Viktor. Dolus touching her only raised bile and not her libido.

"We would have powerful children," he whispered before he pressed his lips hard against hers, his tongue stabbing at her lips and finding them clenched shut against his attempted invasion. Pulling away a scant few inches, he smiled and shrugged. "Worth a shot."

Hopping up from where he had kneeled before her, he moved around his desk to grab something from the drawer as Hera resisted the urge to retch. Rage simmered in her veins. Hera would light the night up with her lightning once she was topside.

"So good to know Persephone is okay after that human attacked her. What a tragedy that would have been had she not been all right." He smiled at Hera as he continued to rummage through the drawer, his words making her focus on his face and not on what he was looking for.

"Did you order that?" Hera shot up to her feet, fists clenched at her sides, as she glowered at the Titan.

A smug smile crossed his lips. "No, kitten, I did not. But I know who did and why."

He slammed the drawer shut and ambled around his desk. She didn't dare take her eyes off him.

A loud booming knock hit the doors, and a panicked man yelled for Dolus through the hatch. A scream rent the air outside of Dolus' office, but he simply shook his head with his smug smile firmly in place.

"In a moment, Gerald," Dolus ordered the man at the door as he stood before her. "We are finishing a meeting here."

"Boss, we have a problem!" The man refused to relent. Hera was stuck between two situations here. She wanted to run out that door, away from Dolus, but with the sound of chaos outside, she had no idea what she would be running into. It could be far worse than in here, and in here, she had one man instead of Fates knew how many she would need to fight off out there.

The doors rattled with the man's fists, still pounding and yelling for Dolus. Hera was surprised at Dolus's reaction, or rather non-reaction was a more accurate description. This seemed like something that should be addressed, but Dolus was not the least bit interested in investigating it.

Warning alarms blared in her head, drowning out the music, drowning out everything but the Titan in front of her.

Dolus laughed.

"Always some fight or argument down here. Sex and drugs cause so many issues." He purred as he reached out and rubbed his knuckle along Hera's cheek.

"Who ordered my sister to be injured?" she demanded again as Dolus tilted his head, looking down her body and up again. As suddenly as she blinked, he grabbed her arms and, with his inhuman power, forcibly turned her to face the door, pulling her body tightly against his. Laying his cheek against her temple, he moved them from side to side in a slow dance.

"My little kitten," he whispered.

Hera knew he would be able to scent her fear now. She could no longer mask it with sarcasm and bitchiness. It was all too real.

"It doesn't matter who ordered it, but why they did."

It had been a trap, and she wanted to laugh at her own stupidity.

Get her here, turn her mortal, kill her.

*Kudos.*

A loud boom sounded outside of his office, before a noise that made her think a body had hit the door caused her to jolt. Dolus was unaffected. He let out a little laugh before singing a song below his breath.

"Should this be my end," he hummed, moving her hips with his and her pulse skyrocketed. "I'll say hi to your daddy for you," he whispered.

Metal glinted in her peripheral. Before Hera could move or blink, he arced the knife down. The icy blade lit a fire inside her as it pierced her chest, sliding through her ribs, finding no resistance.

Hera stared in shock at the pulsing door in front of her. She abstractly realized that someone else was hitting it now. The rhythmic pounding at the door matched her rapidly increasing heartbeat as her body had yet to realize she was as good as dead.

"I'm sure Cronus sends his regards," he whispered, his cheek still against her head.

Trying to focus through the shock of pain, a pain she had never known, she grabbed the blade he still held. Her hands, now slippery with her own mortal blood, tried to pull at his as if that would save her.

"What ... you and ... my father," she gasped, blood dripping from her mouth. Her throat pushed her to cough, but her lungs were not strong enough to pull in the air she needed, leaving her gasping.

"Boss!" Someone new banged on the door, rattling the knob as they desperately tried to get it open.

Dolus held Hera as her knees buckled and her vision faltered, everything wavering like water in front of her.

"Not now," he growled, pulling the knife out finally.

She knew without a doubt that once that knife left her body she was done for.

"Bo—"

An explosion rocketed the underground, dirt and debris falling from the walls. Hera knew something hit her, but she didn't know where, or how hard, as everything was starting to happen outside of herself. That was probably a really bad sign.

Dolus ripped the knife from her, and she fell, but he grabbed her again, or at least she thought he did, as she still saw the door in front of her. Her vision was blackening from the sides, and she was vaguely aware of her rapid attempts at breathing. Each inhale was thick and wet.

She sounded horrible.

The doors imploded, sending shrapnel through the office, and a fiery form stepped through.

"Prometheus," Dolus whispered, his voice awed. "I have no issue with you."

Her mind whirled and blurred, yet she tried to narrow her vision on the almost familiar fiery form.

*Viktor?*

No, Dolus had called him Prometheus.

But even in her state, something in her recognized the man in the fire. She tried to catch his fiery eyes before she took her last breath.

To say what she wanted before she died. If only words instead of blood would leave her lips.

A roar rent the air, and something calming moved over her. Perhaps Thanatos was here.

*Time to go*, she thought, her body falling a bit more, Dolus having a harder time keeping hold of her through all the blood.

The heat that came over her body next was not as terrifying as she thought it would be. Hera had thought burning alive would hurt more, yet when Viktor—or Prometheus—stepped up to her, she only felt a deep and soothing calm. She imagined it was Viktor. Hoped it was him. Whoever it was, he didn't use words, but somehow, she knew he was asking her to trust him.

"I trust you," she whispered, more blood coming from her lips than could be good, and it was getting more difficult to keep her eyelids open.

Glowing hands shot over her shoulders, grabbing Dolus.

Everything around her lit on fire. The scream Dolus unleashed as he burned, immolated in his own domain, would have haunted her for the rest of her life. Should she have lived, of course.

The body behind her was gone now, and yet she was not burning. Had not been touched by the flame.

Her mind screamed that she needed to breathe, panic overtaking her now. So far gone in the panic, she almost didn't even notice that she was now being held against the fiery body as he walked them out of there. The moment he passed where the veil had been, he pulled them into a light jump.

And the pain that followed as her power moved back through her battered body tore her apart.

# Chapter 17

### **<u>Hera</u>**

Screams of pain tore through the air, and a distant part of Hera realized they were her own. Her nerves coming back to life scorched her insides, but a warm, deep voice steadily soothed her.

Dolus kept her close to him as her strength left her, holding her and whispering it would be all right while he swayed with her dying body. The voice ... was it actually him?

Hera tried to pull away, but their hands held her, the voice begging her to stop and rest. No, that wasn't Dolus holding her anymore.

What an idiot she had been to come here. How would she protect her sisters now?

"It'll be over soon, kitten, and you can join your mother and your other sisters. Just let go," Dolus whispered into her mind.

But how? Another voice in the background begged her to stay with him, growing stronger behind Dolus's words. Numb. She suddenly felt so numb. Shouldn't there be horrible pain? Hera knew she was *in* pain, but she didn't feel it. What an odd thing to know...

A sudden light hit her eyes. Perhaps it was a hallucination. Still, when she tried to focus, she could only see fire. No, it was a man in the shape of fire.

"Viktor..." she tried to speak, but water, no, blood poured from her mouth. Why was this happening?

He wrapped his arms tighter around her, or at least it felt like he did. Slowly, the heat around her dissipated, and she was being carried by Viktor now. But was it truly him? What had Dolus called him?

"Something needs to be done. She is too far gone and without her power to heal."

Who had said that? Hera no longer heard Dolus. No, there was Viktor's voice now, too.

"Run, Viktor, run!" She tried to buck away from the hands, and the voice called her back again.

"Hera, stop. I need you to stop. I cannot heal you if you—"

Suddenly, something touched her head, and she was finally able to keep her eyes open. Viktor was leaning over her, tears rolling down his cheeks as he begged forgiveness. Why was Viktor crying and why were they in a cave? The stony walls, reminiscent of the one she grew up in with Themis, surrounded them.

"I am so sorry," Viktor sobbed. "If I had known you were going to do this, I would have stopped you."

A cry left her mouth as the world distorted around her again, her vision of the cave and Viktor lost.

Light cracked through Hera's body. She saw Viktor in her mind, standing before her as a man, not an immortal, just as he had been in his garage when they had made love. He was standing over her again, this time in a room, but he somehow looked different from the man she had just seen.

Hera needed him so much, and she would lose him and her memories to the Underworld. Another bolt of power ran through her veins, tearing her away from the heartbreaking thought.

Screaming, *now* she felt the pain. As if her body was being pulled apart piece by piece. Viktor was yelling her name, his voice choked with tears, as he begged Hera to stop.

Her hand, alight with gold, reached out for Viktor, who held his head in his hands as he fell to his knees, cursing everyone.

Looking back up at her, his eyes red and swollen, she begged him to forgive her, but no words left her mouth.

Suddenly, the world exploded around her.

### Viktor

Viktor watched as Dolus became a living ball of fire, turning to ash before his eyes. As Reaver's Paradise exploded, people screamed and trampled each other to get out.

None of that mattered as he grabbed Hera and cradled her against his chest. He needed to hurry and get Hera to the surface so she could heal. Who knew how much time she had left?

Pulling every ounce of power left in him, he light jumped to his home. He tried to ignore the clothing on her body burning away, but he couldn't help but notice her flesh was untouched by his fire.

That had been a gamble, since pretty much anyone else would have been engulfed. He had spent most of his charge toward Dolus's office, both praying it would work and fighting off Dolus's flunkies.

*"She is near death's doorstep."*

Nodding at Nyx, Viktor carefully laid Hera down on top of his bed, grabbing a blanket from the chair beside it, draping it over her as he checked her wounds.

As he laid his hands on her, she started screaming his name, begging for him to run. Her body arched painfully as she shoved at him. Her legs twitched as if she were trying to stand on her own, but she was far too weak to escape Viktor's hold.

A battle was being fought in her mind. Her body thought she was dying as she yelled for him to get away.

"Hey," he soothed, placing his hands on her cheeks, trying to send her calming energy, wishing there were a more direct way of doing so.

Viktor tried to mend her as she lashed out. He begged Hera, pleaded with her to calm down so he could help her. He wiped futilely at all the blood, desperately trying to see the wound the damned Titan had given her, but she moved too violently and there was a shocking amount of it, some still liquid and some dark and dry on her skin from his heat.

He worried over her prone form. Had her power been returned to her long enough to heal?

There, between her ribs and just under her left breast, was the entry wound. His breathing halted. What a small cut, and it did all this.

He nearly fell back when her back arched high off the mattress, almost levitating over his bed, and erupted with an explosive, crackling light. The light Hera threw off blinded him, and his heart sank.

Was she gone? Had her power flared as a final violent outburst?

When the light faded, he almost passed out with relief. The wound knitted itself up from the inside, and he fell into the chair next to the bed, completely overwhelmed. It might take several hours, or even days, for her body to heal enough for her to regain consciousness. He'd had enough of his own close calls to know that.

Now he knew that she would return to him.

*"I assume her being naked means she survived your fire?"*

"Yes," Viktor breathed out, agitated it was brought up as he was trying to not focus on such a huge and important fact. Hera needed him right now.

Watching her as she finally fell into a peaceful sleep, he made sure she was covered from her toes to her chin. Pushing a lock of hair from her brow, he turned to face Nyx.

"Why are you here, Nyx?" he demanded. Exhaustion had sapped him of the energy to interrogate her as he would have before Reaver's Paradise. "Not just now, but at all? Why don't you take your true form and do ... anything else?"

*Help*, he thought. *Help me, help Hera. Heal her, please.*

*"I made choices long ago, deals and oaths of my own that led us to this moment in time. I told you—"*

"Yes, that's what you said before." He sighed. "Your power has nothing to do with fire, yet you were the familiar of a fire priestess and now hold some of her power within you."

*"As I said, deals and oaths with both of the people who knew far more than you about this upcoming war with the Titans. The Titans who wronged my fellow Primordials long ago."*

"In other words, you're not going to tell me," he said, watching as Nyx lowered her head. He understood Hera's frustration more now than ever.

"Sucks, huh?" Hera said weakly from behind him.

Viktor spun around and lowered himself to the ground next to the bed. Without thinking, he was cupping her jaw in his hand, looking over her face for the fatigue of the wound she'd just healed from.

"How—" Hera coughed, a little bit of dried blood on her lips flaking away, and Viktor quickly moved his thumb to wipe away the rest of the blood without a thought.

"Ew," she muttered. She took a deep breath, a look of relief on her face before she continued. "How am I not a melted puddle of goddess right now? You ... saved me." Her vision dulled, and he knew she was pulling together whatever memories of the past few hours that she could. She blinked up at him, looking so sweetly surprised Viktor could kiss her.

"I should be dead," she breathed.

*"She survived the fire. It's time."*

His heart was beating so loudly he was sure she could hear it, plain as day.

Stalling, he pulled the chair closer to the bed and sat beside her, his elbows on his knees and hands clasped, looking between his feet on the floor.

*No, I need to feel her*, he thought as he took her hand in between his. Stalling for a moment, he watched his thumb stroke over the back of her hand.

"Do you ... feel different or..." Viktor started, but he wasn't sure how to finish as Hera arched an eyebrow at him. Did the curse not unravel and put everything back in its place? Or was it up to him to finish removing it somehow?

Running his free hand over his face, he tried to focus on what her question was again. Obviously, he needed more information on how to fully remove the curse and its counter effects.

"How were you able to use your power down there?" she asked, her voice barely above a whisper, but the demand for an answer was clear.

"My father. When Amphitrite told me West could not go into that place because Oceanus was not welcomed, I took the chance I might be because of who my father is. Even if my power didn't work, it was worth a shot to make sure you came out of there, even if I had to fight with fist instead of fire," Viktor stated, his voice low.

Looking back up at Hera, he could hear the question before it even left her lips.

"Who is your father, Viktor?" she asked, her hand pulling a bit from his grasp, as if she were readying herself to disappear.

Sighing, he looked up at her again, his expression pleading as he watched closely for her reaction. It was the first of many secrets he had to tell her. And he knew each one would bring him closer to Hera never forgiving him.

"Prometheus."

# Chapter 18

### **<u>Hera</u>**

HERA CLOSED HER EYES, searching herself for a reaction. She'd seen his pure elemental form, suspected he had Titan blood somewhere to override having a godform. *But his father?*

And not just any Titan father, but Prometheus.

*Prometheus.*

Her mind prickled as she tripped on a memory, and she recalled some of Dolus's final words. He'd mistaken Viktor for Prometheus.

*Fates damn it.*

Hera opened her eyes and stared at Viktor. He looked like he was bracing himself for a lightning bolt, and she couldn't deny that she wanted to deliver one. A tired laugh left her lips as she looked from Viktor to Nyx. It occurred to her that she was between a half-Titan-half-god and a Primordial god, two of the most powerful beings in the world, and yet they appeared to be a simple man and a house cat.

At that, her laugh turned a little brittle, sounding more crazed than amused.

Viktor frowned. "Perhaps you could let me in on the joke?"

She shook her head.

"You wouldn't get it." How could he? "I'm hoping you didn't save my life just so your father can use me to win favor with my dear old dad," she said tiredly, and she nearly slapped a hand over her mouth for admitting something so true.

He shook his head harshly, his expression aghast.

"Of course not, Hera," he told her. "Prometheus has no allegiance to Cronus or his followers."

"Prometheus?" she echoed. "Not 'father'?"

"I hadn't seen him in around two hundred years … until last week."

Hera would have sat up in bed if she didn't feel so weak.

"He's Earth side?" She hadn't seen Prometheus in many centuries, and now she had to worry about another Titan hanging around. She could scream for all her bad luck.

"He's unpredictable," Viktor said wryly, like it was an inside joke, but one he no longer found funny. "I went to see him in the hopes he could provide a prophecy that could help us."

Hera swallowed the odd emotion clogging her throat. Right then, Viktor looked at her so earnestly that Hera nearly grabbed his face, to either pull him closer or hide his expression. Why did she love the way he said 'us' so much?

Viktor continued without pause. "As usual with him, I couldn't get anything useful."

His eyes darkened for a moment, and Hera pushed. "What did he tell you?"

"It's important that we win. So, nothing I didn't already know," he said stiffly with a shake of his head.

"Helpful," she noted.

"Exactly."

In the brief lull that followed, Hera tried raising herself higher up in bed. Viktor reached over to help her right as the blanket fell down her chest, baring her breasts. He jerked his hand back in time, and she quickly righted the blanket, but a breath shuddered out of her.

Normally she would have been fine with him seeing her naked, especially since they had already been intimate ... but ... something about being so close to death—and close to him—made her skin tingle. Hera knew something deep inside of her had shifted, but she was far too exhausted to ruminate on it. Not when she already had far too many questions for the Titan progeny in front of her.

"Dolus mistook you for Prometheus," she said, her tone going acidic at the thought of the now-dead man.

He nodded, sensing the question in her statement. "Very few deities know Prometheus had a son."

She gestured down at herself. "Why didn't I burn like Dolus did?"

Viktor looked down at her arm where it rested on top of the blanket. Unmarred, except for the blood drying on her skin. "I don't know," he murmured thoughtfully. "My curse ... I think it's broken."

Hera straightened at that, gathering the blanket around her and pressing her back against the headboard.

"What?" she breathed. "Like *broken,* broken? Is that how you can tell me about Prometheus?"

"*The curse dies in the fire,*" he said lowly and flexed his hands, as if the curse were something he could feel and stretch—and for all Hera knew, he could. "That's what the Moirai told me."

They locked eyes, and Hera's heart raced. *Finally.*

Fates damned finally she could have what she needed. To trust him. To feel closer—*no*, she chided herself.

Trust was needed to go into battle together. It was needed in order to win. *That was all.*

"If it's broken, then you can tell me…" she let her voice trail off. "You showed me before. Your mother placed the curse on you, didn't she?"

His eyes shut, and she couldn't tell if his expression was one of relief or pain.

"My mother was a priestess, the leader of our clan," he began slowly. "She's the one who carried Hestia's power and passed it on to me." Viktor laughed dryly. "She had the gift of foresight, and I'm still wondering how much of this she saw."

He would have had to inherit it through his mother, she knew, but Hera was still wrapping her head around his parentage.

"How long had her line carried my sister's power?"

Viktor swallowed, watching her carefully. "She was the first."

Hera's eyes widened. This meant that his mother had received Hestia's power directly from her sister. That Viktor was much older than she'd ever thought. As old as her. Her first instinct was a fresh wave of anger. He'd been hidden for so long, keeping his power from Olympus, while they'd toiled away for their regime and for humanity.

Her second thought, however, was that to live with such a curse for so very long sounded incredibly lonely.

Quickly, she pushed aside that thought, since she didn't truly know if he'd actually been alone all that time. Hera motioned for him to continue, but he still kept his evaluative gaze on her.

"My mother made sacrifices to Prometheus in the fires as a priestess who worshipped him. Perhaps he felt something in her prayers and sacrifices, something that was different, or maybe he had his own vision. But one day, he visited her." Viktor paused, his chest rising with a deep breath. Both of them knew what a visitation from a Titan meant in the days of old. "I was born nine months later. Prometheus stuck around though, but at odd times. Now, I know he was making sure I stayed on the path he'd foreseen." Frowning, he shook his head in frustration with his Titan father, and Hera empathized deeply. "He made sure I ascended, so he didn't waste all the effort he put into my conception," he scoffed. "My village was invaded by Romans, and my mother burned it to the ground along with the Romans—"

"I saw that in the fires before you started seizing," she whispered, and he gave her a slight nod. "When she was singing, that was the curse, wasn't it?"

Viktor broke his stare and looked away as he leaned forward, his elbows on his knees.

"She wasn't just a priestess; she was an elemental witch who knew enough spells to be dangerous. Enough to protect our clan. Always protecting, that woman. But she also knew enough about the Titans to fear for me once I'd ascended. Before she died, she put this curse on me, hoping it would keep me off the Titans' radar."

"It definitely worked," Hera said, her voice sounding flat and tired. What an understatement. "How else did you stay hidden? You were right there the *whole time.*"

A pained expression crossed his face, and she guessed he was remembering the horrible early days of ascension.

"I was angry for so long after she died. I resented not being able to tell anyone about my powers, about my true self. I tested the limits of her spell, trying to tell even a human child, but her burning magic stopped me every time."

Hera nodded, remembering how severe his reaction had been from simple scenes, not even spoken words.

"I burned down my share of places until Prometheus came back and worked with me on my powers," he said. "Training finally brought me around. When I saw glimpses of the future, he worked with me on using the power bestowed through my heritage on both sides. To use it to see into the fires as my mother did."

"You receive prophecies?" she asked, leaning forward.

"I see visions in the fire, like the ones I showed you. And I only see what's given to me. By the universe. The Moirai. Hell, maybe even by my father. It's not as reliable as I would like." Viktor glanced out the window before looking back into her eyes to continue. "You have asked about my powers before ... precognition is not all I can do. I have a sensitivity for magic from my mother, not just from her blood, but from watching her work my entire life. I'm the last known speaker of my mother's ancestral tongue—"

"The chanting song," she interrupted. "You broke the spell on the humans. You need to show Hecate how to—"

Viktor placed a calming hand on her arm, and she realized she'd jerked forward in her eagerness. A wave of exhaustion swept through her, and she leaned back against the headboard. She was tired, but she had to hear more.

"I can," he told her. "These powers ... the god, the Titan, the witch's son ... they used to battle within me. But I learned to control them, bring them together. In my empowered form, pure fire, I can construct weapons from my flames. My father and I may appear similar, but he could never do that."

She raised her eyebrows. "Who taught you then?"

He paused for a beat. "Themis."

And here Hera thought he was completely boring.

## <u>Hera</u>

Hera was unable to stay awake long enough to give him the full interrogation he knew was coming.

Being that her body had been mortal and at the precipice of death so very recently, so it needed more time to heal than normal.

*"You did not tell her the truth. You did not tell her everything."*

Viktor tried to rein in his temper. The goddess of the night was relentless, but he knew she was right. Hera only had a fraction of the story, and it looked like it was up to him to find a way to tell her. He may not feel the scorching pain of the curse, but he would feel another type of pain entirely when he told her the rest of his tale.

The Fates couldn't be kind enough to do it for him. No, the curse was still working on those around him, even if he was free.

"I am aware, and I will. Eventually."

*"The longer you wait, the worse her response. She is one whom, when angry, is impulsive. Why could it not have been the stoic and level-headed Persephone? I like her."*

Looking back at Nyx, he raised an eyebrow, feeling some of their old comradery return to their banter. The way it was before he found out who she truly was. However, that thought plunged him back into the hurt he felt about the familiar's identity being kept secret from him for so long.

Was it hypocritical of him? Maybe. Did it change his feelings? No.

He looked back to where Hera was sleeping, an arm flung over her face, an almost innocent look in her sleep. Her relaxed expression soothed him.

"Why didn't you help me with all this sooner?" he asked quietly.

*"Have I not helped you, child? I did not leave you to do this alone."*

"You know what I mean, Nyx. Why did I have to go through the loss—" Viktor swallowed the flood of emotion back down before he continued "—of the woman I loved and the loss of our future together..."

*"As I said, I have my own oaths. I gave you the darkness of night so you could see her in your fires after she was lost to you. So that you could pray to Chaos for her soul."*

Turning to tell her how much she had cost him, how he couldn't be what Hera needed because of that loss, and how trying to explain it to Hera when she was growing close to him was wrong, he realized Nyx was gone.

Defeated, he slumped in the chair, his heart begging him to finally take enough care to stop feeling. To do as Hera did in building a wall between herself and everyone else.

A whimper broke through Hera's lips, and he straightened, concerned for her as he watched a nightmare pulling her in. When he grasped her hand in his, she calmed, the nightmare she was lost in lessening its hold on her. Viktor *knew* he should put a wall between himself and the woman in his bed.

Yet, as he looked at her, he didn't want to. He wanted to know if there was a chance with Hera. If there was even a small chance that he could find love again. A small chance he could have this woman and actually keep her.

A chance even after all they had lost.

# Chapter 19

## **<u>Thanatos</u>**

Having only been home for five seconds, Thanatos was more than a little annoyed at the knock on his door. He had dealt with deaths all day, most of them refusing to cross. They'd been absolutely obstinate in their belief that he was wrong, that they were, in fact, still alive.

Growling, he pulled back on the shirt he had just tossed off and marched to the door of his home. His tattoos were more than pictures, and if anyone were able to read them, they could own him. Not something he was willing to chance, so he made sure his tattoos were covered if anyone other than Persephone and Hecate were around. No one had ever seen his tattoos aside from the two women, not even his mother, as reaper tattoos were earned.

Walking to the door, he opened it with a growl but blanched at the small black house cat sitting on the front step. Looking out over the cat, he was confused about why a very alive cat was sitting in front of him in the Underworld.

*"Where is your witch?"* the small cat asked as it slunk between his legs and into his house.

Shocked, Thanatos slowly shut the door and turned to where the cat sat on the rug of his entryway.

"Mother?" he asked, trying to take in the fact that his all-powerful mother was ... a cat.

*"Yes, I understand you are confused, but that will have to wait. I need your witch. Now, where is she?"*

Thanatos rubbed his face in disbelief. "I do not have a witch. Why are you a cat, Mother?"

*"The witch, the one from the crossroads."* Nyx looked around his home, her shadows swirling around her.

"Hecate? She is a friend. Not *my* witch. A friend is someone who—"

*"Where is your brother?"*

"Hypnos is not here. Only your intelligent and attractive son."

*"I thought you said Hypnos wasn't here."* His mother gave him a smirk, which on a feline face appeared as a snarky twitching of her whiskers, and she padded around his home, her tail flicking back and forth.

Thanatos snorted as he folded his arms and leaned back against the door.

*"Why are you dressed like a juvenile mortal?"*

Thanatos looked down at his shirt. A reaper counting money with the words 'Stupid people are great for business.'

"Hecate and I like to enjoy the more wistful aspects of life," he stated as he pushed away from the door and squatted down to his furry mother.

*"Then before your next little shopping trip to the children's section, you can tell her I need to speak with her. It is important to us in making sure Cronus stays where he should be."*

Thanatos let his smile drop.

"What do you know?" he growled out, not caring that his mother was infinitely more powerful than him and could take him out with a snap of her dainty fingers. Or claws. And yet, she only sat on her hind legs as she looked up at him, her eyes swirling with a galaxy of stars.

*"Bring me Hecate and I will tell you what I can. Everything I had planned for is changing and, with it, the rules of this game."*

"You sound like the Moirai," he replied.

His mother hissed at the comment, flickering her tail. *"Perhaps I have more information than those spaced-out entities people so love to believe have all the infinite wisdom of the world."*

Now Thanatos smiled. He got his humor from somewhere. His mother was just not always one to show that side of her.

"Then, let's go get my witch."

## Hera

Hera opened her eyes back up to a room lit with the last sleepy rays of the day. She was unsure if it was still the same day, or if she must have been so incredibly weak to need more than one to heal.

Either way, Viktor and Nyx were gone, which worked out perfectly fine in her plan to escape. Pulling her power quickly to her, thankful that she had recovered enough to do so, she light jumped to her home before Viktor could return.

Landing on the edge of her bed, Hera sat up, rubbing her temples with her fingers, and letting her mind process all the new information.

Viktor was more powerful than she ever could have imagined. And now, with his curse burned away with her clothes—and Dolus—he could speak freely.

Dolus.

"Fates damn it!" she groaned, falling back on her peacock-colored comforter. He had information that was now lost along with the den of sin that bastard ran. Or perhaps he never had any intel, and it was all just an assassination attempt.

An assassination attempt in the name of her father was all the same, no matter where that bastard was. Even if Cronus was not free, he had people ready and willing to do the dirty work for him. Devon was a shining example of that after having been killed by the Titans in some ridiculous plan to convert him to their side.

Idiot Titans. All of them.

If they lost this war to them, it would be horribly embarrassing. Hera would have to hide in shame. If she lived, that is.

Running her hand over her chest where the dagger had pierced her, spilling her lifeblood onto the floor, she remembered how she'd known in that moment she was dead. The pain, the fear for her sisters, and something else. Her regret was that she didn't spend more time with Viktor. That she had shut him out instead of working through it with him.

Then Viktor had risked his life to save her from death. Walked into that horrid place with the intention of getting her out one way or another. With or without his power.

Sitting up, Hera recalled more of what Dolus had said, her mind not clear enough to realize the meaning of the words at the time.

"I'll say hi to your daddy for you," she whispered the words aloud, and the hairs on her body stood on end.

Cronus.

If they were trying to get Cronus out, why would Dolus kill her to send her to the Underworld? It was not like anyone could escape Tartarus when a new soul went through. And even if she were mortal still, had died mortal, that did not mean she wouldn't get the choice at the crossroads to return to her body. She didn't know what would happen should she have actually died, an already ascended goddess stuck in a mortal shell, so she knew for Fates damn sure Dolus didn't either.

So, how would that help them break the piece of crap masquerading as her father out? Had her death been meant as a blow to the war effort on their side or another distraction? Or both?

But if they sent all the goddesses to their final death, it wouldn't be hard to get Cronus out in the end, would it?

A panic Hera had only felt once before took over her. With ragged breaths, she tried to calm herself so she wasn't an absolute mess, but the panic was far stronger than she was.

Sitting back down on the floor, she tugged her knees to her chest, trying to pull in deeper breaths. Trying to slow her heart rate and rationalize that they couldn't harm her now that she was no longer mortal.

Hera was not powerful enough to stop them all. There were so many Titans that she had no clue the status of. If they were loyal to her, her father, or themselves.

A sudden bolt of clarity hit her.

She might not be powerful enough now, but she knew how she could be.

# Chapter 20

### <u>Viktor</u>

VIKTOR HAD RETURNED TO an empty bed and been relieved, which he felt some guilt over. It meant he had time before he had to tell her everything.

Time that he needed to use to think of his next step in explaining his history to Hera and sitting around here was not cutting it.

Light jumping to the edge of the city, he walked down the empty streets of Halcyon since all the businesses were closed and boarded up.

The silence of the city and the exercise would help him think.

However, it was an incredibly depressing sight to see such a normally lively city frozen, only the breeze flowing through the bushes creating any noise.

A quick whistle had him turning to see West and Devon standing near where he and Hera had battled the humans under the control of the Titans only days ago.

Approaching the men, Viktor pushed his hands into his pockets and took in the area. His focus fell onto the shattered concrete where bolts of lightning had struck.

"Where ya been?" West asked with a knowing look on his face.

"Dealing with the same messes you both have been," Viktor replied, seeing the exhaustion evident on Devon. His eyes were not on them, his mind gone somewhere else as he looked over the destruction. Knowing, most likely, that the larger battle would do far worse to the city.

"My apologies if you've needed me in a professional capacity. As with everyone else, I was ordered to close my doors."

West waved him off.

"Easy fix. You're fired. Now you don't have to feel guilty that you've neglected my mental health and worry I am on the edge of doing something crazier than normal." West smirked again and Viktor felt the hair along his arms stand up. "I'm pretty sure those lines are blurred anyway now that you're sleeping with my wife's sister."

Viktor startled. "She told you?" Viktor asked, wondering if Hera was confiding in her sisters about him. *That would be a good thing, right?*

"No, but you just did." West winked at Viktor.

"Hera?" Devon asked, his eyebrows high on his face and shock in his voice.

"What? You think I'm talking about Persephone?" West laughed, slapping Devon on the back.

"Seems more realistic ... no offense. I just imagined—" Devon broke off, but Viktor motioned for him to continue.

"That she was like a praying mantis," West finished. "But you still have your head, so we were confused."

Viktor looked away, unable to keep the small smile from tilting his lips up.

"The Reaver's Paradise is ash now," Devon declared as he looked at Viktor. "But I suppose you already knew that."

The smile dropped from Viktor's face, hating that he had to think of that place again. Hating that the image of Hera's prone, bloody form flashed in his mind.

West turned his shocked face to Viktor with Devon's words.

"And Dolus just ... let it burn down?" West asked.

"Dolus is dead. I burned him," Viktor confirmed, with little to no remorse. The man deserved far more than the quick death Viktor had given him. Had he more time, perhaps it would have been slower. A lot slower.

"You burned him? There was nothing there. Just ash," Devon stated, his eyes narrowed on Viktor.

"Humans cremated their own long ago. How is this different?" Viktor replied, thinking perhaps that was the wrong response by the shocked look on West's face and Devon's scowl.

"Holy Fates..." West whispered, his eyes wide and on Viktor. "You ... burned him? Bones and all? You *melted* that scary bastard?"

"I predict you just broke one of your patients, Viktor. I am pretty sure there is some oath about doing no harm to the more fragile minded ones." Devon smirked at West.

Viktor simply stared at Devon.

"He is no longer a patient." Viktor waved to West. "He just fired me."

"Holy..." West put his hands in his hair, tugging at the strands before he looked back up at Viktor. "That's your response? *That?* The humans did it? He was a damn demon!"

"If he were a demon, fire would not have hurt him." Viktor tried to bite back a smile at the aghast look on West's face.

"I feel like you're not truly comprehending my concern here," West replied in an almost theatrically loud whisper. "I am really Fates-damn glad you're on our side. I need a drink."

Devon gave Viktor a slight smile at West's antics. It was apparent the two men were close, and if Viktor remembered correctly, Devon was the friend murdered and brought back to life, giving them a second chance at their friendship. Of course, West had been through so much since he had sat in Viktor's office and unloaded the troubles and trials he dealt with. The man before him had come such a long way, and Viktor felt a sense of pride in what West had become.

Standing back and listening to the banter between the old friends, Viktor found himself roped into the conversation whether he wanted to be or not.

After some friendly ribbing, Devon and West started speaking about the war, giving Viktor the details of what they had seen with the people ensorcelled by the Titans. A strategic meeting that he had happened upon, but the men listened to him, gave feedback, and accepted his.

Having never truly been with people he considered friends before, it felt like this might be the comradery that men shared in a friendship.

They might never know it, but Viktor was thankful to them for including him and giving him this moment before the Titans brought down their torment in the coming days.

Even if it was simply discussing such a future.

### <u>Viktor</u>

The flash of gold light startled Viktor from where he was reading over reports Devon had left him with before light jumping back home. Viktor was trying to understand some of the issues with the humans under the spell of the Titans. A last-ditch attempt to find a way to replicate what he did that night with Hera. That Hecate and her witches could learn about it and make a widespread attempt to pull the humans from the thrall of the Titans.

"I didn't expect you back so soon after you ran," he stated as he turned. When he took in the panicked look on Hera's face, he took a step toward her. "What happened?" he asked as he took her shoulders in his hands and pulled her to sit down in the chair across from him in his home office.

Hera didn't flinch away from him this time, and he wasn't sure if she was beginning to trust him or was just that panicked.

The squeak of the leather as she sat was all he heard, and her quiet stillness unsettled him.

Finally, she gathered herself enough to look up at him.

"That was an assassination attempt ordered by Cronus."

Viktor knelt in front of her, his hands over hers on her knees.

"Did Dolus tell you that?" he asked, keeping his voice calm, even though alarm shot through him.

He had failed to get any information before he left Reaver's Paradise with Hera in his arms, but he knew deep down they would continue to try everything until they succeeded. Nodding at his question, he watched in shock as her eyes teared up before she closed them, looking away.

"In a roundabout way. It would be easier to free him without me, without my sisters, in the way. I cannot protect my sisters and this city if I'm dead," Hera whispered.

"You will not die," he swore, taking her chin to make her look at him again. "I will do everything in my power to make sure that doesn't happen."

"You're right. I won't die—because I have a plan." Her eyes were almost manic as she spoke, scooting forward as her hands grabbed his, dragging them into her lap. "When Persephone and Amphitrite were weak and needed more power to help them fight, they did a soulbond with Devon and West. Their powers merged. If we do that, we would be *unbelievably* powerful."

"But—" Viktor tried to calm the situation he knew could grow out of control far quicker than he could contain it. "Those bonds only work if the two parties are meant to be. If they are both in love and care for each other in a way that makes them one…"

Watching Hera withdraw was painful, but he knew better than to pull her back to him. She stood so quickly he had to catch himself before he hit the ground.

"We can still try! Perhaps Eros will allow such a thing in order to take down those damn parasites!" She clapped her hands together, pulling them into a light jump.

Viktor caught himself on his throne's armrest and glanced around. Olympus was empty, save for them. Hera stood at the center of the throne room, and he rushed over to her, grabbing her shoulders again, but she cut him off before he could say a word.

"I need you to try, Viktor. It's the only way I can make sure we're powerful enough to win this fight," she pleaded.

A vulnerability she never showed the world was plain on her face. A tear trailed down her cheek, and he knew no one saw Hera like this, ever. She was trusting him with a huge part of her right now, and he was an idiot if he didn't at least try to help. Turning from her, he threw out his power with a yell that shook Olympus.

"Eros!"

Viktor had never had to summon the deity, but he knew how it worked from every single time he had shouted for and cursed his father. The Titans responded to power, not just words, which always made him wonder how the early humans ever won favor or found blessing with the deities unless they held some latent power. Of course, from all he had seen over his very long lifetime, the mortals held no favor unless they could give the Titans something in return.

His thoughts turned to Hera and how she viewed the mortals under her care as she moved even higher in his regard. She refused to leave her city to their demise and would stand between Halcyon and the Titans even if it meant true death. Her people were under her watch, and she refused to fail them. How many times had the Primordials and Titans looked the other way when tragedy befell the humans?

Hera was putting aside her pride to find a way to save her people. How many rulers had he known would do the same?

None. Viktor had known none.

A sudden and bright flash of light flared in the throne room, making him squint and throw a hand over his eyes. There was no need to see who it was since he knew Eros had heeded his call. Hera's tightened grip on his elbow confirmed it.

Releasing him, Hera stepped forward, straightening her shoulders as she stood before the ageless deity, who appeared so bright in his resplendent power that the details of his tall form were ambiguous.

"Eros, I need you to bind us through a soulmark," Hera stated, getting right down to business. One of the things Viktor truly appreciated about Hera was her lack of small talk. But now, as his heart raced under the gaze of Eros, he wondered if a hello would've helped their cause.

Eros said nothing as he stood before them. His eyes, discernable as white pinpricks of concentrated light, were piercing. The god simply studied Hera, before taking in Viktor. He wished he could see the expression on Eros's face, but he was still blindingly bright.

"You would force a soulmark?" he asked as he turned back to Hera, his tone even and without the judgement that his words held.

"You bound my sisters to increase their power, to save them. If you do this, Viktor and I have a chance to defeat the Titans."

Something in her voice tore at him. How often did this woman ask for help, much less beg? No, she always ordered. She thought they wouldn't win this war without this bond.

Stepping forward, Viktor let his arm touch Hera's in solidarity, and though Eros caught the movement, he still made no move toward them.

"Others have attempted to force such a joining in the past, something I will not condone. To have a true soulbond, both parties must be open and willing for it to work. If there is any doubt, the mark will mean nothing ... or worse."

Viktor was confused by what that meant, but Eros held up his glowing hands before either of them could question him.

"But we shall try."

Eros stepped toward them both, holding his hands up in the air, and a beat later, a small pillar rose from the center of Olympus between them. It wasn't tangible, the pillar only materializing from Eros's power.

Words moved unbidden through his mind, his lips moving of their own volition as he spoke the magic into existence. Words that Eros was pushing into his mind. And Hera's too, as she recited them in tandem with him.

"We bind ourselves, mind, body, and soul. We let the mountain of Olympus take our bound selves upon this stone for it to remain for all of eternity, never to break, as our bond will never break. As long as Olympus stands, so will our bond," they spoke in unison as they placed their hands upon the stone.

The moment their hands settled over the ephemeral pillar a slice of pain lanced his palm. He flinched, but an unseen power pressed his hand firmly onto the pillar's surface. Their blood flowed, following the curves of the pillar as Eros reached forward and covered their hands with his own.

A hiss left Eros's lips at the moment of contact, and he pulled away.

His eyes were even brighter now as he looked between Hera and Viktor, then down at the stone.

"Your bond was not accepted. Both parties must agree and be wholly open to the bond to receive it. I am sorry, Queen Goddess."

Without another word, Eros and the pillar dissipated in a whirl of light and air, leaving Viktor and Hera in the silence of the throne room.

Viktor looked at Hera, but she did not turn to him, only stared straight ahead. Unsure of how to address this, he tentatively put his hand out, but she moved away from him, not allowing him the contact.

"We need another strategy then," she stated, as if she were completely unaffected.

Viktor was a decent enough therapist to know it was for show, and that she was hurting.

If he were to be absolutely honest with himself, he was upset too, but he had known there was a large chance the bond wouldn't, couldn't be, accepted. Too much was unresolved between them. Hera still didn't know all his truths.

Viktor knew he had to tell her, but he knew the truth might very well drive her away, and after the failed soulbond, he wasn't sure they could recover.

Her eyes met his for the briefest moment before she light jumped away, leaving him alone with his miserable thoughts.

# Chapter 21

<u>**Hera**</u>

Hera looked at her arm once she was in her office at the Senate building. A mark was there, but it was in no way a soulmark. Black ash was smeared over her wrist, some streaks of blue coming from it. She was marked all right—with a failed soulmark to add to her increasingly horrid decisions.

Now she had a permanent reminder to look at every single day.

Viktor was not receptive to their binding, but how could she blame him? Hera was a nightmare on the best of days. Why would he even want to attempt it?

*Because*, Hera thought, *I had forced his hand into this, begging like a whimpering child.*

The last time she had begged in such a way, she *was* a child. Pleading and begging with her father...

No matter the outcome, that would be the last time she would allow her vulnerability to be seen by anyone. Even him.

Why Viktor, of all people, knew how to pull at that part of her, expose that soft underbelly, she did not know. Probably that psycho-analyst side of him figuring out how to widen all the exposed cracks in her psyche.

Hera cut that thought off immediately, focusing her wayward thoughts back to the issue at hand: the upcoming war.

She seated herself at her desk, which was currently overflowing with paperwork sent in from all over the continent. So many issues and concerns were coming in from every corner of Zephyr. Anything and everything.

The notices were full of people begging to volunteer for the military, people needing to understand why their own loved ones turned on Zephyr, people angry at her for not doing anything, and people angry at her for doing the wrong thing.

To protect them, Hera did not allow anyone to join the military. Unable to explain who their true enemy was, she knew it was for the best, but that left her with plenty of people questioning her position. It was too dangerous to allow the humans they had left, the ones not spelled, to walk out among the masses. She had no idea how the Titans were able to enchant them yet, but as of now, she had Hecate and her witches among each and every military camp along their borders.

The remaining Halcyon army was all that stood between the large mob of human puppets and the last remaining city in the whole of Zephyr. She needed those witches to make sure no more of her soldiers involuntarily defected.

Edie had sent her visions, and the world was again torn to shreds. Buildings on fire, crumbled shelters, scorched fields, people weeping in the streets. Weeping from the loss of their home, family, everything. Hera recognized it all too well from the Great War, but this time, she knew the Titans were to blame.

Lightning struck across her desk, hitting her lamp, and knocking it to the floor.

Groaning, Hera put her face in her hands, trying to bring herself back from the images she kept seeing replayed in her mind over and over. She had done everything she could after the Great War ruined this world. To bring it back, to help the humans, and now she was the greatest threat to them. Her decisions could make or break this whole continent. One wrong step and they were under the control of the Titans ... or dead.

Honestly, Hera wasn't sure which was worse.

A loud explosion blasted outside the Senate building, her windows imploding. Hera swung around in her chair and shot up to her feet, rushing over to the shattered windows as she pulled a piece of glass from her shoulder, the wound healing immediately. Yelling and screaming assaulted her ears from the shattered windows.

The street below was full of humans trampling each other to get out of the way. The mass of people moved in a wild panic, animalistic in their need to find safety.

*Why in the Fates were the humans even in the city right now when there is a strict lockdown? I can't protect them if they are too stupid to listen to me!*

Hera knew for a fact that in the direction they were coming from were two Halcyon units with four powerful witches on site. So, how the hell did the mob of humans make it past them into the city center, and who in the Fates-damned hell was blowing up her city?

The guards were gone when Hera ran out of her office—all of them, from where she stood to the great entrance. Not a great sign of things to come. She heaved the doors of the hall open and exited out into the street.

People ran past her in pure terror, mindlessly knocking each other over in their attempt to flee. Their clothes were worn and their faces exhausted, as if they had been running for a while. As if they had been *chased* into the city.

The zing of bullets through the crowd halted her steps. She whirled in the direction the bullets had come from. More chaos. Or was someone driving the mob with gunshots? Where was her army? Had the mobs taken them *all* out of commission?

Stepping out further, Hera looked out over the people, and her heart stopped at the sight. The confirmation of what had happened to her soldiers and witches guarding the city stared at her from blood-red eyes.

A pained noise came from Hera as the soldiers ran on the heels of the people, their guns aimed at the civilians, bullets blasting into the crowd. Witches shot streams of dark magic into the crowd. Magic these witches may know but had sworn to never use.

Halcyon was being attacked by its own military.

### <u>Viktor</u>

*"You know why the bond didn't take. Honestly, men never seem to grow more intelligent through the ages regarding women."*

"Enough, Nyx, not right now," he growled, trying to focus on a spell Hecate had sent him from a coven not far from his homeland only that morning. It wouldn't work, not like the ones Viktor could do. Still, he might be able to change it up a bit to help, though not as well as his since he had more than the power of the witch running through him. But it would be enough. If he could just find the right words...

Suddenly, panic flooded him, and he dropped the orb of power from his hands.

*"What is it?"*

"Hera ... she is incredibly upset. Something is wrong. I need to go."

He spun around but was immediately caught in an invisible web. He felt like he had walked into an immensely powerful pocket of magic, his muscles moving so slowly that he was barely moving at all. Nyx was holding him in place.

*"You feel her emotions from this far away?"*

Annoyed he couldn't move or respond, Viktor only grunted until Nyx finally let him go, and he took a deep breath, his lungs having been slowed as much as the rest of him.

Looking over his shoulder, he nodded to Nyx, his jaw clenched. "I always have."

Not allowing her the opportunity to question him further, especially when she would demand to know why he'd kept it from her, he light jumped to where Hera's power pulsed like a beacon.

The scene before him halted him in his tracks.

Hera was holding an entire army back with a wall of lightning. She stood between frantic, huddled citizens and hundreds—if not thousands—of soldiers.

"Find shelter! Go home if you can!" Hera yelled, the push of the army gaining ground on her as she spoke. She wouldn't be able to hold them back for much longer.

Running to stand next to her, Viktor encircled the army with fire, yet they did not seem phased by it. They completely ignored the dangers to themselves and others as they attempted to fight through the lightning and fire, killing themselves.

The most worrisome aspect of it was that Viktor felt no spell running through them when he reached out. They seemed almost...

"Drugged. They are on Nectar of the Gods, Ambrosia, or whatever Fates damned new name they came up with. Dolus set more than my potential death into motion," Hera yelled over the fire, electricity, and screaming that rent the air.

*Fates-damned Dolus!* Just when Viktor thought he couldn't hate the deity more.

He swung around, his gaze darting around the crowd. Their expressions were dazed, but not completely slack like they'd been under the spell.

Their eyes though—they were wrong. Unnatural, bright red. Huge, glassy pupils.

Putting a mental wall between him and the scared humans, Viktor focused on the soldiers and could feel the drug pulsing through them.

A blast of black magic made it through the fire and hit Hera in the side, her lightning flickering as she tried to push through the pain and keep her wall of electricity up.

A push of power from behind them told him that her sisters and their soulbonds were there, ready to battle. Hera, feeling it too, looked over her shoulder in shock before turning back to the fight. He could feel the bone deep sorrow from Hera, knowing she would not be able to save them all like she did when Viktor was able to undo the spell. This was taking a toll on her mentally as well as physically.

Another bolt of black magic shot out and Viktor stepped between it and Hera, absorbing it into a ball of his own magic. The black magic burned up in a blue flame before going out completely.

Either they would die, or she would. The moment the thought crossed his mind, Hera turned her face to his, the light casting off their mingling power reflected in her eyes.

"I will not leave, so don't even try to match power with me," Viktor whispered, knowing that she would understand what he was saying, even if it was far too loud for her to hear.

"Then die with me, you idiot," she growled.

"Can't die. Sorry to disappoint you should that have been in your master plan."

A fresh wave of screams had the hair on his arms lifting. Arms still braced against the army, he craned his neck over his shoulder to see a new deluge of humans flooding into the street from alleyways and stores. All behind the barrier of lightning and fire.

Viktor swore. He should have seen this! They'd waited until a moment of vulnerability to strike at them, and there were hundreds of them. Full of illicit drugs and ready to die for a cause they did not care for.

How had the Titans managed to drug these people? Had they spread it over time, or just when they were distracted by working on a counter to their spell?

In less than a week, they had completely changed their method of control. Such a quick response meant they had been watching—had realized Viktor could break their spell—and planning. Planning for who knew how long. It couldn't have taken a small amount of time for Dolus to stockpile enough ambrosia to drug this many people.

"They changed tactics," he murmured, but it was pointless.

Hera was already calling on her goddess. Her body lifted into the air as lightning streaked around her, arcing and hitting everyone rushing her. Her skin was pure electricity, her eyes golden light. Her royal blue gown materialized from nothing as she transformed into the goddess, her golden feathered pauldrons and corset following shortly behind, glinting over her curvy figure. Her hair that had been neatly tied back came loose, her natural golden curls falling around her shoulders. A crown of lightning danced in a circle over her head.

The form she took on Olympus was the queen. The one she wore now was a warrior goddess.

And, at that moment, she looked every bit like the vengeful goddess full of wrath.

Viktor called his fire, letting it engulf his body until he transfigured into his hybrid form, a single, massive flame with a bright humanoid core. Should anything try to touch or move through his fiery form, they would find no purchase and be immediately incinerated. As he transformed fully, the drugged humans charged at them, all manner of weapons in their hands, from small knives to military grade guns.

Vines shot out and grabbed several people, pinning them to walls as they struggled. Shadowy ghouls rose from the ground and swirled around them, diaphanous claws swiping for their heads. Viktor turned away as the wraith-like entities took hold of the humans. He did not need, nor want, to see exactly what those monsters were capable of.

"I need to know how to help without rendering you powerless," Amphitrite stated as she moved to stand beside him, West on her other side.

"My fire cannot be taken out by any other measures than my own willpower. Feel free to flood this town if need be."

"Holy shit," West exclaimed. "I thought you were dull, but you turned out to be pretty badass. When I write my memoirs, remind me of this moment. When my therapist turned into a human torch." He threw his hands up, and water started to come in from the docks.

With the others working, Viktor turned back from them and focused on the people closing in. A huge wave of water swept across the back of the crowd, wiping out a good twenty people. Arcs of lightning struck out, rendering plenty of the more advanced weapons useless. One person swung their knives at Viktor, but his fire melted the metal in mid-air.

When the lightning came down from the sky and not Hera, he looked over to see her in a power meditation; she moved her middle and index fingers in circles around each other, her eyes lit so bright that she was lighting the people's faces as many as three rows back from her. The wind shifted sharply, and he watched as a tornado came down from the sky, taking out most of the humans left in the back of the mob after the giant wave hit.

Moving in to cover Hera as she summoned the storms, Viktor let the fire strike out in flares from him as people continued to move forward, melting the weapons and burning their arms and legs.

It was a never-ending group of people from all areas of Zephyr piling down on them.

Creating balls of fire in his hands, he threw them out as Hera pulled a torrential rain from the clouds above. With her rain and the Sea Guardians' power, they were up to their waists now in the water.

His fire raced over the top of the water as if there were an oily accelerant within it, and the people swimming to them went under, finding nowhere to come back up for air before they ran out.

Slowly, in what felt like hours but could not truly have been more than thirty minutes, the humans thinned out enough that even in their mindless state, they were aware of the losing battle on their side. Even more were coming down from their high, running from the wrath that gods and goddesses were bringing down on the city. On them.

Viktor slowed his attacks, turning back to Hera. She was still fully engulfed in rage, but Viktor saw the pain—he saw *her*. He always did.

"Hera, come back," he whispered as he let his fire die out, the cold rain hitting his now bare shoulders, and sizzling, steam coming off him until his body heat cooled to a more human temperature.

West and Amphitrite pushed the water back into the ocean as Devon called his vines back. Persephone's wraiths had thankfully disappeared beforehand.

Hera's head snapped to look at him, anger twisting her beautiful face.

"They dare come here, to my domain, wreak havoc and kill my people?" she hissed. Turning to the sky above, she let out a scream full of wrath. "What must I do to prove my worth to you? Must my eternity be nothing but the suffering of those around me?"

The words hit Viktor directly in the chest. He took a deep breath at the impact of her emotional distress, but he didn't cut her off as he normally would. No, she needed this. It had been too long repressing the fear and pain, and she needed someone to help carry it for her.

Viktor looked back at her sisters, who were slowly making their way to her, and shook his head. He would handle this. Amphitrite placed her hand on Persephone's elbow, giving Viktor a scrutinizing look before she finally nodded. The look Persephone gave him was not one of confidence, but she allowed her sister to pull her back, and that was all he could ask for. Using portals, they left, but before Amphitrite allowed her magic to take her away, she gave him a look that said everything her mouth did not.

She would be nearby and watching. Acknowledging her unsaid words with a nod, he turned back to Hera as Amphitrite light jumped from behind him. Focusing on Hera, who was breathing heavily, he realized it was not from exhaustion, but from emotional overload.

Another scream tore through Hera, her lightning arcing around them, hitting the empty businesses and knocking out the streetlights. The only light on the street now came exclusively from her.

Without an ounce of fear that she would hurt him, he stepped forward and touched her hand. Her eyes moved down to his hand, and so did her body, as her feet touched the ground once again.

Tilting her head to look up at him, he watched as a tear slipped down her cheek, and his other hand came up to cradle her face, his thumb wiping away the tear.

"What must I do to stop death from following me? I've cut myself off from everything. From my sisters. My people. Myself."

Cradling her face in his hands, he looked her in the eyes.

"Heavy is the head that wears the crown," he replied, and her eyes shut tight to avoid another tear from falling. "No, please listen, Hera. You are the only one strong enough to do this, and so you will, but not without me. Never again."

Leaning forward, Viktor took the chance and lovingly touched his lips to hers. Lips that were salty with the tears that had already fallen.

What he wanted was the simple human touch, but Hera needed violence. Grabbing at his neck, she yanked him into a frenzied kiss, pushing him until he was against a wall.

"No," he grunted, grabbing her, and pulling her into a light jump.

As soon as they appeared in his room, he let her fall back onto his bed. He had thought of her here, in this way, for so long—since even before she leveled that fierce gaze on him in the senate chambers—but he'd initially missed out by having sex with her in his garage. On a work bench of all things. He was thankful for a second shot, to say the least.

Viktor removed his pants as she willed away her clothes, leaving her naked chest rising and falling with the quickening of her breath. She wanted it to be violent and all-consuming. He wanted to savor and worship her. Just like always, it would be a battle of wills between them.

Leaning over her, he ran his hands over the curves of her body. She was the voluptuous sister, and in that moment, he thanked every deity to have ever existed for making her this way. Before she could make a move, he kissed her as he took the full weight of her breasts in the palms of his hands, reveling in the feel of them.

Hera pulled on him, letting him land on top of her when she managed to knock him off balance, kissing him hard and quick with an intensity that fogged his mind. Trying to refrain from going too fast, he shifted back to look in her eyes.

"No, none of that," Hera growled, pulling him down into a kiss far harder than the one before. Grabbing her hands from around his neck, he folded his fingers between hers and moved them above her head.

"You do not always get your way, Goddess," he murmured, but his last word ended on a gasp as she leaned forward to bite his lip.

"In this? Actually, I do," she replied with his bottom lip between her teeth. She nibbled before releasing him. "You just seem a little slow in figuring that out, but don't worry." Her legs hooked around his hips, pulling them together. "I will teach you."

Viktor was in a losing battle. No matter how slowly he wanted to take it, she was far too riled to be calmed. This was not the intimacy he wanted, but he would give her what she needed and take her slowly next time.

The way he wanted to do it.

He released one of her hands to give her movement, but Hera darted her hand faster than he anticipated. Before he could blink, she was between them, lining him up at her entrance. When she shoved her hips up, he groaned and followed through with the movement she had started as he thrust into her without thought.

Losing control of his more advanced intelligence, he felt like an animal, but Hera was far further gone than that. Her nails dug into his back, and her teeth latched onto his neck, biting just enough that he could feel a slight edge of pain, and it only managed to arouse him further.

Dangerous. This woman was dangerous. Alluring. Beautiful. Broken.

"Mine," he grunted, shoving aside all his training to keep others out of his mind. He opened up his emotional link, letting her desire crawl through his mind, deepening his drive as he did the same to her. Hera consumed him, and he was happily allowing her to do so.

Suddenly, her body went rigid, squeezing him, and she threw her head back as she screamed a name. A name that was not Viktor.

Shocked at the name that left her lips, Viktor was too close to the edge to do anything more than follow her and lost himself to his release.

Pushing his face into her neck, he took in deep breaths of air, the smell of her calming the inner beast that had been let out after centuries of containment.

Rolling onto his back, he pulled Hera to his chest, his mind overloaded with all the sensations he had just experienced. The fury of battle. The exhaustion, and then pleasure. The bliss of both him and her, the physical and mental connection. Barely able to keep his eyes open any longer, he released a sigh.

Tomorrow. Tomorrow, Viktor would tell her.

As much as it terrified him, he would tell her about his past.

All of it.

# *Chapter 22*

### <u>Hera</u>

A TEAR SLIPPED OVER Hera's cheek.

What had she done? As usual, she went emotions first, logic second.

She had slept with Viktor again, and looking down at her arm, it did nothing for the bond. They were well and truly unmatched. She wanted to play like it didn't hurt, but it did. *Fates, it hurt something deep.* It burned to know the man that she was falling for did not feel the same.

An idiot. She was a Fates-damned idiot to fall for a man who couldn't accept her into his heart. Viktor wasn't hers and never would be, even if he'd called her his in a moment of passion. If he truly felt anything for her, the soulbond mark would be full and thriving on her arm.

It would figure the Fates would screw her like this and make her fall for a man she would never have.

Maybe she should have been nicer to them? Or meaner. If she was going to be penalized with this torture, she had far more creative ways to earn such a punishment. They had no idea that they had been playing with nice Hera until this point.

Wiping a tear away before Viktor woke up and caught her crying like a baby, she jumped when he shifted and put an arm around her to pull her to him. When she didn't come quickly enough, he let her go and lifted himself onto his elbow to look down at her.

"Are you alright?" he asked, his eyebrows furrowed.

Nodding, she gave him a smile. One that she didn't even need to look at herself to know rang well and truly false.

"How could I not be? Finally getting that itched scratched not only once, but twice." Those were apparently the wrong words to use with him, as his face turned to stone.

"Glad I could help scratch that itch," he stated, and fell onto his back next to her as his hand on her hip slipped away.

"I'm sorry," she found herself saying, the apology almost an out-of-body experience. When had she apologized for her behavior before? Would she get hives now? "I'm ... not alright."

Sitting up, Hera tried to tame her riotous curls, more to distract herself than out of actual concern about her appearance.

"Understandable. You're being stripped vulnerable by the actions of others—"

"Can we not do the patient and therapist thing and just be ... us? Lovers ... fuck buddies ... whatever this is?"

"Not fuck buddies, but I will take lover if this means more than once ... twice. I don't count the first time since that was hardly ideal."

Biting her lip, Hera said nothing since she refused to promise him another time. She was already in too deep as it was, and she knew better than to ever attach herself emotionally to another person. Having gotten this close already to Viktor had proven insanely dumb on her part. She wished she could tell him there would be a thousand more times. That they were more than lovers. But the mark on her arm stayed her lips.

So, she decided to avoid the topic entirely.

"Thank you. For standing with me and not leaving when shit hit the fan out there," she whispered, working to keep her emotions under control.

Maybe he would attribute all her distress to the battle, and she would let him. The fact that he had her back without asking for anything in return was yet another reason she found herself drawn to him. Another reason she hadn't cut him off like she should.

Her sisters had her back because they were sisters, Devon and West because they were protecting their mates. She would not delude herself into thinking if the situation were different, if it was Hera in trouble and not Amphitrite or Persephone, that they would come to her aid.

"Always," he whispered, pulling her into him, tightening his hold around her as he slowly dipped into sleep.

Hera was not quick to follow, her mind spinning, her emotions a whirlwind.

"Calm yourself, Hera, and rest. We'll speak tomorrow and figure out what to do next," Viktor whispered, not fully awake, and he turned onto his side, facing away as he slipped into a deeper sleep.

Not a cuddler. Good. That would make leaving easier.

And how could he tell she was struggling? Looking at the dormant mark, Hera knew he should feel nothing from the non-existent bond.

Calming herself, releasing her thoughts from her mind as if he could truly feel them, she took a deep breath. Waiting until he fell into a deep sleep, she carefully slipped from his bed.

She knew she would have to address what happened eventually, but it wouldn't be in his house. She needed neutral territory.

Perhaps, she was lucky, she thought as she light jumped to her home, letting her thoughts move through her mind without focusing on one in particular while she dressed. Perhaps the dormant bond was saving her from herself. Perhaps Eros foresaw that he was someone else's, and even if Viktor thought he was willing, it wouldn't work since Hera would be hurt.

Maybe her soulbond was out there somewhere right now. Waiting for her to finish this war and find him.

"You need more than the people you have at your back to fight this war," a voice she hadn't heard in years said from behind her, making her jump.

Hera spun around and sucked in a gasp. Themis stood in the middle of her bedroom, looking just as she had when Hera was a mere mortal. She stepped forward and clasped Hera's shoulders, squeezing comfortingly before moving down to hold her wrists. Her fingers skimmed over where the dormant mark lay upon Hera's skin.

"Everything should be further along now."

Pulling her arm back, Hera pressed a palm against her failed mark as if it was an open wound and stared at Themis.

"Hello to you too, Themis," she said, shock still working its way through her voice.

The old deity nodded in acknowledgment. It had been ages since they'd seen each other, and something in Hera stirred at being around the woman who had protected her as a child. Who had raised her into an adult before her ascension.

"What in the Fates do you mean, Themis? And please, be a lot more detailed than the damn Moirai. I am living on the edge of a breakdown daily now."

"It means only your sisters are at their most powerful," Themis responded.

Hera huffed out a frustrated breath, but her tone held a tinge of bitterness when she said, "We tried to bind ourselves, and it didn't take. Thanks for reminding me."

"Hera..." Themis whispered.

"No! It's true. Plus, you know me. I cannot feel that bond Persephone and Devon seem to have or any of the mushy shit Amphitrite and West spout off at each other. Who has time for that shit when we are in the middle of planning a war!"

Taking Hera's face in her hands, Themis leaned forward until their noses touched.

"Ask the right questions of him. He is no longer bound by the curse, and he has left some pertinent information out that you need in order to move forward."

Shock stole her breath before Themis stepped away from her.

"You helped train him," Hera recalled. Just before she'd fallen back into her healing sleep, Viktor had told her he'd learned to merge his forms from Themis. Of all the deities! "Why did you never tell me that Hestia's scion was out there and fully ascended? We could have used him!"

Themis shook her head slowly. "There is only one who can answer your questions, Hera."

She frowned, tempted to push for more, but she recognized the finality in Themis's answer.

"And don't worry," Themis continued. "I assure you the humans remember nothing of seeing your goddess form. I took the liberty of wiping the memories of being chased from their homes as well."

Themis disappeared in a flash of light leaving Hera alone.

So, Viktor was still holding back even with his curse broken. Well, that figured.

The old anger she'd felt upon first meeting him built up in the pit of her stomach yet again. Still holding back on her after everything? Well, now, as far as she was concerned, he was someone to help win the battle against the Titans and then he could screw the hell off after.

Hera was done playing games.

### <u>Viktor</u>

Viktor was not at all surprised Hera had left before he woke up. Had he not been pulled into a lull of post-orgasmic bliss, he might have had the strength to speak with her and calm her mind, but he was beyond exhausted, and the hold sleep had on him had refused to relent.

Sitting up, he rubbed his hands over his face. Viktor needed to find Hera and confess what he hadn't after his curse broke at Reaver's Paradise. He had to step up, stop being so terrified of her reaction, and give her the information they both needed to be shared. He'd been an idiot to think he could hold off any longer in telling her the whole truth. Last night had been the perfect opportunity, but he'd tucked tail and went to bed.

A scared idiot, but an idiot all the same.

While they had been able to hold the humans off, they would never be able to do so with the Titans unless he did the one thing he feared.

Which meant hunting Hera down and forcing her to listen. Viktor knew enough about her that she was in an emotionally volatile state right now and was most likely doing something she really shouldn't be doing to try to remedy the sadness he could feel from her.

Closing his eyes, he let himself move fully into her mind. Letting her feelings and intentions move through him. Finding her, he let all that was Hera at that moment move over him.

Opening his eyes, rage ignited inside of him. He could actually feel her putting a wall between them again. One that was built to keep him out emotionally. He knew all too well the feel of it as she had been keeping that wall firmly in place until just recently.

"Fuck!" he yelled, slamming his fist into the headboard, losing control in a way he rarely did.

Something on the bedside table caught his eye as he pulled his fist back. What in the Fates? Had Hera left this for him?

Reaching over, he grabbed a small vial of purple liquid, almost like mercury in its consistency. Hovering his hand over the note next to the vial, he felt his father's power on it. He could feel his father's interference all through the liquid as well, someone else's too, but not anyone he knew well enough to place their signature feel of magic.

Clenching his jaw, his anger already peaked, Viktor grabbed the note and read it over. With the words on the paper, he felt his heart plummet to the ground.

Crumbling the note in his fist, he looked at the potion in his hand against the sunlight coming through the window and made a game plan in his head.

He would hunt Hera down and fix his mistake first before she made one ... or several, of her own.

Then he would make sure this potion was never put to use.

Viktor would protect Hera in a way he never had before. Even if he had to sacrifice everything they were finally building between each other to do so.

# Chapter 23

### <u>Viktor</u>

VIKTOR DRESSED AND LIGHT jumped to Hera's home where he felt her power. To say she was less than pleased to see him was a gross understatement. Her first reaction was cursing before she threw a pillow at him and told him to leave.

He was just relieved it was a pillow and not a bolt of lightning.

Now he stood in front of a very irate Hera, her hands on her hips, arcs of electricity coming off her skin. This was it. The moment of truth and the fear that she would never forgive him was riding him hard. At least if this all went wrong, he had some time to remember her by.

It was the whole reason he had been scared to tell her about his curse. That he would ruin any happiness they could have found as Viktor and Hera. Not the god and goddess with a war on the horizon. He was ignorant enough to think he could wait until it was all over to tell her everything, but it was now a brick wall between them, and he needed it all out in the open. Total honesty.

"Why are you following me?" she growled, putting space between them by moving to the mantle of her fireplace. The furthest away she could get from him without actually leaving her living room.

"We need to talk," he said lowly, a silent prayer going up to Chaos that this was going to work out and he could keep Hera in his life after this.

"Oh, Fates," she laughed, turning away from him. "Sleep with a guy and you're committed." Spinning back to look at him, she snarled, "We had sex. That was it. Move on. We have far more important things to worry about."

"I can't!" Viktor roared, before tempering his voice. "I need to tell you ... everything."

Crossing her arms across her chest, she took a deep breath.

"Perhaps I shouldn't know. As much as it fires me up to say this, we need as much distance between us as possible. We will fight next to each other, be allies, but after that, we walk away."

"No," he growled as her eyes met his.

"I've trusted before. I won't again. You had a chance to tell me the truth, but you decided to withhold even more." She shook her head. "I just want to make it through this war, and then you can keep all your secrets to yourself."

When he stepped closer to her, she threw her hands up and her eyes went golden.

"No, Viktor! I've been hurt enough. Just stop, please. Light jump away, and we can meet up when we've both calmed down to discuss what we will do about the Titans. *Only the Titans.*"

She turned away, but he could feel her emotions raging. Refusing to shut down their connection, he let himself feel everything she felt.

No matter how small, he needed to know there was a chance she would forgive him.

"We're not lovers," she continued. "Barely friends. Allies only. And that is something I will deal with, but not with you. I have to focus on my people's survival, and I cannot do that when I am having conflicting feelings regarding you."

Hera looked away from him, and panic zapped through him. He was losing this battle before he even had a chance to fight.

"No, you may think you get the last say in this, but you don't," he argued roughly. He had one chance at this. "Do you remember that you yelled out another name in the throes of passion last night?"

Turning, she looked at him with her eyes narrowed.

"I did not..." He watched the confusion enter her eyes. "Who? I don't remember saying a name..."

Stepping forward, he placed his hands on her cheeks before moving his fingers to her temples.

"Please, please don't hate me," Viktor whispered as he swept his thumbs across her forehead. "Please," he whispered one last time, and then the ancient words of his mother's people left his lips.

He watched Hera's eyes widen with pain.

## Hera

A searing pain slashed through her head, and Hera's vision went white. Her knees buckled, and she landed on the ground. Not on the carpet of her living room, but on dirt and rocks.

When her vision cleared, Hera blinked rapidly. She was in a cave similar to the one she had spent years hiding in with Themis after her sisters were killed. Hiding from her father. Unknowingly waiting for her sisters to find her so they could banish Cronus. Their fresh powers had been too chaotic to do so alone. No, they'd needed something to funnel and direct their power, and that had been Hera. Mortal Hera—her latent powers called to her sisters', her body alive enough to be the sacrifice needed.

And they had done it. Her sisters had pushed their power through Hera, catching her latent power in the process, and condemned Cronus to his fate. The effort had been too much for her mortal body—too much power—and she'd died, only to ascend. With their father trapped in Tartarus, her and her sisters' powers had stabilized, and so began their reign.

It had been a victory. A painful one, they told her, but a victory, nonetheless. And tell her they did. Harnessing so much power in a mortal form had overwhelmed not only her body but also her mind, and she had no memory of several years before the battle, of the battle itself, and of her ascension as a result.

Part of her mourned the loss of that memory, but a larger part of her was glad for it. Many of her mortal memories were lost to the centuries, especially the ones after her father's rampage. Too much trauma, Hera reckoned, although she certainly remembered the day Cronus murdered her family.

And she recognized this small, sad, ancient place.

The snap of a twig had Hera turning, and she saw herself as a young woman, still mortal and just barely past the line that defined adulthood.

Her mortal self stared into a small fire at the cave's center. She looked lost. And suddenly, Hera knew what this was. This was the day she'd returned to her childhood home and burned it to the ground in her anger.

She shut her eyes tightly, wanting to forget that day, that house. Opening them back up, she saw Viktor was in the cave with her.

When she opened her mouth to call to him, to ask why he was showing her this and how he'd inserted himself there, she stopped abruptly when she realized something. Viktor wasn't looking at her—he was looking at the other her, the younger version, and he looked so incredibly sad that the urge to reach out and comfort him was stronger than she would have liked.

"Why am I here?" she asked, voice shaking.

Viktor looked at her with tears shimmering in his eyes.

"To see the truth of your past," he answered, and he waved his hands over the fire, disappearing.

Suddenly, the cave appeared different, and she realized she was looking at it from a closer angle.

Getting to her feet, Hera looked down and saw that she was in the body of her younger self, covered in freckles, much like her sister Amphitrite, wearing a colorless shift and barefoot. A part of her soul trembled at seeing herself—being herself—like this again.

The sound of footsteps came in from the opening of the cave, someone running at a panicked pace. From inside her mortal body, Hera watched herself grab a knife from under the pillow of her pathetic makeshift bed and hide behind a large rock. A shadow shifted around the entrance as someone neared.

A moment later, a young man covered top to bottom in ash filled the entryway, as he fell to his knees, coughing.

Her younger self didn't move until the man rolled over onto his back, taking in deep breaths to try to calm himself

"I won't hurt you," the man said, his voice raspy as if he'd inhaled too much smoke.

"Forgive me if I don't believe you. You hardly look like you went for a stroll through the fields," she replied.

Still, she slowly came out from behind the rock, her knife in her hand, and Hera wanted to slap her younger self at her inept grip.

The vision faded out before she could experience her younger self approach the stranger.

Fading back in was a similar scene: she sat by the fire again, and the young man from the vision before came in through the entrance, this time cleaned up.

It was Viktor. He looked slightly different—no glasses, longer hair, shaven face, and wearing the tunic, pants, and belt of the old Slavic people—but it was doubtlessly him.

Hera had known Viktor. Her stomach churned. Not only had she known Viktor, but she'd also met him while she was still mortal.

"Ah, good. Fire's not out," Viktor's voice cut into her thoughts.

He smiled at her younger self and pulled out pieces of metal from a sack as he sat across from the fire from her. He melted them with his own fire in his hands, before placing them in the hearth before him. She watched him, his hands moving with a grace she loved watching. Shaking her head at that last thought, she stood.

When had she watched him do this before? In his studio? No, his back was to her when she had light jumped into the garage he worked in. Viktor looked up, with eyes full of concern.

"Are you okay?" he asked as she moved to settle on the ground next to him. Seeming unsure of her words, she simply nodded.

Shrugging, he handed her the object he had been manipulating with the fire. A small bird he made with his own hands. An eagle.

Suddenly, Hera remembered Edie coming to the cave, bringing her things from the world beyond while she hid. Settling with her on her bed, listening to her talk, and Hera wishing Edie could talk back. Which she would in a way ... once Hera ascended.

"Thank you," she whispered, and then the world spun out around her, throwing her into another memory she couldn't recall.

She was in a field, running and twirling as her long blonde curls flew around her in the breeze. She paused when she saw Viktor sitting under a tree, his hands working on something yet again.

Running at full speed toward him, Viktor looked up and laughed, standing and bracing himself. Jumping up at the last minute, he caught her, spinning them around until he fell back. She rolled off him, collapsing next to him when she caught a flash of gray between the fingers of his fisted hand.

"What nonsense are you on about now?" she heard her young voice ask him.

"Nonsense?" he laughed, his voice deeper than it'd been in the last memory. "Everything you do not understand is nonsense." Holding his hand out, he presented a stormy grayish-blue stone. "I found it when I was hunting. Don't laugh, but it reminded me of your eyes."

She'd wondered why he was showing her this. But she understood now.

Hera was watching herself fall in love with Viktor thousands of years ago.

Before she knew it, he leaned over to kiss her, surprising them both before she took hold of his shirt and kissed him back. The world spun again, and she was looking up into Viktor's eyes as they were making love with the cave walls shimmering around them.

"I love you," he whispered as he took her lips in a kiss.

The tender moment felt all too real, and her mind struggled to process it.

"I love you, too," she whispered, her hand moving to his cheek as he leaned down to kiss her again.

Suddenly, the pain in her brain sharpened, and her memories started to overlap with those of the girl, no longer just watching them happen, but her mind remembering them. Reliving them. A scream tore through her, and then Viktor was next to her—the Viktor from her time and not her memories. She was on her knees, and he was holding her.

"Why, Viktor?" she cried. The pain in her head was too much. They were still in the cave, but the visions of Viktor and herself were gone.

"I need you to understand," he whispered, kissing the top of her head.

Hera wanted to shove him off but was too weak to act on it. As her confusion turned to anger, she watched her sisters come into the vision, the Viktor of her memories gone, and Hera once again watching her younger self instead of looking through her eyes.

It hardly took a genius to know what was next, especially as Viktor pulled her tight against him, his strong chest pressed against her back.

"Just ... watch," he whispered into her ear, his voice shaking as much as her body was.

Hera was about to watch herself die, experiencing it for the first time. Even as her memories pierced her living mind, this event eluded her. Distantly, she wondered whose memory they tapped into now, as Viktor was nowhere to be seen.

"You'll have everything now," he whispered against her ear, kissing her neck as he let out a small sob.

Cronus was pinned against the stone wall by Persephone's wraiths as Amphitrite tried to summon water to help, but her powers were still new and hard to control. Streams of water formed from droplets condensing on the cave walls, but they lost their shape every other moment. The wraiths kept hold of Cronus, but they faded in and out. Her sisters fought to maintain hold over their powers, but they were unable to focus their magic.

"No..." Hera whispered, pushing away from Viktor.

"No!" she yelled, running to her sisters.

"Stop!" Turning to Viktor she yelled, "Stop it Viktor!"

Viktor only shook his head, tears in his eyes.

"I can't," he choked out.

Hera froze when the Hera of the past walked between her sisters and toward Cronus, standing in front of them. Trying to protect them, even as a mortal.

Hera's heart actually stopped at the look of fury on her face. Even if she was seeing this memory for the first time, she knew she'd been prepared to die for justice. For her sisters.

Shock continued to hold Hera hostage as she watched herself raise her arms against a grinning Cronus.

Her sisters each grasped her shoulders, flinging their free arms out at their sides. Pure power roared from her open palms, nearly blinding her. Flashes of color, blues and blacks and purples, danced through the stream of raw power, but after a moment, the shades merged into a dazzling white.

Hera held her breath, something in her soul restless at the scene before her.

Her death, but also her eternal life.

Gold bindings materialized around Cronus, glinting at his wrists and ankles. As their combined power battered him, the bindings coiled around him; his limbs, his torso, and his chest. The more their power contained him, the weaker past Hera appeared.

Hera watched the humanity leave her, and the goddess being born. Her back arched painfully—unnaturally, and surely broken. Her feet lifted off the ground until her toes barely skimmed the stone. Her levitating body shimmered, and her younger self threw her head back violently. Her mouth parted in a silent scream, and bright golden light beamed from her lips and her eyes.

A scream tore through the air as Hera died.

The crack of thunder broke it all apart, and the scene went from chaos to quiet. Cronus disappeared, and the shell that was Hera's body hit the ground. Without the combined power blinding her, the cave seemed incredibly dark. Her sisters crawled to her prone form, crying and holding her. Begging her to forgive them.

As was the man behind her as he sobbed into her neck and held her tight.

"I'm so sorry, my Hera," he rasped.

She felt nothing. Hera was numb from the scene before her and the memories slipping back into her head. She blinked dazedly, everything clicking into place as if the missing pieces had never been gone.

A whole portion of her life, her mortal adulthood and the end of it, had been lost to her for so long, leaving her empty in a way she didn't understand until now.

Turning, she pulled away from Viktor to look at him fully. His eyes overflowed with tears, and his hands reached out as if to grab her back, but he was smart enough to stop before he touched her.

"Why? How?" was all Hera could manage to say. Even her voice sounded so unlike herself, completely cold and unemotional.

Closing his eyes, Viktor dropped his hands.

"The curse my mother put on me was to protect me. That much of what I told you is true," he said, throat sounding raw. "Prometheus had told her that the Titans were planning to use me or kill me. She made it to where another deity would not know I existed. That I would be non-existent to them. If they met me with the knowledge that I might have power ... they forgot me just as quickly. I was taught to hide my power ... but it took hundreds of years to learn the curse and wear it down enough to tell you anything."

"When I ascended and became a goddess—"

"The curse took your memories of me."

Now it was Hera who closed her eyes, but Viktor kept speaking.

"When the Great War started, I came to find you. I was determined to help you and your sisters, but when I met you, you just forgot me again the next time I saw you. No matter how hard I tried ... no matter what I did."

Hera opened her eyes, shocked that he was there during the Great War, and he met her stare with a steely resolve.

"Still, I tried to help. I pushed through the curse because I worried what would happen to you, and..." Sighing, Viktor pinched the bridge of his nose, taking a deep breath before dropping his hand. "I pushed the curse too hard and met the brink of death. It took me two years to recover from that."

Hera's heart stuttered at the thought of him being so close to his final death. And she never would have known. "And yet, you still tried. You gave Amphitrite clues..."

"I learned the parameters of the curse. It was not without consequence, believe me, but I was determined to fight at your side." His hands curled into fists in his lap. "Even when you and your sisters couldn't remember me—couldn't even see me—I ventured into the battlefields. If I found you at one front, I would take the other. I used my curse to my advantage then, hiding in plain sight. Decades after the Great War, I'd weakened the curse enough to allow deities to remember me when they saw me—not my true self, but my mortal persona." He looked so, so tired. "That was what allowed me to speak to Oceanus, then West, then Amphitrite, and then..." Viktor pinned her with his gaze. "You."

When he stepped forward, Hera put her hands up.

"I need time, Viktor." She knew she was on the verge of a breakdown once the shock faded, and then she needed to think.

Viktor took a deep breath and nodded.

"I can understand that," he said.

"What else is there?" Hera asked carefully.

After all of this, she couldn't handle another round of revelations. Viktor took another deep breath.

"For me, there is little else. I came back to the cave from hunting, having seen the light of your ascension. I was met at the opening by Themis." He gave her a sad smile. "We had just decided to marry the day before... so there was nothing for me there any longer."

"Fates," she murmured, pushing her hands into her hair.

"I went on a bit of a manic-depressive episode ... and the rest you know. Prometheus found me, and here we are."

"*Here we are*," she echoed dryly. Only Viktor could summarize thousands of years with such a brief phrase. "This curse ... how did your mother have so much power? You were only able to weaken it in the last century."

A shadow passed over his expression at the thought of his mother.

"She was extremely powerful for a mortal—even for a witch. You saw her curse me with her final breath that day in the fires." He gestured to the cave around them. "That was before all this. Before I met you. She'd received Hestia's powers from your sisters when you were still a mortal child. I was mortal then, too, but as she was dying, she passed Hestia's power to me along with the curse." He shook his head at the memory. "I'm not sure if she meant to but doing both at the same time strengthened her curse with the power of the goddess."

"Making it last millennia," she finished for him, her voice empty.

"Precisely," he said. "Even Prometheus couldn't break it, but I'm not sure if he even wanted it broken. I tried to use my powers to find a future where I broke the curse, but those visions never came. Until a few years ago. The fires told me to finally return to Halcyon, and so I did. In the years that followed, I searched my visions for something more exact. When I saw you... *I knew*... that I'd figured it out somehow." His eyes glistened. "And that's what kept me going." A small chuckle burst from his lips. "After all that work, it ended up being the Moirai who prophesied how I could break the curse."

Hera wanted to laugh, but she was still too overwhelmed. He'd seen her. He'd strived for her. Fought for her. Protected her. Fought against a centuries-old curse for her. All without her knowing.

She closed her eyes, needing a moment. This man she'd known the past few days—the man she'd made love to—she knew him far less and far more than she ever thought possible. All of this that he'd been hiding, and she never could have guessed the truth of.

That they were lovers separated by millennia and a mother's curse.

"Emrys," she whispered, opening her eyes and looking into his. "The name I spoke when we were together ... it was Emrys. You are Emrys."

Giving a slight nod at his name, she felt all the walls of the cave closing in, and stumbled back, falling into the emerald chair of her living room. Safe in her home once more. Hera was going to throw up.

"I need you to leave," she demanded, pushing to stand and turning away.

When he grabbed her elbow, she ripped her arm from his grasp, refusing to turn and look at him.

"Oh Fates, Hera. Please don't hate me. I love you..." His voice broke, but she still didn't turn.

"Give me time, Viktor. You owe me that much."

The tension in the room rose, but she felt his power leave. Waiting a few more minutes to make sure he was gone, she stumbled to her bedroom and collapsed onto her bed, clutching a pillow to her stomach as she cried.

Fates, the man had waited centuries for her to remember, and guilt rode her hard that she had sent him away. But she was feeling so much for a man she barely knew. All these feelings of the love and passion of her youth that she'd forgotten. Yes, she'd been falling for him before her memories were returned, but now she felt a love that belonged to a much different version of her.

The sun had moved, telling her she had cried for several hours, but she didn't care.

She was taking a mental health day, and everyone else could screw off. The humans. Her sisters. The Titans. The war.

"You really should get up, Hera." The bed moved as someone sat on the mattress behind her, and Hera froze.

*No. She was dreaming.*

"Come daughter, time to greet the day." A hand touched her hair, and she rolled and jumped away, meeting Cronus's eyes. The bed between them now.

Grabbing her lightning bolt necklace, she glowered at Cronus and called her power, but it was dismal at best, and her eyes widened as she realized she was unable to pull any of the electricity from the world around her.

"Mortal as mortal can be, my sweet." He smiled, all teeth, and it was a smile Hera knew well. She'd gotten her own predatory smile from him, after all. He stood and moved around the bed, Hera frozen in shock, her body unable to move. Adrenaline pushed through her veins as the panic spiked inside of her. She was a sitting duck, and Cronus knew it.

He neared her, getting right into her face, and she tried to break free of her invisible chains, but Cronus had some sort of spell on her.

"Time for a reunion, don't you think?" he whispered, his breath hot on her cheek. He grazed his fingertips across her temple, down her jaw, then wrapped his long, thin fingers around her throat.

"Watching you take your last breath has been the only thing keeping me sane in the hellscape you sent me to," he growled as she tried to pull in air, and his hold only tightened. Black dots appeared before her, but then there was someone else there with them.

Viktor stood behind Cronus.

"Wake up, Hera. Now," he demanded. "Wake up!"

Cronus spun away, dropping her, and she collapsed to the floor. Closing her eyes tightly, she blinked them open to see Viktor standing over her.

Pushing up, she looked around her room, seeing there was no Cronus. It was just the two of them; her and Viktor.

"He was here," she rasped, and Viktor pulled her into him, his arms tight bands of steel around her.

"It was a nightmare. I felt your panic and thought you were being attacked. I shouldn't have left."

Grabbing his face, she looked into his eyes.

"I am a very stubborn woman," she started, and Viktor laughed.

"Believe me, I know—"

"No, please listen. I am stubborn, I make horrible decisions without thinking, and I am not that innocent little lamb you were with before ... before I died—"

Now he cut her off, taking her face in his hands.

"I know who you were and who you are now, and I love both."

"You should run while you still can, because if I get attached again, there is no hope of you ridding yourself of me this time. You step back into my life as anything more than the god sitting next to me on Olympus, you forfeit any future women and the possibility of them surviving should you take them on as lovers. I am not great at sharing, nor do I play well with others."

Viktor, no Emrys, gave her a soft smile as he moved a curl from her forehead, pushing it behind her ear. A touch she allowed. A touch that was like a balm to her soul.

"I will be the biggest pain in your ass," Hera told him. "I'll become the same irritating barnacle of a lover as my idiot brothers-in-law. My point is, you'll never be rid of me." She took a deep breath.

"So?" she prodded. "What do you say?"

She knew she had just pushed him away, but who was she kidding? She was ready to go for it before she even had her memories back. Sadly, it took longer because she was just a damn stubborn woman with serious issues. Thankfully, he was a therapist and could handle her crazy ... she hoped.

"Hera," he spoke, his voice thick with emotion as he looked into her eyes. "That's not even a question. I am already yours. I've been yours forever."

Viktor—no... *Emrys*—leaned in and took her lips in a kiss similar to the one in their memories. Passionate and hopeful and loving. She opened to him, feeling every nerve ending in her body come alive.

Undressing each other, they shuffled quickly back to her bed, and she fell back onto her rumpled comforter, pulling him down on top of her. The first time a man had been in her bed. It was as if she'd been waiting for Emrys without even knowing.

As they kissed each other, she ran her hands down his back, comparing it to the body she'd known before they were lost to each other. He had more muscles than when they were younger, and as she kissed him, the scruff of his unshaved face was another difference. He used to keep himself cleanly shaved before.

When he moved to merge his body with hers, she gasped, the feeling of his pleasure hitting her at the same time as her own.

Swallowing her moan, he moved slowly, taking her in such an intimate way that she felt tears gather in the corners of her eyes.

"I love you, Emrys," she whispered, feeling her soul become whole. A smile crossed his face that shone like the sun, like the brightest fire. She smiled back, laughing a little at how she now completely understood her sisters' besottedness. *Love.* Finally, she knew—and remembered—what it felt like.

Kissing him before he could say anything back, Hera truly lost herself to his touch for the first time in millennia.

Lightning struck out from her, arcing over their skin and between their bodies, but not hurting him in the slightest. His fire did the same, lapping at her flesh harmlessly, warming her deliciously. She knew when her arm tingled that their bond was completing.

Pausing, Emrys straightened and looked at his arm, holding it between them. Where a blurry failed mark was before, a beautiful swirl of fire and lightning was now vibrantly etched into their skin. The same as was on her arm.

His eyes moved to hers, and Hera saw the absolute joy in them before he kissed her, pulling her closer as he lost himself to their lovemaking. She struggled to delay her pleasure, wanting to bask in their reunion more, but her body quickly drowned in sensation.

All too soon, she was as lost to her bliss as he was, but this time, he did not roll away. He held her tighter, pulling her to him as he rolled to the side, not leaving her body.

Pushing a lock of hair from his eyes, she kissed him.

Emrys. Her Emrys. He was who she had been waiting for and never knew it.

Curling up into his arms, they held each other as they fell asleep.

For the time lost, and the unknown of the future, they would hold each other close and for as long as they could.

# Chapter 24

### <u>Hera</u>

A TUG ON HERA'S consciousness pulled her from sleep. Rolling over, her hand hit something solid. Something that made an *oomph* when hit.

"Still a violent sleeper." A deep chuckle and a soft kiss on her lips brought a smile to her face.

Slowly, she opened her eyes and looked at Viktor as he settled back, putting his arms behind his head. She shuffled closer to lay her head against his chest as her hand wandered underneath the covers, exploring a very naked Viktor.

*Viktor.* Should she still call him that or by his real name?

She looked out the floor-to-ceiling window of her penthouse bedroom, seeing only clouds and a few buildings poking above them. Laying her in her bed, wrapped in Viktor's warmth, everything felt so perfect. Nothing outside of the room was, though, and war knocked at her door.

But in this moment, Hera was content. It was all as it should be, and she wished she could bask in it for longer as the sun rose over the city, a beautiful sight to behold from her home.

"I feel like I missed so much," she murmured against his skin. "You remembered. You were able to watch, even from afar. I really only have the last several days with you and the memories of our brief time together ages ago. What did you do after training with Prometheus and Themis? Before you came back?" she asked, and he opened one eye to look down at her.

Hera moved her hand up, so he wasn't distracted, and ran her hand over his chest, through the coarse hair there, trailing her fingers lightly over his pecs. He sighed thoughtfully before answering.

"I was a nomad for a while. Moving from place to place, learning about the world. Through the centuries, I pursued the intellectual developments of the time. Reading and discussing philosophy on existence filled the hours I was forced to spend away from you. I found people's behavior fascinating and decided to become a therapist long before the Great War."

"And Nyx? How did she come into all of this?" she asked, her hand stopping over his heart.

Viktor let out a huff of air.

"That, I'm still waiting on the explanation for. A cat that looked like my mother's familiar showed up one day. She communicated telepathically and said things only her familiar would know, so in all my infinite wisdom, I didn't question it."

Suddenly, the tug in Hera's mind that had woken her became a full-out alarm.

Pushing up to her elbows, she looked around for clothes, but a flash of aquamarine lit up her bedroom before she could rise and dress herself.

Before her now stood Amphitrite, her eyebrows raised to her hairline as she took in a very naked Viktor in Hera's bed.

"You should see him without the sheet." Hera winked at her sister, earning a groan from Viktor. Oh yes, she remembered how fun teasing him was.

"As much as I would like to taunt you about this, we need to go," Amphitrite stated as she picked up Hera's shirt and threw it at her. "Now."

"You, too." She pointed at Viktor.

The serious tone in her sister's voice had her jumping up, not caring she was naked as the day she was born, and grabbing the pants Amphitrite now held in her hands.

"What happened?" Hera asked, trying to balance while she dressed, but Amphitrite was staring at Viktor with an eyebrow raised.

"If it's all the same to you, I'd rather dress without an audience," he replied as he sat up, settling his elbows on his knees, the sheet covering the lower half of him.

Looking back to Hera without answering Viktor, Amphitrite grimaced.

"Another attack on the city," she said darkly.

"Humans again? Are they still drugged?" Hera asked as she pulled on her shirt, completely forgetting her bra. Unlike her sisters, she was far too endowed to get away with it, but there wasn't time. The ladies were going free today.

"No." Amphitrite shook her head. "We need to go to the city center. It's Perses. He's tearing Halcyon apart."

Shock ran through Hera, her skin going cold.

"How exactly?" Hera asked through the terrified knot in her throat.

Amphitrite took a deep breath and squared her shoulders.

"As the Destroyer."

"*The* Destroyer? The one that sent Atlantis to the bottom of the ocean?" Hera asked, earning a nod from Amphitrite in response.

Hera sat back on the edge of the bed, and Viktor's hand immediately went to her back in comfort. She could not compete with the Destroyer. Her entire childhood had been stories of how he was unbeatable. A large rock monster of sorts, lava for blood, taller than the tallest building in Zephyr.

A sense of doom was not going to help, and her people needed her.

*Get your shit together, Hera.*

Standing abruptly, she nodded to Amphitrite.

"Summon everyone who has vowed to stand at our side. Em—Viktor and I will follow," Hera ordered, but Amphitrite barely waited for the words to leave her mouth before she light jumped.

The moment she was gone, Viktor stood from the bed, walking around it to Hera and pulling her into his arms.

"We do this together," he whispered into her hair, and she pulled him tighter against her in a near-desperate embrace.

"This could end badly. I am not sure how we can defeat him," she whispered back, earning a squeeze from Viktor and another kiss to her head. He said nothing more as he turned away to dress.

"Also, you can call me Emrys. That is the name you knew me as from before," he stated, his back to her as he put on his pants, and she eyed his bare butt. She could die soon, so she should enjoy it while she could.

Turning back to her once he finished dressing, he raised an eyebrow, and she savored the small moment of levity before the battle.

"But if you'd like to call me Viktor for the sake of everyone else, you can call me Emrys when I'm between your legs."

Her eyebrows rose. "Confident, are you? Think I'm all yours, huh?" She smiled as she reached for his hand.

He gave her hand a squeeze, his cheeks slightly flushed, and his eyes in awe of her.

"Oh, I know it. You're mine forever, Queen Goddess." He leaned in and pressed a kiss firmly against her mouth.

"Then let's go end the Destroyer once and for all," she whispered against his lips, as she pulled them both into a light jump.

# Chapter 25

<u>**Viktor**</u>

VIKTOR STOOD IN THE middle of the main street running through Halcyon, Hera next to him, and looked out at the damage already done to the city before Hera pulled them to where the battle was happening.

The giant beast made of rock and fire was smashing buildings like kids would sandcastles. Lava flowed from its eyes and mouth, melting anything it touched as it dripped to the ground.

Hera's sisters were fighting alongside Devon, West, and Finley. Calling his fire, Viktor looked to Hera, who had summoned her goddess form, and they both rushed forward to join the fight.

Everywhere lava fell, West hit with water, minimizing the damage. A giant dragon of green light moved around the Destroyer as vines tripped it up from the bottom, causing the monster to stumble, but it found purchase before it crashed onto the street. Mostly by grabbing onto buildings, demolishing them as he straightened himself.

Persephone's wraiths darted through it, crushing through glowing-hot rocks, but the injuries they created healed as quickly as they could deal out the damage. A massive sea serpent snapped from the docks, its long tail thrusting waves towards the beast, causing towers of steam to rise from the Destroyer's back.

Viktor realized that they were slowly pushing it back with their attacks toward the water where the serpent waited. Tentacles would reach out from the water every so often, indicating that another beast lay beneath the surface as well.

Viktor threw balls of fire, which exploded on impact, doing hardly any damage at all. Turning to West, who watched the lava flow with a calculating eye, Viktor made a harpoon with his fire, hoping West caught on.

By the nod, and sudden making of a giant water harpoon, West understood. Viktor motioned him to aim at the eye, and West unleashed the watery projectile, hitting the Destroyer dead center in the eye.

A loud, horrible yell came from its rocky throat, its hands moving to grab at the weapon that had already evaporated.

The eye became lava again, and the only thing they had managed to do was anger the beast further.

Finley, seeing what West had done, pulled her arrows of moonlight from the air and hit the Destroyer in each of his eyes and mouth. Where the arrows hit, the rocks went black before igniting again, fire replacing the stone that had blackened and died. At least it distracted the beast long enough that Hera could get closer to aim her lightning. She struck the areas that were cracked open along the rocky beast's skin.

Hera aimed a bolt of lightning at where its heart should have been. Nothing happening except some rocks falling. The Destroyer was in the center of the city, so Perses most likely knew that her summoning a tornado would only cause more damage, and Viktor could almost guarantee the Titan was counting on that. He knew Hera would try her best to keep the damage to a minimum, meaning she would be on the defensive. In their battle outside the senate, Hera had only used her tornado at the back of the crowd, away from the buildings.

Here, that was not possible, and guaranteed nothing, as none of their powers seemed to make headway in tearing the Destroyer down.

Hera threw her hands into the air and called on the rains, clouds moving in with thunder that shook the earth around them.

The rock monster howled as the water cooled the lava. Every time the Destroyer tried to pull his lava to the surface, the relentless deluge cooled it, giving the Destroyer no quarter. The Destroyer fell back, flailing its arms to find something to hold on to, but the buildings around it crumbled. When it finally hit the ground, the entire street trembled, and large plumes of dust flew into the air.

The Destroyer stilled, its glowing heat fading under the smattering of rain.

Only the sound of the storm could be heard as each of them stepped forward to see if they had managed to put the Destroyer out of commission.

A voice broke into the silence, one he did not recognize, but by the look on Hera and her sister's faces, they certainly did.

"I will finish what I started, goddesses. The end is near, and my beast demolishing this pathetic city was only the beginning."

When the dust settled, the Destroyer was gone, leaving nothing but rubble everywhere.

### <u>Hera</u>

Breathless, Hera turned in a circle to look around. Nothing stood. Everything was … gone.

Before she knew it, Hera was running, her feet moving faster than she could ever remember. As she sprinted from street to street, she realized there was nothing left of the city center. The Moirai building was destroyed, knocked down onto its side. No power from the ancients could be felt anywhere near them. For once, she would have gladly listened to their drivel if only to know that her city was alive and well, but nothing. Silence.

Suddenly, Viktor was there—she hadn't felt him following her, but she should've known. He tried to catch her arms, but she slid past him, her eyes filling with tears as she moved closer to what was left of the Senate building.

It was completely gone. Only fragments of the building remained. As if the Destroyer had not only knocked it over but kicked it all over the place, scattering its remains. The statue of Themis had been reduced to rubble, as if the Destroyer had crushed it in its fist.

Slowly stepping forward, there was a motionless hand in the rubble of the building.

"No," she whispered, pressing her knuckles against her mouth.

Viktor stood beside her, and she felt the power of her sisters join her as well, which meant Devon, West, and most likely Finley too. But she couldn't focus on them.

She could only see the pale, lifeless hand.

"No!" she yelled out, throwing herself down and pulling the large rocks off until she saw who lay beneath. Calista's normally beautiful eyes were milky and staring unblinkingly at the sky. A bone deep sorrow ran through her as Amphitrite pushed past her, grabbing Calista under her arms, and pulling her free.

"Calista!" Amphitrite cried out as she laid the woman flat on the ground. Her hands skimmed across the prone body, trying to bring her back even though it was obvious the senator was gone.

The world around her swayed, and she stumbled as the men moved into the rubble. Finley and Persephone dug on the other side of her. Each member of Olympus worked to pull her senators from where they had met their end.

"Kiran!" Finley screamed, pulling Hera out of her shock.

Kiran resigned, so she had hoped he would have been spared since he had no reason to be here. Looking over, there was a man covered in dust, but not only that.

Slowly, she moved to help as Devon and West pulled Cassandra and Ryder out.

As her family laid out her senators, she looked at them, their faces masks of death. They had not met their demise from the building falling on them, though their bodies showed the marks of such an event. Each of them had their throats slit. The greenish hue around the wounds was indicative of hydra poison.

A dark shadowy presence came, and she felt Thanatos's hand on her shoulder.

"Would you like a moment longer?" he asked in his gruff voice, the voice of Death—not the man she knew.

It made it all too real to hear him right then, to feel this. To know they were gone.

Stepping out from under his hand, Hera went to each senator and closed their eyes. Paying her respects to the people she had worked with for years to protect this country, their home.

Kiran. Cassandra. Ryder. Callista.

"No..." Persephone whispered, pulling everyone's attention to her as she lost herself to emotion. Something Persephone never did. "I have to get to the Underworld! Now!"

Before anyone could respond, she shadow jumped, Devon right behind her.

Urgently, Thanatos turned back to Hera, crouching next to her.

"I need to check on this, but I will be back to care for your friends. I promise," he whispered, giving Hera a kiss on the forehead. The man had always acted like a brother to her and her sisters, even when she acted out, annoying him with her sarcastic barbs. And Hera was never more grateful for him than at that moment. Placing her hand over his, she squeezed his fingers as the shadows took him away.

Standing up, she turned to a crying Finley, who had collapsed in Amphitrite's arms. Viktor stood next to them, attending to the mourning twin. He was close enough to touch, but he was giving her the space that she needed to grieve her people.

A flash of light and shadow surprised her. Persephone reappearing so quickly did not bode well, but nothing compared to the words Persephone said next.

"Cronus is gone."

# Chapter 26

### <u>Viktor</u>

PURE TERROR FROM ALL three sisters hit Viktor at once. Enough so that he had to sit back on a piece of rubble to keep from falling to his knees.

It was an emotional onslaught, but he understood why. He was there when Hera was hiding in the mountain and knew what had happened to her and her sisters.

Still, he felt faint, trying to close the empath pathway to his mind, creating a wall to keep him from feeling their emotions all at once. It was hard enough to feel it when they found the senators, but now it was amplified.

Suddenly, a hand was on his arm, right over the soulbond mark, and a soothing sensation moved through him like a salve spreading over his raw and overstimulated nervous system.

Looking up, Viktor caught concern in Hera's eyes and knew then that she could feel him through their established soulbond. Could see in her eyes that she understood him now, and that he could feel others' emotions so strongly. He felt her terror subside, just marginally, and he somehow loved her even more for pushing through such fear for him. No one had ever been able to help him when his empathic senses were overloaded, not even his parents or Nyx.

His strength returned, Viktor stood, taking Hera's hand in his and interlocking their fingers. As long as she was touching him, he was unable to feel her sisters. As long as they were connected, she soothed his soul.

Hera's panic still mingled under the surface of her attempt to calm him, but he knew she needed him, otherwise she would bottle it up as she always had. He was the only one who could pull her from her own self-destruction. Wrapping her in his arms, ignoring the looks sent his way, including an incredulous one from West, he held her tight against him. His heartbeat calmed, and hers synced with his.

"We can handle anything together. We are stronger than we were, and for that reason, Cronus doesn't have a chance now. Regroup, break it down into small steps, and we will get a plan in place that will guarantee his defeat. Do not let the idea he is free overwhelm you," he whispered into her hair.

Her hands were digging into his back, reminding him that he was without a shirt from having called the fire. Giving a small nod, Hera released him and stepped back to look up at him.

"Then let's go plan how to kick my father's ass, shall we?"

## <u>Hera</u>

Hera seated herself on her throne as everyone else, including Finley, approached their own. As Viktor passed by her, he touched her hand where it lay on the armrest, giving her a sense of comfort through their bond that she desperately needed to make it through this day.

When she gave him a small, sad smile, Viktor nodded and moved to sit on his throne. Now that she knew who he was to her, she had a hard time wondering why his being in the second seat of power on Olympus had bothered her so much. He had belonged there all along. Hera was just too selfish to realize it at the time.

As each person seated themselves, their clothes and appearance changing as the crowns sat upon their heads. Hera readied herself to address them.

The atmosphere was cloying, and she wasn't sure how to start. Everyone there had seen loss that day.

"It is going to take me a while to get used to..." West waved at Hera and Viktor. "All of this."

Hera exhaled a laugh, one that for once was not sarcastic, but sincere. West read the room and chose to be his lovable, idiot self. And she loved that about him, unable to keep from smiling at the man.

"Do not start being nice to me, Hera. I cannot handle that," West said with fake reproof.

"Don't worry, water boy, I'll continue to make you regret your existence," she replied, but it held none of the heat it normally did.

"There she is," West said with a wink.

Thankful for the break in tension, she took a fortifying breath and called on the globe. As the floor opened, the large projection of the globe materialized at the center of the throne room as Hera stood and walked to it.

"Devon, please update us on the current developments you and..." Hera took another deep breath. "Cassandra were able to discover before Perses's attack on Halcyon."

Without a delay, Devon stood up and pointed to each of the areas he knew the current enemy encampments to be. It was far more than she anticipated, but she wasn't surprised.

Even on the globe, when zoomed in on the city, it was reduced to rubble, and encampments surrounded them. How were these people being controlled long enough to stay there? Drugs wore off, and the witches were hitting them with counter spells. What else did the Titans have up their sleeves?

"Are these people loyal of their own volition?" Persephone asked before Hera could.

"That's the question of the day. I am assuming there was an on-going campaign to win certain people to their side, perhaps military personnel that Perses worked with in his General Olethros disguise, creating dissent among the ranks," Devon replied, folding his arms across his chest. "It wouldn't be out of the realm of possibility."

"Kiran, before ... I left," Finley started. "He had a concern that he thought was all in his head, one he was watching closely before bringing it up to the rest of the senate. In Sereia, the emperor had begun making some noise about how things were run in Halcyon. When Kiran went to investigate, there was never any proof, but he had plenty of suspicions. It makes sense now that the issues all began over in that region of Zephyr."

"We have been far too lenient with that pompous ass. I knew he would never hold to the truce!" Amphitrite's temper hit a boiling point, and West grabbed her forearm, running his thumb over the soulmark.

"So, you're telling me the Sereian Emperor, that sneaky bastard, could be using his army to help the Titans?" Hera asked, needing it to be said outright.

"Looks like it," Devon replied, looking between everyone, and earning nods.

"I would," Amphitrite sighed, running a hand through her hair. "Calista ... she was the one with the spies near there. She had been having issues gathering intel recently since the mess with Eurybia, and now I know why."

"They turned," Hera growled, and Amphitrite nodded. "And they know things that could win this war against us. We're exposed. Our weaknesses, our strengths..."

Amphitrite slumped in her seat, looking defeated. Hera felt an urge to comfort her sister, as this was not her fault, but in the past, that had gone wrong. She never knew the correct thing to say, so she kept quiet. West was quick to whisper comforting words to her, and she was thankful for that.

"Then, we need people they do not know about." Hera turned back to the globe, looking it over. Her godfire lit in her eyes as an idea came to her. One that may not work, but she would try anything at this point.

"That look screams trouble. I'm in. What are we doing?" West asked, leaning forward as he continued to rub Amphitrite's back.

"We have your army, correct?" Hera asked.

West confirmed she had the power of the Atlantean army behind her. She did not want to send them in on the front lines, as they were close enough to human to be killed quickly, but they could fight the other humans well enough.

"Does Perses turn into the Destroyer, or does he control it?" Hera asked West and Amphitrite, the ones with up close and personal experience with the Titan.

"From my memories of his last venture in death and destruction, he controlled it," West replied darkly, catching on. "He was blind while looking through the eyes of it, so if we can find him while he is possessing the Destroyer—"

"He's vulnerable. We kill him, and we kill the Destroyer," Devon stated with a nod. "We have to get to him through all the other Titans, though. We can safely assume with Cronus free, they will not be afraid to make themselves known now."

"We need more people. As much as it annoys me, we need Olympus's power, and to have that, we need more people sitting on thrones," Hera remarked and paced. Devon stepped out of her way but stayed near the globe, examining it.

Hera remembered the oath her mother had made with Themis to keep her sisters from having power until death. Themis may have a solution that could help them, since her entire job was to make sure the playing field was even so that true justice may prevail, and it most certainly was not even right now.

Not to mention, each of the deities now sitting on Olympus would need some help in making sure their powers were battle ready, especially since half the people sitting in front of her were new to their godhood. She knew three brothers who could help with that.

Three brothers who could create magical instruments that harnessed raw power.

"Viktor and I are going to find Themis." She turned to the thrones. "I need Amphitrite and West to find the cyclops and meet us back at my place. I do not know if Olympus will accept Themis or the cyclops, and I'd rather not find out the hard way. Persephone—you, Devon, and Finley, go and see what can be done to reinforce the gate at Tartarus and repair any damage the Titans made."

Everyone looked at her with wide eyes, but she was already mentally preparing for what was next.

"Now!" she yelled, and multiple colors of light flashed as everyone jumped through a portal at once.

Looking back at Viktor, Hera held her hand out to him, and he took it without any hesitation.

"Let's go find a way to win this war."

# Chapter 27

## <u>Hera</u>

L IGHT JUMPING TO THE cave where she had spent her mortal youth, Hera was only mildly surprised to see Themis was already there.

Themis's eyes caught on Hera's soulmark, and the Titan gave a small, pleased smile with a nod of approval.

"The truth has been told then?" She raised an eyebrow at Viktor.

"It has. All of it," his voice was low as he spoke, his emotional turmoil at the memory still strong as ever as it came through the bond. "She knows the curse created the separation and erased her memories."

"Themis," Hera started, walking towards the woman who'd really raised her. As much as her mother tried to save her, Themis was the one who actually did it. "We need more allies. I know if anyone can put us on the right path—"

Themis held up a hand to stop Hera.

"My ability is simply to keep everything balanced. I cannot step in to assist in this war more than to make sure both sides are on equal footing," Themis stated, and Hera felt the argument on the tip of her tongue. "But"—Themis gave a small smile—"I do see the Titans having an unfair advantage in numbers."

At her side, Viktor threaded his fingers through hers. Probably a good idea because Hera was feeling her temper rise. She wondered if Themis was planning to have them jump through hoops for this.

"How?" Hera asked as she narrowed her eyes at Themis.

Themis slowly walked around the pair of them, taking them in.

"So many things have been foretold long before you both were even born."

Hera rolled her eyes and looked at Viktor, who was considering Themis with narrowed eyes. She felt better that he was as unimpressed as she was.

"It was foretold that the sisters would die, that others would rise in their place." Themis stopped in front of them. "That the balance would come when the queen found her king again after the tragedy of time and loss."

Hera squeezed Viktor's fingers and felt some relief that their story was meant to be this way. No matter how much she felt she'd missed out on the centuries without him, Chaos had set them on this path.

Themis placed one hand on Viktor's shoulder and one on Hera's. Lights danced around them before they were once again on Olympus.

"So, now that we have our queen and our king, let's set up the rest of the players on the board, shall we?"

Turning away from them, Themis faced the thrones and lifted her arms into the air as the ground beneath them rumbled, just as it did when a new throne was being created.

Hera gaped as four new thrones, two on each end, came up from the marble floor of Olympus. Each throne etched with symbols: wings with a caduceus; two spears crossing under an owl; arrows crossing through a sun; a knife through a rose.

"Oh, you've got to be kidding me." Hera rolled her eyes.

Themis turned back to them, a look of inquiry on her face.

"Really?" Hera waved her hand at the thrones. "The symbols for the mythical Olympians?"

Themis gave her a patient, maternal look.

"The symbols were foretold long before thrones were created upon Olympus. There was always meant to be these gods and goddesses, just not for some time and not exactly as people, or goddesses, thought." Themis raised an eyebrow at the end of the sentence to make her point.

Looking back at Viktor, Hera rolled her eyes.

"It's true," he agreed, surprising Hera. "The fires have shown these symbols for many centuries. I thought maybe it had to do with the myths, but it seems it just simply hadn't happened yet."

Hera grunted, corrected, before turning back to Themis.

"So, they have powers now? They can fight alongside us?"

"They have powers, but as for their loyalty, that is up to you. Do you feel like you're worthy enough of a leader for them to follow into battle? Do you believe Kiran has forgiven you?"

"Wait, these are for the senators?" Hera asked in disbelief. "They're dead—murdered. Thanatos took them ... unless you intervened." Hera paused and sighed.

"Of course," Hera snorted. "Thanatos takes them to the Underworld, and you catch up and throw them in the river Styx, working your ancient mumbo jumbo on them."

Themis nodded; her hands folded in front of her.

"Yes, that is close to how it happened. I intervened on his way to the Underworld, but I allowed them the choice to ascend as opposed to throwing them in and using my... mumbo jumbo." Hera chuckled at Themis's poised, elegant voice quoting her with distaste. "They were always meant to be here, Hera. When will you learn that, quite literally, everything happens for a reason. They will follow you, at least most. I am unsure of Kiran, as his soul was quite angry."

"I did not kill Finley," Hera growled, but Themis only tilted her head in acknowledgement.

"No, you did not. She was felled by a Titan, Perses, or General Olethros, as he calls himself. Prometheus and I stepped in to keep her from true death."

"So, they all died, and you took my senators on a field trip to the river Styx and brought them back to life?" Hera clarified again, not believing she would have her senator's back. Not daring to hope.

Viktor stepped closer to her, his hand going around her waist and pulling her into his body.

"That, I did."

"And now, instead of senators, I have Olympians?" she inquired with a raised eyebrow and smirk.

Themis gave her a wink that would have done the old Hera proud.

So, they had their thrones, yet they were not here to claim them.

"My Olympians, then. Where are they now? Why are they not here to claim their thrones?" Hera asked, turning to Themis. The Titan closed her eyes as if in answer, and her hands went up into the air, holding them out like scales, as if weighing the sides of the battle in front of her.

Slowly, little lights like fireflies flew up the mountain and swirled around the throne room, becoming almost tornadic.

Separating into four distinct groups of lights, they formed human shapes, and she watched as the senators she had just pulled from the rubble so very recently stood before her with godfire alight in their eyes.

The knot in her chest loosened at the sight, relief pulsing through her. She could feel their eyes boring into her, the demand for answers on the tip of their tongues. Or perhaps that was her own guilt.

She had failed them, all of them, and knew it.

Slowly, Hera made eye contact with each of them. Ryder gave her a nod. Calista, a wink. Cassandra gave a tilt of the head, indicating without words that she would follow Hera.

Last was Kiran. His face was stoic, a stone mask that told her nothing of what the man was thinking or feeling.

"Welcome back," Hera started, unsure of how much Themis had told them.

When she glanced back at Themis, all she was given was a smile and a nod of approval. Hera stepped toward the senators, and they split apart, letting Hera walk through them as she moved up onto the dais and took a seat upon her throne.

In her soul, she knew that if their power was strong enough to create a throne, it was strong enough to tell them which one was theirs. She trusted Olympus to guide them.

Calista took the lead and approached hers without hesitation, confident in her movements just as she had been in life. As she sat on the throne etched with the dagger and rose, her long dark hair loosened, and a soft petal pink dress wrapped around her body.

Cassandra followed, sitting on the throne etched with spears and an owl. Her hair braided back like the warriors of old, and a leather corset and flowing white skirt materialized over her body, more practical for combat but no less beautiful.

Shrugging at Kiran, Ryder moved to the throne with the wings and caduceus. He transformed, now covered in golden tattoos all along the skin that wasn't hidden by his white button-up and slacks. His hair was longer too, she noticed, but it was tied in a bun at the base of his neck.

Kiran was the last to move, his hesitant step so different from his usual overly confident swagger.

"I had assumed, correctly, that the caduceus was the symbol for medicine," Kiran stated, staring at the rod with the snakes wrapped around it, their faces meeting, wings topping it off.

Ryder smirked. "It was actually the symbol for thieves back in the old days."

Hera turned to look at Ryder, raising an eyebrow.

"What is it you actually did as a human, Ryder?" she asked, unsure if she truly wanted to know.

Ryder only gave her a wink as he settled back on his throne. Hera had known he stole secrets for Amphitrite's network, but what else had the man gotten up to? Shaking her head at Ryder, she watched as Kiran finally started toward the throne with the sun and arrows.

A bright flash of light engulfed him, making him jump back before he looked down at his golden button-up and slacks. Shaking his arms out, he snuck a look at Hera before he finally seated himself completely.

Once each of the newest goddesses and gods was seated, Hera felt a connection forming with them through Olympus, the power attaching to her with strings made of light from every throne, even Devon, West, and Viktor's. She hadn't realized until now that the three gods had yet to form a strong link to her through Olympus.

Hera closed her eyes and allowed the connection to flow through her in a way that hadn't happened since she first took her throne alongside her sisters so very long ago. As the connection steadied, she felt Devon and West even stronger than before, able to call for them directly now.

But the connection with Viktor was by far the strongest, even stronger than the one she had with her sisters, and Hera felt him send a wave of calm to her that she appreciated. As if he knew exactly what was happening, what she needed, from afar.

Finally, the lines of power, the new and the ancient ones from her sisters, joined, melding together into a single cord.

Her eyes flashed open as Amphitrite sent her own call out, but this was for Hera to come to Atlantis.

Amphitrite must have rounded up the cyclops since the call was not one of panic, but smug satisfaction.

And for the first time since they had found Hestia's power, Hera thought they might have a chance to win this war after all.

# Chapter 28

### <u>Viktor</u>

VIKTOR WALLOWED IN FRUSTRATION as he tried to pull images from the fires, receiving nothing for his troubles except some sparks and irritation.

*"The fires will not show you what you want them to, Viktor. You are now far too close to the situation at hand."*

Ignoring Nyx, he pushed a little more of his power into the flame. He needed an alternate ending to this story than the one his father had predicted in yet another damn note left on his bedside table, where the vial had first shown up.

The moment Olympus took on more deities, the timeline had changed according to Prometheus, and now the vial was guaranteed to be needed. Viktor had hoped it was wrong and went to the fires himself, but nothing happened because Nyx was right. He was in the middle of it now and no longer an outsider.

It was the same premonition his father had with his mother. He would not lose Hera to a similar fate, not again. She may be a goddess, but she was not going to be able to withstand this. Falling back on to his butt, he stared at the fire, nothing showing him the future or even a glimpse.

*"As I said—"*

"Shut up!" Viktor roared at Nyx. Her hackles rose as she hissed back at him. He pushed himself onto his feet and paced. "All you ever do is tell me how things aren't going to work, or how I'll fail, or what I'm doing wrong!"

He stomped toward Nyx, where she perched on a branch and thrust a finger in her feline face.

"You are one of the most powerful deities out there, and you're doing nothing!"

*"I'd suggest you calm yourself now, Fire God."*

"No!" He kicked dirt at the fire, his temper causing sparks to fly from his hands. "No, for once I want some damn answers! If you've been here this whole damn time, why didn't you save my mother? Why aren't you helping now?"

Hands on his hips, sparks popped as he tried to pull himself back from the brink of a rage that would burn this entire forest down. Nyx looked away from him, unable to hold his stare, and he deflated. If she had fought back, his rage would have been far easier to hold on to.

A shadow moved over the sun, and Viktor startled, glancing up to see what was causing the unnatural darkness.

There was not any eclipse coming that he knew about, but when the shadows lengthened and a pale woman stepped from the darkness, he knew this was no act of nature.

The stranger wore a sheer black veil and black form-fitting dress with sparkles that looked like starlight. A black jeweled crown sat atop her veiled head, and black feathered wings came out from her back. Though he had never seen this woman before, he knew she was Nyx.

"I was not there when your mother died and I was not there when Hera ascended," Nyx spoke aloud for the first time to him. Her voice was not unlike the one he'd heard in his mind, but it was somehow louder, deeper, and more real.

"Your mother had a familiar, but it was a mortal cat," she continued. "When your mother was killed by the Romans and her own fire, and you were burning down everything in your anger, your father came to me. I was living in the Underworld, bringing night to the world, and working to keep my children in line. You've met Thanatos," she said as an aside, and Viktor fought a delirious laugh at the implication that Thanatos was as difficult to control as an errant toddler.

"Your father worried you would continue on the wrong path, and as I was the only Primordial he trusted—because I kept to myself—he asked that I watch over you. I knew in order to do so, I'd need to gain your trust, and I saw my opportunity when her familiar died."

Viktor waited a moment to study her before he spoke.

"You are one of the most powerful deities to have ever lived. Why have you wandered the world with me for so long?" Far longer than he was at risk of burning down the world.

"In the beginning, yes, it was temporary. I chose to bargain with your father. Should I ever need a favor, he would owe me. But, with time, I saw something in you that I wanted to nurture, so I stayed, leaving at night not to hunt, but to bring darkness to the world for humanity to rest. My own children no longer needed me, and I saw in you something great." The deity then shrugged. "Plus, I was relatively bored."

"Did you just make a joke?" he asked, laughing a little.

"I did," she replied. "I raised some of the most annoyingly sarcastic children, and I cannot blame their father for that."

Shaking his head and looking down, Viktor let his hands drop to his sides.

"This is not over. What your father saw in the fires is not written in stone, Emrys," she told him, serious again. "And he gave you the tool to undo it all if it comes to fruition."

Viktor put his hand in his pocket, wrapping his fingers around the vial.

A vial that was his failsafe.

# Chapter 29

## <u>Hera</u>

HERA HAD BEEN TO Atlantis several times since West had revived the small island kingdom from the depths of the Thalassian sea. When she visited, she checked in on West's mother and the massive rebuilding efforts, but she hadn't been to the palace since Amphitrite had first moved in as wife and queen.

She'd figured there would be far too much coupling going on, and she had no desire to see either Amphitrite or West naked and in the throes of whatever weird sex stuff the two of them got up to.

Stepping into the foyer of the grand palace with Viktor at her back, her eyes settled on three figures she hadn't seen in far too long, and a lightness lifted her spirits at seeing their familiar faces.

"Brontes, Steropes, and Arges," Hera greeted the three cyclops brothers, a slight hitch in her throat at the sight of them. They had created Hera's lightning bolt necklace that allowed her to control the electricity in the air and channel it into her lightning bolts. Amphitrite's ring that allowed her to harness her power to take control of the sea. Persephone's earrings that could render her invisible should she need it.

But seeing them also reminded her of being a young goddess with out-of-control powers. They'd given her what she needed so desperately at that time: control. Now she needed control again. In such a short time everything had changed—her relationship with Viktor, and with herself, and the installment of new goddesses and gods on Olympus—but it was guaranteed to change even more.

Hopefully for the better.

Before Hera could think better of it, she stepped forward and was immediately pulled into Arges's embrace. The large man lifted her and twirled her in the air.

The cyclops did not look like what mythology had deemed them to look like. To any passing observer, they had the appearance of overly large men around seven feet tall and had two eyes, just like any other human. They blended in as long as one ignored the slightly too long canines, which most humans did.

But, when the brothers were calling their power of the forge, letting the universe tell them what weapons needed to be made, their eyes sealed shut and a large eye opened in the center of their forehead. It gave them a second sight, giving them the ability to see the magic they fused with the weapons they made.

"We've been missing you, love," Brontes stated, stepping forward to pull Hera from Arges, and soon after, Steropes was holding her.

While her sisters had gone to their realms soon after they were given their earrings and ring, she had wanted to spend time with the three cyclops, feeling safe in their forge with them. Many nights she would sit and watch while they worked. They sang songs that would lull her to sleep. They conversed with her to help with her anxiety. It was like having three loving uncles, and the fact they allowed her to stay when no others could enter meant the world to her. She'd felt loved and protected.

Hera never understood what drew her to the fire of the cyclops' forge until she had stood in Viktor's garage. Until she regained the memory of watching him work and manipulate metal over the fire. Somehow, her subconscious had found a way to remind her of Viktor, feel his essence, even when she couldn't have him with her. So much, so many choices she had made, were finally making sense.

Steropes lowered her back onto her feet and patted her lovingly on her head.

"Rumor has it we have a new war brewing," Brontes stated as he leaned back against one of the stone walls of the palace.

"Yes, and we have new gods and goddesses on Olympus," she replied. Viktor stepped up next to her, placing an encouraging hand at the small of her back. The brothers' eyes lit up, as if they knew exactly what she would ask of them next. "Could you make weapons for them? Items to help them harness their power?"

"Yes!" they answered unanimously, making her smile. Amphitrite, who was walking back into the room, jumped at the loud response.

"Anything for our little lightning bug." Arges winked at her.

### Hera

After the cyclops went to their forge, Themis promised to take the Olympians there so the cyclops could work their magic.

Once they were gone, Amphitrite took Hera and Viktor to see the progress the army was making.

The Atlantean army had come such a long way in such a short amount of time that seeing them practice out in the open, Hera knew whoever trained them should have been promoted to the highest rank in the Halcyon military long ago.

"Want me to have them take off their shirts?" West asked from behind as she stared out over the field of men battling with swords. Viktor simply grunted his displeasure from her side.

"Sure. Do you provide refreshments for the show?" she retorted.

Hera knew Viktor was probably rolling his eyes, but his arm around her waist gave her a playful squeeze, and she shuffled closer to the man she wouldn't mind seeing shirtless every single day.

West chuckled as he leaned his forearms on the railing of the balcony that they were observing the training yard from.

"If I did that, then I'd have to serve Amphitrite every time she stood here and stared, pretending she was watching simply for the purpose of research. My fragile ego couldn't take it if I thought she was enjoying it."

Hera let out a tiny snort as one man hit the ground on the field and rolled out from under the strike coming right at him.

"Your ego would be just fine. In fact, you might actually be tolerable should you think you have some competition," Amphitrite piped up from the other side of West.

"I think you remember what happened the last time I thought I had competition. I know most of the people at Enigma do," he replied, referring to their local club where Amphitrite used to meet with her informants.

Amphitrite looked away from him, her face going red with a blush. West only smiled at her before winking at Hera and looking back out to the field.

"I think I'm better off not knowing that story," Hera stated as she looked back out to the men. Several of the lower-ranking officers were setting up targets for practicing with the military-grade weapons. They did so at her insistence, since most of the soldiers who'd never served only had knowledge of swordsmanship, and basic knowledge at that.

"I think I like you a lot better now that you and Viktor are tangling the sheets together."

When she raised an eyebrow at West, he only grinned unapologetically.

*The cheeky bastard.*

Before she could formulate a reply, their attention was pulled to an approaching figure. One of the men who she had watched fight ran toward them, up the stairs to the overlooking balcony. He squared his shoulders and saluted West, who beckoned the human closer.

"Ah, General Alexander Markos, let me introduce you." West gestured to Hera. "You recognize Archon Zenovia Quinton." The general nodded at West. "She is also Hera, Queen of Olympus," he told the man.

The general's eyes widened, and he bowed before her, an arm across his chest, before straightening once again to meet her eyes. His were the color of honey, his skin olive, and he wore his long black hair in a braid down his back. The tattoo around his arm looked similar to the cuff West always wore. The one he wore as a symbol of his status as king of their people.

"General, were you a part of the Halcyon army?" she asked, not letting her eyes wander from his. She had a type, and as hunky as the general was, he was not it, but he was still nice to look at with his tight short-sleeve shirt and leather pants.

"I was in special operations, Archon," he spoke, his voice a smooth bass. "I resigned when I took my post training the Atlantean army."

"You're doing a damn fine job by what I've seen so far," she replied, and the general looked out over his people.

"I did what I could. I only hope they will be victorious in the battle ahead," Markos stated, worry pinching his brow.

The worry of a leader for the troops he had grown to care for. She knew the feeling well. Stepping up to him, Hera placed a hand on his shoulder.

"Your people honor Olympus and Halcyon by standing with us in battle, and should any fall, they will be honored among Olympus."

The look of shock slid across the man's face before he bent into a deep bow of respect.

"Modest man. Not only is he an amazing general, but he also handcrafted some of the weapons the men use for practice," West boasted, and Hera watched a blush cover the general's face before he cleared his throat.

"Impressive," Viktor finally spoke.

"Building weapons was a hobby of mine before I joined my brethren," he stated with an embarrassed air that made Hera smile.

"I will have to introduce you to some friends of mine one day and their magical forge," she promised, and the general's eyes widened at the prospect. He must know she spoke of the not-so-mythical cyclops.

"It would be an honor, Archon," he replied, turning to look back over his soldiers on the field, but Hera did not miss the smile of excitement on his face.

"I'd like to speak with you about your methods, as well..." Viktor started, and General Markos moved to begin what Hera assumed would be a very long and boring conversation about metalworking.

She leaned over the railing once again, watching the training continue below.

Hera wished she could guarantee that future for him. That she could guarantee that everyone on this island would make it home, but she had learned long ago not to wish for such things.

The Titans would take their pound of flesh.

### <u>Viktor</u>

In the middle of his conversation with General Markos, a ripple of power hit Viktor, raising the hairs on his arms. He vaguely recognized the feel of it.

A Titan call of power.

It was not directly sent to him, but his Titan blood stirred in response, and Viktor knew exactly what it was.

Stumbling back when the power pulsed through him even stronger than before. He quickly searched for West, another Titan progeny, and found him gripping the railing with an unsettled expression.

"You felt it?" West asked before Viktor spoke.

Viktor nodded and looked to Hera, who glanced back and forth between the two men.

"Felt what?" she asked as she moved to Viktor's side. Across from them, Amphitrite held West by his shoulders, and the general stepped back with an alert look on his face.

The call surged again, and Viktor felt the Titan in him begging him to respond, begging him to send his own power back, either as friend or foe.

"Your eyes are fire," Hera whispered, placing her hands on his chest. "Viktor, what is happening?"

"They are ready," West replied, his own eyes a dark blue instead of the whiskey color they were normally.

"The Titans?" Amphitrite asked, and the general stiffened.

"Yes," Viktor whispered as the pull of power continued to agitate the Titan blood in him. The longer he didn't respond, the stronger the pull.

"I'll prepare the army," General Markos replied, earning a nod from Amphitrite before he took off toward where the rest of the soldiers were gathering, noticing the change in their king above them. He was sure he and West were giving off a sense of unease that the power-sensitive people of Minoan descent could feel.

"Fight it," Viktor growled, seeing the hazy look in West's eyes taking back over again.

The call grew bolder, sharpening with urgency. It was the call of Cronus to every Titan still on the Earthly plane.

"Oh, I am not feeling at all like I want to do anything other than blast that asshole apart. Don't worry about me," West gritted through his teeth.

"We need to gather everyone in the city center now," Hera ordered, nodding to Amphitrite and West as she pushed out her own call to their people. To the Olympians. The Underworld. Anyone who had offered to stand beside them in battle.

"The cyclops will not have had time to make the weapons!" Amphitrite exclaimed with a look of panic.

The three giant men, who had obviously been close to Hera by their warm greetings, joined them on the balcony, slightly out of breath from running across the island, heeding her call.

"Oh, lightning bug, we have been preparing long before you asked." The one in front smirked as the two behind him crossed their arms and nodded. Viktor looked from them to Hera, who smiled in relief.

"Thank you," she told them before she closed her eyes and threw her head back with the force of her call. The power that pushed out from her was almost visible, like the haze of heat coming off the metal in his garage.

Another pulse went out, not from the Titans, but from Hera. Not one to gather forces, but a battle cry to her people, one that Viktor could feel reaching far beyond their borders.

The war had begun.

# Chapter 30

### <u>Hera</u>

IT WAS TOO LATE now to do anything more than gather her troops.

Hera had thought—no, she had *hoped*—she had more time to prepare for battle, but Hera knew there was no point in wishing for such things when it came to her father. He would work to catch her off-guard, and had Viktor and West not felt that call, he would have managed.

Edie sent her the image of the Titans moving into Halcyon, the Destroyer back and already finishing his work in demolishing her city. The fire was now completely out of control and spreading rapidly to the far edges of the capital, near both the docks and the forest.

Her home was gone. The penthouse she had worked to make her own, that towered over her city, was buried somewhere in the rubble. Hera was never more relieved that she had evacuated the city than she was then. They may lose businesses and buildings, but human life was far more important.

The tether between her and Viktor pulled tight, and Hera didn't fight him when he pulled her into his arms, kissing her forehead as he turned her away from the destruction of her home and city.

"We will rebuild, Má lásko," he told her as he leaned in to kiss her.

"What does that mean?" she whispered against his lips. "Má lásko?"

"My love," he replied, and her eyes opened.

"All this time." She gave him a small smile before placing another kiss on his lips and letting herself be completely wrapped up in his arms.

"All this time," he repeated back to her as he held her. Viktor light jumped them to the place on the mountain where the view of the city was clear, yet they were away from the danger. It was a ledge near his home that she recognized. From a gap between the trees, she watched her city burn, and despair shook her sobs free.

Squeezing her eyes shut, she held him tighter, soaking up all the comfort she could before she had to face her enemy. Taking in everything he had to give so that she would remember what she was fighting for. Storing his love for when the battle reached its peak.

Amphitrite and Persephone materialized at her side, light and shadow jumping from wherever they had just been. They looked out over the city with her as the Destroyer released a blood-curdling scream and slammed his fist into the Maritime Administration building. Amphitrite let out a horrified gasp at the sight of her building being reduced to rubble.

Hera stepped out of Viktor's hold to embrace her sister. Over Amphitrite's shoulder, she caught Persephone's teary gaze, and her other sister joined the hug. She tightened her arms around them as their city, the one they had built back up after the Great War, fell to dust.

Closing her eyes, Hera tried to hold her own emotions in, to stand strong, but when Viktor rubbed a hand over her back, the tears fell.

"I hate them," she whispered against Persephone's black hair.

"Then I shall walk them into the Underworld myself when we kill them all," Persephone replied, pulling back enough to look at Hera and wipe her tears away, as Amphitrite squeezed Hera's waist.

"We will walk out of this alive this time," Hera demanded, but she knew her sisters understood she was asking them to make a promise to her.

"All of us," they responded in unison.

Her sisters held each of her hands, and they stood there in almost prayerful silence. Helpless. They were helpless until their armies came in, when the plans they made were in place and they felt the call to put them into action. Hera was glad for this moment to just hold her sisters in case this was the last time she could do so.

"Time will tell," voices chanted from behind them, and the sisters all turned slowly to see the Moirai's ethereal forms standing at the edge of the forest. "All the players are now on the board, and so now... time will tell as everything finds its balance."

As murderously annoyed as the Moirai made her, she was glad to know they still lived. She glanced over her shoulder at her city once more before focusing back on the Moirai.

"Finally got your shit together enough to be useful," Hera replied as her voice broke on a sob.

The Moirai morphed into one being, their face in various states of aging as they stepped forward, reaching out to touch Hera's face.

"Step into your destiny, Queen of Goddesses, and make it fast," the Moirai said with many voices.

Suddenly, the wind picked up, blowing and whipping Hera's hair around her face as the Moirai swirled into a vortex.

Just as quickly as they had arrived, the deities were gone, and the air stilled. Hera swallowed thickly as she heard the Moirai's words echo in her mind.

They had a chance. This wasn't the end.

She faced her sisters, setting her expression to stone.

"You heard those specters of fate. Let the battle begin," she growled, her body floating up as her goddess form took over. Lightning sparked off her body, her eyes alight with gold.

Amphitrite and Persephone took their places at her side and transformed. Persephone's eyes went black as inky veins crawled up her arm, and her black wings and horns appeared from shadowy whorls. Amphitrite's eyes glowed bright aquamarine, and a dress like a waterfall poured over her figure.

Beside her, Viktor lit up like a torch.

The mountain top was lit with the power of the Olympians like a beacon to her allies and a threat to their enemies. They were coming.

It was time to beat some Titan ass.

It was time to face their father.

# Chapter 31

### <u>Viktor</u>

W HEN THEY OPENED A portal to the city center where the battle would take place, they found West and Devon already there. In an instant, Persephone and Amphitrite moved to their soulbonds' sides as the men transformed.

West became a being of pure water, currents shifting and sloshing within the bounds of his figure.

Devon's aura flashed green, and a dragon made of emerald light encircled his shoulders like armor as vine tattoos crawled over his skin.

All of them peered up at the oncoming Destroyer. The monster of lava and rock shifted toward them like a predator who'd scented its prey, having felt their power flooding the area.

"No one here dies today. Do I make myself clear?" Hera's goddess voiced the words as she stood in the center of their group, lightning dancing around her, with her sisters on either side of her. Wraiths flew around Persephone as water swirled around Amphitrite.

Viktor squared his shoulders, ready for battle, but a low, slinking figure that entered the rubble-covered street pulled his attention. Nyx appeared in her jaguar form at his side, flame and all. Shocked she had shown up, Viktor wasn't sure what to say, but she was quick to give him a feline smile.

*"I have waited a long time to put these little upstarts in their places."*

Viktor sent a feeling of appreciation to the Primordial Goddess, but his gratitude was cut short as the Destroyer roared and swung out toward them.

Vines punched through the large monstrosity, flying from wide cracks in the city's surface. West light jumped forward, now standing on a bare tower frame next to the rock beast, calling all the water he could to him. Viktor watched in awe as West accumulated massive waves, growing to the size of the Destroyer, and began fighting the lava beast in his giant watery form.

The two giants pummeled each other above the city, sending eruptions of steam into the atmosphere.

While the water wouldn't kill the Destroyer, it would keep it busy while Finley looked for Perses.

Suddenly, boulders rocketed in from the mountains, hitting the Destroyer and surprising everyone. The Destroyer roared, and they all turned to where the rocks had come from. Viktor's eyes widened at the sight of the creatures moving down the mountainside toward them.

Giant men, with more hands than they had time to count, came into the city in a stampede, picking up rocks and boulders and flinging them at the Destroyer. West quickly retreated from the onslaught and released his watery form as he moved in beside Amphitrite once again.

Viktor watched as Hera's head swung around to Persephone, who did not look at all surprised to see them there.

"Where did you find the Hecatonchires?" she asked, and Persephone shrugged.

"They found me. The cyclops told them what was happening, and they wanted to help since we released them from false imprisonment, as well," she replied to Hera.

"See? Kindness counts, Hera." West smirked, earning an eye roll from Hera in return before they moved their focus back on the Destroyer.

"Now!" Devon yelled, his eyes pure green and his hands shot out, sending thick, massive vines out from the earth to hold the Destroyer's rocky legs in place. Devon continued to send more and more vines as the monster broke through them with its substantial strength. Meanwhile, West summoned more water as he and Amphitrite continued to douse the Destroyer.

Viktor turned to Hera, holding out his hand of flame to harmlessly grasp her arm, the one with the mark.

"Has she sent the call yet?"

Hera started to shake her head, but then her eyes burned brighter, and Viktor could feel Finley's call through his bond with Hera. For a moment, he marveled at the connection that only went between Hera and the Olympians, but Hera quickly pushed the location Finley had provided into Viktor's mind.

Viktor and Amphitrite nodded to each other before they light jumped to where Perses was hiding while he controlled the beast, leaving his body vulnerable. Viktor glanced around, noting they were in a cave somewhere in the mountain. Finley materialized at his side, glaring at Perses.

"My ghost hounds scented him from above," she whispered darkly.

Viktor approached the Titan carefully, almost afraid to wake him, as Amphitrite watched him closely.

The Titan's eyes were hazy and fogged over, his focus solely on controlling the Destroyer. Without Finley's skilled hunting and spectral animal crew, they never would have found him, holed underground like this.

Still, it seemed far too easy that he was here unguarded.

A sudden hit of black magic to his back told him that Perses was, in fact, not unguarded.

Spinning around, he called his fire, a ball of flame in each hand. Amphitrite touched her ring, which gave off a bright light and transformed into a trident in her hands. Finley pulled her silver bow from thin air and sent a moonlit arrow toward the direction of the black magic.

Amphitrite arced her weapon toward Perses, but she was cut off by a soldier coming from the shadows. Viktor punched a flame at the soldier, and Amphitrite swung her trident to his middle, but the soldier ducked beneath both his flame and her swing. Suddenly, four more soldiers and three witches were between them and Perses.

Viktor felt the moment Perses was aware of their presence, his eyes still somewhat foggy as he tried to keep control of the monster he had created, but also aware enough that Viktor knew it would not be easy to kill him.

Before the soldiers and witches took another step, Viktor created a wall of fire between them.

"New game plan," Amphitrite rasped. "We have to take the witches and render the guards useless ... hopefully without killing them. But if we have to..." She let the thought trail off as the witches pushed a wall of black magic against his fire.

"Careful of their magic. It would kill a mortal, but if you were to be hit by it, you would be paralyzed for at least a good hour," he warned, particularly concerned for Finley, who was so incredibly new to their world.

Amphitrite turned to water, still holding her trident, and Finley nodded, transforming her bow into a sword that worked better for close combat. Viktor let the flame barrier fall, and the soldiers immediately charged toward them for a fight.

Knocking them aside, Amphitrite fought three soldiers with her trident while Finley took the other two with her sword, and Viktor threw his flames at the witches. He made orbs of the hottest flame he could create and waited until the strongest witch opened her own hands to create an orb. Taking the moment of distraction from when she worked to create her weapon, he hit her with the flame, and her body immediately immolated. Her screams pulled Perses even more from his trance.

"We have to work faster!" Viktor yelled at the goddesses.

Amphitrite gave up trying to save the men as they sliced at her with their broadswords, and took her trident, stabbing it into them. Finley struck down the others, crying out with the effort of her swings.

Viktor was able to push in on the weaker witches, having taken out their coven leader. Fear grew in their eyes as he stepped closer to them. He sent another tirade of fireballs at the witches and their shields burned up between them. They looked into each other's eyes and nodded silently.

The next moment, the witches wasted away, dissolving into a husk of black magic. He gaped at the empty space where they'd stood, perhaps troubled that they'd end their own lives instead of retreating.

Viktor stepped back to regroup with Amphitrite and Finley. Just when he braced to make a killing move against Perses, the Titan woke fully, his eyes clearing and his lips curling in a horrible smirk.

"Well, well, well, what do we have here?" A sword ignited in Perses's hand as he spoke, its initial bright flames solidifying to a matte, shadow-like blackness.

Amphitrite charged forward, the cold metal of her trident meeting his blade as Viktor conjured a whip of fire that hissed through the air, narrowly missing Perses as he twisted away. An arrow whizzed past, nearly grazing Perses's ear.

Perses laughed, spinning his blade before taking on a battle stance. "I honestly thought you might present a challenge. I was wrong."

He lashed out with his sword, nicking Viktor, who then burst into flames, while Amphitrite lunged at Perses, her trident slicing into side as he swung his sword on her.

As Perses snarled, his sword sparking with untamed power, Amphitrite retreated, her trident held high as she fell back to where Viktor stood, readying himself for another attack.

Older than all of them, Perses was immensely powerful. They would have to figure out a way to catch him off guard in order to have a chance of winning this fight.

Viktor held his hands out, letting an orb of pure fire grow between his palms, nodding to Amphitrite and Finley, hoping they caught on to his plan. He would distract Perses while they came in from both sides to attack.

Finley nocked her arrow from his left while Amphitrite readied her trident on his right.

"Are you even tryi—" Perses's eyes widened before a soundless scream tore through him. Two hands of blue flames gripped his head, and the Titan crumpled to the ground, lifeless. His death mask was frozen in a scream, his eyes wide open.

Persephone suddenly appeared, touching her earring as she stepped over his crumpled body.

"I apologize for taking the kill from you three, but I felt my way was easier. Once you did away with the obstacles, I was able to slip in and handle it before he fully recovered from controlling the Destroyer." Her eyes held Amphitrite's in apology, as if killing Perses was somehow Amphitrite's job.

Shaking her head, Amphitrite called her trident back into her ring.

"Whatever, he's dead. I don't care who got to kill him as long as he's going to the Underworld and not coming back."

Persephone gave a calm nod.

"Hecate is currently escorting his soul to Tartarus."

"Good, let's head back and finish this shit," Amphitrite stated as she light jumped away, followed by Finley and Persephone.

Viktor looked down to where Perses's body lay on the floor of the cave the Titan had found to house himself while he destroyed an entire city with his creation.

Without an ounce of remorse, he lit the body on fire, careful to contain the flames to the dead Titan, and light jumped when the immortal flesh quickly fell to ash.

His only goal now was to get back to Hera.

# Chapter 32

### <u>Hera</u>

S LOW CLAPPING SOUNDED FROM behind Hera, distracting her from where the Destroyer had disappeared in the middle of battle, fading away like literal dust in the wind. The others must have managed to take out Perses, and while that was a relief, the asshole currently walking up behind her was a whole other level of bullshit.

Feeling the oily taint of his presence, Hera stood taller before she turned to face her father. Never again would she cower before the man who had murdered her family.

As she turned, she took him in. The first time in millennia she had looked upon his face. He looked the same ... only not as terrifying as he had when she was a little girl. She remembered clearly the long black hair and purple eyes, but he seemed nowhere near as large as he had when she was a child.

She felt like Tartarus should have done something to change him. Hera supposed if you were already an evil monster, hell wouldn't do much to change anything. All the evil in him was already there.

Hera had never faced him as a goddess, though. No matter what he tried to do, she needed to remember who she was now. She was no longer the mortal child that he had hunted.

*No*, she thought as her lightning built back up in her palms, *I am powerful*.

She would destroy this man, father or not, she thought as thunder rolled over the city.

"Ah, then let the battle begin, daughter!" He laughed, standing in the center of the road several yards in front of her. She watched as massive portals opened behind her father, and people in Sereian uniforms passed through into the city. They were led by Atlas and Crius, who she had hoped would never see the light of day again after the battle in the Underworld. Other Titans, like Cronus's brothers, not by blood like the myths stated but by their greed, followed. She watched Iapetus, Hyperion, and Coeus as they took their places beside Crius and Atlas.

Behind her, she felt the arrival of Viktor's light jump, and he provided a warm, supportive presence at her back. Iapetus watched Viktor with a familiarity that made Hera uncomfortable. Looking from Iapetus to Viktor, she saw the similarities. *Ah*. It looked like she was not the only one fighting against her own blood. She remembered then that Iapetus was the father of Prometheus, making Viktor his grandson.

What a normal, happy, and healthy family tree they had all sprung from.

There were many other Titans Hera could hardly remember the names of, but it didn't matter. They were standing on the wrong side of the battle and would join Cronus in returning to the nightmare that was Tartarus soon enough.

Hera eyed the many enemy soldiers, and she was finding it difficult not to show her concern. Though they stood behind Cronus, their eyes clear—not in a spelled or drugged haze. She wondered how many of them knew *why* they were fighting.

Were they fighting because they believed the cause? Or because they feared death and retribution?

"I see the emperor decided to cozy up to you. I knew he was an idiot," Hera gritted out, staring at the Imperial insignia.

Coeus barked out a laugh. "The emperor has been dead for well over thirty years, silly girl."

With her heart rate picking up, Hera took a step forward before a staying hand grabbed her elbow. Viktor.

"Let me guess, you've been playing emperor for him?" she asked, already knowing the answer. How else could the Titans have sown dissent so deep in the land? How else could they have an entire nation's army at their backs?

Coeus changed before them, morphing into the Sereian Emperor she remembered: the dark eyes and thinning hair, short and fat. Coeus let the illusion go, returning to his tall, blond, curly-headed self, and smirked at her. "So, you see," he said, gesturing back to the Sereian Army. "You've always been outnumbered."

Hera glowered.

"We have this," Viktor whispered as he placed a hand on her shoulder, picking up on her shock and fear through the bond. "Stay with me and don't let him get into your head."

Nodding, Hera lit her hands with lightning, the electricity buzzing around her skin as it moved up and over her body. She was done talking.

Cronus lifted his fist into the air, and the army behind him, whether willing or not, all shifted into position, widening their stance. The movement sent a menacing ripple through the mass of humans.

"You are outmatched, daughter. I would say you need to get more people, but the less you have, the quicker this nasty business will be, and the sooner I will reign victorious. And I have such grand plans."

Almost as if Cronus's words summoned them, the last remaining part of the Halcyon army loyal to her moved in behind her, led by Cassandra in her goddess form, her leathers creaking as she marched them into battle. Edie flew over the army to Hera, bringing her attention to another army coming in from the sea to the South.

The Atlanteans wore modern gear for warfare, bulletproof vests, tactical gear, all in black, but their hair was braided in honor of their culture, the war bands on their arms matching West's cuff. Edie sent her an image of West greeting General Markos, grasping forearms.

Cronus hummed thoughtfully at the sight of the Atlanteans, looking unsettlingly hungry.

"I was wrong. Let's get this started then!" Cronus yelled, throwing his hands to his sides, and the armies at his back ran toward them, clashing with the Halcyon forces behind her. The Atlanteans moving in as reinforcement.

Hera and Viktor light jumped past the mortal armies to the Titans who hid behind them. Amphitrite, West, Devon, and Persephone followed.

A contingent of soldiers abandoned the fight against the combined army to protect the Titans. The Titans let the humans throw their bodies at the Olympians, which only managed to further enrage Hera. Once again, the Titans proved how little they cared for the mortals.

Hera hit them with bolts of lightning, and West flung them out of the way with waves of water as vines pulled them into alleyways, where wraiths waited in the darkness. But they kept coming. The soldiers renewed in an endless line, each new round running full steam ahead even after seeing what had happened to those in front of them.

Bolts of silver and gold whooshed past her, hitting the humans closest to her, and Hera looked up to see Kiran and Finley on the rubble above them, Finley of moonlight and Kiran of sun, striking the people down with their arrows.

One of the Atlantean soldiers fell to the ground, having taken a knife to the throat, and Hera felt a helpless rage at his death. Kiran turned and hit him with an arrow of light, the man's body arcing off the ground and lighting up.

"Kiran!" Hera shouted in reproof, but when she looked back at the soldier, he was standing back up, blood no longer pouring from his body. Hera turned back to look at Kiran, who only gave her a smirk and salute.

"He has always been such a righteous, pompous asshole. Good thing he is on my side, or I'd fry him," she muttered to herself as she concentrated on the battle.

"Behind you!" Amphitrite yelled at Hera. She spun around just when Calista showed up, slicing a man's arm as he snuck up to attack Hera while she was distracted by Kiran's frustratingly helpful magic. Behind Calista were some of the most beautiful women Hera had ever seen, all of them radiating the lusty power of the sirens.

Amphitrite's spies. Spies who looked more like they belonged to Calista now that the woman was immortal.

"Let's get to work, ladies," Calista ordered, and the spies moved forward, following close behind the goddess. The men in their path suddenly halted as if in a trance. Calista walked up to the one right in front of the group and ran her fingers over the man's chest before she whispered in his ear. Turning, the soldier fought the men on his own side, making sure to protect the gods and goddesses instead of attacking them.

"Alright, that is pretty damn useful," Amphitrite stated as she watched the sirens move through the small crowd that had formed around them, entrancing them to protect the people who were their enemies less than ten minutes ago.

A blast of heat tickled her shoulder, harmless to her, and she whirled around to see the end of an enemy projectile being incinerated. She looked at Viktor in his fiery form and mouthed a thank you to him for having her back. Two close saves in such a small amount of time rattled her, but she continued to send out bolts of electricity.

Farther into the battlefield, the Titans grouped together, and dread curdled her stomach. Hera needed to get to her father and end this once and for all, but there was an entire war happening between them. She stomped her foot on the hard ground and a static force field expanded from her footprint, pushing the combatants around her a few feet back.

The chaos of everyone converging on each other, swords and bullets flying, nearly overwhelmed her. It was an absolute mess Hera was unable to keep track of. Worrying for her people, fighting for her life, and trying to keep the Titans in her sight all at once was proving far more difficult than any battle she had fought alongside the mortals in the past.

West shouted, and Hera looked over to where several Atlantean soldiers were fighting a Titan. One of the soldiers separated from the group and charged the deity. No, not any soldier. General Markos. She darted forward, sending a bolt of lightning at the Titan, but she was too late to stop the Titan before his blade went through the General's thigh, cutting his leg off.

"Get him help!" she yelled, unsure of who she was yelling at. A flash of light was there and gone, General Markos gone with it. Her lightning had struck the Titan after his attack, and now his attention was back on her, allowing the Atlanteans to continue the fight.

Their numbers dwindled more than Hera liked, and she hoped it was just injured parties being taken away to get medical attention, but she knew that was wishful thinking.

"Still not enough, daughters!" Cronus yelled as the Titans moved out from behind him, now fighting alongside the army they had just been hiding behind as they gathered strength.

Amphitrite and Persephone flanked her now, filling in the space she'd made with her static field. The three of them lifted off the ground, levitating with the force of their goddess forms.

A sudden earthquake hit, causing soldiers on both sides to stumble. Hera shot a look at Amphitrite, who shook her head. *Not her doing then.*

The earth to the left of them cracked open, sending black smoke into the air. The Underworld army, a company of wraiths and Furies, spilled out behind Thanatos, his black armor glinting and moving like a second skin as he marched at the front, his eyes narrowed on Cronus with an intensity Hera had never seen in the Reaper before.

Turning back to her father, she smiled with all her teeth. On either side of her, her sisters transformed into their purest forms—beyond the goddesses, they became entities of raw power.

Water. Darkness. Electricity.

"We are far more powerful than we were as the innocent children you murdered!" she shouted, her voice traveling far with the force of her will. Cronus took in all the armies working their way to him, ready to unleash hell on his minions before sending him to Tartarus where he belonged. His eyes met Hera's, and he called up a purple orb of power, smoke billowing out from it, before pulling it back and sending it sailing toward Hera.

Hera thrust her palms out, sending an arc of electricity to meet his orb in the air. White and purple static exploded midair, thunder following. She grunted, her aggression rising, and cast a bolt of lightning down on her father. Cronus shielded himself, redirecting the bolt to the humans and killing several of them.

Hera's hands curled into fists as her sisters threw their own hits at Cronus and his brothers, but the Titans seemed impervious to their strikes—they even seemed to flourish from them. Cronus sent more orbs of dark power their way, sending them like grapeshot cannons; rapid and random.

Her sisters advanced toward Cronus while the other gods and goddesses handled the clash of armies. Hera wanted to search for Viktor, to make sure that he was okay, but she knew nothing could break her focus on Cronus.

Persephone aimed a beam of pure shadow at their father, and the hit landed, necrotizing Cronus's shoulder before it healed almost instantly. Cronus roared, and Hera felt satisfaction come off Persephone in waves.

Hera sent her intention to Amphitrite as Persephone cast her deadly power toward the Titans. Amphitrite nodded, her liquid form wavering with the movement, and she gathered all the many streams of water she had in the air into a single deluge leveled at Cronus. Hera summoned a storm above them, and the dark cloud released heavy rains to feed her sister's assault.

Levitating higher into the air, Hera couldn't see Cronus and the others through Amphitrite and Persephone's attacks, but she hoped this attempt would be enough to weaken them. She blasted pure electricity into Amphitrite's water, lighting it up and jolting the angry currents.

After a few moments of maximum effort passed, Hera and her sisters drifted back to the ground. At some point, they would have to cease the assault to see how the targets fared. At the same time, the water and lightning dissipated, leaving soaked and scorched ruins behind.

Hera gaped at what she saw. Cronus and his brothers crouched beneath a purple glimmering shield. The ground they stood on had been pushed nearly a foot deeper into the earth, the circumference of the shield lined with pulverized concrete.

Slowly, the Titans rose and straightened to their full height. Breathing heavily, Hera fell out of her purest form, back into her goddess, as her sisters did the same though they were in shock and exhausted. How could they defeat them if they couldn't even make a dent?

In a rapid move, Cronus pulled his shield into a massive scythe and swung it at Hera before she could throw up her own barrier.

Preparing herself for the hit, she was shocked when a giant cat made of fire jumped in front of her, roaring at Cronus as she absorbed the power meant for Hera.

Stunned, Hera tried to feel the power emanating from the animal, the realization of who had just saved her, shocking her even more.

"Nyx?" she asked, and the feline turned her fiery eyes on Hera, lowering her large head in a nod before turning back to Cronus. Gratitude and fear mixed within her. She hoped the Primordial came to fight for Viktor—and for her son, Thanatos—but she also knew her complicated relationship with Nyx just got a bit more twisted as she now most likely owed the old goddess a life debt.

Beside Nyx came Themis and who she assumed was Prometheus. He looked a lot like Viktor, and he was holding fire in his hands, so the odds were good she was right.

"Traitors!" Cronus roared at the Titans as Hera light jumped in front of Nyx and the others.

She refused to hide behind anyone.

"Hey, asshole," Hera taunted, "Looks like you get one chance to go back to Tartarus before I rip you to shreds and send you there, piece by piece."

"Tonight, you die, and so do all the traitors who stand beside you," Cronus growled as he unsheathed a sword covered in vibrant hydra's blood and brandished it in front of him.

"If I die, I'm doing everything I can to take you with me. No matter what, your ass rots in Tartarus. So, the question is, are you ready?" Hera yelled, her words echoing with the goddess's voice. All the troops, deities, and even Nyx roared a battle cry as Hera finished. The air along Hera's arms stood up at the pure power her people threw into it. The power they pushed into her, their queen.

For a small moment, less than a second, Hera shot a prayer to Chaos that she could save as many of her people as she could. That her army would stand strong through it all.

"End them!" Cronus yelled, his Titans moving in.

Hera opened her hands, lightning gathering between her palms.

It was time to finish this.

# Chapter 33

### **<u>Viktor</u>**

Keeping people off Hera was Viktor's main focus in a battle as large as this. And they came for her in droves.

He managed to use some of his fire to create boundaries around the humans fighting on their side, as well as to melt the guns that would end this fight far too soon. Viktor watched as Ryder zipped through the fight, moving faster than any immortal he'd ever seen, extracting the injured before they could be killed.

Devon fought alongside the Underworld army; vines and wraiths moving through the group.

Kiran and Finley were taking them down from the rooftops with their arrows of sunlight and moonlight.

Cassandra worked her way through the deities who came too close to the humans alongside Calista, who would catch a soldier and press a kiss to his lips, rendering them unconscious or dead. He had some questions about that, but that would obviously have to wait to be addressed until after the battle.

Hera's lightning struck farther out, her powers not great for close range combat, but that was why he was staying close. As was Nyx, who tore apart plenty of Titans, leaving them far too injured to heal fast enough to do anything more than lie there as Hecate showed up with silver bonds to take them to Tartarus.

The emotions, the screams, and the fear bled into him, even with the wall he had built in his mind. There was no ignoring the macabre essence of war. No denying the echoes of the dead and dying. Even he was not powerful enough to shut that out.

One of the Titans unleashed a herd of rams made of dirt and clay, which trampled people as they ran toward the goddesses, but Persephone called four horses up from the ground, horses that looked far too similar to the fabled four horses of the apocalypse. They met the ram's head on with shadowy hooves, returning the creatures to dust.

Looking out over the battle—the humans, Atlanteans, harpies, Hecatonchires, witches, new Olympians, and Titans all in one chaotic clash—Devon's green dragon flew over them, shielding where it was needed. Edie was in the air too, swooping down on the humans, picking off weapons, saving many mortals mere moments before being beheaded. She was much larger than her bird form had been when she'd been at his house, watching over him.

He knew West had his sea creatures at the docks should anyone try to run to the water, and from the way he put it, it would not end well for anyone, mortal or immortal, should his Leviathan get a hold of them.

The Titans had come prepared, yes, but the goddesses had deities and creatures in all shapes and forms fighting for them.

Sensing a spike of animosity toward Hera, he spun around and melted a poisoned dagger in mid-air. His heart raced as he took his place next to Hera once again, close enough to see Cronus's eyes.

And he was staring at Hera with a hatred that Viktor could not imagine a father feeling for his child. But Viktor knew better—he remembered Hera's mortal days well. This was no father; this was a monster.

Cronus roared and threw his hands out, and purple threads of magic expanded around his fists. He charged toward Hera, and his power deepened to something darker, transforming into a beam from his hands as he held them forward. Anyone in his path—on his side or not—fell like dead weight.

Viktor knew that Cronus held his own death magic. Magic not of the witches, but of his own power. The power that was bestowed on him as Titan. And distantly, a part of him recognized that this was it. Cronus's real move. He was going to strike in the confusing crush of battle after luring Hera closer, making her fight through armies to attack him.

Everything seemed to move slowly and quickly all at once.

Before Viktor could do anything, Kiran was in front of her, and the beam of death magic hit him right in the chest, his body taking it all in before collapsing to his knees. A nearby human in bloodied Sereian regalia took his chance and sliced at Kiran, sending his body falling to the side from the blow.

Viktor watched in horror as Kiran fell to the ground, not moving.

Hera let her power go, sending out an air-shattering lightning bolt that forked above them. The soldier burned from the electrocution and collapsed, but the other, more powerful, bolt pushed Cronus several yards back before he could land another hit. She fell to where

Kiran lay, the battle still raging around them as she tended to her senator.

Viktor and her sisters stepped up and covered Hera. He sent fireball after fireball at Cronus, but the bastard was already behind his barrier of power again.

Devon's dragon came down from above and settled around them, creating a shield to protect from any other bursts of power from the Titans.

They would keep Hera safe.

All of them.

### <u>Hera</u>

Hera fell to the ground, crawling to Kiran and rolling him onto his back as she smoothed the bloody hair from his face. He was in horrible shape, the blast of magic leaving raw, exposed, burned skin on his chest. Some areas so burned she could see bone and his face had been sliced in half, temple to neck.

"I ... saved you..." He tried to smirk, but his face was far too injured. The blood was pouring from him, puddling around his exposed teeth before leaking out of his mouth. Hera let out a mix of a sob and a cry as she held him.

"You stubborn idiot," she cried. "You've been so mad at me, and I've hated every minute of it."

Reaching up to touch her hair, he tried to give her a weak smile, his hand falling as he was unable to keep it up long, his body losing strength.

"Someone help!" Hera yelled, looking around and seeing that everyone was busy fighting while she was being guarded by Devon's dragon. Out of the corner of her eye, Finley was still picking people off with her arrows, but she was distracted, going between the fight and her brother.

Hera looked back to Kiran, holding him as he tried to speak more, the war raging around him so loud it drowned out the words he tried to push out. He was getting far too weak. Shouldn't he be healing at least a little bit?

"Was … never mad … at you. I…" He coughed, blood splattering her clothes, but she didn't care. "I was … mad … at myself."

"Don't you fucking die, Kiran. You're immortal now. Don't you dare give up so easily when I know you're a stubborn bastard through and through. Stay with me, okay?"

Kiran tried to say something, but his body was weakening, and Hera watched, her heart dropping, as Kiran's face went slack.

"No, no, no…." she whimpered. "You're my friend. I need you here, please!"

A hand landed on her shoulder, and she looked up to see Ryder standing over her in his godform.

"I will take care of him, Hera," he whispered.

Not Archon, but Hera. Tears sprang to her eyes as she placed her hand over his, squeezing it before letting go so that Ryder could take Kiran.

Pushing up from where she knelt on the ground, Hera tried to compose herself as she stood. Swallowing, she looked up to see Cronus smiling at her through her friends and family. The ones who remained. The ones he planned to kill. His smile broadened before he took a bow, as if to end a scene of some morbid play he had going on in his own mind. He had killed her friend with a blow meant for her, and he was taunting her. It was all a game to him.

As Ryder disappeared in a blur with Kiran, Hera called all of her powers. The sky responded to her as rain showered down upon them, and thunder shook the ground as she walked through the green energy field of Devon's dragon, past the wall of protection that her friends and family had made. She stopped to stand in front of them. To stand between her father and her family.

Hera began to glow brighter, pulling in all the electricity from around them, the city, the atmosphere, even the earth. It all streamed into her, leaving her skin shining like a star before a loud scream tore through her body, the buildup of so much energy tearing her apart at the seams. Finally, unable to take it any longer, she looked down at a smirking Cronus, her power having made her levitate above them all, and let out a battle cry as she unleashed a wave of power that blew back all of his remaining army and Titans. Some of them turned instantly to dust, while others fell onto the ground in broken heaps, and those at a distance tumbled back several feet. Hecate and her witches moved in fast to contain the felled Titans.

But, somehow, Cronus withstood it all. From the dust scattering around him, he had used his own people to shield him.

Lowering to the ground, Hera stared at her father. The world went quiet between them as she focused solely on him; the battle continuing to rage with the ones that survived her powerful blast.

Fewer pieces on the game board, as the Moirai would say. Their deaths were all a cosmic joke between powerful deities.

Looking over her shoulder, she found Themis and gave her a look, to which Themis nodded in understanding. Finding Viktor, she gave him a smile, one that had him shaking his head. He could always read her so well.

"I love you," she mouthed, knowing that if she gave voice to the words, she would break down and call off her plan. She clenched her jaw and faced her father.

"Hera!" Viktor yelled, and she used his scream as her starting pistol. She darted toward Cronus, who smiled at the challenge and sheathed his sword dripping with Hydra's blood before he ran toward her.

When they met in the middle of the battlefield that had been her city, the whole world lit up with the power of her light jump.

# Chapter 34

### <u>Hera</u>

Meaning to take Cronus from the battle to the Underworld with her light jump, Hera was shocked when they landed in a familiar field. Somehow, Cronus had managed to subvert her light jump at the last moment before their location was determined.

And now they were in the field of her childhood home. The one she had razed to the ground herself in anger after her sisters had died here, burning the house filled with the stench of death and dried blood.

Glaring down at Cronus as he laughed, she pulled her fist back and punched him in the face before jumping up, grabbing his sword from the sheath as she did so.

"We finish what we started, where we started it." Cronus smiled as he stood up, gesturing around them. He stretched his fingers as he prowled toward her. One of them would be going to the Underworld as a resident and the other a visitor. She just had to make sure she was on the temporary side of that arrangement.

Hera was exhausted, her body sparking, and she knew before she looked down that her soulmark was once again dormant. Not the same as it was before, the connection was still there, but something was blocking her from accessing it.

"I learned that trick long ago so that your mother would never suspect anything." Cronus nodded to her dormant mark.

Hera's eyes widened. She thought Persephone was the first to forge a soulbond since the ancients ... but perhaps her parents had been. That betrayal stung even deeper. The thought that not only had he betrayed his children, but he had also betrayed his soulbond. Then something Eros had said when she tried to bond with Viktor clicked in her exhausted mind.

"You forced mother into a soulbond? How?" She looked at Cronus's arms and saw nothing. There was no mark to indicate he'd ever had such a connection with another person.

"I never said I was her soulbond, but as you've seen yourself, it is possible to live an alternate life thinking yourself in love or not in love with someone." He laughed. "Honestly, how do I keep surprising you?"

As bone-tired as Hera was, it took her far too long to put it all together. Eros had stated there had been people before who forced the bond. Could someone trick another into believing they were meant for each other in that way? Eros would not have joined such a pair. Another puzzle piece clicked into place.

"You bastard! You forced a fake bond with her! You messed with her memories."

And Hera knew he'd done it. Knew he was capable of it. Somehow, he had created a bond that didn't exist, a fake soulbond, using magic to create a false mark and connection that was one sided. Her mother never knew she was a prisoner in her own marriage.

Her lightning sparked up her body again before flickering out almost instantly, and her hands clutched the hilt of his sword at her side until her knuckles went white.

Cronus let out a laugh.

"I thought you were powerful now, daughter!"

Cronus was in her face the next moment, and she stumbled back, falling to one knee when she tried to push herself back up again. She blinked slowly, the field around her blurring. Cronus grabbed her by the throat, pulling her up to meet his eyes.

"You shame me," he spat in her face. "To see my progeny so *weak*." He tightened his hold. "So pitiful."

Hera tried to swallow, but he held her throat too tight, and her vision darkened at the edges. How long had she been fighting? Was it hours or a thousand years? Two thousand? Three? Her limbs felt like stone, but she lifted her sword arm marginally.

"How have you managed to rule for even a century?" he snickered. "You, the runt of the pack. Always so desperate."

Hera grunted as she thrust the sword into his side. A hiss left his lips, and he dropped her, grabbing his sword out of her hands.

"This toy is too dangerous for you, my darling daughter," he sneered as he sheathed the blade.

Hera struggled to rise from her knees. She had used too much of her power throughout the battle and had only been able to run at him on pure adrenaline. She needed a few minutes to repair the damage she had done to her own body.

Cronus had other plans, of course. Grabbing her chin, he bent over to get in her face.

"How does it feel to fail them all again? To lose everyone you love because you are too weak to finish the fight. The punishment for that weakness is *guilt*, daughter. You had to live with the guilt of being the only one to survive." At his words, she felt his powers lock on to her, keeping her motionless and unable to fight him back with the remaining strength she had left.

The world froze around them as he leaned into whisper in her ear, "How does it feel to live life as a failure? A killer by inaction alone? I love the feel of your suffering, almost makes me want to let you live..."

Cronus shoved her away, releasing her as she fell.

"But I won't. I will release you from my power in a moment. You are weak, and I hate it when my prey does not fight back," he growled before his eyes glazed over as if reminiscing. "Oh, it was a joy to kill Amphitrite. She was good at holding me at bay, as I am sure Persephone would have been had I not surprised her. Demeter and Hestia went to their deaths like the boring little lambs they were in life."

Stepping forward, Cronus shoved her, and she fell back, still bound by his powers. His foot landed on her chest, pushing down on her sternum with his boot.

"Actually, I'd rather just be done with it all. I still have to finish off your sisters, anyway." He closed his hand into a fist and aimed it at her, before opening his hand and she felt a tug deep in her chest. She watched as her power streamed from her, his eyes beginning to grow a bright lavender.

"You are so dense." Hera let out a groan of pain, feeling like her muscles were separating from her bones as her back arched off the ground. But she still found the ability to open her hands, palms up.

His eyebrows furrowed as she pulled her magic back.

"How is that booboo on your side feeling?" she asked, voice rough.

Cronus looked to where his skin was turning black from where she had cut him with his own blade. The blade covered in hydra's blood.

Lifting her head, she looked him in the eyes as hers glowed gold.

"I am the queen, you piece of shit," she growled, feeling some of her power return.

"Bitch!" he yelled, releasing her powers and pulling his hydra blood covered sword from the sheath.

Her body was far too weak to do much more than lie there. She laughed at him as he raised the blade over her, smiling the same smile he had earlier on the battlefield.

"Checkmate, asshole." She laughed as his face contorted with pure wrath. Staring him in the eyes as she whispered words in the language of her youth.

As he slammed the sword into her, she grabbed his ankle and pulled them into a light jump, hoping she didn't miss her moment, as the timing had to be precise. Hoping and praying the small amount of power she took back from Cronus didn't fail her. That it was enough to take them both to their final destination before he shoved the blade into her body. Then she did the only thing she could think of.

Her Plan B in all of this.

She allowed herself to die.

### Viktor

"Where is she?" Viktor roared as West tried, and failed, to calm him down. Devon stood in his way, his hands up as he tried to keep Viktor under control. His entire body was on fire, his chest heaving as his anxiety climbed with every moment she was missing.

A sudden tingle had run through Viktor's soulmark mere moments after she disappeared, and when he had looked down, the mark went dormant, turning black again. He could still feel a connection, but he couldn't call out to her, and he couldn't trace her power to go to wherever she was.

"We will find her." Devon tried to keep Viktor's focus on him as the battle around them calmed. The Sereians that were left were overtaken, waving the white flag once Cronus was no longer there.

Apparently, Cronus alone was the one holding the leash on his mindless armies.

Without their leader, the humans and witches, who had been enthralled were confused and angry. The humans who had fought under their own volition tried to run, but the Underworld army moved faster than they could, and either killed them or brought them back to be jailed.

The injured, humans and mortal deities alike, were being cared for. The dead were being taken to the Underworld.

The Titans had no one to hide behind any longer and were taken down by the other gods and goddesses, as well as Hecate, who bound them and moved them to the Underworld.

All except Finley, who lay next to her brother, holding his hand. Viktor had no idea if he had crossed to the realm of the dead, but he would worry about that after he found Hera.

Suddenly, Viktor couldn't feel Hera anymore at all, and the loss sent a bone-deep pain through him. One that rivaled the pain he'd felt when he lost her the first time.

The first time, it was his curse that took her from him. Now it was Cronus.

Anger boiled his blood, and he spun around to find Persephone and Amphitrite. From the looks on their faces, they could no longer feel her anymore, either.

Thanatos stepped up to them, his black armor covered in blood and his brow heavy.

"Go," he told Persephone. "I will move the souls through. We need someone on Tartarus right now," he told her before he turned and started shouting orders at a man Viktor guessed was Thanatos's second in command. Shadows that were very corporal soldiers just moments ago streamed along the ground, making their way to the base of the mountain. Turning back to them, Thanatos looked them over. "I can handle it from here if you need to split up to find her."

"Yes, please keep me informed if I am needed." Persephone stepped forward, placing a hand on Thanatos's shoulder, which was the only part of the man not covered in someone else's blood.

"Of course, but I am taking a very, very long vacation after this," he stated, and Viktor was almost sure the death deity was not joking. Thanatos' eyes held a fatigue that Viktor knew was soul deep. He couldn't fathom how long Thanatos had been in dire need of escape. It was the look he saw on the faces of soldiers who'd returned from war; not broken—past broken.

Persephone nodded thankfully, and as she turned back to face them, her eyes suddenly went black, and she stumbled. Devon was immediately there to hold her up, his hand around her waist, but her black eyes only stared off before a pitch-black tear bled from her right eye.

"No!" Persephone cried out so suddenly that Viktor jerked his head around, looking for another enemy encroaching on them.

West and Amphitrite had similar responses, and Devon already reached for his weapon. Persephone clutched at her chest and fell to her knees.

Viktor looked over at Thanatos and saw that his eyes were black as well. No scream left him, but instead a curse left his lips.

"Hera is in the Underworld," Thanatos whispered.

"How?" Amphitrite stated, "If she light jumped there, we would have felt her."

Turning to look at Viktor, her eyes having returned to the mortal blue, Persephone gave him a look that froze his heart and soul.

With watery eyes, Persephone spoke the words he hoped to never hear. That he had spent lifetimes trying to keep from ever hearing.

"She is dead. I felt her soul cross over."

# Chapter 35

### <u>Hera</u>

"Fates damn it, death shouldn't hurt," Hera groaned, rolling onto her hands and knees, trying not to throw up. Themis had better know what the hell she was doing, or Hera was going to haunt the damn Titaness for all of eternity.

"What did you do?" Cronus yelled from behind her.

*Oh, right. He was here, too.*

Pushing up onto her feet with wobbly legs, Hera tried to reorient herself. Dizziness and battle fatigue made her off kilter. Apparently, death wasn't as restful as she'd hoped.

"I got the express pass," she tried to joke, but wow, she was done for. She had never known such exhaustion before. "Straight past the judges, straight past the Lethe." She waved her arm from where she was bent over, trying to fully stand up. "And here we are. First in line for eternal damnation!" she exclaimed as she threw out her other hand.

Joking would keep her from breaking down. Keep her from remembering the look in Viktor's eyes when he realized she was apologizing for what was about to happen. For the sacrifice she was about to make so she could make sure they all lived.

Chaos couldn't have them. Not yet anyway.

*No, don't think about them now or you'll break. Stay strong.*

Hera was an idiot, but she was doing what she had to do to protect them.

Being that Cronus would never willingly go to Tartarus, Hera had only one choice left when she realized letting him stay in that battle, protected by his minions, would mean they would lose.

And that was not a loss she was willing to let happen.

She had tied her goddess to him through a blood bond, one that he solidified by stabbing her with the same blade she had cut his side with.

He was tied to her, and when the Hydra blood slid into her heart, she let the call of death have her.

Hera took in the terrain behind her father, the whole of Tartarus. The sky was a murky purplish black, yet still light enough to see the dead trees and hellish landscape with pits of fire and a dilapidated castle. In the distance, red lightning struck the ground, throwing up chunks of earth, fires starting from where it hit trees.

A hellish nightmare.

*Fuck,* she thought, as several of the Titans she had just sentenced to eternity here slowly walked up to watch her face off with her father.

The prison warden was with the inmates for eternity. She was not looking forward to the time she was about to spend here. Not at all. Maybe after five or ten thousand years, they'd get bored with torturing her and find a new hobby. Crius looked like he'd take up knitting. Atlas looked like maybe he'd be good at home repairs.

Cronus looked like the type to kick puppies for fun.

"You bitch," Cronus growled as he stalked toward her.

"No one to get you out now, Daddy. As soon as I moved past the veil of Tartarus, it was sealed back up twice as strong by Hecate." She hoped. She was relying completely on Themis to keep everyone else alive long enough to make sure this war was done and over. "Looks like most of the gang is in here with us."

Themis would have a Fates-damned nightmare of a time with Viktor when he found out her part in all this.

As Hera looked down at her arm, a whimper left her lips. Now that she was beyond the veil, her soulmark was black ash once again. The connection severed by death.

Such a short time with Viktor after such a long wait to have him again.

Allowing herself a moment to wallow, Hera let a single tear slip down her cheek before pushing the feeling away and wiping her face.

"I will make sure you regret this for all of eternity," he seethed as he pointed his finger at her.

"That's the thing. I chose this, and in doing so, I saved everyone I love." Stepping into Cronus's personal space, she spat, "So. It. Was. Worth. It. Asshole."

Cronus laughed again; the laugh was far too maniacal for her liking. Had he always been this unhinged? Or had his time in Tartarus pushed him even further out into insanity?

Putting two fingers in his mouth, he let out a sharp, piercing whistle.

"I made friends when I was last here, so I guess if I am stuck with you, I might as well introduce you."

Hera watched as black, oily creatures crawled out of trenches, ignoring the Titans standing around as they clambered toward her.

As much as the terrifying landscape troubled her, the oily creatures stilled her breath. She took in their strange anatomy: their sharp needle-like teeth; six legs that cracked as if breaking each time they put weight on them; necrotized skin hanging on their odd skeletons; their limp, bat-like wings that looked like they were broken, dragging behind them. The oil dripping from them seemed to be acidic as it hit the dirt.

"When you first sent me here, I met these lovely creatures. Sadly, they truly love flesh, and I never had enough to feed my pets. Took several times of being shredded apart myself before I figured out how to control them. But with you here." Cronus smiled. "I can give them fresh meat as often as possible."

The creatures let out an excited noise that was bordering between a grunt and a chitter. The closer they came, Hera noticed they had no eyes. Their faces, if they could be called that, were dominated by a massive snout that twitched as they picked up her new scent.

Stumbling back a step, she kept her eyes focused on the three monsters. Her father laughed, as did many of the Titans behind him.

"Feast my little beasts!" Cronus yelled, and Hera tried to stand strong, bracing herself for the attack as they launched in an awkward gallop toward her at his words.

Oh, this was going to hurt.

*A lot.*

## **<u>Viktor</u>**

Viktor had no idea if a goddess's soul left their body like the mortals.

Having not realized he had asked aloud, he jolted when Persephone answered him.

"When I was close to death, I left my body, but I had not yet died. I, too, am unsure of how it works with immortals since we are not meant to know true death."

"My father's body is still here..." West whispered, and Amphitrite pulled him into a hug that he reciprocated. Placing his head atop hers, he held her tight, both of them keeping each other up. They were both dead on their feet, battle fatigue evident on their faces, yet they refused to leave the war zone.

Devon stood off to the side, arms crossed. Viktor was sure he was just as tired but was better at hiding it. Viktor had seen him fighting with a skill that was borderline scary. Stopping bullets with a green shield, he'd thrown out vines to pull the enemies away from Persephone as she summoned her wraiths. It was when an enemy got close enough to attack him with a knife or sword that he moved in a smooth cadence, taking the enemy down in hand-to-hand combat as if there was nothing to it.

"Maybe she is at the crossroads? Like you, when you were injured?" Devon asked, but Persephone shook her head.

"No, she's still in the Underworld. Only just got there, actually."

"Where?" Viktor asked. Maybe Persephone could get there quick enough to intervene. "Where in the Underworld is she?"

Persephone closed her eyes, shadows rising around her as she concentrated. When her eyes opened again, they were pure black. The goddess was looking at them now, not Persephone. And she wouldn't have any of the concern or familiarity that would allow her to break the news of Hera's position to them gently.

Viktor prepared himself, ready to light jump wherever he needed to in order to get Hera back.

"Where is she?" Viktor asked the goddess this time.

"Tartarus," she replied, her head twitching toward him, and he assumed those black eyes were studying him. Closing her eyes, Persephone took back over, and Devon took her arm as she blinked her blue eyes back open.

"Tartarus," Persephone herself whispered, horrified. "With Cronus."

Before he could ask how to get there, how to get Hera out, Persephone disappeared into shadows. Viktor was quick to follow on her heels, letting the feel of her power pull him to the Underworld. He had never been there before and wouldn't know where to go otherwise.

Fire wrapped around him and disappeared again, leaving him on the banks of a river of pure flame, the sand along the bank inky black.

Finding Persephone quickly, he followed her as she walked down the shore, carefully moving around bones sticking up from the sand and the creatures sorting through them. It did not take long for Viktor to realize this was a graveyard, the bones of dug-up bodies or from others just not bothering with burying them in the first place.

He felt the power of Amphitrite, West, and Devon follow him, and together they walked past huge boulders that looked out of place among the sandy cemetery. Before he could comment on it, Persephone approached a gate, alone in the middle of the burial ground, out of place just as the large boulders were. He was assuming the boulders were to hide the gate, and when Cronus escaped, this was the result of it.

"Is that the gate to Tartarus?" he asked Persephone, who stared down at it. Persephone only nodded as she knelt by it, her fingers moving lightly over the runes. "If you open it ... we can get her out?"

Persephone bowed her head. A drop of water hit the runes, and he realized she was crying.

"That would release everyone we've put there," she responded, her voice low and solemn. "All of the work during the battle would be undone."

Viktor fell to his knees beside the gate, staring at it in shock. She was down there with every enemy she had put away. There was no way she would be in any shape to slip out should they even attempt to open the gate.

Devon walked to Persephone's side, kneeling next to her, and pulling her against him. Turning her head into his neck, she trembled and sobbed.

Amphitrite was crying behind them, with West speaking soothing words to her as he held her tightly in his arms as well.

Viktor put his head in his hands, his own eyes tearing up. Hera was gone. She had sacrificed herself to make sure her father was secured in Tartarus. How it all went down, he had no idea. But the surety in Persephone's confirmation that Hera was there ... he wanted to balk and tell her she was wrong. There was no way that Hera was in there. That the universe would never be so cruel.

Now his soulbond was gone, and he didn't have a tether to the mortal world to pull his soulmate back. To bring her back to life. To this world. To him.

But he knew that as selfish as the world thought she was, Hera did all this for the guaranteed safety of her family.

She was in there, and she was not going to be able to escape. If he were to open the gate and the Titans escaped, her sacrifice would be in vain.

"Why..." he croaked, his word breaking on a sob as he laid his hands on the stone gate. "Come back, please..."

"If she died and her soul crossed, what happened to Cronus?" Devon whispered to someone nearby.

Viktor didn't care what happened to Cronus, didn't care where that bastard was rotting away for eternity.

Memories of his time with Hera ran through his mind. Of the time before she ascended, when they were young lovers, to the time when he saw her again in person, standing tall as Archon. He had always known she was strong and capable, and she had made herself into someone important through all her guilt and pain. She'd said she felt weak, like a failure, but she was strength and fire. Everything he both loved and needed.

But she was gone. Her power. Her essence. Her soul. All gone, leaving him alone once again.

"How did he cross into Tartarus then? Maybe that is the answer to retrieving Hera?" Amphitrite asked.

"She died and took him to his death through a blood bond," Themis spoke, startling him. Viktor, so engrossed in his own pain, hadn't felt her power mingling with the rest of them. But now, he lifted his head slowly to glare at Themis with all the rage burning in his soul.

"You knew about this?" Amphitrite asked, her voice holding a lethal edge, but Themis ignored her as she focused on Viktor.

"If all other plans failed, she was to create a blood bond, get him as close to Tartarus as possible, and let him kill her. Then she could take him with her beyond the gate. Should she mistime any of it, she may end up dead by herself, which would mean going through the gates, the judges, and ending up in Elysium instead of Tartarus. She needed Cronus with her since the Underworld would recognize he had escaped and put him back where he belonged. She ... piggybacked, so to speak."

"And you let her do this?" Persephone asked in such a terrifying tone, her goddess form taking her over and making her look like a fallen angel bent on vengeance.

Themis simply closed her eyes before opening them again, revealing an apology there. One he had no intention of accepting or even listening to.

"I promised her," Themis replied.

Devon stepped up and put his hand on Viktor's shoulder to stop him from moving closer to Themis.

"And what promise was that?" Amphitrite demanded.

Themis shook her head slightly, tears in her eyes.

"That if I thought the war would not go in your favor, I would give her a way to make sure Cronus would not hurt those she loved." As she finished this statement, she looked right at Viktor. "That she would be the one to cross the gates, so you didn't have to."

Tears streamed down his face as he looked at the gate. Themis had confirmed his suspicions.

Sacrifice. She had put herself into actual hell to protect him, her sisters, Devon, and West.

"How do I get her back?" His voice broke as he looked from the gate to Themis, but Themis only shook her head, not looking at him any longer.

Closing his eyes, Viktor imagined holding her, making love to her, playing with her hair while she laughed and joked, and him telling her to be serious. He wanted to feel lighter again, like he had when he'd been so relieved his fire had accepted her as it did before. Like he had the night she gave herself to him, but slipped out before he could catch her, playing her cat-and-mouse game.

His thoughts stuttered to stop on the last memory. Of him rolling over to a note from his father and a vial sitting on his bedside table. He'd been too angry at the time to really take in what it had said, his mind more focused on finding Hera. He had read the note, but not really allowed himself to see it as more than an alternate timeline to avoid.

As Themis stepped back and the sisters took comfort in the arms of their soulbonds, Viktor pulled the object from his back pocket and looked at the vial in his hand. Opening the note again, he read Prometheus's scrawl. His handwriting had always been barely legible.

*Sometimes the field must burn, the land must die, as it did for your mother, as it will for your heart's soulmate, for there to be rebirth. Trust the fire. -Prometheus*

As usual, it made no sense. Was Viktor supposed to light himself on fire? That wouldn't kill him, and he certainly wouldn't rise from the dead.

Looking at the purple mercurial liquid, Viktor pondered what it all meant. What did he have to lose at this point? Trust the fire, right?

The fire could show multiple lines of possibility, and his father was asking him to trust that he'd done all he could do. Now, he had to take a leap of faith.

Damn, he hated it when his father was right.

# Chapter 36

### <u>Hera</u>

H ERA FELT THE FIRST bite into her flesh, the ripping of skin and muscle. The whole time, she could see Cronus in her peripheral, laughing in glee as the creatures tore at her.

A cry ripped from her lips unbidden. Her body arched in pain as another one of the beasts tore into her side, piercing vital organs.

How could she feel such pain without a physical body? Oh, but pain in the soul was so much worse, and this was the perfect torture. Absolute, perfect torture. Her sister was a genius.

The ear-piercing whistle sounded again, and the demonic creatures stopped, stepping away from her. The blood dripping from their mouths was all hers. She did not want to focus too much on the meat between their teeth.

As they stepped out of her line of sight, Cronus leaned over her, his hand slamming her shoulder down as Hera tried to flip back over onto her stomach.

"Shh, no. Fighting while they eat you alive is fine, but right now I need you to focus and listen, darling," Cronus whispered, his hands moving hair out of her face like she wasn't a bloody mess. All perfectly normal.

"Fu..." Hera tried to speak, but her mouth kept filling up with blood. Knowing it would cost her, she realized she didn't care and spit the blood into Cronus's face. Before it filled her mouth again, she spoke. "Fuck you. I may have to be here..." Blood dribbled out. "But at least I know you're here with me."

Cronus tapped her on the nose after wiping the blood off his face.

"And that, darling, is going to turn out to be your worst nightmare." As he leaned over near her ear, she felt her body repairing itself, but she knew he would remedy that after his next words. "Because now I have you forever. *Forever*. And I plan to take that time to destroy your soul."

The whistle sounded again, and the demons were once again upon her.

This time, Hera did not bother to hold back her screams.

## Viktor

"You have no idea what that vial will do to you." Persephone stepped in front of Viktor. "For Hera, I cannot let you do something without knowing what it could cost you. If you were to die, it would not honor my sister."

Looking Persephone right in the eyes, he saw the concern, but also the hope that maybe, just maybe, Hera wouldn't be alone in her torment if the liquid did in fact hold the key to her survival.

"If Devon was in there, what would you do?" he asked, watching emotions flicker over her face. He had put up the wall once he had remembered the vial, unsure of what exactly would happen. He did not need their mental anguish over the loss of Hera overriding his decisions, making him second guess this.

Viktor was in enough anguish all on his own.

Persephone stepped away from him, and Devon moved to take her into a hug, running his hands over her back.

Stepping forward, West put a hand on Viktor's shoulder. They were saying goodbye, which was probably for the best since Persephone was right—he didn't know what would happen when he consumed the contents of the vial. He hadn't thought to ask his father, and he doubted Prometheus would've told him.

"In case..." West took a deep breath and gathered himself. "Thank you for everything. You saved me in more ways than one. So... thank you."

West pulled him into a hug, and though Viktor was not used to such things, he allowed it. West needed it, and most likely, Viktor did too, if he was being honest. He could not guarantee survival. For him or Hera. Viktor gave West a pat on the back and stepped out of the embrace.

Amphitrite gave him a smile. Her eyes dropping tears down her cheeks with every blink of her aqua eyes. Being the person she was, getting anything past her was almost impossible, which was why he knew she was his best bet in reuniting with Hera. It was worth the hours of agony he had spent in the night after he dropped his bread crumb. He knew then everything would be worth it when he held

Hera in his arms again. And this would all be worth it if he could bring her back.

Looking at each of them, even Themis, who nodded, gave him the sense that he was making the right choice.

That was all he needed to start the trek to his damnation.

Taking the vial, Viktor popped the cork out and swirled the liquid in front of him before putting it to his lips. He took a small breath and tilted the vial back, swallowing all the contents.

His vision distorted, blackening at the edges as his body went numb. The world tilted sideways as everyone ran to catch him. His lungs tried to pull in air, but he couldn't get any oxygen in.

As he felt his heart slow and finally stop, he understood.

He finally understood.

It wasn't Hera's death the fires had seen.

It was his.

# Chapter 37

### **<u>Hera</u>**

KICKING ONE OF THE oily beasts, Hera tried to grab enough of the vile ground to pull herself out from underneath them, having healed enough to use her extremities finally. Cronus was allowing her small breaks, enough time to recover to fight the demons off, but not enough that she could do much more than try to crawl away.

*Nice of him, really. Asshole.*

She spit out blood, and the beast growled, dripping noxious spit. It moved to lunge again when an inferno suddenly overtook it, making Hera cover her eyes and look away. A horrible squeal left it before the beast went quiet, leaving only the two remaining demons.

When she opened her eyes, the demon was gone. Now, it was just ash floating in the air, adding to the ambiance of the hellscape.

The other beasts turned away from her, now scrambling to where their ugly brother had been preparing to make her his next meal before he was scorched.

Pulling herself away enough to roll onto her side, she tried to crawl with what little strength there was left in her broken body. She glanced back into the darkness where the demons held their grotesque noses in the air.

Shuffling on their weird legs, they moved to the black wall that was the edge of Tartarus, sniffing and looking for their new prey. Another beast blew up when it got too close, throwing the last member of the pack of demons into a frenzy of panic. The ugly thing struggled to run away, going in feverish circles, unsure of where the threat was.

Hera didn't care. She lay on her back, unable to move anymore as she let her body knit back together enough to make another attempt at escape. Anywhere was better than this. She needed to find a place where she could hide until she came up with a game plan.

At least she still had the ability to heal a bit quicker than a mortal down here, but not for much longer, as her power weakened by the minute.

"No! She is still alive!" her father yelled, whistling over and over again to get the attention of the remaining creature.

The other Titans shifted restlessly, getting antsy that the show could be over so soon.

In an instant, his shouting stopped.

Feeling intact enough to push up on her elbows, Hera saw why her father had stopped squealing like a stuck pig. A man of pure fire walked out of the darkness at the edge of Tartarus.

Was she hallucinating? He couldn't be that much of an idiot, but in that moment, she really hoped he was.

"How did you get in here?" Cronus seethed, and the man lifted a hand, sending a stream of pure white fire at Cronus. Hera kept her eyes on the figure as Cronus burned, his angry yells turning to pained screams. She wanted to laugh or cry, but she only had the energy to put her head back on the ground. The dizziness of her blood loss made her woozy, her healing slower now.

When Hera felt a gentle weight on her head, she blinked her eyes open, not having remembered closing them. The man of fire stood over her with his fingers brushing along her temples.

"Emrys?" she choked out, remembering her Emrys from the mountain. The one that held her so tenderly. *Viktor... he's called that now*, she remembered as her brain worked to come back online after nearly losing all her blood.

But in that moment, between life and true death, he was Emrys. Her love. He was not the man who pretended to be a cold, sterile therapist. He was fire and warmth and safety.

"Shhh," he soothed. That his fiery lips were able to make such a noise baffled her, but her bafflement turned to fear as he stood up, pulling his face from hers. She felt the words on the tip of her tongue begging him to stay, but in her heart, she knew he would never leave her. No, they had learned from their past. It took her a moment longer to realize he had placed himself between her and her father.

"You can try, Cronus, but you don't have the ability to do anything here. I have everyone on the other side of that gate ready and waiting should you try anything."

"You cannot escape either, bastard offspring. That gate is a one-way ticket. Once here, you're stuck," Cronus said smugly.

If Hera had the energy, she would have gotten up and broken every bone in the man's body.

Turning her head, she saw Cronus healing from some serious burns.

How come he wasn't healing as slowly as her? Oh, right ... she had already had to heal several times already, both on the battlefield and in this hell.

Cronus started walking towards her, his demon pet following closely behind.

Hera smiled as Emrys unleashed his fiery wrath on them all.

### West

"Is he dead?" West asked, poking at Viktor's shoulder.

Devon was next to him, pressing his fingers to Viktor's neck before shaking his head sadly. West jerked back and leaped to his feet, shaking his own head in denial.

"No, nope. The man was an emotional health nut. He would never kill himself," West responded, wiping his hands on his pants.

"Did he go to join her, or to bring her back? Is that possible?" Amphitrite asked, looking from Themis to Persephone.

"For once, I do not know the plan here," Themis said, her brows furrowed. "I had nothing to do with any of Viktor's choices here in the Underworld."

"Can you do something?" West asked, looking between Devon and Persephone. "Aren't you, like, queen and king here?"

"What would you suggest?" Persephone asked, and they all watched as West began miming a movement—intertwining his fingers, one hand on top of the other, and pulsing his arms up and down as he blew air loudly through his mouth.

"Make fish faces?" Devon guessed, as Amphitrite asked, "You want Devon to kiss him?"

"What? No!" West threw his hands up, walking past Persephone, who looked at the gates with contemplation, her arms folded.

"They know what you mean. They are choosing to let you act foolish for their own satisfaction," Persephone stated without looking at them, her entire focus on the situation at hand.

"Wow, thanks *friends.* Also, not the time," West muttered as he paced back and forth in front of the group, and Amphitrite grasped his hands with an apology in her eyes. West put his arms around Amphitrite and held her, kissing the top of her head.

A flash of silver and a dusting of shadows appeared, and Hecate and Thanatos materialized where Viktor's body lay outside the gate of Tartarus.

"Is he in Tartarus?" Hecate asked as she leaned down, feeling for Viktor's pulse and finding nothing.

"Did you have something to do with this?" Persephone asked as she swung around to look at Hecate and Thanatos, who did not look at all surprised that they had Viktor's body between them.

"I told you nothing happens in the Underworld that I do not know about," Hecate responded.

"That is not an answer to my question," Persephone retorted, a thread of anger in her voice.

Darkness slid over their group, moving like a dense fog across the sands, and a beautiful female formed, covered in black.

"She did only because I made a deal with her. A deal in everyone's best interest," the woman spoke.

Persephone shot a look at Thanatos, who held his hands up. "I only did it because my mommy made me."

"Not long ago, I asked that Hecate make a potion," Nyx stated bluntly. "I was concerned over some of the visions Viktor and his father had, and I wanted to be sure when the time came, he would not lose the woman he loved again." Nyx stepped forward and knelt beside Viktor across from Hecate, gently placing her fingers over his head.

"Will he come back? Can he bring Hera back?" Amphitrite asked, still secure in West's tight hold. His fingers dug into her side as if letting her go might result in him losing her, too.

"That is... not likely," Nyx stated, standing again. "It was for him to cross the veil to his love. The veil is stronger now, layered. He would not be able to move through it. Not without his powers, which Tartarus will leech from him as it does the others."

Hecate moved her hands over Viktor's chest.

"See? It was a good idea," West whispered into Amphitrite's hair.

Hecate placed her hands on Viktor's chest, a silverish glow coming from her fingers and spreading over him.

She looked up to the sky of the Underworld, and her eyes turned to liquid mercury.

# Chapter 38

<u>**Viktor**</u>

KEEPING CRONUS AND HIS flunkies back was taking too much of Viktor's energy. Not to mention the countdown ticking in the back of his mind. He still had his powers, but they would lessen the more he used them, since there was nothing to replenish them.

Cronus moved in on him with at least twenty other Titans behind him, their eyes brimming with blood lust at the prospect of finally taking down the goddess who had sentenced them to Tartarus.

A shiver ran up his spine when he felt the rocky terrain even out under his feet. He was near the edge of Tartarus.

And he just hoped he had enough gas in the tank to try for a trip home.

Cronus launched into a run, and Viktor threw out the last of his power reserved for fighting. His body strained as he fought not to overuse, to protect that last ember he'd need for later. If there was a later.

"Come on, come on," Viktor mumbled, hunkering down as he pushed even harder.

His feet slid back in the dirt, and he was careful not to step back onto Hera behind him. A sudden horrible pain in his leg had him looking down to see the cursed creature, the same one that had been on Hera, now biting into his calf. A surge of raw anger ran down through his body as the image of her prone, bloody form flashed in his mind. His fires flared even brighter with his anger, and his body's flames lashed out at the beast, sending it yelping.

Cronus was within mere feet now, and Viktor braced himself, meeting Cronus's glare with his own, as he called on the last of his power.

Nothing happened.

"Fuck," Viktor swore.

Cronus was now within reaching distance, and Viktor knew he wasn't going to make the light jump. There was not enough power left in him to do it. He glanced back to see Hera's face, her eyes straining to stay open, and he knew what he had to do.

If he couldn't take Hera home, he wouldn't leave her to this. He would take them out of here, but it would be by his fire. The very fire he promised to never let burn her.

But he wouldn't leave her here. They would just have to return to Chaos and hope, somehow, their souls would find each other again.

## Hera

Hera felt herself being shifted in Emrys's arms; unaware she had closed her eyes once again. She really wanted to sleep, but the movement and screaming was keeping her from finding her rest.

"Stay with me, my love. Almost there."

Where? They had been bound here for the rest of eternity. This was not some minimum-security prison where the guards were lax. With Cronus's escape, they had doubled up on security and made the veil infinitely stronger to avoid him ever escaping again.

There was just no way to pass back through the veil, especially since they would lose their powers here.

Hera's eyes flashed open.

"You still have your powers. You're not supposed to be here! Why would you ... how could you?" She was not at her most eloquent when she was healing from being near death, but she was finally catching up on the situation. "Doesn't matter though, does it? Maybe having your power will keep Cronus from messing with us down here. Even Persephone wouldn't be that much of an idiot to open the gate for us and risk the war starting all over again. At least, I hope not."

"Where you go, I go too. And, she isn't opening the gate," he replied, now standing still as he looked into her eyes, or she thought he did.

It was hard to tell when he was pure fire.

As he held her, she felt warmer and warmer, but not the familiar kind of heat she was used to feeling with him, and panic stirred in her chest. Her eyes widened as her skin burned, and Viktor held her tighter to his chest, apologizing over and over again.

Viktor was burning her. He was burning her alive!

"Emrys? Viktor!" she yelled as the intense heat stole her oxygen, the pain beginning to sear her nerve endings.

"I am so sorry, Hera, so damn sorry," he cried as they burned. "But I refuse to leave you here. True death is better than being here for eternity."

Once the pain hit a critical point, she lost consciousness.

*Finally.*

## <u>West</u>

Devon and West refused to leave until they knew what was going on. Hecate had given up thinking she could help him move across the veil with a light jump.

"He's officially dead, then?" West asked as Hecate sat back on her heels.

Thanatos stood behind her, rubbing her shoulders. The woman looked like she was about to lie down and take a nap right there.

"I thought I would be able to boost his powers, giving him enough juice so he could light jump if he made it close enough to the gate, but I wasn't able to," she whispered, her eyes downcast.

Persephone let out a cry of pain, and from the way Thanatos flinched, something had happened in their shared connection to the realm.

"What is it?" West asked as Devon rushed over to Persephone, who bent over like she was going to throw up.

Thanatos dropped to his knees, and his head fell into his hands.

"What is it?" Amphitrite yelled, her voice sharp with panic.

"They are no longer in Tartarus," Thanatos whispered.

A foreboding sense of dread filled the air. They were not going to like what came next.

"Well! Where are they?" Amphitrite demanded as she moved to Thanatos, standing over him with her arms across her chest. West joined her side but didn't touch her. She would turn to him for comfort eventually, but right now, she needed to get angry and get answers.

Thanatos met her prying gaze, and the tears in his eyes made Amphitrite's knees buckle, her hands hitting the ground as she sucked in desperate breaths. West moved to grab her, holding her as she let out a scream.

"Hera!" she yelled. *"Hera!"*

Nyx approached Viktor's body once again, squeezing her son's shoulder as she passed. Kneeling, she placed her hand on his chest, over his heart, and then on his head. A simple gesture, but one that felt ancient.

"May the Fates be with you and Hera in death. Bless you both on your travels to Chaos. May you both find your place among the stars," Nyx whispered, blessing him before standing and reaching out for her son's hand.

Shaking his head, Thanatos stood.

"I need to give him funeral rites ... both of them," he whispered hoarsely.

He wished he had Hera's body to bury, but he supposed if she was with Chaos now, she would not wander the Styx if he was unable to give her physical form a final resting place. Still, she would be honored in death.

Devon joined Thanatos's side, stalwart and ready to help carry Viktor's body. He knew that Thanatos could easily have lifted him alone, but he understood why they needed to do this for him. West came up to help as well, shock still written all over his face even as he honored the man who'd become a close friend in such a short period of time.

West and Thanatos held Viktor's shoulders as Devon grabbed his feet, and they lifted when suddenly Viktor's body heated up.

Dropping him and jumping back, they watched as his body combusted, flames reaching high into the air.

Then Viktor's body collapsed into ash, while at the same moment, a bird of pure fire soared up from where his chest had been. The bird flew in a circle above them before diving to the ground where Viktor had been, vanishing as it hit the black shore. The men dove out of the way as flames burst forth, burning so brightly that they all threw their hands over their eyes.

The fire burned out quickly, fading to the Underworld's normal darkness. Everyone dropped their hands to look at the scorched spot where the bird had landed.

On the ground, in the ash left behind, were Hera and Viktor.

Both very much alive.

# *Chapter 39*

### <u>Hera</u>

Hera's eyes flew open, and she tried to scream, but there wasn't any oxygen. Trying to pull in air, she gasped desperately. Her hands curled into fists with the effort, and she felt sand between her fingers, not the packed dirt of Tartarus.

And even as she struggled to inhale, she realized her body was no longer being torn apart or melting.

The more she regained the sense of wholeness in her body, the more oxygen she felt in her lungs. Her head rolled to the side, and Viktor was next to her, struggling to pull his own air in. His face was covered in ash, sand, and blood ... and he was very naked.

So was she. If she had the energy to be embarrassed—who was she kidding? She never cared before and wouldn't start now.

Viktor was speaking to her, but she couldn't hear him through the ringing in her ears. She could only focus on the trails of tears running through the ash, sand, and blood on his face.

Suddenly, the ringing stopped, and she could hear everyone's voices at once. Amphitrite and Persephone's were the absolute loudest.

She focused on Viktor as she tried to ignore everyone else.

"Hera?" he asked, voice rough. She coughed in response, her lungs feeling like they were still on fire.

"You idiot," she croaked out through her cracked lips.

"She is most definitely back," West said from nearby. "Personality and all."

"Let me check her out," Hecate's voice came seconds before the probing touches, but Hera could only stare at Viktor as he rolled to his side and took her hand in his, his other hand touching her jaw.

"I swore to you on that mountain I would always care for you." His voice was low and held so much meaning that she let out a laugh that sounded weak. Almost like a sob. Viktor pulled back enough to wipe away the lone tear that escaped her eyes.

"I've changed from that innocent girl you made that promise to," she rasped. "Thank you for saving me."

His hazel eyes, dirty and red as they were, softened, and it made her feel weaker and stronger at the same time.

"I love you," he said simply, as if it explained everything he'd done—and perhaps it did.

Another half-laugh, half-sob wracked her body.

"Well, I love you too, even if you were an absolute Fates-damned idiot to come after me."

A small huff of breath left his mouth as a smile tilted his lips. A bit of blood from where they were cracked welled up.

Viktor leaned in closer, but let out a hiss, and they both glanced down to see why their arms were burning. A small firestorm of electricity danced over their arms where the soulbond flared back to life, even stronger than before. Hera looked up into Viktor's eyes as the soulmark reformed on her skin, her hand going to his cheek as he moved his lips to hers.

It was a chaste kiss that meant more to her than any other kiss she'd had with anyone else.

"I get it now. It really is nauseating," West muttered from somewhere nearby as she kissed Viktor.

"That idiot survived, too?" she asked with a small smile against Viktor's lips. She glanced over her shoulder, looking past Hecate who knelt by her legs, and spotted a grinning West.

"Yes, but this display of affection between you and another living being might just kill me," West retorted, but he looked incredibly relieved. "Also, can we get Viktor some pants? I'm feeling my masculinity is being threatened right now."

Closing her eyes, the urge to sleep was growing more powerful.

"Persephone?" she called out, unable to keep her eyes open.

"Yes," a soft voice came from beside her, a light touch on her shoulder.

"Can you please take me and Viktor home?" she asked, not bothering to open her eyes back up, just basking in the feel of the safety, comfort, and love she only ever felt with Emrys.

"Of cou—" Persephone started, but she was cut off.

"I'll do it." The feminine voice came from nearby. "You make sure everything down here is secured. My son has gone back to the mortal realm to handle some lingering issues. I'd rather not ask him to come back again so soon."

Hera didn't recognize the woman's voice, but something tickled in the back of her mind.

Once again proving he could read her thoughts, Viktor whispered, "Nyx."

If Hera had the energy to roll her eyes, she would have.

### Viktor

As Viktor tucked a sleeping Hera into his bed, he felt a peace he'd scarcely felt before. For the first time in millennia, he was truly relieved. They'd done it. Somehow, they'd come out the other side of the war together, alive. And he was never letting her go again.

Everything was perfect—well, almost. Viktor had absolutely drained himself and wasn't sure he could reach that part of him at all right now. He really hoped he hadn't lost his powers entirely when he returned from Tartarus.

But if it was a choice between Hera and his powers, it would be Hera every time.

For a moment, he considered joining her in bed to rest, but he had one more thing to do.

Making sure she was sleeping peacefully under the covers, Viktor stood and walked out to the deck off his bedroom overlooking the forest.

"She is well now?" Nyx asked as she turned to him, tilting her head. It was weird to hear her speak outside of his head—and as a woman, no less. He couldn't see the look on her face through the black veil she wore, but there was concern in her voice. Even though they had their differences in the past, she still cared.

"Getting there. No longer a feline?"

Nyx let out a laugh that sounded too surreal. "No, I am no longer in need of that form."

"You were bound?" he asked, surprised such a powerful being could be bound in any way.

"It was by choice, I assure you. No one would dare force such a thing on me. They would not live to tell the tale if they even so much as tried."

"Huh," was all Viktor thought to say.

Nyx gave another laugh before leaning forward on the deck railing and releasing a sigh.

"Your mother may have been a fire deity, but she could only read the fires when night came," Nyx started, and Viktor's attention sharpened. "She prayed to me, or who she thought I was, so many times. Prometheus told me that the priestess who called for me was the mother of his child. The child that would fight the Titans, and I was all for taking those devils down, even if it was far, far in the future."

Looking out over the mountainous terrain, they both watched Edie soar in the dying daylight. She was the size of a natural eagle again, weaving a celebratory flight path through the trees surrounding his home. Nyx turned to him, placing her hand on his forearm.

"Prometheus foretold your mother's death. That she would use her fire to burn the village, herself, and the Romans invading it, to the ground. That you would survive and that she would bestow Hestia's powers on you. After a long chat, mostly arguing and possibly some maiming, I finally agreed to watch you for him." She shrugged lightly. "By that time, my sons had decided to go their own way in the Underworld, and I chose to stay with this new little Titan that held the fate of the world in his hands. I saw my young sons in you as you helped your mother tame the fire, night after night. I called night for her even during the brightest part of the day, just so she could have what she needed to ensure you were safe. Of course, I couldn't be near you as powerful as I am *and* remember who you were after your mother cursed you, so, like I said before, I took the form of her familiar once it passed on." She squeezed his elbow with affection. "I became your protector."

"You voluntarily took the form of a cat all this time to protect and guide me?"

She smiled at him, letting a small amount of her power leak out, and he felt a chill. Her power was *immense.* No wonder he was amazing at hiding his own powers when the person who taught him had been able to pass herself off as a simple feline spirit.

"You had to be hidden from the Titans who looked to use you. So, yes, I became a familiar. Instead of holding my own power close to the surface, I could push it deep as long as I was in the form of the Ovinnik. Something few of us can do, and most likely the biggest reason your father sought me out, and I was able to teach you. In doing so, I was able to be near you, guide you, and not trigger the curse."

"Did he have to clean your litter box, too?" Hera's voice came from behind him, and he looked back to see Hera holding herself up against the door frame. Even though he moved quickly to Hera's side, he did not miss Nyx's huff of indignation.

"Thank you, Nyx," Hera whispered to the Primordial Goddess with sincerity. "For everything."

Wrapping Hera into his arms, he looked to Nyx, who gave a small shake of her head.

"I hope you realize that your children will give you as much grief as you've given me, Queen Goddess," Nyx prophesied before leaving in a swirl of shadows.

"She is a powerful hellcat, I'll give her that, but I am glad she was on our side," Hera murmured into his shirt as he held her tighter.

"Me, too," he agreed.

"And she is right," she said as she looked up into Viktor's eyes. A small smile twitched at her lips. "Our children *will* be absolute terrors."

"I think some of my DNA will offset yours and calm them a bit," he stated as he brushed his lips against her forehead.

"I seem to remember a wrathful Fire God who's not so calm. Reaver's Paradise and Tartarus ring a bell?" she laughed quietly.

Viktor chuckled and pressed another kiss to her temple.

"Fine. I'm calm until you're in danger. I did wait thousands of years to break a curse and get you back, so I would say I'm at least *patient*."

"Well, when you put it like that..." she murmured as she pulled him into a searing kiss. His mind went blank with passion before he finally remembered what he was planning to do once she woke up.

Viktor finally gathered the strength to pull back, and he held up a finger, indicating for her to wait.

"Give me a moment. I have something for you that I promised I would give you as soon as we finished ... well ... winning this war."

"Wow, you actually thought we would win?" she asked, leaning back against the glass door as he moved to his briefcase on the floor. He flicked open the latches, revealing files for work. Work that was waiting for him. Waiting for the world and their lives to return to some semblance of normal.

Looking up at her, he smiled. "I never doubted it. You are far too stubborn to die."

"You mean to stay dead? Pretty sure I died two times now."

Viktor felt a coldness at her words. He wanted to plead with her to never allow that to happen again, but, with them together and her father locked away once again, he hoped their future would hold better things for them.

Stepping toward her, he handed her the small metal box. Giving him a surprised, but skeptical, smile, she took it from him and gave it a small shake.

"Hmm, I wonder ... is it my dignity? I could use some of that back after giving West the best show of his life, coming back from the dead naked as the day I was born."

"Just open the damn thing." He laughed as he leaned against the back of the couch and folded his arms across his chest. She raised her eyebrows in surprise.

"Oh, he swears? I need to up my game in the bedroom and get you to loosen up there, too. I could use some dirty words." She winked and opened the box, her face going from mirth to shock. "Vik—Emrys," she corrected and looked up at him with shining eyes.

"I made it before I lost you to the curse," he said quietly.

"I remember now. It wasn't the most romantic proposal." She laughed.

Viktor could only shrug.

"I was a young man with no money and trying to make sure I made it all official before we took off on some idealistically grand adventure."

"You had just gotten laid, you mean, and were in a state of post-orgasm bliss." She chuckled, taking the metal ring from the box. He had made it long ago—at least the band. Recently, he'd added two stones, the kind he would never have been able to find or afford as a mortal nomad: a deep red ruby and a bright yellow diamond. The two stones orbited each other on the ancient metal.

"It's perfect," she whispered as she stepped into his arms to kiss him. She only pulled back to put the ring on. Looking back up at him, she gave him the widest smile he had seen on her since he'd made his way back into her life.

Taking her face in his hands, he kissed his wife.

After so very long, he had her back.

His heart finally found the peace he had been searching for.

# Chapter 40

### <u>Hera</u>

"THERE IS A MEETING in fifteen minutes about the reconstruction of the Fates Consulting building. The Moirai have been ... difficult for the construction team to deal with. They are requesting things that are not easy to obtain," Hera's assistant rattled off as they walked to the new Senate chambers. Turning to the young demigod she had hired to help her as she rebuilt her city, she paused with her hand against the chamber doors.

"Relay this message to them: if they want a new building, they get what they get. If they cry about it, they can live on top of the mountain with the goats again like they used to."

Her assistant stumbled but caught himself as Hera pushed open the chamber doors and walked through, her head held high.

Each of the senators were seated, all of them there. Even Kiran, who gave her a half smile.

The idiot had to be a hero and get himself half-dead at her expense. Though they had gone toe-to-toe so recently, he had proven himself a friend, just as she knew in her heart he had been since they met. Damn him. It would have been easier if she hated him, but he was here. His face had been sliced, and the resulting scar crossed from his right temple to the left of his mouth. His right eye no longer worked, but he was alive.

And that was what mattered to Hera.

Stepping up on the platform, she made her way to her chair in the center. Her hand touched Kiran's shoulder as she passed him, and his hand went up to squeeze hers. In that small touch, she knew they had forgiven each other. She met Finley's gaze, and she could see her eyes were watering, but she was trying to stand strong. Hera gave her a nod of support, to which Finley replied with a small smile.

Looking from senator to senator, Hera nodded at each of them, appreciating the people who had stood next to her in battle. Hera would no longer shut them out, not now that she was healing. Both mentally and physically.

Though the nightmares still came, they were few and far between. She had closure, protecting her sisters and people, and Viktor really enjoyed playing therapist with her. She usually had to get naked and distract him to make him stop wanting to discuss her thoughts and feelings and use his mouth for other, more fun endeavors.

Once she sat down, the guards opened the doors, allowing the public to come in. Hera took a deep breath and felt relief roll through her that they had made it to the end. The threat was gone. They were rebuilding their city. They managed to save most of her people, and although there were still losses, they could heal as a country, as a nation, together.

Now that they had control of the Sereian Empire in the absence of the Emperor and the destruction of the army, they needed Kiran to step completely into the role of governing the reformed country. He was a senator in truth, not just a liaison to a false emperor any longer. But the empire was big, and it was in need of a lot of restructuring. Which meant Kiran could not do it alone.

Hera called the meeting to order and moved to the first order of business.

"I'd like us to vote in our newest senator. After a lengthy discussion, we'd like to call General Alexander Markos. His experience and knowledge in military logistics, as well as the restructuring of Atlantis, will lend him the expertise needed to bring a peaceful resolution to the chaos that the Sereian Empire has endured."

Markos stood before the senators, a crutch still needed as the cyclops worked on a prosthetic for his missing leg. He gave a steady half bow, and a chair was added to the end of the table. Waiting until Markos was seated, Hera opened the meeting to the citizens of Zephyr.

There were plenty of people asking for assistance, and Hera was more than happy to grant it. The fact that some of her city still stood, that most of her people were here, and that they had vanquished the Titans gave her heart a sense of peace.

As the meeting concluded, people filed out, and Hera approached Markos at the other end of the table.

"You ready for this next part?" she asked with a smile, and he seemed a little taken aback by her expression. Perhaps Hera was more enthusiastic than she should be when she had spent so much time complaining about adding to the power structure, but that was the insecure, terrified Hera of before. When she glanced over to see Viktor waiting in the wings, he gave her a nod.

"Sure. Let's see why Themis thought it was wise to take me for a dip in the river Styx when I was all but dead," Markos replied, beginning his walk to the doors, but Hera pulled her and the other Olympians into a light jump. Markos, the poor man, wobbled as he suddenly stood on the marble floor of the throne room.

"Sorry, habit." She reached out and steadied him until he reliably got the crutch under him again.

"Is my stomach supposed to feel like it's been turned inside out?" he asked as they walked toward the thrones.

"Not when you do it yourself. Give it time," she whispered, halting him gently when the floor shook, announcing a new throne was being placed. A little overdramatic, the mountain was.

Every goddess and god watched silently as the throne formed from the mountain. Hera's eyes went to the symbol at the headrest: a war hammer. Each of the now so-called Olympians, as West determined they should be called, stepped forward to take their seats. Why the man was allowed to name anything was a mystery to Hera, but she was dropping it... for now.

"Balance ... and now there are twelve," Amphitrite intoned. "A new throne gained while we fought a battle to secure our rule."

Finally, Markos seated himself on his throne, and shock rippled across his face as he transformed, just as the others had. He wore burned orange slacks and a button up that was not in fact buttoned all the way up, a metal crown with blunt edges, which looked strikingly similar to the metal flames of Viktor's crown. The most marked aspect of his transformation was his leg; though it was still missing from just above the knee, a diaphanous orange light took the form of his lost limb.

But Hera was sure every woman in the room was too busy staring at his very muscular chest to notice.

"Shirt did not button all the way, General," West said in a bored tone.

"I don't think I like you anymore, West." Calista pouted as Markos buttoned his shirt up, only to stop and cut a smile to Calista, leaving the rest of the buttons undone.

Hera let out a laugh, the first real one not in private, and not in the happy bubble she and Viktor lived in. Everyone's attention snapped to her, surprised at the authenticity of the sound, which made her laugh again. Viktor and her sisters smiled.

She looked around Olympus, at all twelve of the thrones filled with goddesses and gods. The space felt full, and she wondered how only three thrones had stood here for so very long.

And she was thankful for each and every one of them.

"Let's get on with the show then, shall we?" Hera smiled as she stepped from her throne and called the globe so they could look over the world they were all going to protect until their last breath.

Hopefully, not for a while ... or ever again.

### **Viktor**

Starting back to work felt wholly different for Viktor after everything they had been through. He wasn't the same man that he was when he started working as a therapist in Halcyon.

His office had been undamaged by the battle being so far from the city center, but he could still look out the window and see dead trees in the distance, lost to the fires. The burned forest would ultimately make the land more fertile, bringing it back to life in a much better state than it had been before.

The ebb and flow of life.

Viktor mentally rolled his eyes, remembering his father's note.

Listening to his patient, he heard all about their struggle to rebuild, the loss of their brother, and their confusion about what all had happened.

That part Viktor could do nothing about. So many humans had lost their memories—from Themis, but also from the Titans. Everyone who had been mind-controlled and drugged had no idea what had happened to them. Their last memory was before the Titans managed to get a hold of them. It took a great deal of manipulation of the press for Hera to work out a story that would appease anyone.

Still, there were plenty that were skeptical, but he knew from the past that if the humans could not pin down something tangible to explain all their why's, they would let it drop. Eventually.

As far as most people knew, there was a biological attack on their food supply by the Sereian Empire, which had resulted in sickness and memory loss. Some people had reactions, even dying, and others not so much. After the death of the emperor, they were able to find the faulty facilities and shut them down.

That was the official story.

After an hour of working through raw grief and loss, Viktor was ready to go home. The home he now shared with Hera, as she chose not to rebuild her old, more ostentatious penthouse and instead chose to move in with him.

She told him that it no longer fit her, and he agreed.

Hera had let the pain and anger go, though not completely, and was finally finding herself after centuries of playing the part of someone else.

And Viktor was so incredibly proud of her.

Light jumping to their home, he was not surprised to find Hera completely naked on the couch, drinking wine and shooting him a smirk from behind the glass.

He'd been worried all day that the first postwar senate meeting would go horribly, so he was thrilled to see her in a good mood. Even more so when that mood meant no clothes.

Standing, she put her wineglass on the coffee table and sauntered over to him. The walk was slow and predatory.

"Hello, doctor," she crooned as she leaned into him, taking his lips before he could respond. Mere seconds later, he was inside her on the living room rug, fire burning through his veins as he kissed and took the woman he was bound to, body and soul. Electricity struck out as she found her release, and he followed closely behind with a growl, sounding more like a jungle cat than a human being. Carrying her to bed, he kissed her, and in his distraction, he barely missed hitting her head on the door frame.

"Luckily you missed. Amazing sex or not, I'll fry you for knocking me sideways." Hera smirked against his lips at her empty threat. Yes, she was healing and finding her true self—but that didn't mean she was changing completely. He chuckled and lowered her onto the bed.

Spending the day making love to her was everything his previous self was sure he'd lost forever.

The road to their reunion was long, painful, and deadly, but they made it.

Everything was becoming whole again in their world.

*Thank the Fates.*

## <u>Hera</u>

The three sisters gathered on a terrace in Olympus, looking out over their world, their city, and their people that they had sacrificed so much to save. The city was still in shambles, but they watched, and helped, the rebuilding efforts.

"It is hard to think that the war is over," Amphitrite whispered, sidling closer to Hera.

Ever since Hera had died, gone to Tartarus, died again, and came back, her sisters had stayed close to her. Always ready to berate her for her brash plans, but then tell her they were glad she was there; it was the closest she'd felt to her sisters since their mortal years.

And Amphitrite was right. It was hard to accept the war with the Titans was finally done. They had lived in fear of the madness that was their father escaping Tartarus for so long that Hera had a hard time believing it was over, and that they could move on with their very long lives.

Persephone with Devon. Amphitrite with West. And now Hera with Viktor.

It was all so surreal to her that something so beautiful came from something so dark and evil. Even though this was one of the worst battles of their lives, they had found their soulbonds through it.

And the irony of it stunk of the Fates.

The Moirai were back in their tower, annoying as ever. She went to check in on them one time and almost blew the building up again. The crazy old crones just laughed and giggled like the insane asylum escapees they were.

"The city is healing," Persephone whispered.

"It is. It will be a slow process. First the infrastructure, then the economy, then the people. They will need to take time to heal from this, especially if they lost someone," Hera said, but her words felt vacant. Like they didn't mean enough in that moment to truly carry the weight of the future.

The humans across Zephyr didn't remember the battle and most of the invasion, although the earlier story of Sereian aggression still held. Themis and Prometheus had made sure the secrets of the goddesses stayed just that. The humans could not handle any more surprises, and the truth that Halcyon had just been a battlefield between gods, Titans, and all sorts of magical beings would be far too much.

Hera held out her hands, surprising her sisters, but they each took hold, each giving Hera's hand a squeeze.

As ridiculous as that simple gesture was, she could have cried. She had never reached out to her sisters for emotional support before, but they did not hesitate to give it, and for that she was supremely thankful.

Persephone sniffed, and Amphitrite and Hera looked over at her.

"Are you ... crying?" Hera asked in shock.

"No ... maybe," Persephone mumbled, wiping tears away as quick as they came. "I'm just really emotional these days. The war ... and Hera actually needing me..."

Hera grabbed Persephone in a hug, earning a gasp from her before she reciprocated with her own bone crunching hug. It was weird to see her stoic and normally unemotional sister so tearful.

Amphitrite moved in and put her arms around her sisters, hugging them both.

It was so ridiculously emotional.

And Hera loved every second of it.

# What's Next?

## Read on for a sneak peek at "Reaper of Chaos"

### Prologue

#### <u>Thanatos</u>

Thanatos stood in front of his home in the Underworld, covered in blood and ash, as the Goddess of the Underworld stood on his porch, her face lined with exhaustion.

He was sure he looked much worse.

Persephone had cleaned herself up, back in her black dress, not a hair out of place, but it wasn't long ago that she'd been wearing as much of their enemies' blood as he was.

They had battled side-by-side to defend the goddesses' rule over the world, and while the danger of her father Cronus's dominance had passed, her haunted eyes revealed the toll it had taken on her.

Thanatos walked up the wooden steps of his gray brick gothic home, the Underworld back in a balanced state around them, to stand before Persephone.

Staying still, quiet as a statue, he could imagine she could read the look in his eyes. Thanatos finally felt the weight he'd carried for millennia become far too heavy. He wasn't capable of continuing his duties of reaping souls, not now. His psyche was fracturing like glass and the slightest pressure would shatter it altogether. Exhausted and weary at such a bone-deep level, he wasn't sure if he could continue as a reaper.

"You've earned time away from here. Will fifty years suffice?" she asked, clasping her hands together in front of her and squeezing them as she bit into her lower lip.

Shock had rendered him speechless at her offer. He would have gladly taken five years, but fifty … fifty meant that he could actually recover, reset, and return to his duties with a fresh mind. He could avoid becoming the jaded reaper he once was before Persephone's rule.

"Thank you." His voice was gruff, from both yelling commands on the battlefield to his army of underworld soldiers, and from the emotion of finally having what he needed to heal.

Taking his hand in hers, she placed her other one on top.

"I will miss you, but I understand. I have backup options in place, reapers from your army, and with them, I can handle the souls in your absence. Go, Thanatos. Discover what it means to be human. You've never had that chance."

As tears broke from her watery eyes, the normally stoic goddess grabbed his shoulders and pulled him into her embrace. He hugged her back and realized how much they had both needed this moment of comfort, which was gone all too quickly.

She squeezed him once before vanishing, her shadows having transported her to somewhere else in the Underworld.

Trying to gather his equilibrium before he took a step toward the freedom he so desperately needed, Thanatos rubbed his hands over his face. When they came away with blood and ash, a veil of depression stole over him.

He'd lost good men and women this day, and he was not only still alive, but getting a vacation.

He slammed his fist into the gray brick of his home, the impact echoing in the sudden silence. Dust and fragments of brick exploded outward, but he didn't care to check the damage.

Snarling, his anger bubbling to the surface, he tore through his home, cursing Cronus for bringing more despair to their lives when the bastard titan should have stayed in Tartarus to rot for all eternity.

The bloody black armor tightened around him, as if a ghostly hand were squeezing him in its fist. Thanatos froze before panic caught up with him, his lungs constricting every moment he wore remnants of the battle on his skin. Thanatos roared, his voice a sound of pure fury, fueled by frustration and fear, as he struggled against the constricting armor. Managing to get his bracers off, he hurled them across the room with the force of a man possessed.

He moved toward the bathroom, leaving a trail of black armor and red blood behind him. Something inside his mind finally cracked. The urgent need to cleanse himself of the remnants of battle before he completely broke overwhelmed him.

His lungs constricted as he turned the shower to the hottest setting, letting the scalding water burn his skin. He slid down the marble wall to the tiled floor. Head on his knees, his arms, covered in runes, wrapped around his legs as rivulets of red ran down his olive skin to the drain below.

Leaning back to rest his head against the white tile, he let the water slam into his face, unable to breathe. He was death. Death could not drown. Death could not die.

# Chapter 1

### <u>Thanatos</u>

After living among humans and pretending to be one of them for so long, Thanatos was ready to resume the role of reaper in guiding souls to their final rest.

A thought Thanatos held onto when he entered Halcyon's city center for the first time in fifty years, observing the altered skyline, reconstructed following the conflict.

Fates Consulting, where the Fates dwelled in their metallic spiral tower that met the sky, and Cerberus Financial, where Persephone managed the largest financial institution in the world, were nearly the same. However, additional buildings now stood between them.

Staring at the new skyline, Thanatos wondered if the world had caught up yet to what it would have been had the humans, long before the battle between the goddesses and Titans, not used horrible weapons against their fellow man.

The scale of destruction caused by the Great War was beyond anything Thanatos had ever seen. Land was ruined, water was sickened, and the human population had been brought down to a fourth of its original size.

The very humans he was walking between as he navigated through the new Halcyon; rebuilt in his absence after the battle. People who gave him a wide enough berth that he didn't need to shoulder his way along the busy street.

Mortals could sense when death was near, and even if their conscious mind wondered why, the primal part of their brain avoided him at all costs.

Pushing his hands into the pockets of his leather jacket, he waited at a crosswalk with several other people who kept a good five feet away from him. Their eyes darting over him until he met their gaze, and then they were quick to look away.

New met old as sleek metallic skyscrapers were woven into the city next to brick-and-mortar buildings standing long before the Great War.

Much like the rest of the continent of Zephyr, and its now-healed lands, without the wastelands and dark waters, he observed the rekindled spirit of exploration reminiscent of ages past. Mortals were working to improve their lot in life and starting new governments that met their needs as citizens. Each new country had its own leaders, no longer under the archon's control, but still under Hera's watchful eye, unbeknownst to them.

Humans remained oblivious to the existence of the goddesses even after the powerful battle against the Titans. Hera, as acting archon then, had spun a story of an invading army that was believable enough for the humans to hold on to instead of trying to make sense of something that might destroy their status quo.

If anyone was aware the gods had fought in the middle of the emptied town, they'd said nothing about it.

His eyes moved along the street and the new businesses now set up there, and he realized he recognized only a handful from before. He wondered if most of the shopkeepers had just decided not to rebuild or if they were among the fallen.

The crosswalk signaled they could go, and when Thanatos stepped onto the road, the man beside him shivered at the aura of death rolling off him. Stumbling away from Thanatos, a fear in his eyes that he probably couldn't explain, he shoved several people out of the way, running down the street.

One of those people was a frail woman, unable to catch herself as she tumbled into the street where cars were still moving. A horn blared. Unable to move through the shadows in full view of mortals, Thanatos used a small burst of magic to reach the woman before anyone else could.

He grabbed her arm and yanked her back onto the sidewalk. The driver slammed on the brakes, burning rubber against the road, and the car lurched to a stop several feet beyond where the woman had been standing.

Her frail body trembled, her milky eyes filling with tears, and as much as Thanatos wanted to blame the shock of almost being killed, he knew it was his presence.

Stepping back, he let her go before her heart failed and she needed a guide. People were quick to swarm in, checking on her, as Thanatos slipped away from view.

Shaking off the morose feeling of being unwelcome, Thanatos continued on. It seemed that Halcyon had finally managed solar-powered vehicles on a large scale. The scientific community was busy after the war, proving once again that necessity drives invention. Their endeavors reached the farthest corners of the globe, even the reclaimed lands. Enough so that Thanatos had seen some of it on his travels.

But now in Halcyon, the hub of civilization, he could see the true extent of humanity's advancements.

So much had changed in the span of fifty years.

There were far more people too. Some were completely absorbed in their phones as they navigated aimlessly through the crowds. Young couples and families were moving from store to store, laughter on their lips and smiles on their faces.

The city was bustling.

Lights flashed in his peripheral, and he turned as a large mobile ambulance passed by, and Thanatos felt the tug of the soul inside the vehicle. A soul that was close to crossing.

It was a bit unsettling for him to feel the pull of his reaper after so many years. Despite his appreciation for the vacation from ferrying souls, he underestimated his need to feel useful in that capacity. Did the Underworld know of his readiness to return, or was it just a coincidence?

Taking to the shadows, he shifted into his incorporeal form, shadow-jumping along as he trailed the ambulance back to Halcyon General.

Unnoticed, he slipped into the shadows and jumped across the road, reappearing near the ambulance as it skidded to a stop at the glass doors marked **EMERGENCY** in red. The doors burst open. People in scrubs rushed out, meeting the paramedics and taking over the patient's care while the gurney was pushed inside. The paramedics ran beside them, giving them information.

As a man administered oxygen to the patient through some sort of apparatus, the woman beside him promptly jumped onto the gurney and began pushing on the patient's chest.

Thanatos' total attention fell to her, a magnetic pull almost taking him from the shadows before he was ready to show himself.

Confused on why this mere mortal would call to him, since she was alive and seemed quite healthy, he called on his reaper sight, giving him the ability to see the souls within people.

The curvy blonde nurse disappeared, and he discovered the presence of two souls within a single body.

*How was this possible?*

Within the nurse's soul, a completely different woman's soul emerged, shifting and flickering like a mirage. Pale skin covered lean muscle instead of the tan of the nurse. Instead of scrubs, the pale woman wore a blouse as if she'd stopped in the middle of a business meeting to attend to the patient. Her dark brown hair was neatly pulled back, the strands smooth and straight, a stark contrast to the blonde's untidy bun.

Thanatos swiftly imagined every conceivable scenario in his mind, particularly after noticing the woman's lack of a blue light. Instead, a soft white glow emanated from the nurse's body. Only souls that were still alive held a white aura, which meant the soul inhabiting her had not passed on yet.

This was not an angry soul possessing a mortal. Not someone who had died with a story to tell.

He truly had no idea how a person could contain two souls and not be absolutely mad in the mind.

Moving to shadow closer to where the gurney had stopped, the woman still working on chest compressions, his runes tingled with electricity when his fingers moved over the magic that had been inked beneath his skin long ago. The runes had been dormant for centuries, and nothing around him could have had the power to trigger them. *Nothing,* he thought, his jaw clenched before his focus returned to the scene around him instead of the nightmarish memories the runes brought.

More people flooded into the room that contained the gurney and dying soul. The woman with two souls continued her desperate attempt at reviving the man, surrounded with more instruments than Thanatos could ever hope of naming.

Numbers and codes were yelled out as people darted around in an urgent yet proficient manner. They paused only momentarily when they ran through his incorporeal form, each of them rubbing their arms or shuddering from the chill of death.

The nurse on the gurney refused to quit, telling the patient in a hushed, melodic voice—whispering so softly that no one but him could hear—that she needed the man to stay with her. To stay and not cross the veil. Not yet.

Thanatos's gaze hardened as he moved through the controlled chaos, his attention fixed on her and her softly spoken pleas.

Did she mean the literal veil of the Underworld? How would one know of the veil and be alive to talk about it? Had she had a near-death experience?

If so, it was exceedingly rare. Most people who thought they'd seen the veil had merely experienced their brains flashing random images as they died. No one had ever crossed the veil and returned to the mortal world.

A man called a time out loud, breaking Thanatos from his trance, and the woman stopped. Her head hung low as she steadied herself with her hands on the sides of the gurney, her knuckles white.

Everyone in the room except her stepped out, moving on to the living souls that were not past all help. All but a tall male who lingered in the doorway, offering to assist her with the now-dead man, but she only shook her head. With a last long look at the nurse with two souls, the man left, letting the door close quietly behind him.

Pushing herself off the gurney, she pulled her gloves off, disposing of them in a biohazard bin before turning back to the patient.

"It wasn't supposed to end like this," she whispered as she stared at his body surrounded by discarded medical equipment. The pads, wires, and I.V. lines were all evidence of the failed attempts to save him. "You were supposed to make the right choice..."

He tried to listen to what the woman was saying, but as Thanatos moved to see more than her profile, something deep inside of himself shifted in a fundamental way. As if his heart was suddenly far too big to be contained within the cage that was his body.

She was gorgeous. Maybe not in the way the magazines would proclaim, but still gorgeous in a way that made him step forward without thought; lost to some magic deep within her. Her eyes, one blue and one green, were captivating. Her face was lightly speckled with freckles, resembling stars in the night sky.

Captivating. That was the word for her, but his study of her was lost as her soul separated from the woman she inhabited. A soul that, just as he thought, was very much alive.

He was immortal yet never had he witnessed two souls within a single mortal body, which left him with countless questions. How was such a thing possible?

As her soul left the body it inhabited, so did the man's who had lost his battle to cling to life, pulling at Thanatos to reap him. Unlike the mystery woman's soul, the man's detached in the characteristic blue light of a soul ready to cross over.

Unable to deny the pull of both the soul and the Underworld, Thanatos clenched his fists and looked over the woman's soul one last time, committing her essence to memory.

Thanatos vowed to find her again once he escorted the man to his final resting place.

Then he would figure out the secrets he knew she held, and maybe ... more.

He stepped up to the man's essence hovering near his body before placing his hand on the soul's shoulder. The feeling of rightness as he pulled the soul to him, attaching it to his reaper side so it would not be lost on the mortal plane, was almost as potent as his curiosity about the woman. Drawing in a deep breath, he readied himself to take a spirit home for the first time in fifty years.

The soul of the woman with mismatched eyes snapped to Thanatos as if she could truly see him.

"Who are you, and why are you taking this man's soul?"

**Want to read more? Scan this QR code**
**or go to https://books2read.com/Reaper-of-Chaos**

# Also By

Want to be the first to know about new releases, giveaways, etc.? Sign up for my newsletterby going to http://www.authorcdbritt.com or scanning this QR code!

***Also By C.D. Britt:***

**<u>Reign of Goddesses Series</u>**
Strings of the Fates (Reign of Goddesses #.5)
Shadows and Vines (Reign of Goddesses #1)
Sirens and Leviathans (Reign of Goddesses #2)
Storms and Embers (Reign of Goddesses #3)
Reaper of Chaos (Reign of Goddesses #4, Blood of Saviors #1)
**<u>Clan of Shadows Series</u>**
Prophecy of Gods and Crows (Clan of Shadows #1)

Blood Debts (Clan of Shadows #1.5)
Omens of Wolves and Witches (Clan of Shadows #2)
**<u>Blood of Saviors Series</u>**
Reaper of Chaos (Blood of Saviors #1, Reign of Goddesses #4)

# ABOUT THE AUTHOR

C.D. Britt has been obsessed with mythology since elementary school. The obsession has only grown, so she started writing mythic fantasy with significantly happier endings than the original lore.

She currently resides in Texas where she has yet to adapt to the heat. Her husband thrives in it, so unfortunately, they will not be relocating to colder climates anytime soon. Their two young children would honestly complain either way. When she is not in her writing cave (hiding from the sun), she enjoys ignoring the world as much as her children will allow with a good book, music, and vast amounts of coffee (until it's time for wine). C.D. Britt is the author of the *Reign of Goddesses* and the *Clan of Shadows* series.

**Stay Connected!**
www. authorcdbritt.com
https://linktr.ee/Cdbritt

# Acknowledgements

Thank you, dear reader, for picking up my book. I am forever grateful to you for giving me a chance and reading my work.

To Chrissy, Ashley and Niki: Thank you so much for editing and making this book the best version of itself.

To my Beta readers: Thank you so much for the kind words and constructive feedback! Some of you had no mercy and I appreciate it! I hope to work with you all again.

Thank you so much to my ARC readers and street team! You are all so amazing! I love to hear from you all and look forward to our next adventure!

Thank you to my book club/author friends for working with me on becoming a better author. I enjoy our weekly chats!

Alyssa, thank you for being my sounding board with names. I should never name anything without your approval.

To my children, thank you for the unconditional love and encouragement. I know I've been busy with this book and all the last minutes details, rushing around like crazy, but you've been troopers and I love you so much!

And to my husband, you're still here. You must REALLY love me. Like a lot.